Ship of Dreams

By Brey Willows

2025

Butterworth Books is a different breed of publishing house. It's a home for Indies, for independent authors who take great pride in their work and produce top quality books for readers who deserve the best. Professional editing, professional cover design, professional proof reading, professional book production—you get the idea. As Individual as the Indie authors we're proud to work with, we're Butterworths and we're *different*.

Authors currently publishing with us:

E.V. Bancroft
Valden Bush
Addison M Conley
Jo Fletcher
Helena Harte
Lee Haven
Karen Klyne
Sydney Lear
AJ Mason
Ally McGuire
James Merrick
JP Preston
Robyn Nyx
Simon Smalley
Brey Willows

For more information visit www.butterworthbooks.co.uk

This trade paperback is published by Butterworth Books, UK

CATALOGING INFORMATION
ISBN: 978-1-915009-78-4
CREDITS
Editor: Nicci Robinson
Cover Design: Nicci Robinson
Production Design: Global Wordsmiths

Acknowledgements

Taking on a new genre is a big deal, and this was quite the challenge. I have to thank my wife and editor, Robyn Nyx, for her incredible patience as I meandered, procrastinated, and researched myself into missed deadlines. I adore the cover she designed too, after much back and forth about concepts. And to all those who gave me other steampunk examples and talked gears and gadgets with me, thank you! It's a fabulous and fun genre that I've fallen deeper in love with. And to every reader who continues to spend time playing in the worlds I create: you have no idea how much I appreciate you.

Dedication

To the captain of our own ship of dreams.
You're my best adventure.

ℙROLOGUE

Late summer, 1898

IT WAS THE SEARCH for the bodies that led to the cave. The pack of scruffy, rough-housing boys had been taking turns throwing rocks from the cliffside and watching them fall to the crashing whitewater far below. Tussling, pushing, playing…children being children, goading each other to the edge of the cliff and then jumping back in fright as they pretended to push each other off. The long shadow of Edinburgh-upon-Wind, the sky city of the capital, shifted and faded as the clouds floated beneath it, blocking it from view. These boys had never, and likely *would* never, get to a sky city. So they made the best of land villages, as children are wont to do. The outskirts of Edinburgh-upon-Sea were remote enough for the boys to feel like they were being adventurous, but near enough so they could make it home for afternoon tea before it got too cold and too wet for playing outside to be fun.

When the lower cities had become too crowded, too full of sickness, and too mired in the industrial smog puffed into the air like oily cigar smoke by the new machinery factories creating yet more machines, the most affluent people in those areas had built the floating cities they lived in now, taking them above the filth and grime. Gears, industrial strength balloons, and steel kept them aloft, so the lords, ladies, barons, and other titled people never needed to look at the poor, the indigent, the desperate.

A cold northern wind blew over the black sea, buffeting the children of the rural land city, making hair stand in tufts and scout uniforms flap wildly. A small airship zipped past, and the children waved and yelled inappropriate things at it, outdoing each other with the filthiest words they'd recently learned (though they weren't always sure what they meant).

When the rumble began, only one boy frowned and glanced back over his shoulder before dismissing the noise as an extra grumpy wave and turning back to his friends just as one tackled him to the wet grass. They rolled towards the cliff edge.

And then there was no cliff edge, because the one they'd been rolling towards was falling in a long, wide shard towards the sea, followed by far more of the land itself, breaking apart to become independent of the earth to which it had been tethered.

The boys didn't have time to stop rolling towards their end before the new cliff was behind them, and the crashing, rock-filled ocean rushed towards them from below.

Chapter One

"Careful," Temp Strud murmured as the underwater dirigible touched the side of the cave, dislodging rock into the inky blackness lit only by the small chem light she'd wheedled out of the maker on the Chimera. The chemicals in it would glow until it burned out or was opened to the elements, and she had to hope that neither of those things would happen while they were underwater. As it was, she wasn't certain how safe the two-seater, glass-domed floating vehicle was. Their trips to the land cities weren't infrequent, but it was rare they needed to go anywhere near the cold, dark waters around the British coast.

"Release air from bags two and four," Duncan said, his face practically pressed against the glass as his mechanical eye zoomed in and out, trying to scan the depth and distance as they made their way into the deeper, almost impossible to see cave at the back.

"Eerie," Temp said, lifting and lowering the handles on either side of her seat to release the air from the bladders attached to the outside. Colour in the cave's side indicated layer upon layer of earth, from the teal of copper to the muted black of slate. "There!" Temp hit her head on the glass dome and swore. "See it?"

Duncan pulled back gently on the lever in front of him, and they floated back until they were level with a drawing of what looked like a bear etched into the rock. "You were right. As usual."

They moved forwards again, and Temp made a mental note of every bit of rock art she could see in the dim cavern. With a memory that seldom failed her, she'd be able to draw them all once she was back on the ship.

"Land rising ahead. Shift air into bags one and three."

Temp did as she was told, and water cascaded over the dome as they rose into a huge opening. "Yes," she whispered, her heart hammering in her chest, and excitement making it hard not to shove open the dome and leap out to explore.

The little craft bumped against something, and Duncan flicked open the release switch to let the dome open off to the side. His eye clinked and whirred as he looked around, echoing off the cave around them like a strange calling card.

"Ladies first," he said, not looking at her.

"Call me that again, and I'll leave you here." Temp swung her legs out of the craft, tipping it precariously, and then slid into water that reached her hips. "Crackers, that's cold." She peered down and held the globe near the water. "Steps." She inched forwards, testing each one, until she was out of the water and standing on what looked like dirty marble.

There was a splash, a swear, and then Duncan was beside her, holding up a second globe. "Tell me again what we're looking for?"

She headed left, and he headed right, the way they always did in these situations. "First, see if there are any braziers. These little globes aren't going to provide nearly enough light, and we need to be away from that cave before the tide comes back in." If there was one thing she'd learned from these expeditions, it was that every culture needed light and found a way to have it. Sure enough, a three-foot round bowl placed on a tripod loomed out of the darkness. She lit a match and threw it in, hoping there'd be enough old oil to catch.

It popped and flared so fast she barely had time to get back. From across the cave, there was another pop and flare, and shadows danced across the walls covered in paintings. And in the middle...

"Bloody hell," Temp whispered, squatting as her knees went weak.

Duncan knelt beside her, and they stared at the perfectly preserved Viking longship settled directly in the centre of the cave.

Wood, stone, and ivory carvings were piled around the base and glittered with the silver jewellery and weapons in the mix.

"I *knew* it. The coastline was different when the Vikings were raiding the British Isles. Norse oral tradition mentioned this area as one of the mystical places that was hidden away, meant to be a portal to the gods, never to be used again."

"You seem determined to anger them gods every chance you get with all your snooping around in the places not meant for us." Duncan stood, wiping his hands on his trousers. "Aside from the treasure find of the century, what are you looking for?"

Temp pulled a folded piece of paper from her pocket and handed it to him. "The Firebird. Norse myth. The Prose Edda says it's a key to finding the Golden Apples of the Gods, and it said it would be in a place borne of every element."

He looked up from the drawing and around at the cave. "Air, earth, water, fire." He turned the drawing sideways, studying it. "What's it do? And what's it supposed to be made of?"

Temp began to wander but didn't go near the ship. She wanted to savour the moment, like saving the best part of a dessert for the last bite. "Some scholars have interpreted the tales to mean it was made of glass, but that seems doubtful. No artefacts have been found to suggest they used glass as a means of art. It's more likely to be silver. As to what it does..." She shrugged. "The tale says that when the gods grew old, they'd bite into the apple and grow young again."

Temp hadn't found a cache this rich in a long time, and while she'd be glad to claim credit when she turned it over to the British Museum, she'd been tasked with finding the Firebird, and she didn't want to leave until she did. The sound of a wave crashing made her look up, and their little craft bobbed hard against the stone. Holding up her hand, she studied the specially crafted compass on her leather gloves. The hands and dials swayed, like they were moving with the tide. "Damn." She hurried towards the ship. "We're losing time and tide," she called out, knowing Duncan would pick up the pace too. She searched for a way onto the ship, but the old rope ladder hung in wispy tatters. She looked around and spotted a plinth holding a stone carving of a raven, which she took as a sign. Carefully, she lifted the heavy carving and set it aside, then dragged the plinth to the ship and set it at an angle against the wood. She stood back, then ran up the plinth and jumped off the top and onto the deck.

Oak timbers groaned, and the smell of rot rose around her, but it was the skeletons that took her breath away. Two sat at the stern, their bony hands intertwined. One was covered in the vestiges of what looked like a red wool dress, and the other wore a blue one and a tattered veil that hung over her skull face.

And there were animal bones everywhere. "A sacrificial graveyard," she said, looking again at the skeletons. A glint caught her eye, and she moved close to see something encased between their hands, cupped in a way that suggested it was something delicate.

She winced as she tried to pry their hands apart, and fingerbones snapped and fell to the wood planks below.

"Temp!" Duncan's scream bounced off the cave walls.

She grabbed the item without looking at it, shoved it in her satchel, and looked over the side of the ship.

Duncan lay lifeless on the stone, water lapping at his side and smoke rising from a hole in his chest. Standing beside him were three men, and she ducked as an electric charge sliced through the air beside her head, sending up the pungent smell of singed hair. She crouch-ran back to the plinth she'd climbed up on and ran down it, making her way towards the sea dirigible. Duncan. He'd been her second, her partner, for so long. She couldn't leave him—

Someone crashed into her, knocking her into the rising water. As she struggled to rise to the surface with one of the men struggling just as hard to keep her from doing so, she looked towards the ceiling and saw it; a glass orb hung from a silver chain at the apex of the cave. And swinging towards it was one of the men who'd killed Duncan. He grabbed it just as she was pushed below the freezing water again.

With no other option, she pulled the knife from her boot and shoved it hard into his stomach, and then into his neck when he jerked away. Gasping, she rose for air and splashed towards the dirigible. She jumped into the foreseat, hoping like hell she could manage the craft alone, and jerked the dome shut. Awkwardly, she reached behind her and flipped the levers to release the air, and the craft plunged beneath the waves crashing harder into the cave. A glance over her shoulder, beyond the black water, showed her one man looking at the orb as the other one urged him into their dark craft. With a shove, she pushed the lever forwards, and the craft shot into the dark tunnel, bumping and scraping against the walls. With nothing but black water ahead, there was no way to know if she was going to drive straight into a wall, but the glow coming from behind told her not to slow down.

She jerked forwards as she was hit from behind and one of the bladders scraped hard against the wall. Bubbles obscured her view out the right side. It had been punctured. The craft tilted sideways, pressing her against the dome. Another hit sent the dome scraping against the sharp shells embedded in the rock, like nails slicing along glass that wasn't meant for a deep-diving vessel.

And then the glow was above, and the other dark craft pushed down on her, forcing her lower, and the scraping got worse. Another bladder popped, this time sending a burst of bubbled air, and the whole back end sank. Her craft slowed.

The other ship moved ahead into the darkness, the glow fading to leave Temp bobbing in a blackness she'd never experienced. She pushed air into the other bladders and kept the forwards level pressed to full capacity. Slowly, the craft inched forwards, buffeted by the waves. Light, diffuse and mild, finally made its way through the water, and she breathed a sigh of relief. The air was getting thin, and spots swam in front of her eyes.

Cracking, like a spiderweb spun from lightning, covered the dome and she barely had time to hold her breath before it shattered, and icy water plunged into the craft. She kicked free and swam hard, her lungs burning. She broke the surface and gasped for air, only to get hit by a wave and carried back towards the cave. Spluttering, she swam forwards again, this time parallel to the cave, away from the pull. Something bumped her, and she grasped for it. A piece of the wrecked craft served as a raft, and she collapsed on top of it, unable to remain conscious any longer.

Chapter Two

There were few things Alexis Minty enjoyed more than stealing from entitled people with more money than sense. One of them was a good bar fight, and as she ducked a poorly aimed mug of beer, she grinned and directed a punch to the middle of a particularly portly man. He doubled over, his already-red complexion turning just a little more beetroot.

The sound of a shot brought an immediate halt to the raucous row that had no real origin nor any real point. The blue smoke steaming from the airgun held by the rather irritated looking barman gave him the kind of halo he deserved for the patience he exhibited when dealing with the particular type of crowd that the Dirty Squirrel catered to.

"Off w'ya, the whole lot. Take yer crews and sod off." He made a vague motion towards the whole room, but there was no doubt as to who he meant.

Alex patted the shoulder of the man still trying to catch his breath after the gut punch and sauntered past him, straightening the blaster holster and then her leather hat. "C'mon, lads. Time to head to the ship."

Despite general grumbling and a few final shoves, the crew of the Devil's Urchin listened to their captain and stumbled into the cold night of London-on-Ground. Alex puffed a whisky-scented breath into the air and watched it dissipate. She'd need to change into her thicker, less hole-eaten tights soon, or she'd get the chills on her thighs like she did a few years back. She reached down to scratch her leg, showing indecently below the beaten leather of her skirt.

"Bend down like that again, boss, and they might mistake you for a pub flower."

Without straightening, she kicked back, catching McGrew in the shin and making him grunt.

She stood. "As though I'd be mistaken for anything other than a proper lady." She wiped her nose with the back of her hand. "Let's get aboard. Too cold to be standing about with you lot."

They set off, and one of them began singing a poor rendition of "God Save the Queen," complete with lyrics that would have gotten him arrested if police bothered to keep a watch over the Low London cityscape. At the metal docking station lurking like a giant in the night, she gently cuffed the lad paid to guard the station and flicked him a coin. He gave her a smile, complete with missing front tooth. He motioned her closer, and she bent down.

"A lass came over. Said you were expecting her. They didn't shove her off from up the ship, so I guess she was right." He bit his lip, staring into her eyes as though hoping he hadn't made a mistake.

"Well, if she wasn't thrown from the ship, then I guess you were right to let her up."

He shoved the coin in his pocket and ran into the night. When he heard the ship was back in town, he'd be there to stand watch. Street kids were always looking out for a bit of extra coin to be earned from the not-so-legal ships that docked in the shadows.

She climbed the eighty-three steps to the mooring line holding the ship to the docking station and whistled. Immediately, the clanking and whirring of gears sounded as the gangplank was lowered. Her night was about to get even better, because one of the other things she liked even more than robbing the gentry was a good woman to keep her company.

The crew, a little less raucous now, headed to their berths. She checked in with the two crew members left to guard the ship.

"You've company." Ted showed no expression, as usual. "Put her in your cabin."

She clapped him on the back. "Good man."

"Cap…" He turned a little to get her attention before she walked away. "Be careful, eh? There's something about this one. Something missing in her eyes."

Alex hesitated. There'd never been a crew member on the Urchin with a better sense of people than Ted. She'd trusted him with her life more times than she could count, and she wasn't about to quit. "I'll keep an eye. Thanks."

He nodded, satisfied that she'd taken him seriously, and turned back to gaze out at the flickering flames of the burning lamps along the city streets below. He always stayed with the ship when they docked, preferring solitude to the rambunctious outings of his crewmates. She knew why that was and so never pushed him to join in. Everyone was entitled to their secrets and ways. The world was hard enough without people trying to change you.

She opened her cabin door and grinned at the sight of the woman lying face down on her bed, as naked as the day God had made her. Her chin rested in her hands, and although she smiled, it was a practiced one that didn't reach her eyes.

Alex took off her hat and tossed it on the table, then shook out her hair. Even a good comb probably wouldn't make it through the mess of snarled curls easily, but it was unlikely the woman in her bed would care about decorum or deportment. "The matron sent you?"

The woman nodded, her blond hair escaping the loose bun and sweeping along her neck. "Said your preferred girl was busy, but I'd do."

The words, while bland enough, made Alex wince internally. "She'd do," like porridge instead of pie. "I find I'm not actually feeling amorous tonight, I'm afraid."

The woman's expression changed. Her shoulders fell, and she slid back, pulling the thick wool blanket with her to cover modesty lost long ago. "Guess I won't do then, eh?"

Alex went to the drinks cupboard and poured them both a

shot. She handed one over. "You know why I like having Emily come over?"

Her eyebrow twitched as she tossed back the shot. "Same as why everyone likes us who work at the matron's place."

Alex shook her head and sat beside her. "Because Emily is always glad to see me. She likes being here, with me. We enjoy each other in the biblical fashion, sure," she laughed when the woman rolled her eyes, "but we have some good talks too." She wrapped a loop of pretty blond hair around her finger. "But, lovely, you don't want to be here. And I never want to be with a woman who don't want to be with me."

The sudden and almost explosive watershed that was let loose from the woman's eyes, along with her low, soft wail, made Alex wince and wish the matron had simply said no one was available tonight. She put her arm around the woman and held her silently until her sobs diminished into soft hiccups.

"The matron would beat me senseless if she saw me this way," she said.

Alex knew that was true. "Well, no need to tell her, is there? What's your name?"

"Polly." She used the wool blanket to dry her eyes. "She'll know I haven't done my duty when I show up without your coin."

"Polly, you got any skills?" Alex tilted her head. "Other than the obvious, I mean."

She shrugged. "I can cook. I like to bake, really. But Pa got in desperate trouble when the automatons started working the fields. No one needed him, and the money dried up. I tried to get a job in some of the fine houses, but there's lots of us trying to find work who have been ousted by them damn machines."

"Well, then you're in luck." Curses and damn her soft heart. "Seems our cook went and got himself put six feet under after a game of poker went bad, and we've been eating food barely fit for dogs. If you're not too proud to work on a pirate ship—"

"Do you mean it?" Polly threw her arms around her in an

exuberant hug. Then she pulled back, her expression darkening. "Would I have to continue the matron's trade with your crew?"

Alex grimaced. "And have you trade one bed for another? Nah. You feed us, and I'll make sure the crew know your role, clear as day. Next time you bed down, it will be with someone *you* want."

Once again, Polly threw her arms around her, and Alex did her best not to notice the soft skin under her hands, or the way Polly's breasts felt against her chest. She'd have to find another willing partner in the next port or work out her frustration in a better pub discourse of the more physical nature. "All right now." Alex patted her back and disentangled herself. "We're upship in the morning." She turned to her desk, wrote out a quick note to the matron, and signed it with the wax seal she kept for official matters like this one. Not every pirate's word was good, but everyone knew the seal of Alexis Minty was solid. "This is your offer of employment. If the matron needs you to pay out any contract or such, let her know I'll take care of it the next time we're in dock. She knows I'm good for it."

Polly leapt from the bed, all modesty forgotten as she pulled on her bloomers, ragged, yellowed petticoats, and coarse linen dress. "Your reputation made me think I was in for a terrible time tonight. But you're nothing like—"

"No." Alex held up her hand, her eyes hardening. "My reputation is well deserved and not one you should ever doubt I worked hard for. Don't let a moment of kindness make you think otherwise. We're pirates, Polly, and there ain't no one on this ship that hasn't got blood on their hands. Make no mistake. If you're joining my crew, you'd better understand that."

Polly paled and swallowed visibly, but then her back straightened, and her chin lifted. "Can't be worse than what I've been doing, and at least this way I have some say over my life."

"You won't have any say over your death if we get caught and captured. They'll hang the cook same as they'll hang the captain." Alex opened her door. "If you're not back by upship at dawn, I'll know you changed your mind."

Polly shook her head and hesitated only a moment before pressing a quick kiss to Alex's cheek. "I'll be here."

Alex closed the door behind her and sighed. Damn it all. She'd hoped for a release and instead ended up with a new crew member. She tossed back another shot and then headed up to the deck.

Ted stood just where she'd left him, and he didn't look at her when she leaned against the rail beside him.

"She'll be back. New cook. Likes to bake."

He snorted. "Soft as butter in summer, you are."

She didn't respond. He was the only one who knew her whole story, just as she knew his, and he knew full well how she felt about the treatment of women in the lower classes. Hell, he knew how she felt about the treatment of women in the upper classes too. "Send Tim to clean out the cook's old room. Make sure the crew know she's not to be touched, or I'll buy her the poison for their food."

He nodded but didn't reply. "Where we headed in the morning? You get any information in the pub?" he finally asked as they watched a group of gutter children run past, chasing a beleaguered and too skinny chicken that wouldn't be worth the energy taken to catch it.

"Word is there's a supply run to New Chelsea. I have a desire for fresh meat," she said, mimicking the accent of those who lived in the air city that rose high above the smog in the north. "And I want some new cloth for sail repair."

He looked down at her tights, showing a hole just between her boot and skirt. "You might want some for that too. You're already a pirate with a reputation that makes mothers swoon and children lose sleep at night. No need to look like you've been dragged behind an airship."

She couldn't argue, and she'd already been thinking about it earlier. "Right. Supply drop it is then." Stifling a yawn, she turned away. "See you at dawn."

He put his hand on her arm. "You did good," he said, looking at her with his deep brown, serious eyes.

She knew full well he was talking about Polly, and not just because they needed a new cook. "We do what we can, eh?" she said, tapping his hand before walking away to her cabin. Dawn was coming, and the excitement of a fresh raid would make it hard to sleep. Like Polly, she'd once had to make a choice, and there was never a day she'd regretted her path. Paying for companionship the way most pirates did was a small price for the freedom she lived with each day, and no one would ever take it from her again.

Chapter Three

"Captain Strud? We've received a crow, sir."

Temp turned to the young crewman and accepted the proffered device. "Thank you." The crow, a beautifully worked mechanical flying messenger with gold inlay in the black metal wings and rubies for eyes, which were also the source of the electrical currents that helped it find its destination, would have been worth a fortune even without the information tucked into the compartment beneath the metal breast. The insignia, an eagle with outstretched claws, made it clear who the missive was from.

"I'll be in my office," she said, leaving the control room and opening the hidden entrance behind the bookcase. She climbed the stairs that led out of the double decker gondola and into the enormous frame of the zeppelin, with its huge metal ribcage and individually filled balloons that kept it aloft. The metal walkway was cold; she pulled the ankle-length duster closed over her suit, as well as pulling her captain's cap lower and putting the goggles over her eyes to protect them from the frigid air.

The engine noise receded as she moved closer to her office, located in the silver dragon's head that fronted the Chimera. Once inside, she doffed her duster and cap and stretched out in the chair behind her desk. The eyes of the dragon were windows, and she watched the clouds pass by for a moment, even noticing a smaller airship in the distance, probably headed towards Cardiff-over-Coal. That wasn't on their itinerary for another two weeks, and she was looking forwards to Welsh cakes and a cup of strong tea, though they wouldn't stay long. Even in the city raised high above its counterpart, the smell and smoke from the mines far below still managed to waft that way.

Her wayward thoughts gave way to duty, and she opened the letter encased in the crow's compartment.

Captain Strud,

Greetings from Stratford-upon-Venus. We understand your mission proceeds as planned, though we were grieved to hear of Duncan's passing. We have reason to believe that both questionable English aristocracy as well as certain Americans have taken an interest in the item we're searching for, and that it was they whom you encountered at the Viking ship site. As you know, should the Apple fall into the wrong hands, and perhaps especially those of our Wild West cousins, it could have quite disastrous and far-reaching consequences. In light of this, we respectfully request that you act in all haste, to the best of your abilities, of course. Should you need further armaments or staff, we are fully prepared to assist. Simply leave word at your next port. If you would be so kind as to respond by crow with an update, it would be most appreciated.

Sincerely,

The Followers

Post script: the Viking ship set sail once again when the unusually high tide flooded the cave, and much of it was damaged as it collided with debris within its confines. However, we have made note of the location and hope that one day we will have the facilities to re-enter the space and retrieve that which you found.

"Wild West cousins." Temp leaned back in her chair and considered that. The likelihood of them finding the artefact before the English was about as likely as Temp donning petticoats. Somehow, the men in the cave didn't strike her as American, though she couldn't say why. And surely they wouldn't be interested in something so far from their shores? That's what she would have thought before anyway. She could still see the expression on the man's face as he looked up at the orb. Were they aware of the connection to the Firebird? Or did they assume the orb was the only piece? How would she go about finding them in order to take the orb back? As was so often the case when she was on these missions, she had more questions than answers.

She stroked the Firebird perched on her desk, noting the delicate nature of it and wondering how they'd managed to create something so beautiful so long ago. *More questions.* She took a fountain pen from the collection on her desk and began to reply. A knock on her door made her look up. "Come."

"Cocktail time, Captain Strud."

"Thank you, Peter." She set the letter aside to deal with later. It wasn't like she had much to report anyway. She straightened her maroon cravat and tugged at her waistcoat before putting on a fine linen suit jacket and picking up her black cane. The tip matched her cravat, an affectation she'd grown to enjoy and employ often. Peter held open her duster for her.

"Thank you," she said. "Have you enjoyed your lessons today?"

He grimaced as only a young man could. "Not really, Cap. The angles and numbers in maths have my head all turned around. Wish I could just read books all day. Have you seen the one about the man in the painting?" He gave a low whistle. "Downright gave me the chills."

She smiled at his enthusiasm for books, one which she shared. "Angles and numbers are important when you work a ship like this one, Peter. You need to understand wind and rise, what it takes for these balloons to lift the kind of weight required, when to use the sails and when they won't be of any use, and what to do when the engines go down. Fanciful stories are good, but they have their place." Visceral darkness and an inability to breathe momentarily assailed her. "You need to know what happens when things go wrong, and you have to get yourself out of a tight space."

His expression downcast, he seemed to understand her

warning came from a place of painful knowledge. "I know. And I'm trying, really."

She ruffled his hair. "I know you are, lad."

Conversation stopped as it grew too loud from the engines on the metal walkway, and they ducked their heads and hurried to the staircase leading to the staff lounge. She tapped a bell that let someone on the other side know she was coming in, just in case they were standing too close and got knocked over. The door swung outward and as it shut behind them, she took off the duster and handed it to Peter, who hung it up beside the door.

The staff stopped what they were doing. The women curtsied, and the men gave slight bows.

"Good afternoon, everyone. Cocktail hour should be an interesting one. Please make certain a staff member is in place at all times. If one leaves to serve a passenger, then another should take their place right away. If anything goes wrong or there are any questions, report to Peter, and he'll come find me right away." She didn't miss the flicker of glances that gave away how they felt about reporting to a person Peter's age. Duncan was gone. He'd been her second-in-command, her friend, and he'd handled many of the delicate aspects of life on the ship. She hadn't been able to face the idea of replacing him yet. Peter, a young orphan she'd taken under her wing when she'd found him stowed away in the cargo area several years ago, was one of the few people she trusted, and he was just presentable enough to be allowed to move among the moneyed gentry they served. She smiled at Joe, who looked back at her kindly. He'd have gladly stepped up, but he also seemed to understand her reticence. He'd handle things quietly while giving her the room to grieve.

She nodded and left the staff area. The dining room was empty but set up for the evening, with crisp linen napkins folded into swan shapes at every seat and crystal decanters ready for the drink of choice.

The moment Temp opened the door to the lounge, she was met

with deep laughter. A quick glance showed staff in place exactly as she'd asked, and the room was spotless. Plush velvet curtains blocked out the evening rain, and thick carpet underfoot could almost make one forget they were flying high above the smog-filled, poverty-strewn world below. "Gentlemen. How is your trip going so far?" she asked, striding to the table and touching her captain's cap in greeting.

"Strud. Sit. We're discussing the merits of art in a world full of shit." Oscar sat with his arm around his lover's shoulders, the ever-present slim cigarette between his lips even as he spoke.

"So blunt, Oscar. There's really no need." Lord Charles Douglas tapped the table as if to emphasise his point. "If we can't embody all that is good and decent in the world, then what chance do the downtrodden have? We must lead by example."

Temp knew better than to join in their argument; doing so previously had led to many alcohol-fuelled nights, heated debates, and more than one morning headache requiring powders. "And your fulfilment rooms? Is everything what you desire?"

Oscar's grin became mischievous, and he planted a kiss on his lover's cheek. "What do you think, darling?"

Charles flushed. "Well...yes. Yes, everything is...sublime, I would say."

His curly blond hair was mussed under his hat, and his soft blue eyes looked at Oscar with such devotion it was hard not to look away, as though observing something meant only for private moments.

"Are you ever tempted to peek into a room, Captain?" Oscar asked, leaning forwards. "Don't you want to see what beautiful perversities your fellow man falls into face-first behind those closed doors?"

Temp grinned. "Who do you think sets up the rooms?"

He threw back his head and laughed, but Charles looked mortified. "Of course. If there's anyone in the world who could send us all to gaol, it would be you." He licked his lips and took a sip of his laudanum-laced cocktail. "I'll wager your stories would put mine to shame, and they'd all be truth."

Temp tilted her head. "Aren't all stories at least a little true?"

"What's yours?" Charles blurted. "Your story, I mean, not...not your desire." He flushed once again and took a long sip of his drink.

"I'd like to know both." Oscar raised his eyebrows, waiting.

"The wonderful thing about a trip on the Chimera is that it's all about you and what you want. The crew are here to facilitate the immersion of your senses into your personal fantasies. Those of us who work here..." She smiled, knowing full well that Oscar had a deep desire to understand his fellow humans, though he protested that he didn't like them very much. "If we shared our lives with you, it might very well ruin the illusions we work so hard to create." She stood, waving off their protests. "Enjoy your evening, gentlemen. Please remember we'll be docking at Chelsea-on-High tomorrow to take on new passengers, and if you're at all desirous of anonymity, I suggest you take your meals and company in your rooms."

She left them to their debates, which were going to become more nonsensical as the opium began to play with their senses and the evening wore on. It was part of what made the illusions so real. Their minds would be fully open to the magic created in their rooms via the décor, the sounds from the recorder, and even the smells which were purchased from trade ships from as far away as Africa. The rest was provided by an artist with no moral compunctions and a vitascope that sent those images into the room. It was true, Temp knew secrets about everyone who could afford a trip on the Chimera, many of which would cause the kind of scandal not easily fixed.

But she was good at keeping secrets, other people's as well as her own. It was what she'd been brought up to do, after all.

"All well?" she asked Peter, who was reading through the nightly desire sheets that dictated what part of the client's fantasy would be played out that night.

He puffed out his cheeks and handed her the sheet. "Well, uh,

Cap..." He shook his head and looked at his well-polished boots.

She frowned. He wasn't easily bothered and mostly just laughed off the clients' demands. Halfway down the list, she saw what had him flustered. "Interesting. Was this part of the original design?" She knew it wasn't, of course. She personally made certain that each room was designed specifically to create the world the client requested. And for this particular client, it had been of paramount importance that everything be beyond perfect.

He shook his head emphatically. "No, sir! I wouldn't have missed that."

"No. Nor would I." She checked her pocket watch and then looked at the list again, along with the specific details of the request. "Guess I better go change."

His head snapped up. "You're going to do it?"

In truth, she was more than happy to do it but seeming too eager was never a good look. "Do you truly think it's a request rather than a demand? If that's what she wants, that's what she'll get."

"Crikey," he whispered, his eyes wide.

"Remember, Peter," she put her hand on his shoulder and squeezed, "nothing you see, hear, or find out on this ship *ever* leaves this ship. We're the keepers of secrets and that's why we have fine food, fine clothes, and a finer airship than any other in the skies. Understand?"

He nodded. "Yes, Cap."

"Okay." She checked her pocket watch again. "I'll change quickly and head to her rooms. Keep an eye on everything, and if you need help, talk to Joe. Unless the ship is going down, don't interrupt me."

"Yes, Cap."

Quickly, she headed to her rooms. A distraction from the land mission and the loss of her friend was exactly what she needed. The questions about what would happen and how long they had could be set aside for a night of make-believe. She pulled on rough, brown leather flying gloves and a matching pilot's cap, and changed her smooth black boots for thicker, heavier flying boots. Her hair, short and slicked back for the cocktail hour, was now artfully mussed. She changed the silk cravat for a simple olive linen. The overall effect was of a rugged and ready pilot. *Exactly what the lady ordered.* And it was a look that she liked herself. It made her feel powerful, sexual, and confident that she could give the lady exactly what she wanted tonight.

She made her way via the back corridors to the lady's rooms and knocked. When it opened, she bowed low, sweeping her hat from her head. "Your Majesty. I believe you were expecting me."

CHAPTER FOUR

ALEX SCANNED THE HORIZON with her binoculars. The Urchin's special black metal skeleton made it invisible in the night, making it the perfect time to raid. The sky was just beginning to lighten, and the buildings of Chelsea-on-High began to glitter. Docking stations made of the same stone were attached to the floating city at regular intervals, via bridges, and Alex wasn't certain which one would be receiving the supply transport ship. Hence, the binoculars and the tension in her shoulders.

"High security today." Ted stood beside her, also scanning the horizon. "See the guard ships?"

Alex shifted her gaze. "I count two at each docking station we can see, so I assume that's the same at the others on the far side."

Chelsea-on-High was one of the wealthiest floating cities. With its white stone houses built back-to-back and side to side, it was something out of a classist fairytale.

Alex hated it.

If she could burst every balloon holding it up and strip every gear that kept it in place, she'd do it before anyone even noticed, and there'd be nothing they could do as it crashed to the ground. Instead, she had to make do with causing them inconvenience. It wasn't nearly enough, but it was something.

"There."

Alex saw it. The small airship cut through the sky, rear gears spinning as the wings banked it towards the docking station furthest from their vantage point. "Call the men."

The crew moved like a well-oiled machine, crawling like ants through the airship to each gear rig. Alex placed the brass voice box beside her and flipped the switch so her orders would carry to every mast. "Clean and quick, boys. Security is tight as the bumholes of the people who live here. No noise, and if anyone causes trouble, deal with it."

The ship picked up speed, and she turned the tiller to pick up the wind. "Out sail!" she yelled, and her heart leapt with the ship as the spike-like sails dropped open all along the sides, thrusting the Urchin up and forwards like a bullet. They careened towards the supply ship, coming up under it to stay out of sight until the last moment. She sailed silently behind on the far side, and the moment it let out its mooring line, she shouted, "Close sail and drop!"

As one, the crew cranked the gears to close the spike sails, then leapt overboard, holding onto the thick ropes attached to the sides. Alex gave the tiller to a crewman, tied a rope around her waist, and flung herself off the side and into the air. Pure exhilaration slammed through her as she hit the deck, duelling sword already drawn in her left hand.

It was a short, unimaginative fight. The supply crew weren't fools, and the moment they understood what was happening, they raised their hands in surrender. The one who'd had a brief moment of insanity and reached for the emergency flare had lost two fingers on his right hand, but aside from the bandaged bloody stumps, he was fine.

"Right, lads. Move fast and sure." Alex looked at the men kneeling on the deck. "We'll be out of your hair shortly. No fuss, no fire."

One of them narrowed his eyes and then looked over his shoulder at the Urchin, which was now moored alongside the supply vessel. "You're Captain Minty." He swallowed hard, fear in his eyes now. "You don't leave people alive."

"Untrue." She waved her sword in a vague manner. "We've left our fair share of warm bodies—just not the ones stupid enough to try to stop us from taking our share."

"Your share?" He ignored the elbow in the side from his

crewmate. "You take and take. Don't give nothing back. Don't work like the rest of us honest folk. Just steal what others have worked so hard for."

She scoffed and looked at Ted, who shook his head as he watched the crew shift the boxes from one vessel to another via the planks laid in a line along the ship's sides.

"You think those dandies up there worked for any of this?" She motioned at the cargo with her sword. "You think they've worked a day in their lives? They're thieves same as us, just dressed in finer clothes." She turned away when he didn't seem to have an answer to that. "Nearly done?" she called out.

"Aye!" one of her crew said, wiping sweat from his brow. "Like candy from a nipper! Plenty to keep us going."

"Right!" She raised her voice, letting it carry to both ships. "Upship, lads."

Ted tilted his head towards the crew, and she nodded. One of them whimpered and closed his eyes. Ted raised his airgun and brought the hilt down on the first man's head, dropping him. The second one looked at his fallen comrade but didn't say anything before Ted knocked him out too.

The third, the talker, frowned. "You're really not going to—"

He hit the deck face first, out cold.

"Good. They'll have a headache and a tale, but we'll be free of the guards until we're safely away." She and Ted were the last to cross between the two ships, and she nodded at the crew member holding the last mooring line. He cast it off the supply ship, and the Urchin quickly rose and banked away as she took her place at the tiller. The sky was turning a pale pinkish blue; it was time to find the shadows once again so they could go through the plunder.

"Cap!" The boy at the top of the main mast pointed. "Look over yonder! A real dragon, it is!"

She looked at Ted, who shrugged. They couldn't see what the boy was talking about from their vantage point, so she angled the ship that direction, curious. Around the far curve of Chelsea, she yanked the lever on the sail, forcing them backwards.

"What in the name of Bell's breasts is that?" Ted crossed his arms.

The ship sitting at the rear docking station, probably the one least used, was enormous. The silver dragon's head at the front turned pinkish purple in the morning dawn, and the eyes almost seemed to look through the skies. The ribbed zeppelin was the largest she'd ever seen, and by virtue of thick silver lines, it held what looked like a double-decker passenger ship below it, nearly as long as the flotation engine itself. At the rear, a silver tail curved along behind it, moving almost like a sail, back and forth in a slow sweeping motion. And if she wasn't mistaken, there were huge, folded sails against the sides, like wings that would snap out and take the ship through the skies exactly the way a dragon would.

"Bloody hell," she said, leaning on the till. "Who owns that kind of ship?"

The crew gathered at the front, and they watched as a flotilla of guards moved up the gangplank to the ship and stood at attention. The railing door was opened, and a woman in a huge gown and full headdress exited, followed by a retinue of servants and more guards.

"Is that…" Ted edged forwards as though he'd be able to see her face from there.

"It can't be." Alex shook her head. "Everyone knows she hardly ever leaves the palace in Upper London. And if she does, she takes the Royal Airship." She snatched up the spy glass out of the drawer by the tiller and focused. "Well, I'll be the bitch of a boot maker." She handed the spy glass to Ted. He whistled as he stared through them and then handed them back.

She looked again, but the Queen of England had disappeared into a carriage and was being carried away, so she refocused on the ship. *Chimera*. What did that mean? It rang a bell, probably from her school days, but she couldn't place it. "Any one of you seen that ship before?"

No one answered, and she wasn't surprised. She'd been sailing the air around the United Kingdom for years and hadn't ever come across it, and it wasn't something you'd forget seeing.

"Um..." a small, quiet voice piped up. "I've heard of it, Cap."

She lowered the spy glass and looked around. It was Kip, the mast boy, who probably wasn't more than ten years of age. "Well? Spit it out, lad. What do you know? Does it belong to the queen?"

He shook his head, his eyes wide as he noticed everyone staring at him. "I worked in a house in London-mid-Upper a'fore I came to the Urchin, Cap. I heard a maid tell another maid that Baron Klasser was takin' a trip on a dragon to feed his sins." He looked towards the vessel. "Other maid said ships like that shouldn't be allowed. That they went against God."

"Well, ain't that interesting." Alex stared at the ship, considering all possibilities.

Ted moved a little closer. "That won't be like taking a supply ship with three crew members, Cap. If they had Her Majesty aboard, then they're well-armed and ready for a fight."

"Aye," she said, sighing. "We'll leave her for now, but I think we might follow her awhile and see who else she might pick up. Could present an opening."

Ted nodded and turned to the crew. "Upsail! Back to yer posts. Drop down to lower masts."

As one, the crew lowered the spike sails and caught the wind. Alex manoeuvred the ship into a wide circle to moor at a docking station at London-mid-Upper, where they could blend into the host of other ships. It took them out of sight of the Chimera and Chelsea-on-High in general but was still close enough for them to follow her silver tail when she left port. Thankfully, Chelsea had felt it necessary to separate itself from London overall, making it a small bastion of wealth floating above the behemoth circle of London. At this distance, they could see people coming and going from the ship but couldn't make out who they were, even with the spy glass.

"Ready to check the take, Cap?" Ted pushed a crate towards her.

"Kip," she called out to the boy, who'd scrambled back up the mast.

"Aye, Cap?" He leaned far over the edge of the platform on which he sat.

"If that ship moves, you say the word, understand?"

"Aye, Cap!" There was no mistaking the pride in his voice at being given such an important job.

Alex looked around and spotted Polly watching at the back of the crowd, her arms folded, her gaze thoughtful. She took the crowbar from Ted and forced one crate top open, then turned and did so to the others as well. Soon, the deck was piled with fine linens, enough food to keep the crew full for weeks, and plenty of dishes and the like to sell at the black markets along the pirate's coast. She took her share, including plenty of the fine material, and had a lad bring it to her cabin. "Polly, get some help bringing this back to the kitchens. Don't let none of these bastards nick anything either. You have my permission to cut off the hand of anyone who tries."

Polly gave a quick nod and started forwards, and two crew moved with her without being asked.

Ted would ensure the rest of the crew got their share and would put down any fights that broke out, as they inevitably did when two or more of them wanted something particularly fine. Back in her cabin, she sifted through the goods. No jewels in this raid, but it was just a supply ship, after all. It was still a good haul. She ran the silks and linens through her hands and was reminded of a time when she'd only known the feel of them and nothing else.

At a knock on the door, she tossed them back into the pile. "Yeah."

Ted came in and closed the door behind him. He raised his eyebrow, and she nodded.

"Go on."

He sat in the chair he liked most, a thick cushioned one that leaned back slightly. She'd picked it up off a raid on a fellow pirate ship, one of the Barbary coast raiders who ran slave ships. The pirate's code didn't apply to those bastards as far as she was concerned.

"Crew good?" she asked, handing him a glass of whisky.

"Aye." He sipped it and nodded, closing his eyes. "Polly's already making something that smells like it might've come off heaven's table."

"A heavenly meal for hell's saints. Sounds right." She sat in a chair across from him. "What's on your mind?"

Ted rarely came to her cabin without reason. Sometimes they'd have a good debate on the state of the world and what they did in it but usually, they kept chat to the business of the ship and what they'd steal next.

"That dragon."

She waited, knowing there was more and rushing him never got them anywhere faster. She couldn't stop thinking about it either.

"A ship that can afford to look after royalty might be just the thing we've been looking for."

She raised her eyebrows. "I wasn't aware we were looking for anything particular."

"Well, maybe you aren't." He looked at her for a long moment. "But some of the crew want to get back to the families they left behind. Have enough money to take home and make it so the kids don't starve."

She scoffed. "If the kids weren't starving when they left, they sure as hell starved when their fathers were gone and had no one to take care of 'em. Bit late to get back and hope for anything else."

"Still," he shrugged a little, looking away, "they can try. Get the kids out of the workhouse, pay off their debts. Start over." He motioned in the direction of the dragon ship. "That there could mean the difference between being a pirate and being a regular man."

"You make it sound like there's something wrong with being a pirate." She glared at him, anger rising. She knew full well he was right, and that what he said made perfect sense. That didn't mean she had to like it.

"No man on this ship turned to pirating because he had other options." He tilted his head. "'Cept you and me, that is. But we had our reasons, and they have theirs. We raid that ship, we give them a choice, and that's a damn sight more than they had when they joined up with this crew."

"Blast." She stood and began to pace. "You said yourself that ship is going to be guarded like the damn palace. Who knows who else is aboard?"

"And ransom pays well when it comes to folks who live in the sky cities." He grinned a little. "That alone might make it worth it."

"If we didn't end up at Executioner's Dock." She looked out the window, thinking. "You know I want to do it. I wanted to do it the moment I saw that silver tail. But I don't want to get the whole crew killed over it."

"You happy raiding supply ships and the occasional passenger zeppelin? Always having just enough to keep us going for a while but not forever?" When she threw him a look, he sighed. "Yeah. I know you are. That's how you're built. If anyone was meant for this life, it was you. Even if you don't get to put that brain of yours to use very often." He stood and poured himself another two fingers of whisky. "But you can't tell me that Polly wouldn't be better off starting her own bakery somewhere than working on a pirate ship where she's bound to go from one bad thing to the worst thing."

"Using guilt is a low punch." She went to run her hand through her hair, and it got stuck on snarls. "Fine. But we're done talking about it for today. When Polly is finished in the kitchen, send her in here, will you?" At his frown, she rolled her eyes. "I need help with this mop on my head, and I could use her ideas on how to turn this cloth into something useful. Isn't like I need a ballgown, is it?"

"All right." He laughed, the frown easing, and left.

She kicked off her boots and noticed a hole in the toe of her left one. Good thing she'd seen plenty of leather in that pile too. Maybe she'd pop into Upper London and get some new boots made. The thought made her smile. She wouldn't be incognito, walking the gentrified, pristine streets in her holey boots and stockings, an airgun holstered to her side as well as to her thigh. And getting caught now, just before the biggest haul she might ever make, would be foolish indeed.

Chapter Five

Temp breathed a sigh of relief as the last of the Queen's Guard left the ship. Oscar and his lover disembarked too. He wasn't scheduled to depart for another week yet but over the years, she'd learned that he moved through the world like a kite let loose in the wind, blowing this way and that, his creativity fed by whimsy and whisky. He'd send word by crow from wherever he was, and she'd pick him up so he could finish the journey he'd paid handsomely for.

Several esteemed passengers remained, though none showed their faces in Chelsea. She waited at the top of the ramp for her next guests, who were already twenty minutes late. That wasn't a problem, per se. She built in plenty of time between stops to make certain she was never late picking up a guest, since they often didn't wish to be seen boarding the ship only spoken about in whispers behind fans or in single-sex smoking rooms.

A small steam car puffed up to the bottom of the ramp, and two young women tumbled out. Laughing, the taller, short-haired one straightened her skirt and rumpled blouse. The other was dressed in a man's suit, not dissimilar to the one Temp herself wore. She took the other's hand, and they hurried up the ramp together.

"Ms Stephen, Baroness Sackville, welcome. I'm Captain Strud of the Chimera. Peter will show you to your cabin, and I'll be along shortly to explain how the next two weeks will progress."

The shorter one, Ms Stephen, gave her a frank once over. "Vee, who knew we'd be right at home?"

The baroness grinned and nudged Temp's shoe with her own similar one. "I might have to mind my manners or lose my girl to the dashing captain!"

Temp simply smiled and motioned towards Peter. "If you wouldn't mind, it would be best if we could upship as soon as possible."

Giggling and with their arms around each other, they moved past her, and she could hear them commenting on the beauty of the décor. Their driver lugged their substantial cases up the ramp, and she smiled at him. "Thank you. You can leave them here, and I'll have a crew member deliver the bags to the appropriate rooms." She held out her hand, and he took it, sliding the bill from her palm as he shook it.

"Are they...I mean, will they be okay?" The driver stepped back and looked down the length of the gondola and then up at the zeppelin dwarfing them.

"I assure you, they're in capable hands. Good journey." She tipped her head towards the car.

"Righto." He backed away, then shrugged. "None of my never mind, I suppose."

She waited until he was off the ramp, then turned and hit the lever just inside the door. With a snap and a hiss, the gears clanked to life and the ramp folded itself into planks that slid into an opening beneath the door. No doubt he'd head straight to the nearest pub to talk about the strange airship with the equally strange captain and passengers, so it was most certainly time to get into the sky.

Picking up the newly installed telephone device, which was attached to its own switchboard in the mid-deck and worked by the most up-to-date automatons, she wondered if the new guests were situated yet, but even if they weren't, she had a feeling they'd consider the tilting and heaving of the ship taking off just another part of the adventure. "Drop mooring lines. Upship." Having given the order, she made her way to the gondola beneath the primary body of the ship and took the tiller from the crew member in place. This was one of the best parts of her job. There was simply nothing like the open air and freedom it provided when they were in flight.

"49.677528, -5.835415," she said into the telephone. "Drop wings when we're over Low Worthing and raise topsail when we move over open water. The wind coming off the Channel will push us straight out to Land's End." She received affirmative responses and took a deep breath when she heard the sound of the wings opening. The ship lurched forwards, and her forearms strained to hold the tiller, which she always thought of as the leash that barely controlled the dragon they were lucky enough to ride.

Clouds flew past, and smaller airships below were barely a blur as they caught the wind current almost always in motion over the Channel. She checked gauges and used the compasses on her gloves to guide the ship along the coast far below. This far south, the only other sky cities beyond London-on-High were Mid-Bristol and Port Portsmouth. Mid-Bristol was a tourist city, a floating town known for its creative types who professed to be nonconformists but who rarely did anything to alleviate the poverty below the floating city. Port Portsmouth earned its name as an airship port that received everything from cargo ships from the Americas to passenger ships from France and Germany. It was heavily guarded, and they often stopped there to refuel and restock when they only had a few passengers aboard.

Fortunately, they'd made that stop a week earlier and had enough to get them through the next month. Now, she could fly out over the water and sail the air waves beyond the coast for the next two weeks until she needed to pick up her next passenger. Or until she figured out how to track down the men who'd stolen the orb. Or she figured out some other alternative that would lead her to the Apple. Whichever came first. In the meantime, she kept up the image of enigmatic captain of the mysterious ship. It was a good cover, and one she enjoyed. The phone rang, and she picked it up.

"Hoisting main sail in two minutes, Captain." The noise was loud behind the upper gondola engineer.

"Thank you. Engage when ready." She held the tiller tightly

and that same rush of exhilaration hit when the ship's sail caught, and they flew through the air like an airgun bullet. Within minutes, they'd left England behind and were headed for the coordinates she'd given. They soon slowed and then bobbed in the wind. "Sails down," she ordered into the phone, and all three sails were lowered, bringing the Chimera to a virtual stop. "You've got the tiller." She patted the crew member on the shoulder and stopped to look in a mirror before she left the control room. She smoothed her hair back into place and made certain the pilot's cap was at just the right angle, then she headed towards her newest guests' cabin but met Peter in the hallway. He almost seemed to be hovering.

"Everything okay?" she asked, looking beyond him towards their cabin door.

"Fine, Cap." He looked over his shoulder, and then leaned towards her. "I just didn't want you to get a surprise, see. Soon as I opened the door, they were down on the bed, and I don't think they'll be interested in bein' interrupted."

She squeezed his shoulder. "Well thought. I'll wait an hour and then go in. Let's go check on tea."

Two hours later, Temp was informed the new guests were in the lounge having drinks, and she checked her appearance once again before going to join them. Deportment and presentation were everything on this ship, from the captain all the way to the lighting in each room. She was adamant it stay that way at all times so nothing broke the illusions the clients paid for.

"Baroness, Ms Stephen. Is your accommodation satisfactory?" she asked, noting that none of the other guests had left their cabins for an afternoon drink.

The baroness pushed out a chair with her foot. "Call me Vee, and please, sit with us. I want to know everything about you."

Temp sat, taking in the entirety of them. Vee, the baroness, wore a loose-fitting waistcoat and trousers with a button-down white shirt beneath. Sitting so close, it would have been difficult to slide a piece of paper between them. Ms Stephen, or Ginny as she asked to be called, wore a stiff-collared blouse and skirt that reached her ankles, but it was clear she'd forgone the corset and waist belt popular with ladies of London. On her sleeve was a leather pocket which buckled around her arm.

"May I enquire, Ginny, about your handsome pouch?" Temp motioned towards it. "I've a fondness for things like that myself." She held up her fingerless leather gloves with the compasses built in.

"I'm a word player, Captain." She opened the pouch and slid from it a fountain pen, a small glass vial of ink, and a sheet of folded blank paper. "If I don't have my implements with me at all times, I feel as naked as a child left to roam a forest."

"An excellent way to carry them indeed." Temp knew full well the power of stories, and it was a shame Oscar had already left the ship, as she had a feeling he and these women would have enjoyed chaotic conversations. Temp pulled a sheet of paper from a leather binder and pushed it towards them. "These are the instructions we were given. If you could read this over and make certain these are still your desires, we can go about getting the first session ready for you."

Giggling, they read it over, and Ginny made a few notes before handing it back. Temp looked it over and nodded. There was nothing that couldn't be easily changed. "Thank you. Would you like to begin before or after tonight's meal? We can always serve your meal in your room as well, unless it will interrupt the dream."

Vee raised her eyebrows. "I enjoy a bit of anticipation. What do you think, Gin? After dinner?"

Ginny laughed and kissed Vee's cheek. "Whatever you want. I'll choose tomorrow."

Temp stood. "Very well. I'm going to leave you—"

"I wanted to know about *you*." Vee's eyes narrowed a little. "Don't think we didn't notice. We notice *everything*."

Temp gave a small bow. "Mystery is part of the journey." She turned away with the leather folder in hand and made her way to the illusionary mechanic's room. "Wade?" she called, when the room appeared to be empty.

"Here." He rolled out from under the Artful Artifice Contraption on a plank of wood he'd attached multiple wheels to. The goggles over his eyes made them appear huge, like an owl's, and the pockets covering his dirt-streaked jacket bulged with all manner of tools. "You have the new dream sheet?"

She handed it down to him, and he read it from where he remained prone on the plank. He'd been the illusion engineer for years and knew exactly how to make the dreams come alive in a way no one else had ever come close.

"Righto." He rolled onto his knees and pushed himself on the plank towards the desk piled with gadgets and gizmos galore. Using a pencil with teeth marks around the tip, he quickly drew new lines on a design sheet as he checked the dream sheet. "Time?"

"Ready by seven, please."

He saluted and blinked his owl eyes behind the goggles. "Everyone else happy?"

She tilted her head, wondering how she'd look in goggles like that. She was fairly certain the ones she wore when she was at the tiller didn't make her look avian. "I haven't received any complaints. Guest room five has been vacated for the moment. They got off in Chelsea."

He nodded and pushed open the board to the far wall that held sixteen switches. He flipped one. "Turned off for now then. Shame. I was enjoying creating that one."

She wasn't sure how to respond, so she said nothing. It seemed a little immoral to enjoy other people's deepest fantasies. That was, of course, absurd given the purpose of the ship. "I imagine we'll get a crow in a month or so when they wish to reboard."

He nodded and fiddled with his wrench. "Anything else?"

She grinned and backed towards the door. "No one else on the ship can dismiss me quite the way you do."

He grinned back. "No one else needs me the way you do." With a grunt, he laid back down and rolled himself under the machine once more.

With nowhere in particular to be for a while, she wandered the ship checking that doors were closed, that no one was somewhere they shouldn't be, and that everything was spotless. The register for the evening said five guests were planning on coming out for dinner, and she was certain at least two of them wouldn't be in their correct minds, given their requests for the voyage. It might make for an interesting night.

With a sigh, she went back to her cabin and looked over her inventory lists, as well as the requests from the staff in the different departments. Then she shoved it all aside and began to draw sketches of all she'd seen in the cave: the ship, the carvings, the wall art. And most especially, the faces of the men who had ambushed them. She hadn't seen one of them really at all, but the other two she was able to sketch out well.

She missed Duncan's company and input. He'd often mention a detail or item she hadn't come across, and that always added to the overall picture. They'd enjoyed long conversations about philosophy and religion, and she'd been able to depend on him to do many of the tasks she was ill-suited for. She'd lost people in her time in the American Airship Military, and it always hurt. But losing Duncan, who was more like family... She dashed away the moisture in her eyes. *Damn it all.* The cost of this expedition was already too high. She'd been studying the Golden Apple tales and locations for years, and when she'd heard about the historical items found floating off the Scottish coast, pulled from the water by befuddled fishermen, she'd known she finally found what she needed. If only she'd gotten there sooner and gotten away with the orb too.

Rubbing her father's gloves between her hands, she forced herself to breathe deeply and remember his words: *Do right by the world, even when it doesn't do right by you. Be someone you can look at in the mirror each day.* Nodding, she set the gloves aside and continued to sketch. By the time she looked up, bleary-eyed, from the drawings that would hopefully lead them to her quarry one day, dark had fallen outside the dragon's eyes, and the gas lamps on shore and along the air city skylines were no more than pinpricks of light in the distance. Thick, heavy black clouds hung in the sky above, and fat raindrops slid down the windowpanes.

Just as she stood to pour herself a glass of whisky, a shadow passed ahead of the glass. She frowned. No other airship should be flying this close, and certainly not in the dark. She hit the switch for the electric lights in front of the eyes. Red film in front of them would make the eyes glow like the fabled monster's, warning off any other ship nearby.

A loud thump made her jump, and it was followed by others. *Grappling hooks. We're being boarded.* She knew the sounds too well, and anger flared through her, hot and dry. She grabbed the phone on the desk at the same time she pulled open the drawer. "Obscure. Immediate Obscure. Repeat. Immediate Obscure." The code would tell every member of staff to hide, and Wade would employ the room locks so no one could leave, and more importantly, no one could get in. Any clients not already in their rooms would be ushered into safe zones with the rest of the crew.

Peter threw open the door. "Cap—"

"How many?" she snapped, grabbing her holster from the closet and clipping it on, before loading a multi-blaster on each side.

"Loads." He ran after her down the hallway as they headed for the cockpit. "Seemed to come from all sides."

"Are you armed?"

"Aye, Cap. Do you think it will come to that?" he asked, his voice quavering only a little.

She didn't answer, but she didn't need to. Pirates taking on a ship this size weren't cowards. They entered the cockpit and found a single crew member holding the tiller, his face pale. "I've never seen anything like it, Cap."

She peered into the darkness and gritted her teeth. There was no mistaking the vessel, with the many sharp sails that stuck out like spikes all over it. In fact, she'd been keeping an eye out for it for some time now. "It's the Devil's Urchin."

Peter leaned against the wall, his eyes wide. "Then we're good as dead."

"The hell we are." Temp looked at the crew member. "Don't leave this room. Only open the door for me or Peter. Understand?"

He nodded, his knuckles white as he gripped the tiller.

"Peter, come with me." She left the cockpit, turned right, and pressed a portion of the wall that looked innocuous to reveal a hidden alcove. Switches, levers, and cranks were set in orderly rows. "See this one? Count to ten and then crank it all the way. When it stops, flip this switch upward."

"Where are you going?" he asked, his hand already on the crank as she strode to the door.

"This ship is sacred, and no air trash is going to take it. Count to ten." She pushed through a far door and took the stairs two at a time to the mid-deck, counting silently to ten in her head. Goggles pulled down and cap firmly in place, she ran down the metal pathway through the rigid ribcage, gun in one hand, cane in the other. Shadows passed the portholes, and thumps sounded as pirates landed on the viewing deck.

Sound exploded, and screams came from outside. Bursts of light showed through the thick canvas as the lightning gun let loose on the Urchin.

CHAPTER SIX

"BLOODY BASTARDS OF BASTARDDOM!" Alex looked over her shoulder and watched as bolts of lightning shot from air cannons on both sides of the ship as well as the hump of the dragon adorning the top. The Urchin, made mostly of metal but with a whole lot of lightweight wood and more than a little flammable gas, caught fire and quickly became a nighttime sun. "Return to the ship! Get that bloody fire out before she blows to pieces!"

Her bellow was loud enough to reach the crew, who immediately swung back on their ropes like pendulums slicing through the darkness.

A voice boomed through the air around her. "That was your only warning. Leave the Chimera immediately, or we will fire again and obliterate the Urchin from existence."

Alex ground her teeth and watched her crew throwing buckets of water on the worst of the flames. Why did a luxury airship have that kind of weaponry? At the very most, she'd expected a few armed guards. Hell, the queen wasn't even aboard anymore. But lightning cannons were top-range. That meant they were protecting more than some snooty passenger ship. She thought fast. The captain of the ship would see the Urchin's crew turning back. This was her chance to sneak in, grab what she could, and get back, hopefully with enough goods to pay for whatever damage had been done to her ship. She loosed her rope and slid down onto the gondola's deck, landing with a barely audible thud.

Crouching, she made certain to slide beneath the portholes. She tried a doorhandle. Locked. Swearing under her breath, she looked around for another way in. There it was: a window only slightly open, just above the door. It was small, but she could squeeze through. She just had to hope there was no one with a blaster waiting on the other side to put a hole in her.

Lifting her hands, she depressed the silver button on the side of her gloves and the claw-like spikes slid from beneath each finger. A quick tap of her boots and a spike came from the front of each one as well, and within seconds, she was climbing the wall to the window. A quick glance showed the room to be dark and empty, and she slowly pulled it open and slipped in, shimmying through and dropping neatly on the other side.

"God's teeth," she murmured. A lifetime ago, she'd lived with these kinds of items in her home. Vases with glass swirls of colour laid in fine silver, paintings by artists long dead and still revered, and even gold candle holders with candles that were unburned. And this was just one room in a ship probably filled to the dragon's eye sockets with finery. She opened the jute sack slung across her back and began filling it with everything she could grab, barely glancing at it before dropping it in. They'd have a good look later, when she was back on the Urchin.

And then she saw it. Rare items were a passion of hers, something she'd once spent hours upon hours studying in the library, and the innocuous-looking stone carving hanging on the wall like an ornament had been on her find-and-steal list for years. Carefully, she lifted it down off the hook and saw the etchings covering it. Why would the captain have it out in the open?

A buzz filled the air, and lights flickered on. "Shite sticks," she said and dove behind a large, red velvet settee just as a door at the far side of the room opened. She cradled the stone carving to her chest, unwilling to drop it in the bag and risk breaking it, but also not sure how she'd keep it safe as she swung off the Chimera and back onto the Urchin.

"You did well, Peter." A deep voice cut through the open space. "If I wasn't so against killing people, even air trash like that, we'd have shot them down completely. But I've alerted Peele's air squad, and the Urchin shouldn't get far. It didn't look like it was moving very well with all those charred sails."

Alex closed her eyes and tried to breathe past the fury that rose like a volcano about to erupt. *They left me. Bastard whores.* Had they assumed she was aboard in all the chaos? That she'd gone back after shouting the order? Unlikely. It wasn't as though she was a softly spoken flower. But Ted wouldn't leave her unless there was no other option. The Urchin must be in bad shape indeed.

"Now. If you wouldn't mind joining us, pirate, it would make it easier for us to have a conversation. The furniture costs more than your life is worth, and I'd dislike the need to shoot through it."

Alex stiffened. *Hell's balls.* It had been too much to hope that she'd be able to sneak away. She rose slowly from her position behind the couch. "I wasn't doing anything wrong. I'm a passenger on this ship. Was just hiding from the pirates, you know." She stepped to the side, and the bag of stolen goods clanked loudly against her, and the carving clasped to her chest might as well have been a beacon. Only then did she really stop to look at the people facing her, airguns raised.

"You're a woman." It would have been hard to sound more daft, but she couldn't help it. The woman wore her hair short and slicked back, but a lock of it fell across her forehead and over her eyes, giving her a dashing, rakish demeanour. She wore an expensive-looking brocade waistcoat over a shirt so white, it might have been made of a summer cloud. And...trousers. Even Alex hadn't gone *that* far. She took it all in slowly, until her gaze moved back up to meet the woman's eyes. She looked amused rather than irate at Alex's improper perusal.

"At least we know you have powers of observation, if not those of timing, given that your ship sailed without you." She seemed to look Alex over in a similar way but didn't appear nearly as impressed. Her eyes narrowed somewhat when she saw that Alex was holding the carving. "Captain Alexis Minty of the Devil's Urchin, I believe? I'm Captain Temp Strud."

Alex froze. It couldn't be. She looked harder, trying to picture the person of that name she'd known an entire lifetime ago. She could see it, a little, in the half-grin and light in the sky-blue eyes. Her gaze darted beyond the pair to the door behind them, then she looked over her shoulder. Without another thought beyond escape, she leapt for the wall, her makeshift claws hitting the wood as she scrambled up.

There was a sound behind her, a whirring, clanking noise, and then cold metal wrapped around her ankles and sent her crashing to the floor, splinters of wood raining down on her as her claws scrabbled for purchase. She twisted in the air and slammed onto her back, the breath whooshing out of her, and the world growing dim. Still, she didn't let go of the carving.

A large form blocked the light. "Now, why would you go and do a thing like that?" the captain asked. "We could have shot you in the back."

"Oomph," was all Alex could get out as she struggled to get her breath back.

"Well, we have agreed that your timing isn't the best, haven't we?" Strud tugged the stone from Alex's hands, giving her an inscrutable look before she turned away. "Peter, get Crispin and Shell. Take Captain Minty to room twelve, please, and then bring me the key. Make certain the necessary visual elements are installed in relation to our guest's situation."

"Yes, Cap."

Alex listened as the young man hastened out of the room. She pushed herself into a sitting position and looked at her ankles. A thick chain was wrapped around them as neatly as if she'd been personally bound. "What's all this? How'd you do that? What's in room twelve?"

"Polite conversation requires one to ask a single question and wait for the answer before asking another question." Strud leaned against the wall, her arms crossed as she looked down at Alex. "I have a maker on board. He's always coming up with interesting new devices, and that's one of his." She tilted her head towards what looked a little like an old-fashioned crossbow. "It links into that and then shoots at the target. Just like that, you have a bound pirate."

Alex glared at her and yanked her skirt down, which had ridden all the way above her knees in her fall. "And room twelve, you pompous cow?"

Captain Strud laughed, a full open sound. "Well, that's not something I've been called in a long while. You'll see when you get there." She looked at the sack containing the items Alex had loaded up. "I don't imagine what's in there will be worth the noose."

Bile rose in the back of her throat. "You'll be handing me over to the bobbies then? Why not just put me out of my misery now?" She nodded towards the gun hanging loosely in the captain's hand. "Would save us all a lot of time."

"I recognise bluster when I hear it." The captain's eyes grew hard and cold. "Your reputation precedes you, Minty. I'm aware of your disregard for life and how much blood you carry on your hands. The Urchin may continue to sail, but at least their bloodthirsty captain won't be there to guide the blade any longer."

The young man, Peter, came in followed by two hulking forms.

Alex pushed back, fear flooding her. "Golems. You've got golems on the ship. And they say I'm the mad one."

Each one had an eye of glowing red and an eye that was black with floating swirls of white. It was hard to know which one to stare in horror at. Normally, golems were blocky things, clearly inhuman. But this moving clay had been sculpted and looked far too human-like to not be the bearers of night terrors. She flinched away from the enormous clay men as they bent on either side of her and picked her up. Ineffectually, she pushed at them until they held her arms in their vice grips, and the young man fit manacles around her wrists.

"Now. We can take the chain off, and you can walk to your room, or we can have Crispin and Shell carry you to it. Which would you prefer?"

Alex swallowed hard. The creatures' cold stone grips made her want to crawl out of her skin. "I'll walk. Just make them stop touching me."

Captain Strud's eyebrow twitched slightly, but she nodded at Peter, who picked up the crossbow and depressed a lever. The chain around Alex's ankles shifted and slipped and then unravelled, and she watched in amazement as it slid along the ground and back to the crossbow, where it then wound itself around the gear.

"How?" she whispered.

"Magnets or some such thing." Strud shrugged. "Quite useful. Now, if you will. I have guests to get back to. Most won't have noticed the minor commotion, but a few will need reassurance." She turned to Peter. "The room is ready?" When he nodded, she turned away. "Enjoy your final nights of freedom, Minty."

Alex walked between the golems like a piece of cheese between thick slices of concrete, and she heard Peter walking behind her. When they left the room, she stumbled. That had been some kind of small drawing room. The dining hall in front of her was decked out in crystal, from the chandeliers with that strange, buzzing light to the glasses on the tables. Everything was pristine and beautiful.

She wanted to break it all, sweep through it like a vengeful god and not leave a single thing uncracked.

Instead, she continued her walk through another entryway that led into a long corridor with doors set on either side. Guest rooms, if she had to guess. All the doors were closed, and small green lights glowed above each one.

"What do the lights mean?" she asked, hoping Peter was close enough behind them to hear her.

"It means the room is occupied, miss." His voice was still a little high-pitched, and there was no mistaking the stress in his tone.

They finally came to a door at the end, and there was no green light. She balked. There was nothing, truly nothing, she hated more than being in a locked room. "Now listen, lad. Let me go, and you can come join me on the Urchin. We share all the loot equal, we do. There's no need to put me in there. I haven't done anything wrong, have I? Didn't get away, so didn't actually steal anything. Neither did my crew."

One of the golems opened the door, and the other shoved her in. Her knees went weak and gave out.

Blank-faced stone walls surrounded a single bed. There were no paintings, no tables. It was a cell like they had in any other prison. A water closet with half-partitions took up one corner. Better than a bucket, at least. She looked over her shoulder. "Please. Don't put me in here. I'll be on my best behaviour—"

"Captain Strud gave orders, miss." Peter stood behind the golems. "And you don't have to worry. She won't mistreat you. She's the best of people, honest. I wouldn't leave her side for all the treasure in Britain. But miss," he shook his head dolefully, "you really shouldn't have tried to take the Chimera. Cap has no time for thieves." He sighed and backed away. "We'll see you have food and water." He looked at the golem on his left, which looked just like the one on his right. "Crispin, take the manacles off, please. She won't be able to escape anyway. And...remove the gloves too. Those claw things could come in useful to her if she gets too close." He glanced at her feet and sighed. "I think we'll leave the boots though. No sense in having the lady walk barefoot from the ship."

The giant moved forwards, and she held up her hands, more to shield herself from the grotesque being than for him to unchain her. Still, the lack of heavy metal around her wrists did feel better. Rather than allow him to touch her, she stripped off the gloves and threw them at his chest. He left, the manacles and gloves swinging from his thick hand, and stood beside Peter once again.

"No!" She scrambled on her hands and knees towards the closing door. "Don't! Please, don't—"

The door clicked shut, soundless and final. Alex slumped against it. There was no way out unless she managed to flush herself down the loo, and if it had been an actual option, she would have taken it. She rolled onto her side and curled her legs against her chest as the room began to close in on her.

Chapter Seven

Far from being upset, the guests who were vaguely aware of the disturbance found it all terribly exciting and wanted as much detail as Temp could provide. When they learned she'd captured the famous pirate, their excitement took on a new level. Once she was satisfied there was barely a ripple and her passengers were happy, she headed back to her office.

Most of what Minty had tried to steal was standard issue pirate bait. Seeing the ancient stone carving cradled in her arms wasn't surprising, but it did confirm something Temp had been wondering for some time. At one point, she'd considered searching Minty out, but now she didn't have to.

"I'm going to turn in, Cap, if that's good with you?" Peter peered at her from around the door to her office.

"Fine, lad. The engineers have let me know there was no damage done to the ship, but I'm going to take her up and away a little further, so we're not sitting here waiting for the Urchin to come back for their fair leader."

He grinned and tipped his hat back a little on his head. "She's right pretty for a pirate, Cap."

Temp laughed. "She is, but if you fell asleep beside her, you could bet you wouldn't wake at all in the morning."

He left, and she poured herself a glass of American Applejack she'd had imported and then sat at her desk, her thoughts whirling. The Firebird sat atop a black, burnished wood cradle, and she studied the markings as she had so many times before, sometimes until her eyesight grew blurry. When she'd sailed the wild skies of America in smaller, less distinctive ships, pirate raids were frequent and dealt with quickly and brutally. But sailing here in England had been soft and pleasant, and she'd grown complacent. Most pirates here were land-bound, and since she rarely docked anywhere lower than Mid Manchester, she'd failed to keep her guard up.

But the Devil's Urchin was supposed to be the most feared ship in the skies, and they'd nearly sent it crashing to the earth with an exhalation of electricity. If that was the worst there was to fear, then there really was no need to fret. Unless, of course, the other people after the artefact figured out who had the Firebird, that they needed it, and then decided to come after it. That could certainly present a challenge.

And then there was Alex Minty. There was something about her that seemed vaguely familiar, but Temp was damn sure she'd never met anyone like her. Torn stockings, wild red hair, eyes as green as spring grass... No, Temp would have remembered crossing her path. And yet...

She tossed back the last of the Applejack and rubbed her thumb over the Firebird. A soft, pinkish glow followed the line of her touch, as it always did, and then faded away. How had they infused that aspect into metal? And how did it fit in with the artefact the Fellows had tasked her with finding?

"Damn it." She stood, straightened her waistcoat, picked up her cane, and strode out of the office before she could think of the many rational reasons to turn back. The communal areas were empty, which was unsurprising. After the initial hubbub, the excitement had led the passengers to swim in their fantasies for the rest of the night.

She took a deep breath and nodded at Crispin, who stood guard outside Minty's door. "Make sure she doesn't bash me over the head or anything like that, would you?"

Crispin's head inclined slightly, but he didn't say anything. Golems were creatures of few words. Probably too difficult to speak with a stone tongue. If they had a tongue. She'd never thought to check.

She stuck the large key in the door and pushed it open. Minty sat on the floor, her legs out in front of her as she leaned against the side of the bed. Her arms were crossed, and her expression was mutinous as she stared at Temp.

"What do you want? Handing me over already? I felt the ship upshift. Afraid the Urchin will come back for me?" Her tone, though cocky, still held some of the residual fear Peter had mentioned.

"Actually, I was wondering if you'd accompany me to my office. I have a situation I'd like to discuss with you." Temp watched the emotions flash over Minty's face and knew for certain how badly she wanted out of this room, though she was clearly also trying to figure out the game. "No tricks. Crispin will join us, of course, just in case you get the urge to open my skull with something we pass along the way."

Minty stood slowly, her gaze darting towards the hulking shadow in the hall. "I don't want it touching me."

"As long as you behave, he'll keep his hands to himself." She stood back and waved the way into the hall. "Please."

Minty edged past her and away from Crispin. "Lead on."

Instead, Temp motioned her to walk beside her, and Crispin walked behind them. "You have a dislike of golems, I see."

Minty shot her a look that might have singed the hair of a lesser person. "Observant." She glanced over her shoulder. "What are you doing with such heavy things on an airship anyway? Most won't let them anywhere near because of the extra weight."

"I only employ two, and the ship is more than capable of handling them." Temp made sure to turn down several unnecessary hallways and double back again. She didn't want Minty memorizing the passageways, should things not go the way she was hoping they did.

"Employ?" Minty scoffed. "They're tools. No different than a hammer, but with an evil burning inside them."

"A superstitious pirate. How disappointing. I'd heard you were actually intelligent, all things considered." She didn't miss the flush of anger in Minty's cheeks. "What burns inside them isn't evil. It isn't even good. It's simply a type of lifeforce, akin to our hearts and brains. They have emotions too, and you insulting them isn't going to ingratiate you."

Minty's jaw tightened, and she didn't say anything further, but it was obvious she was taking in their surroundings as they approached the dragon's head office using the public route instead of the one leading through the dragon's belly. Temp pushed open the door and waved her in. "Thank you, Crispin. If you'll wait here to escort Captain Minty back to her room when we're done, it would be much appreciated."

His head tilted slowly, and he seemed to look beyond her.

"I assure you I'll be fine, and I'll call out if I need you."

He turned away, putting his back to her door and taking his place like a guardian. She shut the office door and turned to find Minty sitting at her desk, feet propped on the edge, the battered, multi-pocketed, safety pin-covered skirt falling back to reveal an indecent amount of thigh, vaguely covered as it was by the tattered stockings. Her black, scuffed boots sat atop a pile of paperwork, and she held the stone carving in her hands.

"You seem to have an affinity for that," Temp said, pouring them both a whisky and passing one over.

Minty narrowed her eyes and waited until Temp had taken a sip of her own drink, as though to make certain it hadn't been poisoned.

"I assure you that if I wanted you dead, I'd simply have thrown you from the ship." Temp sipped and watched as Minty tossed back the whisky in one gulp without letting the stone out of her grip. "A waste of expensive whisky, I see."

"This..." Minty held up the stone, turning it so it caught the light and sent long shadows along the walls. "What do you think this is?"

"We both know what it is." Temp debated the wisdom of her decision once again but again shoved it away. She had to trust her instincts. "The Cippi of Melqart inscription is instrumental to our understanding of the Phoenician language and a map to the sword of Hercules."

"It's worth a fortune. Hunters have been looking for that sword for years. Why would you just have it sitting out like that?" Minty traced the carving with her fingertip, like she was memorizing it.

"Because the sword was found two years ago." Temp sipped her whisky and smiled at Alex's look of surprise. "I found it using that stone, and then I turned it over for safekeeping." She shrugged. "Now I keep it out as a conversation piece and because I enjoy the beauty of ancient artefacts." She looked at Minty, hoping she was right. "I was about to search you out for a quest of a more... nebulous nature."

"Nebulous." Minty said it slowly, as though sounding it out. "Afraid I'm just a simple pirate, Cap. Not real sure what you mean."

"Your reputation precedes you, Minty. Let's agree not to play games. I'm aware of the fact that you're considered not just ruthless, but also crafty and intelligent. If you weren't, you'd have been caught long ago."

Minty grinned, and it lit her eyes. "Well now, that's a compliment I hadn't expected." She looked Temp over, and this time, the emotion in the glance was clear. "And as for games, I won't agree to any such thing. You look like you'd be fun to play with."

Temp ignored the twitch of desire. Dangerous women led to dangerous situations, and she didn't have time for that, no matter how interesting it could be. "The Golden Apple of the Norse. What do you know about that tale?"

Minty tapped her boot heel on the paperwork. "I know it must be worth an awful lot."

Temp crossed her arms. "Oh?"

"Oh." She took her feet from the desk and sat up. "I know it's strange that a person such as yourself is so interested in something like this. And I do know more than the average pirate about the arcane." She shook her head, her red curls sliding over her shoulders. "But I admit, this particular one I don't know much about. I assume it has something to do with this?" She set the carving aside with a brief, sad look and then turned her attention to the Firebird, sitting on a table beside Temp's desk.

"I'd rather you not touch that." Temp moved it out of Minty's reach. "Do you know anything about it?"

"I know it's part of a map." Minty stood and began to wander Temp's office, picking up this and that and then setting it back down under Temp's watchful gaze. She stopped in front of a large, ornately drawn compass overlying a map on the wall. "I know that it takes someone with knowledge of the arcane to use it, but to this day, no one has figured out what it goes to or what to do with it once it, whatever *it* is, is found."

"Mostly accurate." Temp moved to stand beside her in front of the compass. "Here, off the coast of Scotland, a Viking ship was discovered in a cave after a landslide. On that ship were two skeletons holding the Firebird. Also in that cave was an orb, which I believe was meant to go hand in hand with the Firebird. Sadly, only the Firebird was recovered. The orb was taken by another team."

Minty leaned forwards and read the section above Temp's fingertip. "Well now, that's interesting. No one has gone down to the Covesea Caves in years. Too hard to get to."

"Not to mention the amount of human remains which clutter the ground like seashells on a beach." Temp took a little satisfaction in seeing Minty grimace. She might be ruthless, but that didn't mean she liked the sight of death.

"Isn't just that though." Minty's gaze slid over the compass map like a caress, her fingertip hovering over it as she traced a line along the Scottish coast. "There's something odd out there. Something's wrong with the wind currents, like they're being moved around by giant hands conducting a band. They don't act right." She dropped her hand away from the map. "Despite you not saying it directly, it's clear you were the one to discover the treasure." Minty grinned. "I'd have come away with a lot more than just this bit of silver."

"Perhaps. Do you know what the orb is supposed to lead to?"

Temp had no intention of giving Minty any information she didn't already have.

"Something nebulous? Or maybe a piece of fruit?" Minty grinned and glanced at Temp before turning away to study another bit of paper tacked to the wall. "I've heard lots of things. The usual guff about immortality. Seems like that's what everyone wanted back then." She tilted her head towards the Firebird without looking at it. "They never seemed to want something as base as gold." She finally turned and stared at Temp, her expression impassive. "What do you want from me?"

It was now or never, and as Temp stared into Minty's eyes, she couldn't help but feel like she knew her on a level she had no right to. "I need to get that orb. But I'm not sure who has it now." She held up a drawing of one of the men. "This is the person who beat me to it."

Minty took the sketch and stared at it hard, her jaw working. "And?" She glanced at Temp and then back at the drawing.

"I'm a rather poor thief. I have no skill at blending in or at taking what doesn't belong to me. You, however, have a reputation for doing both. And given your connections to the undesirable elements of society, I thought you might be useful in helping me retrieve what I need."

Minty lowered the drawing and stared at Temp for a long moment, and then her expression began to change like a tide coming to shore. A smile spread over her face and a laugh erupted as she understood. "You're asking me to steal something for you. Self-righteous prig born with a silver spoon up her bum needs a filthy air pirate, so she doesn't get her soft hands dirty." She flopped into a chair and tossed her head back, still laughing. "The gods do have a sense of humour after all."

"I admit to a strange element of serendipity." Women rarely unnerved Temp, but something about the total lack of decorum Minty exhibited left her flummoxed. She was well aware of the irony, given her own decision to snub society's expectations of femininity.

"And what's in it for me?" Minty set the items on the desk and crossed her hands over her stomach. "Why should I do anything for the person who set fire to my ship and is going to hand me over to be hanged the moment we make port?"

"I imagine we can find agreeable middle ground." Temp sighed at the look Minty gave her, which could have pierced a steel hull. "Very well. You work with me to figure out how to steal the object I need, and I'll leave you at whatever port you designate when our deal is completed." She held up her hand before Minty could agree. "But, if you fail to obtain the object, if you steal anything other than the object, or if you double-cross me in any way, be assured I'll make certain you hang. I may even pull the lever myself, if it comes to that."

Minty's jaw tightened, and she glared at her without saying anything.

"Or you can refuse to help me, and I'll simply hand you over when we make port, and you can stay in your cell until I lead the police onboard to arrest you." She leaned against the doorframe, not breaking eye contact. "Your choice."

"Not much of a choice, is it?" Minty's eyes were hard when she stood and stuck out her hand. "You have a deal. I steal whatever it is you're looking for, and then I go on my way. Simple."

"Simple indeed." Temp went to shake her hand, but Minty pulled it away.

"No cell." At Temp's hesitation, Minty backed up a step. "It's not like I can go anywhere, and even if I pocket anything, I can't exactly sell it on from this monster of a ship, can I?"

Temp smirked a little. "There is that. Very well. No cell."

They shook, and Temp found she liked the feel of Minty's smaller, calloused hand in her own larger one. "We won't make port for a while yet. That will give us time to work out the details and make a plan. I've made certain we're well away from where your ship left you, just in case they decide they want you back for some reason.

So we won't be interrupted."

Minty looked away, and her shoulders fell slightly. "Fantastic."

"Now, it's late, and I need my rest before I deal with my guests tomorrow. Excuse me for a moment." Temp picked up the phone on the desk and dialled zero. "Wade, please." When he answered, she said, "Set up room twelve for vision seven, please. Right away."

She ignored Minty's questioning look. "Follow me."

Minty stood with her hands on her hips. "You said no cell."

"And I meant it. I'll remove the guard, and you'll be free to come and go as you please until we get to port. But I have to insist you leave the other guests alone and don't communicate with them in any way." She looked Minty over. "You don't exactly fit in."

Minty rolled her eyes. "Fine. You're not the type to go back on your word, are you?"

Temp jerked back slightly. "Never. If I give my word, it's sacred."

Minty laughed. "Sacred, eh? I'm sure you've made many a woman take the Lord's name in vain in a *sacred* kind of way."

Temp couldn't help it. She laughed, unsurprised by the assumption that she preferred the fairer gender. The question was, did the captain of the Urchin prefer her companions with beards or petticoats? Not that it mattered, obviously. "Perhaps. Shall we?" She motioned towards the door, and then led the way back through the maze of corridors to the room Minty had been in before.

Minty stood back, staring hard. "What's this?"

Temp opened the door. "Have a look."

The room was, of course, completely different. Wood panelling covered the walls, the bed was dressed in thick covers, and a porthole showed the clouds beyond. It looked very much like a room that might belong to an airship captain.

Minty frowned, scanning it from the doorway. "What in the devil's arse is this?"

"Welcome to the Chimera, Captain Alexis Minty. We're the ship where dreams come true." She tipped her captain's hat slightly and backed away. "Sleep well."

She walked away, smiling as she heard Minty mumbling about black magic, and headed back to her office. She'd made a deal with the captain of the devil's airship, and she could only hope she didn't turn out to be the devil herself.

Chapter Eight

If falling to her death wasn't so unappealing, Alex might very well have taken her chances and flung herself over the side and simply hoped for a landing that didn't break every last bone.

But that was, in fact, *un*appealing. She touched the wall, and it didn't feel like wood, but her brain told her it was wood because it *looked* like wood. It didn't feel like the concrete blocks that had been there before either. What the hell did Strud mean that the ship made dreams come true? The bed was real enough, and she sank into blankets softer than any she'd slept on in many years. Lying there alone in bed made her think of her captor. She was dashing, intelligent, and without question, a keeper of secrets. That, at least, was something she could respect.

She turned over and stared out the porthole window. Stars blinked in their black blanket, and she wondered where her crew and ship were. Probably had to land somewhere and assess damage. They wouldn't come after the Chimera again, as there was no way on hell's plains that they'd match that fire power. And that left her stuck here.

Stuck wasn't really the word for it though, was it? The ship was sumptuous, and no doubt the food would be excellent. Strud said she was free to roam but not to interact. Easy enough. That didn't mean she couldn't lurk and see what kind of person booked passage on a ship that changed its design while you went for breakfast. And maybe she could find out more about the mysterious captain too. She rose when her stomach rumbled and tentatively opened the door, expecting to see one of Satan's golems standing guard. But the hallway was empty, just as Strud had said it would be. Slowly, she walked along the corridor, and as she passed a painting, she stumbled and stepped back to look closer.

It was *moving*.

Or rather, the horse was running along an open field, and a girl sitting on a fence was waving a white scarf against a blue sky. "What in the blazes," she whispered, peering at it so closely her nose nearly touched the canvas.

"Fabulous, isn't it?"

She jumped and reached for her sword, but it wasn't there, so she crouched into a fighting stance. The man standing there glanced at her, nearly expressionless, and then looked back at the painting.

"Nothing on the Chimera is left to chance. Nothing to ruin the dream, to take away the sense of fancy and freedom." He raised his hand as though to touch the horse, then let it drop. "And so, we lose ourselves." With barely a shrug, he turned away, put a large key into a door, and disappeared into one of the guestrooms. The light above the door turned green.

"I'm sailing in bloody Bedlam." She took a breath and shook out the feeling of strangeness, then continued down the hall, decidedly not looking at any more paintings. They could do what they wanted to without her knowledge. Better that way.

At the end of the corridor, she heard voices and turned that direction, careful to stay in the shadows of the larger rooms that remained dimly lit. That infernal buzzing continued, louder as she passed beneath the strange lanterns that didn't have a flame. She finally came to a room with brighter, but still subtle, lighting and stood to the side as she listened to the voices beyond.

They sounded...strange. Too loud, too excited, too slurred. She pulled her skirt up to give her room to move and squatted before she peeked around the doorframe. Four women sat at a table, raucous laughter sliding out between sips of an amber-coloured drink. One woman had her arm around another, who leaned into her and looked into her face, clearly besotted. Two men sat nearby, looking barely conscious as they ate and seemed to mumble things to each other. All of them were dressed in clothes more expensive that most anything she had on her ship, including the ship itself. Her palms itched as she thought of what they'd have in their rooms that would feed her crew for months. They probably wouldn't notice, and she'd need a way to buy passage back to wherever the Urchin was once she'd completed her deal with Strud. Fortunately, she had a couple weeks to make that happen.

Platters of food were placed on various tables, and her stomach rumbled once again.

"Er, 'scuse me, Captain Minty?"

She jumped and banged her head on the sideboard, upsetting it and nearly knocking an expensive-looking vase from the top. "Bollocks and cheese, lad. Does everyone sneak up on you on this damned ship?" She put her hand to her chest as she stared at Peter. She could see him blush, even in the dim light.

"No, ma'am. I mean, we don't mean to sneak up. But we do things real quiet, so we don't disturb the guests. Try to remain invisible, right? That way, nothing interferes with their experience."

Before Alex could ask what experiences these people were having, her stomach growled loudly.

Peter smiled. "I knocked on your door to see if you wanted something to eat, but you didn't answer. I was going to bring a tray and set it outside your door, but then I saw you here...watching." He held up his hand. "That dining room is for guests. But if you want, you can come eat with us in the staff kitchen."

She glanced back into the room, which looked like a lot more fun than she'd have with the silent crew. But it wouldn't be good to get Strud's back up this early in the voyage. "All right. Lead the way." She followed him to a door marked Crew and into a small, cozy lounge. A few staff members sat at tables. One, an older man with thick glasses, looked at her over them.

"Captain Minty. Please join us." He moved a newspaper out of the way. "Peter said you might be along."

She looked around. "Can I get myself a plate of something? I'm fit to eat a bear."

A woman came out of a kitchen just visible off to the right. She was holding a plate full of steaming food. "Here you go. Nothing fancy, but it'll fill a hole."

"Thank you." Alex sat down and tucked in, nearly moaning out loud at the taste of the thick brown gravy that covered perfectly cooked mash. The pie had a thick crust and was full of meat and veg, though what kind she couldn't tell through the mountain of gravy she poured over it.

"I'd just hired a new cook on the Urchin, and I bet whatever she was going to make wasn't as good as this." She finally stopped to take a breath and sat back.

They were watching her like an animal in a zoo, expressions amused and curious.

"What?"

"I don't think we've ever seen someone devour food in such a manner," the man said. "I'm Joe. Chief steward."

"Why are you being so nice to me?" Alex asked, eyes narrowed. "You know who I am. And that I'm a prisoner here."

His smile was surprisingly gentle. "Jackup John is my nephew."

She laughed and smacked the table. "How is Jackup? It's been years since he left the Urchin to make his way in Mid Manchester. I've never found his like again. He could jack the sails like no one I've ever met."

"And he continues to do so. He runs his own passenger transport between the Tri-Manchester ports." He leaned forwards and looked at her with kindness in his eyes. "He told me an awful lot about the demented Captain Minty and how she handled portions of the loot she stole."

She leaned back and tapped the side of her nose. "And that's a detail that should stay with you and Jackup."

"And that's why you're welcome to dine with us anytime." He nodded at her empty plate. "Victoria sponge for pudding?"

She grinned. "Always got time for Victoria, eh?"

He didn't take the bait, though there was a gleam in his eyes. There wouldn't be any gossip about the ship's royal passenger then. The pudding was brought out, and she shook her head at the perfect sweetness of the cream. "How do you keep this on an airship?"

"You'll find the Chimera to be a beast unto herself, Captain."

"Call me Alex, please." She pushed the empty plate away. "What the blazes is this ship, Joe? It gives me the creeps."

Rather than answer, he looked at Peter, who gave a small shake of his head.

"Now, why would you defer to a lad so much younger than you?" she asked, genuinely puzzled.

"There's plenty for you to learn about how this ship runs, Alex," he said, standing and tucking the newspaper beneath his arm, before adjusting his spectacles.

Only then did she notice that his left hand was metal, with slender silver fingers.

He moved them, clearly seeing the direction of her gaze. "But my understanding is you have plenty of time to get to know us and our ways. I'll enjoy trading stories with you, I think." He gave Peter a short nod. "Good night."

Peter gave him a weak smile. "Night."

The rest of the crew left as well, and she turned towards Peter but couldn't deter the yawn that overtook her.

He stood. "I'll lead you back. Until you get the lay of it, the ship can get confusing."

She followed without complaint, looking forwards to crawling into the deep bed. "And you're not going to tell me about my strange captor or the stranger ship she sails?"

He shook his head. "That's for the captain to do." He shot her a quick glance over his shoulder. "Just...mind where you go and who you talk to. Things here aren't always what they seem."

She frowned and was going to press, but they'd entered the

corridor of rooms.

"Here you go." He stopped and then backed up a few steps. "Breakfast is anytime you want to come get it. I saw you taking note of the way here, and I think you can find your way back, no problem." He grinned back at her when she laughed. "See you tomorrow."

She opened her door and then locked it behind her. Fortunately, it was just as she'd left it, and she kicked off her boots, removed her skirt and corset, and flopped into the bed. She was asleep seconds after her head hit the pillow.

***

She woke to a sky the blue of robin's eggs and had a moment of panic as she tried to figure out where she was. When it came back to her, she groaned and pulled the thick down pillow over her face. Captured and forced into a deal she could only hope the captain kept her part of.

A soft knock at the door had her up and out of bed. Without thinking about what she must look like, she opened the door. No one was there, but there was a small pile of clothes with a note on top.

Given the likelihood of you bumping into my guests as you skulk about, perhaps you'd consider dressing appropriately. T. Strud.

She snorted and took the pile into her room. Carefully, she unfolded the pieces and laid them out, shaking her head at every new item. A combination shift caught her eye though. The one-piece linen undergarment would make it easier to slip in and out of her clothes at night and wouldn't slide around when she was climbing rigging or swinging onto other ships via a rope. She also pulled out the silk stockings and pressed the softness to her cheek as memories flooded her mind. There was no time for that kind of sentimentality. Her old stockings looked like rags on the floor as she dropped them and pulled on the new silk ones. Beneath the shift, they looked absurd, but it felt good to be wearing quality, and new quality at that. She picked through the other items. The bustle could be set fire to for all she wanted to wear a big pillow over her bum. The puffs for the sleeves could be thrown into the pit too.

That narrowed it down to the simple black A-line skirt, paired with a beautiful blue brocade corset with black stays and black satin trim. Over it, she wore the long black jacket with a single button that allowed the beautiful corset to show beneath. She looked in the mirror beside the water closet and very nearly didn't recognise herself. Though it was painful, she dragged her fingers through her hair, trying to comb it into something manageable. The curls had a mind of their own, however. Glancing around the room, her gaze fell on her old corset, which had seemed fine when she'd worn it a day earlier. Now it looked barely fit for a match girl. She yanked the stays from it and turned back to the mirror. Quickly she threaded the black cords through her hair, managing to pull it back and into a loose chignon.

Why do I care what my hair looks like? Abruptly, she turned away from the mirror and pulled on her old boots. They were comfortable and well-worn and had served her well. She'd had them custom-made by a maker in London-on-Ground shortly after she'd escaped her old life, and she had no intention of getting rid of them. So they didn't look right with the new clothes. No one on this vessel would bother a wit what she looked like. And her own crew would simply laugh at the expensive clothing and wonder what she'd get for it when she sold it on. But clothes didn't make the woman. Pirate captain Alex Minty was just as deadly in a fancy corset as she was in one with holes. She'd just look better when she was killing someone, that was all.

She stopped and looked at the painting again. The girl was sitting beside the horse now, both relaxing in a field. The horse nuzzled the girl's hand as she fed it an apple, and Alex jerked back when the girl seemed to look directly at her from the painting.

"Bedlam," she muttered and continued on towards the kitchen.

Peter had been correct the night before. She'd watched closely as they made their way back, and despite Strud's attempt to confuse her by going down multiple unnecessary corridors and doubling back, she could still find her way to Strud's office with no issue. There'd been no need to say so out loud, however. It was often best to play dumb and allow people to underestimate you.

Still, she noted the uncharacteristic nerves as she ducked into the staff kitchen. Joe was there, once again reading a paper. He smiled when she came in and moved his plate away from the seat beside him. "There's porridge in the tureen there," he said, pointing. "And tea in the pot."

She fixed herself both and sat beside him. The porridge was creamy, clearly made with real milk rather than the oft-boiled water they used on the Urchin. Instead of diving in the way she had last night, she savoured each bite. The tea, too, was the kind you got in London-on-High, not the sweepings you found in London-on-Ground. "I need to steal some of this tea for my ship," she said, sitting back and closing her eyes.

"Or I could simply arrange for you to take some with you when you go." He sounded amused. "You might want to consider asking for things here instead of simply stealing them."

She grinned and opened her eyes. "What fun is that?"

He laughed, and they both looked over as Peter walked in.

"Cap would like to see you when you're done with breakfast, miss." He looked between them and stood awkwardly for a moment. "I'll come back."

Alex looked at Joe. "So why is it you aren't the one in charge?"

"What makes you think I'm not?" He smiled and stood, taking her bowl and mug into the kitchen area and then returning to sit opposite her. "Temp is training him, and to train him well, she needs him to think he has more responsibility than he does. That way he learns to think on his feet, to make decisions, and then learn from his mistakes. She knows I'm always here watching, in case

I need to step in. But I'm happiest in the background, making sure everything moves the way it should. I'm no second mate." His expression turned sombre. "She had a good second, a man with integrity and a good soul. But he caught the fever when we stopped for supplies, and we had to leave him behind. Temp didn't show it, but I know it hit her hard."

"You call her by her given name instead of by captain." It wasn't a question, but one was implied.

"We've sailed together for many years. I knew her father as well." Again, there was a shadow in his voice that spoke of a sad state of affairs. He flexed his metal fingers, almost as though a memory made his hand move.

She studied him. If he knew Strud's father, then it was possible... "How long ago did you meet?"

He looked surprised at the question. "Shortly after he took ship in the Americas. Temp was a young hothead then, always stealing the family flyer and sneaking off to the western ports. Her parents despaired of raising her as a proper young lady. When it became clear that was never going to be possible, her father trained her to fly airships properly. I was on his crew and became a good friend of the family. That's when this happened." He held up the metal hand, gears moving as he wiggled the silver fingers. "We got caught in a storm over the Atlantic, and I got it trapped in the rigging. Took it right off when a gale hit." He gave her a rueful grin. "It happens. Still, I watched Temp become the kind of airship captain other men wanted to be."

It had been after the family had left England then. Her secret remained safe, and clearly the time abroad had wiped away memories of English society from Strud's mind. "How unusual, and how lucky," she said, truly envious of Strud's upbringing. "What I wouldn't have given for a family who understood me so well."

"He was an unusual man, that's certain." He stood and held out his hand, pulling her up as well. "Enough galley gossip. She can get surly when she doesn't get what she wants."

And what she wants right now is me. The thought made her smile, and she gave him a jaunty salute before heading out and making her way through the labyrinth of corridors to the dragon's head office. Peter hadn't come back, but she hadn't needed him to. She knocked and entered on hearing the command.

Temp looked up and stared for a moment. "That suits you." She looked away, her cheeks ruddy.

"I should probably find it strange that you have this kind of outfit available in my size." She took a seat and frowned at the lack of give in the skirt. Maybe she'd cut the sides. "But that seems like the least strange thing about this ship."

"And you'd like to know more?" Strud asked, eyebrow raised. "That doesn't seem like a good idea, given our deal. I'll let you off the ship, and you'll be able to tell everyone all about it. That would be bad for the necessarily private nature of our doings."

Alex shrugged. "Whatever you say."

"I say we get down to business." Temp stood and pulled a book from the shelf behind her, and the wall slid open. "This way."

"Well now, that's handy." Alex stood in the doorway, trying to work out how the hidden door worked in such a small space. "I bet you've got these little contraptions all over the ship."

"A ship that deals in secrets must have plenty of secrets of its own." Temp stopped beside a table in the small extra room. "There are things I prefer to keep private."

Alex moved around the windowless space, looking at the walls. Or reading them, to be more accurate. News clippings from around the world, pieces of articles torn from books, photographs and drawings, maps and more maps... The walls were a collage of research from the scientific to the fantastical. Arcane items were circled in red pencil, and she automatically began to make connections between the marked items and the notations around them. "I stole that one." She tapped what looked like a simple smooth rock covered in glyphs. "Sold it to the British Museum for enough to feed my crew for two months. Even got some new sails."

"You stole an ancient Honduran stela? From whom?" Strud looked genuinely distressed.

"Dead guy." Alex shrugged. "Mason someone or other. He took it from an archaeological site, then he got back here and died of consumption. I went in, paid my respects, and decided his numpty of a son wouldn't have any idea what he had in his possession. So I rescued it, took it to the museum, and made them an offer. He was dead, after all. He didn't care what happened to it."

"You don't know that." Temp squeezed the bridge of her nose between her thumb and forefinger, her eyes closed. "Sometimes these relics need to be kept safely away from the public."

"Like this one." Alex picked up the Firebird and cradled it in her palm. "And what's this? Oddest table I've ever seen." Deeply carved lines bulged and squared off in places, but it didn't seem to have a logical pattern. She moved closer. "What is this?" she said again.

"Step back, please."

"What, you think I'll steal something right in front of you?" Alex crossed her arms, wishing she had a weapon of some kind.

"For goodness sake." Strud shrugged. "Fine. But don't say I didn't warn you." She leaned over the huge carving and flipped a small, innocuous-looking switch in the middle.

Gears ground to life and the concentric circles of the wood carving moved, shifting in waves, one section rising and then another, while another fell and yet another popped up. Alex jerked back as a portion close to her lurched upward, nearly hitting her chin. She threw a quick glare at Strud when she chuckled, but then turned back to watch the show.

"This is a Parameter Piercer Wade came up with. It's a map of the UK that moves with the location of the ship, showing where we are in relation to the land below us. It helps with navigation in storms, but I also find it useful when I'm looking for certain items of importance."

Alex leaned in again, reading the small lettering etched into the expensive wood. "This kind of craftmanship...I've never seen the like." A piece lowered ever so slightly, and she looked up at Strud. "Is it that delicately attuned to the ship's movements?"

Strud nodded, her gaze moving over the intricate map. "He tried to explain it to me once. Something about magnets and lines that cross the earth. He updates it every time we dock somewhere. He walks through the city taking notes and making diagrams, then he spends weeks in here updating the pieces." She smiled. "It's a spectacular piece of art, isn't it?"

Alex had to agree. She walked around it slowly, taking note of the different places and markings, of where cities were higher or lower. A map like this would be worth thousands. To know where you were in relation to the land below you and be able to plot a route so clearly... Military, cruise ships, even pirates, would pay handsomely. "Is this the only one in the world?"

Strud laughed. "It is, and it's too big and heavy for you to steal." She held out sketched portraits. "These are the men who have the orb."

Alex tilted her head as she looked at the beautifully drawn pictures, and a frisson of dread burbled in her stomach. She nearly groaned out loud. "Baron Willoughby. Of course."

Strud's eyebrows rose. "Baron? I didn't think you had much truck with nobility in any form. Other than to rob them, of course."

Alex pulled the breakfast knife from her jacket pocket and slammed it into the wood on the edge of the map. "Enough insults. You've made me a deal and I'll honour it, but I do not need your pithy comments nor your assertions of my inferior being." Hands on hips, she glared at Strud, daring her to argue, hoping she would, and wondering if she could take a swing at her and lay her out, just for the sake of satisfaction.

Strud's eyebrow rose, and she looked thoughtful. "I was stating facts, Captain, and I meant no insult. That you take it as such is somewhat confounding but also interesting." When Alex didn't respond with anything other than a continued glare, she shook her head. "Please refrain from stabbing my furniture. As for Willoughby, what do you know about him?"

"How do you know he has it?" She wasn't about to explain *how* she knew him, but the fact was, it wasn't going to be nearly as easy as Strud thought it would.

A flicker passed over Strud's eyes, and she glanced away, but it was so fast it almost mightn't have happened. "Servant gossip. One of Willoughby's maids overheard him talking about it at a party he was throwing and saw it in his hand. We'd spread the word far and wide that we were looking for it, and she sent word via crow. In return for a finder's fee, of course."

"Of course." Alex knew, without a doubt, that Strud was lying. Her jaw was too tight, her hands pressed too firmly to the outer circle of the wood table. But so what? Everyone lied. You just had to be certain those lies wouldn't get you killed. She wanted to flop into the deep leather chair by the bookcase, but the skirt didn't allow for that kind of freedom. Instead, she sat on the arm. "So we're going there based on the word of a maid you paid before you even verified her information? You're not very good at this secret organisation business, are you?" She took some small pleasure in the red that suffused Strud's cheeks.

"I'm quite certain the information is sound." Strud pulled out another sheet of paper. "This is what you're looking for."

Alex picked up the fine linen paper and studied the drawing, which had been done with a fair hand. "Strange," she said. Whereas the Firebird they had in front of them was intricately carved silver, the piece in the drawing was perfectly round, with a small knob on the side that would clearly allow the Firebird to perch atop it. "What are these markings?" she asked, tracing the whorls that ran in smooth patterns along the middle.

"I'm not sure." Strud picked up the Firebird and moved her fingers across it, the pink lines following her touch. "I'm wondering if it's something like that."

"The colour might be there, but they look almost like

hieroglyphs..." She glanced at the Firebird. "Or maybe Norse figures." Alex nodded when Strud simply looked back at her implacably, ignoring the idea that Strud's fingers would trace lines like that along her skin. "Willoughby's estate is a fortress. And Low Nottingham is nothing but dark back alleys and thieves around every corner, most of whom work for Willoughby. That's why he put himself in the middle of it. How do you expect to get in and out without a fight?"

Strud grinned and leaned against the bookcase behind her. "I wouldn't want to take away all your fun. Though I'm hoping you're better at robbing an estate than you were my ship." She held up her hands. "Just a fact, not a judgement."

"You can stick your facts in dark bodily places." Alex grinned back. "Do you have a plan?"

"I was rather hoping we could come up with one together." A chime sounded, soft and sweet, and a green light flickered above the door. Strud looked at her pocket watch and then tucked it back into her waistcoat pocket. "I need to see some guests. Please don't take, stab, or break anything while I'm gone."

"And who are these guests?" Alex asked. "Anyone I know?"

Strud shook her head, a smile touching her lips as she pulled on her captain's cap. It shadowed her eyes and made Alex shiver. Strud might come across as a dapper dandy, but there was something of the dangerous in her, a predator lurking beneath a svelte façade.

"Unlikely, but I have a feeling there's more to you than you let on."

"Et tu," Alex said softly as Strud left the small room. It was true that she had secrets aplenty, but Strud was running some kind of crazy cruise ship while also seeking out rare artefacts. Alex had been the primary predator for so long, she'd forgotten what it was like to be prey. And she had a distinct feeling she didn't even know what might be hunting her.

Chapter Nine

As a rule, Temp didn't have physical relations with the Chimera's passengers. Every once in a while, she dallied, and in the case of the queen, she wasn't exactly in a position to turn down the request. Overall, however, it was bad form. The passengers had specific requests, and the Chimera usually exceeded expectation in delivering on those. Seeing a crew member aside from the waitstaff, even Temp, outside of their rooms could sully the experience.

But as Ginny sat on Temp's knees, her bum moving provocatively as Vee watched with half-lidded eyes, Temp was having serious doubts about her commitment to her own policy. The writers had been making full use of the ship's entertainment, and Temp had been informed they'd also made use of the lounge, drawing room, kitchen, and viewing deck. Most of that use had not included clothing, or at most, quite minimal covering. They were certainly the most open passengers she'd had aboard in many years. Even Oscar had kept his fantasy world mostly private.

"Come along, Captain." Vee sipped her whisky, her expression lascivious and hungry. "You don't want us to go away unsatisfied, do you?" Her unlaced boot slid up the side of Temp's pantleg. "Surely you want us to have everything we desire?"

Yes I do. "I'm afraid I'm not on the menu tonight."

Ginny pressed her bum harder against Temp's leg, then shifted so she straddled Temp's thigh but faced Vee. "Perhaps it's us she doesn't desire," she said, reaching up and unravelling the bun at the base of her neck, letting her hair spill loose down her back.

Temp grabbed Ginny's hips, mostly to stop the maddening

rocking rhythm that was setting her on fire. Long, luscious hair was often her downfall. The way it slid over a woman's naked back when she arched, her voice raised in pleasure…

"I'm so sorry to interrupt, but I'm afraid the captain has plans tonight."

Temp closed her eyes and swore, but she wasn't sure exactly what she was swearing at. Alex's appearance among her guests or the fact that she was helping Temp out of this situation.

Vee's gaze slid slowly away from Ginny and Temp, like it was taking concentration to look away. Then her smile widened. "Well, if we'd known there were other playmates aboard, we might have left the poor, beleaguered captain alone." She stood and grasped the table to steady herself and then held out her hand. "Vee."

"Alex Minty."

This time, Temp knew full well what she was mentally swearing at.

Ginny stopped her unsubtle grinding, and her head snapped around. "Well now, this night has just become even more delightful." With more determination than grace, she climbed off Temp's lap and joined Vee in front of Alex. "Ginny. And you're the famous woman pirate."

Vee took Alex's hand in hers and kissed her knuckles, once she managed to find them. "Bewitching creature. I don't mind telling you that we had our scripts changed once we heard you'd been captured." She looked over her shoulder at Temp but didn't release Alex's hand. "If we'd known what secret you were keeping to yourself, we'd have insisted on meeting her sooner."

Ginny rested her head on Vee's shoulder as she continued to stare at Alex. "Maybe we could convince the captain to join us if our glorious pirate wanted to as well. She has to keep an eye on her, after all…"

Alex looked past her admirers at Temp and smirked, one eyebrow raised in question. Temp rolled her eyes and shook her head emphatically. Alex gave a small shrug.

"As much as I'd love to see what kind of interesting things you get up to, she's promised that we'll have time together tonight, just the two of us. And with a woman like that, you don't want to share when she's sure to have you hanged later. You want it to be all about you, eh?" She winked at them, making them laugh.

"How delightfully dark," Vee said, leaning a little against Ginny, like it was hard to stay upright.

Temp crossed her legs and tried to look casual, but hearing three women talk about enjoying intimacy with her, especially three extremely attractive, intelligent women, was making it hard to think objectively about anything at all. Acquiescing would make for a night she wouldn't forget, that was certain. Maybe she'd have to make use of the ship's design once she was rid of all of them and allow that fantasy to play out in a way that wouldn't get her killed or fired. *But what a way to die...*

"Very well." Ginny tugged on Vee's arm, leading her away. "We've plenty of time to convince you before we leave the ship. For now," she bit her lip and swung her hair over her shoulder, "we can play make-believe."

She gave a little yelp as Vee dashed towards her and chased her from the room, leaving Temp and Alex alone. Temp swallowed and stood, pulling her trousers away from her nether regions. "Thank you for intervening. I was having some difficulty dissuading them."

"Right. It certainly looked like you were trying very hard to get her off your lap." Alex's wry smile suggested otherwise. She looked past Temp towards the door they'd gone through. "If I'd known that was the kind of passenger you had here, there's no way I would've stayed in my cell so long."

"And now that you know, you're still relegated to your *room*, and I'll ask you to stay away from the guests, as fetching and willing as they may be." Temp stood, her hands in her pockets, and noticed for the first time how much smaller Alex was. She had such a big presence, it was easy to overlook that she was a storm in a teacup. "Did you actually need something? Or was it simply that you wanted to bother my guests?"

"I didn't bother anyone though, did I? I saved your tight arse from having to give in and get naked. And I did have a question about our little adventure." Alex looked beyond Temp again. "What was all that talk about desire and fantasy?"

Temp sighed and pinched the bridge of her nose. "I may as well show you and explain, since we're going to be together for some time, and you'll just nosy about until you get answers anyway."

Alex grinned and tucked her arm in Temp's. "You already know me so well."

"But Alex," Temp said, looking down at her and stamping out the feeling that she fit well against her, "you can't tell anyone about what you see here. It's of the utmost importance, and I've already taken a chance by showing you the research room. This," she motioned vaguely towards the rest of the ship, "is a private matter and could get people in serious trouble."

Alex winced. "I'm well aware of the legalities involved in relationships like the ones we have. Like those of Ginny and Vee. You need not remind me." She mimed locking her lips. "On my honour as a pirate, I'll take what I learn on your oversized ship to my grave."

Temp stared at her for a moment, debating the wisdom of questioning a pirate's honour. But they'd come this far and had a long way to go yet. "Very well. This way."

She took them along the primary corridors until she got to the entryway for Wade's workspace. The backways and false-fronted doors were out of the question. If the Urchin's crew did come back for Minty, she wasn't about to have provided a way for them to get through the ship like rats. At Wade's door, she stopped, still uncertain. "You swear—"

"Bollocks and bells, Strud. It isn't like you're guarding the crown jewels." Alex pushed open the door and strode in.

Temp shook her head. People's fantasies and the way they

played out were worth more than the crown jewels of any country. She moved up behind Alex, who had stopped and was staring in fascination at the machines machining and gears gearing. "Wade?" Temp called.

"Seven!" he called from further down the row of machines.

"This way," Temp said, leading Alex down the furthest row.

"What is all this?" Alex asked softly, her fingertips lightly brushing a bright copper tube.

"This is the Illusionary Mechanic's Room. It's where fantasy becomes reality." She stopped at the large, blackened window for room five, which had been Oscar's. She flipped a switch, and the room illuminated, showing the small trio of vitascopes placed at different levels in the window. "What do you see?"

Alex studied the room as well as the vitascopes, her brow furrowed. Her long red hair was escaping the black cord she'd used to tie it up, and Temp wanted to pull it out the rest of the way and run her fingers through it.

"It's a...well, it looks like a college room of some kind." She looked at Temp. "My room looked like a cell, and then it looked like a ship's cabin. But it didn't feel like one." She tapped lightly on one of the vitascopes. "Is it to do with these? What are they? How do they work?"

"You are truly terrible about asking questions and not waiting for answers." Temp motioned for them to keep walking along the row of machines. "Those are called vitascopes. They're hooked up to the Artful Artifice Contraption, where all the main images are loaded. The scopes themselves use those images, stamped on a type of film that projects what we want people to see into the room. The more delicate the illusion, the more vitascopes we use to overlay the images, so it feels real." Temp stopped and tapped a metal machine at her feet beneath another window. "We also extract scents into vials and then pump the scent into the room. Olfactory senses can complete a scene in a way that pure imagery can't."

Alex stared at the machinery, clearly contemplating the information. Temp wasn't worried about her seeing anything she shouldn't, as Wade kept the windows black unless he was altering an illusion. It was the first time she'd been able to show someone behind the scenes, and she acknowledged the sense of pride.

"Fantasies." Alex tilted her head, her eyes narrowed. "You design these rooms to fulfil people's fantasies, whatever they might be."

Temp nodded, uncertain as to why Alex was looking ever so slightly like she wanted to punch her.

"Rich people pay you to create a place they can play out their dirty little dreams. Down there," she pointed, "people are scraping by with barely enough to eat, and up here," she pointed, this time at Temp, "people are spending cart loads to do the dirty however they want to."

Now Temp understood. Not only had she captured a bloodthirsty pirate, she'd also captured one with a social conscience. "It isn't for me to tell people how to spend their money. They earned it, it's theirs to do with as they wish. I simply provide an unusual outlet." She tapped on a vitascope. "And for people like us who prefer the company of our own sex, I provide a place of safety as well."

Alex snorted in a rather unladylike fashion. "For people like us with money, you mean. People who already live in London-on-High and don't have to worry about not having a place to sneak off with whomever they want up their skirts."

"That's life." Temp shrugged. "At least with me, they get something when they spend their money. You just take it."

For a moment, it looked like Alex was going to argue, but her shoulders dropped, and she turned away. They walked the rest of the way to where Wade sat on the floor, a pile of copper tubes and gears between his legs. His muttering stopped when they neared, and he looked up, his giant owl eyes taking them both in. She felt Alex jerk back a little and then relax again.

"Those are some glasses, handsome." Alex started to kneel but the skirt pulled tight, forcing her to stay upright, and she made a sound of irritation.

That bit of stretched material across a very pert, very nice-looking bottom made Temp take a deep breath. "Wade, this is Alex. Alex, this is Wade, our illusion engineer."

His already wide eyes widened further, and he tugged the goggles off and shoved them onto his head, forcing his hair into sweaty spikes. "You brought the pirate back here?" Without the goggles, his eyes became tiny black pinpricks as he squinted at them.

"She was going to find her way back here anyway at some point. She's rather obnoxiously determined that way. Plus, she's going to assist us with the orb issue. We now have a location for it, thanks to Captain Minty."

He squinted at Alex. "No good will come of having her back here. And don't you go telling anyone about my makings, eh? They're for the Chimera, no one else."

"You make it sound like the Chimera is a person." Alex peered past Wade at the length of rooms, and then her expression changed. "This is how you changed my room from a cell. You've got a window that lets you see inside." She glared at them both. "You spy on people in their rooms? That's...that's..." She shook her head. "And *I'm* supposed to be the immoral one."

If apoplexy was a person, Wade now personified it. His face turned a mottled red, and he struggled to his feet. "Now listen here—"

Alex took a single step back with her left foot, and Temp immediately recognised the fighting stance. Had it been any woman other than Alex, she might have been surprised, but she'd heard plenty of tales of Alex's prowess with knives and fists, though she looked far too small to affect any real damage. But that kind of thinking could get Temp a knife in the back, and she'd do well to remember it. "Enough." She moved between them. "I need both of you, so you're going to need to table your dislike of one another until we've accomplished what we need to do."

Wade moved to look around Temp, as he wasn't quite tall enough to look over her shoulder. "I'd never hit a woman, even one such as that. But be assured, miss, I fix the fantasies and manage the mechanisms, but each person's business is their own, and I don't never interfere. Cap tells me when the room is to be up and running and when to shut it down, and that's that."

Alex's posture relaxed. "I'd damn sure have a peep."

Wade paused, and then laughed, and the tension dissipated.

Temp took a breath and shook her head. "Now that we've cleared that up—"

"Could you make my room something more interesting?" Alex frowned slightly. "Could you put someone in it that wasn't real and have them interact with me?"

Wade raised his eyebrows at Temp but didn't say anything.

"In a manner of speaking. Now, if we could—"

"What does that mean? In what manner?" Alex folded her arms and looked about as moveable as a boulder.

Temp looked at the ceiling, trying to marshal her patience. "You don't need to know all the details, Alex. We can change the scenery in your room, if you wish."

"In. What. Manner." Alex's eyes were hard, her lips pressed into a thin line. "You said you only have two golems on the ship, so it can't be those. I'm not leaving here until I understand. It's my way. I hate being in the dark about anything."

"I regret making you the deal. I should just leave you locked in your room and be done with you." It was fleeting, but Temp didn't miss the tiny flinch around Alex's eyes. "Fine. Wade, are any of the rooms empty?"

He turned away and opened a cupboard with a multitude of tubes. Some were green, some weren't. "I could open ten, if you wanted to show her that specific thing."

Temp nodded, and they followed him further down the corridor, stepping over the multitude of copper piping that led from the Artful Artifice Contraption to the vitascopes at each of the windows. At room ten, he flipped the switch that allowed them to see into the room.

Alex leaned so close to the glass, her nose nearly touched it. "What is it?" she asked, pointing at the humanoid shape wearing a voluminous cloak.

"It's an automaton. We use them throughout the ship specifically for the type of situation you mentioned. Automata have come a long way since Jaquet Droz created The Writer, and we use similar clockworks to those used in the seventeenth century, with some upgrades, of course. While the actions are still somewhat limited, using the overlayed vitascope imagery, we can make it seem quite like a real person. Real enough to fulfil the desire required."

Slowly, Alex's head turned so she was facing Temp, a wicked gleam in her eyes. "Any desire?"

"You won't be finding out." Temp gave her a look that telegraphed playtime was over. "Turn off the room, Wade, in case the passenger returns."

He did so and then shoved his hands in his pockets. "Need anything else from me right now?" He toed a pipe, making it chime. "I've got to see to tonight's visions."

"You made the table." Alex turned towards him, her eyes wide. "You're the artist who created that sublime map."

His smile started slowly, growing like a sunrise until it covered his face. "That's me."

"Extraordinary." Alex motioned at the room around them. "It seems a travesty for you to be trapped back here. You should be making millions in Upper-New Chelsea, getting people to pay loads for what you can do."

Temp gently took Alex's arm and turned her towards the exit. "Thank you for your time, Wade. If you need anything, we'll be in my office."

He mumbled something about staying well away from them and then ducked behind the Artifice, disappearing from view.

Alex seemed to take everything in on the return journey, though she didn't ask any further questions. She stopped short in the corridor, however, at one of the paintings. "Another vitascope creation?" she asked, as a boy ran through a field, a red kite bouncing in the air behind him.

"No. That's a pictorial prompter. They're often specific to the details of the person whose room is closest to the painting. Even if they don't pay it much attention, it sticks with them and adds to the illusions of their experience."

"And someone wants to be a boy flying a kite?" Alex tilted her head. "A little tame, I would think."

"It's not for us to say." Temp held her elbow and pulled her gently along the hallway, hoping to get her back before they ran into more passengers.

"Have you ever made use of one of those rooms for your own interests, Captain?" Alex walked a little closer, her hip touching Temp's. "A little slap and tickle with a house maid, or a rumple of the sheets with a washer woman far below your lofty station."

"I assure you, I can have those things in reality and have no need of illusory options." Temp gritted her teeth at the tone in her voice, which was so uptight, she could have stood a spoon in it.

"Touchy." Alex allowed a semblance of space between them again. "What I wouldn't give to watch whatever was going on in Ginny and Vee's room." She gave a low whistle and then looked sharply at Temp. "But you know, don't you? You set up those scope thingies, and they have to tell you what it is they want."

Temp didn't answer.

Alex placed her finger to her lips, as though thinking. "The secrets you must know. Pirates can come in many flavours, Captain. Perhaps I'm not the only one here."

Again, Temp reminded herself not to let Alex get under her skin. "You're here because I need you to help with a specific secret." She opened the door to her office and waved Alex in. "What do you need to get it done so we can be rid of each other?"

Alex moved away to look at the walls. "Do you have an architect's rendering of the estate?" She'd been there, more than once, but she didn't need to say as such because even so, she'd only seen two of the main rooms. That left twenty more, plus four towers and the underground cave rumoured to be there.

Temp shuffled some papers and then placed it on top. "It's the best that can be found. The hall is old and has gone through several restorations and renovations."

Alex glanced at it and then yawned, not bothering to hide it politely behind her hand. "I think it's time for me to turn in. Let's pick this up tomorrow, yeah?" She moved to the door and looked over her shoulder. "No need to walk me to my room; I can find my way." She grinned. "And I'll be sure to sleep naked tonight, just in case you're looking in my secret little window." The door closed behind her, and she was gone.

Temp slid into her chair and lightly banged her forehead on the desk. This was going to be the most difficult assignment of her life, and it had nothing to do with the artefact and everything to do with the woman she needed to get it for her.

Chapter Ten

Golems. Automatons. Rooms that were changeable, and illusions catering to desires people couldn't fulfil on land, high or low. And you could do an awful lot of questionable things in the low cities. Alex had done her share, so she knew that to be true.

And then there was the art, the jewellery, the machinery and maps... Everything on this ship was worth a fortune. Not to mention the secrets. What could she sell that kind of thing for? Not the women's secrets, sure. She had her limits, far reaching though they may be. Granted, it wasn't an option right now, but down the road? Who knew how things would turn out.

She slid the new clothes off and laid them neatly over a dresser, which was real enough. That hadn't been in here when it was a cell, which explained some aspects of the changeable rooms. They still used real pieces of furniture, but that was minor comfort. She stripped down to bare skin and turned in a full circle, her arms raised, her hands behind her neck, just in case anyone was actually at the peep window. She doubted it though. Wade's outrage had been genuine, and Strud seemed far too uptight to have a peek, no matter how curious she was.

Flopping onto her side, she continued to think, her mind whirring with all she'd seen and learned. Mostly though, her thoughts kept returning to Strud. Damnation, that woman was unlike anything Alex had even dreamed up. Her strength, her charisma, her seeming comfort in her own body and bearing were beyond attractive, and Alex's heart had raced so many times, she wondered if it might simply up and kill her. She laughed against the pillow. To survive all the years living as a pirate, only to die of attraction.

An attraction that was going to have a terminal end, for certain. When she'd managed to get the other part of the Firebird, Strud would let her go, and she'd return to the Urchin. Assuming that Strud kept her side of the bargain. This would be a strange tale she'd only tell a select few people. Maybe just Tom. How was Polly getting on anyway? Was Tom keeping the crew away from her? Had he taken over? Or had someone else taken advantage of her absence and claimed captaincy of the Urchin? If they had, she'd damn well make sure they hung from the bow when she got back. No one would ever take that ship from her. The waterfalls of blood on her hands made it hers by right.

She turned onto her other side and punched the pillow into a more pleasing shape. Stealing from Willoughby was a risk in more ways than one. The only real option was to get in and get out without him noticing. Without her crew, she'd need a good plan, and she had no doubt that Strud would be waiting, safe and sound, on her ship while Alex took all the risks. She sat up, her mind racing. But if that was true, then why go back to the ship at all? Hell, she could steal the piece and then head off into the dark and never see Strud or this mad ship again.

Why did that thought make her feel...something? Something she couldn't name, but something that wasn't the elation she should feel at the idea of escape. Sure, she'd made a deal with Strud, but she was a pirate, after all. And they only held to deals made with other pirates. There was, in fact, honour among thieves, if only because they understood the ramifications of betrayal.

She threw the pillow on the floor and pillowed her head on her arms. What was the orb? What did it lead to? The moment she'd seen it, she'd known it for an artefact, a map, but even the old stories didn't say what exactly it was supposed to lead to. And when Strud had asked her, she'd given her opinion...but Strud hadn't responded with what it *actually* was. Bollocks and tar. Carried away with wanting to impress the captain, she'd missed an opportunity to get information.

What if it did lead to treasure, as some thought? What if it was enough to...to... Huffing, she flipped onto her other side. Tom's words came back to her. Not everyone wanted to be a pirate. Maybe she could pay some debts for her crew, help them settle the way she had Jack. Do some good in the world. That felt right in her gut, but was it a stupid plan? If she got caught, she'd hang, and for what? The promise of a treasure others had already died for. Ah, but that would make her name, wouldn't it? The pirate who'd found the elusive treasure. Perhaps she could convince Strud to keep her on for the whole search, assuming it didn't take too long. Faced with the treasure, she could then decide how to deal with Strud.

Maybe then she'd finally feel like she'd made something of herself, despite the assurances in her old life that it could never happen.

***

She woke, bathed, and dressed quickly. Her dreams had been filled with action, motion, and plans. They were slipping away already, but the feeling of being shot from a gun filled her with a need to get into Strud's secret little den. Her stomach grumbled.

After breakfast, that is.

She headed down the corridor but stopped abruptly at the sight of a man's prone body on the thick carpet, blocking her way. The man had figures and what looked like sums drawn in black all over his body, and before she looked away, she noted the paintings of ducks on his wide backside. Then she really looked at his skin and blanched. She knew that blotchy blue pallor all too well. Frantic, she looked around but couldn't see any sort of button or lever to call for help. The door to his room was cracked, however, and thinking quickly, she dashed in. The buzzing light came on, and she winced at the glare.

There. An automaton dressed in what looked like the clothing of a ballet dancer turned towards her. The face, a porcelain painted mask with gears at the temples that moved when it blinked, turned towards her.

"There's been an emergency. The passenger in this room is unconscious in the hallway, likely from a poppy overdose."

The thing blinked, the gears whirred, and it turned towards the wall, which Alex assumed was the window in Wade's work area. She waited, unsure if anything was happening, and the window suddenly appeared in the wall, Wade's giant owl eyes looking at her.

"Word has been sent. No need to hang about." His voice filled the room around her, booming off the walls.

She nodded and left the eerie scene, stepping gingerly over the body. Laudanum. That was probably why Ginny and Vee had seemed so unsteady. It was a dark drug, one that took people into dark places. Gritting her teeth, she made her way to the staff quarters, where Joe was moving quickly from coffee urn to silver pots.

"Some passenger wake up with the need for a posh breakfast?" she asked, noting the way the rest of the serving staff moved almost silently in and out of the kitchen.

"Unexpected guests," he said, glancing up and giving her a brief smile. "Help yourself to porridge and coffee."

"How do you get unexpected guests on an airship flying over open water?" She frowned, spooning a healthy portion of porridge into a bowl. "Assuming they're not about to attack, that is."

Joe handed a tray full of mugs, milk, and cafetieres to a waiter. "Sometimes it's best not to ask questions." He stopped this time and really looked at her. "For the continued health of your spine, I suggest you stay put. These aren't the kind of guests who'd take to you. Or rather, they'd take to you and then take you away."

She sat at the table and ate, watching the quietly organised chaos around her. Joe handled it with aplomb, but the tension in the room could have smothered an elephant. Suddenly she found herself alone, and the silence gave her goosebumps. She scraped the bowl clean, threw back the coffee in three gulps, and left the kitchen. Staying close to the walls, she moved slowly, staying in the shadows and glad the clothing Strud had provided was all black. The corset leather creaked if she moved too much, but that was good as it kept her movements small. At a porthole, she glanced out and froze.

The small flyer docked against the Chimera's deck was innocuous-looking, however, the insignia was anything but. The Hermetic Order of the Golden Dawn was the only organisation to use the Rose Cross, with all the attendant symbols covering all four arms. Fear—cold, fierce, and deep—made it hard to breathe. *It can't be.*

Forcing herself to keep moving, she made her way towards Temp's office. Once there, she bit her lip in frustration. One of the golems stood directly in front of the door. There was no way she'd get close enough to hear what was being said.

A hand on her shoulder made her jump, her heart leaping to her throat.

"Sorry, miss," Peter whispered, holding up his hands. "This way, if you don't mind." He walked past her and down an almost invisible corridor to the left, hidden behind a fake wall.

She followed and could have sworn the golem's gaze followed her, though it didn't move. Peter stood next to a simple door of thin wood and waved her over, then put his finger to his lips. When she stood beside him, she realised she could hear the conversation inside. Why was he allowing this? Surely he wouldn't go against Strud? Right now, that didn't matter. She listened.

"Thank you for seeing us. I apologise for arriving unannounced. I'm aware you dislike disruptions in your schedule, but this is of the utmost importance."

His voice was nasal, as though the words were trying to get out through his nose but weren't quite managing the feat. It was a voice she'd heard before, and she closed her eyes and swallowed against the bile that rose in her throat.

"It usually is by the time you get around to asking for our help." Temp's voice was level and distant, and utterly lacking in its usual warmth. "What can we do for the Dawn?"

"It's the Golden Apple. We're aware that you're looking for it, and we assume you know that the American cowboys are interested as well." There was silence in response, and he cleared his throat. "Well, we felt you should know that one of those Americans has turned coat and fed the information to the Germans. Kaiser Wilhelm the Second is gathering an expedition to find the orb and has offered a healthy sum to anyone who gives him information on its whereabouts."

"And?" Temp asked.

"And we feel it prudent to request your expediency in the matter. Her Majesty sends her regards and requests that you leave your current post to pursue the matter at hand." He hesitated. "Captain Strud, if anyone other than Britain gets their hands on the Golden Apple, it would be catastrophic."

"Oh? Why is that?"

Alex had to admire Strud's calm and uninterested tone. She played the game nearly as well as Alex did.

"Because not only does it provide immortality, but it also provides youth and a type of...of charisma that makes it so people want to follow the person, even if it goes against their nature. A ruler who wouldn't age nor die. One who could convince people to do whatever they wanted them to and make them think it was their own free will in the process. A god among men would mean world domination within a generation, and there'd be no way to stop them. Her Majesty quite insists that this become your priority."

"And, for the sake of argument, say I find the Apple. What then? What would you have me do with it?" Temp's tone remained even, but there was something of the threat just below the surface, suggesting there was both a right and a wrong answer.

"You would turn it over to us." That came from another voice, one that held the kind of force only a man used to power could emit. "The Golden Dawn would hold it sacred and keep it safe, away from unworthy hands."

"And Her Majesty agrees with this, does she?" It sounded like Temp was moving. "She thinks the Dawn should hold that power? That sounds rather unlike her, I should say."

"No monarch should have that power. Not even our beloved queen." The strong-voiced one said *beloved* as though it was something found on the bottom of his shoe. "No, it will be placed in the Dawn's vault for safekeeping. As a person well known to acquire and rehome artefacts of this nature, we know you understand." There was no mistaking the notion that he meant her to fall in line, whether she understood or not. "You will have unlimited funds, transport, and whatever manpower you need. Name it, and we'll see it done. You have our permission to do this in our name, if it helps you get through otherwise closed doors."

There was silence, and Alex would have given her left molar to see Strud's expression.

"Oh, well if I have your permission..."

"There's one further thing, before we go." Mr Nasal spoke again. "We understand you were recently in an altercation with the Devil's Urchin, and that you may have come into contact with the captain of that foul vessel. That you, in fact, may have captured her. Is that true? If so, we've been ordered to take her off your hands."

Alex held her breath. *Please, please don't say yes.* She leaned against the wall, her knees suddenly refusing to do what knees had been created to do, which was to keep her from falling. If Strud handed her over now, her life was as good as over, even if she didn't hang.

"I'm afraid your information is faulty, gentlemen. Yes, we had a run-in with the Urchin, but the captain, in her hurry to get back to her burning ship, fell overboard. The last I saw of her, she was falling through the clouds like a dark angel."

Alex put her hand over her mouth to keep in the sigh of relief. Peter gave her a small, sweet smile. Not only was Strud *not* going to turn her over, she'd killed her off. No one would be looking for her anymore, and when she made it back to the Urchin, she'd be a legend. A dead pirate come back to life. She liked that an *awful* lot. But...how had they known to ask about her at all? She'd functioned under the Alex Minty name for years without suspicion. The man with the voice she recognised...somehow, he'd put together that Alex was the woman from his past. There'd be no other reason for him to ask about her under the name she'd been living under since her escape. There was no filthy swear good enough for how bad that could be for her health.

"Ah. Very well." Mr Strong Voice came nearer the door she was pressed against, and it vibrated as he spoke. "Shame. It would have been nice to see her hang. Still, it was a death worthy of a pirate. I doubt she made her peace with God as she fell. May she rot at the devil's feet."

Peter winced, and Alex rolled her eyes. How very dramatic. But she knew full well he meant every word.

"Thank you for your hospitality." Mr Nasal set down a cup with a clatter. "We can tell Her Majesty you'd be happy to take a leave of absence from your ship in order to take on this most profoundly important task?"

"You can be assured I'll do my part. I'll walk you to your ship." The office door closed with a click, and then there was silence.

Peter let out a whoosh of air. "Can't imagine Cap's gonna like them being high and mighty with her. Good though, that she got you killed off." He led the way out of the corridor, and they watched through a porthole as the men boarded their ship and pulled away, steam flowing into the sky behind them, the odious symbol blinking in the sunlight.

"Peter, can you please tell Joe and Wade to meet me in my office after lunch?" Strud came up behind them. "Minty, let's talk."

Alex kept her expression impassive, but the tone in Strud's

voice worried her. Did she regret not handing Alex over? Was she going to change the terms of their deal? Her heart thudded in her chest. Or had she finally remembered that they'd met a very, very long time ago?

Chapter Eleven

Temp sat behind her desk, questions and plans battling for supremacy in her mind. Alex sat in the chair opposite, forced into a proper position by the corset and skirt combination. As much as she appreciated decorum, she found that she missed the wild-haired vixen who'd boarded her ship.

"Why did you have Peter bring me through to listen?" Alex asked.

"Coffee?" Temp got up to pour it for them, unable to sit still anyway. "Because if the Dawn was coming, there could only be one reason. They've often been on the sidelines or in the shadows when I've been looking for something. I expected them days ago, and I'm not a believer in ignorance. You're helping me with this situation, and therefore you should know who the players are." She handed Alex a mug and stared down at her. "What I didn't expect was the questions about you."

Alex grinned, hoping it masked her concern. "You should have. I'm quite the popular girl in these skies. Everyone wants me, but no one can keep hold of me."

"Except me, apparently." Temp sat back down. "What's your connection to the Golden Dawn?"

Alex spluttered in her coffee and started coughing. Temp passed her a handkerchief and waited patiently. She didn't expect the truth, but she could hope.

"What makes you think I have one?" Alex finally said.

"One of the gentlemen, the one who sounds like he's got a permanent cold, wasn't asking for Her Majesty. His interest was personal. I could see it in his eyes. Same for the other one. But when it was clear he wouldn't get to strangle you himself, he looked like an angry toddler who'd had his toy taken away." She sipped her coffee. "I did you the service of keeping the authorities from coming for you. The least you can do is tell me the truth."

Although Alex's expression gave nothing away, Temp could see the struggle for an explanation in her eyes. Finally, Alex's expression hardened, her guard clearly up once again.

"There's no connection. I probably stole something that bizarre cult wanted to get their claws on, and it put a stick in their arses. No doubt they wanted to carve all those weird stars and symbols into my skin and offer me up to whatever deity they're sucking the toes of this week." She shrugged and studied her boots.

Temp sighed. "Very well. Keep your secrets. But our schedule has changed now that we know the Germans are after it too. We need a plan."

"We need a crew." Alex folded her arms. "I could try to do it alone, but those walls are high, and there are armed thugs everywhere. At the very least, we need lookouts." She tilted her head. "I'd assumed you'd be staying on the ship, so you didn't get your pearly white hands dirty."

"Never assume anything about me. *Never* think you know me, Minty." Temp once again saw Duncan's lifeless body being covered by rising water. "Let's look at the hall and make a plan."

They headed towards the research office, and Temp mulled over the conversation with the Dawn. How had they known she was after the Golden Apple?

"Why you?"

Jolted from mental meandering, she looked at Alex. "What do you mean?"

Alex ran her finger over a map on the wall. "You're the captain of a strange luxury ship. The queen herself sends emissaries to ask for your help. You deal with rich people, but you have an interest in the arcane for a reason you didn't name when I asked you before. Yes, I noticed. Forgive me, but you wouldn't be the person I'd seek out to go hunting an ancient artefact from a fable. With the world at stake, at that. So, why you?"

There was no way on earth Temp would tell Alex about the Followers and what they did for the world. Organizations like the Followers and the Golden Dawn, both of whom claimed to have the world's interests at heart, survived thanks to the secrecy they required from anyone who worked with them. Her father had been a Follower, and there'd been no question she'd become one too. The Golden Dawn, however, had always seemed to operate with status and hierarchy as the primary motivations, and she'd always been distrustful of their ultimate aims. It wasn't unusual for both organizations to go after the same artefacts, but once one of them was in the lead, the other usually backed off. This time, that wasn't happening, and that made the situation more complicated than Temp liked. And clearly, Alex had some kind of history with the Golden Dawn, and that raised questions she obviously wasn't about to get answers to.

Temp might need Alex right now, but when this was over, she wanted Alex to leave with as little useful information as possible, and that included anything to do with the Followers, especially if Alex had some tie to the Golden Dawn. "Just like you have a reputation as a ruthless, cunning pirate with an uncanny ability to find the unfindable, I too have a certain reputation for finding things of importance. My services are expensive and specific."

"Unlike mine. I'm happy to grab any old thing." Alex shot a look over her shoulder. "As you say, we all have secrets."

There was a knock at the door, and Wade and Peter came in, followed by Joe. "Thank you for coming. As you know, we had visitors today, and the information they brought with them was both useful and concerning. I thought we had time to plan slowly and methodically, but apparently that won't be an option."

"What do you need from us, Temp?" Joe asked.

"Captain Minty has given us a person and likely location for the orb. Low Nottingham, Wollaton Hall, Baron Willoughby." She held up the drawing of him. "So that's where we'll be going."

"All of us?" Peter asked, the glow of excitement making his cheeks pink.

"No, lad. I need the three of you to keep the Chimera running without incident. I don't want anyone to know I'm not onboard. With luck, we'll be in and out within a day or two, and my absence will hardly be noted. Once we have both pieces, we'll have time to work out if it truly is a map of some kind, or if it works in some other way."

Peter looked at Joe and Wade, his eyes wide. "But...but who is going to watch your back, Captain? We're your crew. We should be there."

Joe smiled and put his hand on Peter's shoulder. "And as her crew, we have to help her in every way, even if it isn't the most exciting part." He glanced at Temp and away again. "There are things she has to do on her own."

"We need *someone*," Alex said, crossing her arms. "I don't want to have to go through that huge place by myself, which means you being inside with me. Or someone else inside with me, if you'd rather play lookout and stay safe."

"You're telling me you don't have a contact in Low Nottingham? I find that difficult to believe. And I don't want a large crew. They make it harder to move quietly and swiftly, which is what we need to do." Temp had already lost Duncan. She wouldn't lose another of her crew, no matter how badly she needed them on the ground.

"Fine. It's your coin. Given your *unlimited resources* from several interesting locations, we should be able to hire someone who won't just hand us over to the baron." Alex tugged at the stiff corset and huffed. "And I'm not wearing this damn outfit."

"Off ship, I don't care if you storm the hall naked as the day you were born." Temp laughed when Alex glared at her. "Three heads are better than one, which is why I've asked you all here. Peter, I need you to make sure everything is stable with the passengers and that lunch is served on time. Joe, Wade, I want your input about how best to get into the hall."

Peter's eyes dropped, as did his shoulders. "Okay, Cap." He turned away, his hat in his hand.

"Peter, running the Chimera is a big job. You'll be in charge of a ship worth more than all of Her Majesty's airships put together, as well as the safety of our high-profile passengers. That's no small thing."

He straightened, and his eyes grew bright. "Yes, Cap. I won't let you down." Straight-backed and chin up, he left the room, closing the door behind him.

"You're good with him," Joe said, pouring himself a small whisky.

"He's a good kid. You'll keep an eye on him?" Temp asked.

"Of course." He stared down at the wood map and moved to the side. "Where is Nottingham? I never was much for going north of the Gap, if I could help it."

"Spoken like a southerner." Temp grinned and shifted the map so Nottingham rose. "Wade, you've been quiet. Anything to add?"

"It's a mistake, and you shouldn't go." He pulled a drill bit from one of his many pockets and rolled it between his fingers. "We've already lost Duncan because of this stupid thing. We lose you: we lose the Chimera. You're the only reason she flies safe. Why we're all safe. Her Majesty can go—"

"You lied." Alex's tone was soft, but there was steel in it.

"Pardon?" Temp said, not looking up from the map. "What is it now?"

"I was told that Duncan got sick when you were at a port." Her eyes narrowed. "You drew those images because you saw those men when you grabbed the Firebird. You got your first mate killed."

Temp felt the accusation like she'd been stabbed in the chest. "There are things you don't need to know, Minty. Things that don't concern you. What concerns you is helping me get that orb so you can get back to your life of thievery and ill repute."

Alex simply glared at her, saying nothing.

"Wade, I'm going. Can you add anything useful to our

information?" This conversation wasn't proving nearly as fruitful as she needed it to be.

"I do." He moved around her desk, opened a drawer, and pulled a fresh sheet of paper from it.

It wasn't surprising that he knew where everything was, but it was always a little disconcerting when it was clear she had no privacy in her office. She watched as he began to sketch, the picture coming to life under his skilful, thick hands.

"Nottingham has more than five hundred caves running through the city, some connected by tunnels, others groupings of their own. Manmade, most of 'em, and they've been used as prisons and for storage and as beer cellars and for tanning leather and—"

"Wade," Temp said, her patience slowly eroding.

"Righto. Well, one of them connected cave systems runs right below the hall. Heard it at a steam convention last year from someone who was looking into the waterways up that way. Went and had a quick look at the city myself for this," he said, tapping the wood, "but it wasn't long enough to get underground."

Temp stared at it thoughtfully. "Where would we enter?"

"Nottingham is a city of doors and openings, holes, pores, and connections, layered knots of space under buildings everywhere. It's a labyrinth like something out of Greek myth. A rats' nest since the sky cities went up." He stopped to look at his sketch. "This here is Beeston Lodge, built a few years ago after the riots. It's on the edge of Willoughby's property, and there are caves all along there. Come up near the lodge and make your way above ground from there." He shook his head and stepped back. "But I don't know if there's water underground, or where it leads. You could drop into a pool filled with shit and have to swim through it all the way to the hall, for all I know."

Temp grimaced. "Let's hope that revolting option isn't the one we're faced with." She turned to Alex. "Do you think we could find a guide to lead us through?"

Alex didn't look up from the map, her expression thoughtful, and her hands on her hips. "If Wade is right, and it's a labyrinth, then we'd better. I have no desire to be trapped underground for the rest of my life."

"It wouldn't be a long one, that's for sure," Joe murmured.

There was a long, thoughtful silence as no one spoke but continued to stare at the map.

"Willoughby is ruthless." Alex finally looked up. "If we're caught, we won't be coming back. But you know that already."

Temp simply nodded. There wasn't anything more to say on that count.

Alex shrugged, and some light came back into her eyes. "Well, let's go steal from the bastard, shall we?"

Two hours later, Temp led the way into the belly of the ship, where a small flyer hung suspended above trap doors. She pulled her flying goggles on, adjusted her cap, and held out her hand to help Alex into the rear seat.

Alex ignored it and bounded onto the wing, showing that she'd cut slits in the side of the skirt up to her knees, allowing her to move more freely. Not only that, but a leather pocket was strapped to her thigh and clearly held a blade. There was another one attached to her upper arm, where she'd cut the sleeve of the blouse to allow for the small airgun, no bigger than her palm, to fit snugly into the sheath. When she saw Temp looking at it, she grinned and patted the one on her thigh.

"You wouldn't send a girl into danger without a way to protect herself, would you? Wade had a few things he said he could spare." She slung a sack from her shoulder and dropped it into the footwell of the flyer.

"It's not you I'm worried about." Temp climbed into the front seat and checked the tiller and bag pressures. "Wade, all the gears are oiled and ready?"

He grunted as he undid the knot from the holding ropes. "Think I'd let you loose in it if it weren't perfect?"

The glass bubble over them clicked into place, though the

engine noise still made it rumble. She gave the signal, and he let go of the rope. The flyer dropped from the Chimera's belly like a stone, and when she gauged them far enough, she inflated the bags to halfway, shifted the lever to open the wings, and engaged the gears to propel them forwards. They shot through the wispy cloud layer, and Temp smiled when she heard Alex laugh with what sounded like real joy. They dropped lower, until they were flying below the level of the mid-cities but well away from the ground. Night came early this time of year and provided welcome cover for a small, unremarkable flyer.

A combination of torches and new electric lighting twinkled below and above them when they made it back to land, sending them even deeper into the shadows between. It was quiet, aside from the rushing wind speaking its own special language. It would take a little over two hours to get to Nottingham, and she wished it was longer so she could enjoy the freedom that came with no immediate responsibilities except flying.

"What city would you live on? I assume it would be an air city. Which would it be for you?" Alex broke the silence after about half an hour.

"I don't ever want to live in a city. I plan to live out my life in the air. I was born to play on the wind," Temp said, almost without thinking and then wondered if she'd given too much away. "Where would you live, if you were ever to settle down?"

"Those words send horror through me. But if I had to choose, I think I'd go with Camden-in-Middle. I like the lack of rules and expectations. I like the way makers and artists and tinkers all mix together to create daring new things."

That was interesting. Temp would have thought Alex would want to live in a rich section, if only to prove that she could. But the place she'd mentioned was one that offered a similar kind of freedom to that which she had on a ship. It seemed like they both craved a certain amount of liberty from the world around them.

They didn't speak any further, and Temp was glad for it. The best part of taking a flyer out was the quiet, and she didn't want any more verbal jousting with Alex to ruin it.

She saw an N, lit up by torches on a hill below, and began her descent. They docked at a nearly abandoned station outside the city, and Temp hoped the flyer would still be there when they got back. The dock itself was rusty and swayed in the mild evening breeze like it was deciding whether or not to lay down and have a nap.

Alex jumped out with the securing rope and tied it expertly. Temp joined her and finished with the front tie.

"This way," Alex said and pulled up the hood on the black jacket, covering her beautiful red hair.

The stairs clanged under her boots, and even more so under Temp's heavy tread. But there didn't seem to be anyone around to hear it. "But the lodge is that way," Temp hissed, grabbing Alex's arm.

"And we need a guide. You think we'll find one lounging on the baron's doorstep?" Alex jerked her arm away. "Trust me or don't. But make the decision now."

Temp's jaw ached as she clenched it hard, then she motioned for Alex to lead the way. Alex held out a small wooden compass with gears that clicked in her hand as she turned one direction and another. It was similar to the one built into Temp's glove, but like the map in her office, pieces rose and fell according to the buildings around them. When had Wade had time to create something so perfect? And why had he given it to Alex instead of Temp? She'd need to have a talk with him about who was in charge.

The paths were hidden by a layer of sickly smelling, unnatural-seeming fog. If it weren't for the sound of Alex's boots, Temp would have lost her.

The thought gave her pause. Alex *could* lose her here. She could disappear, take the flyer, and leave Temp to fend for herself. Which Temp could do, of course. But it would make the whole situation far more complicated. When she'd told Alex she wasn't a good thief, it was true. She could hunt things down and clamber through caves and ancient temples, sure, but sneaking in and out, or having to face a criminal underground without wanting to take out the air rifle and shoot them wasn't in her nature.

A hand on her arm stopped her, and mist swirled around Alex's cloaked form, painting her like a wraith out of a dark fairy tale.

"Turn here. Hold my arm like we're lovers taking a walk. But let me lead."

Temp didn't reply. Any response would likely just cause an argument. And this was, after all, why she'd needed Alex in the first place. They moved through a number of narrow alleys, each smelling worse than the last, until they opened out into a small square.

"Don't say anything," Alex murmured, stretching up to kiss her cheek as though they were a couple. "This is my world."

Temp's cheek burned where Alex's lips had touched it, and she tripped a little as Alex pulled her forwards and into what sounded like possibly the most raucous pub in all of England. The Old Angel had left heaven behind some time ago.

Inside, it smelled of beer and bodies used to a hard day's labour. She struggled not to take out her scented kerchief and press it to her nose. Alex looked around, smiling, her hood pushed back to reveal her face and tendrils of hair. She pulled Temp along to the back, where they sat at a worn, well-nicked table still sticky from the patron before.

A woman with an apron covered in all manner of things hurried over and looked at them expectantly without saying anything. But then she seemed to look closer. "Well, I'll be a headless chicken in a pigsty." She wiped her big, chapped hand on her apron and held it out. "Captain Minty, what brings a legend of your sort here?" She shook her head quickly. "Ay up. Never mind me asking. None of me business, is it? Glad to have you." She let go of Alex's hand and frowned at Temp, tilting sideways to look her over from her boots up. "If you don't mind me sayin', this don't seem your sort."

"She's my sort where it counts," Alex said with a rakish grin. "Two pints and some pickled eggs."

The woman threw back her head and laughed. "Well now. Good to know there's at least some truth to the rumours. Be right back." She walked off, still laughing.

"What are you doing?" Temp asked under her breath, frustration and anger making it hard to sit still. "Everyone will know who took the orb when it goes missing right after you arrive."

Alex cupped her cheek in what would look like a tender touch from the outside. But her nails were too close to Temp's eye, her touch too firm. "You think we'd be able to hire someone to take us through the caves to Willoughby's place just because we asked? These people are place proud, and they protect their own. My reputation is the only thing that's going to get us what we need. And you look like the person who is willing to pay for whatever we need."

Temp gave a quick smile to the woman who set down their beer. So be it. She settled into Alex's plan, and she'd deal with the fallout later. They might know Alex, but no one knew Temp. If she could keep it that way, she wouldn't be followed back to the Chimera, nor would anyone be able to tie her to the theft.

They drank in silence, and Temp noticed the way Alex scanned the bar as though simply enjoying the atmosphere, but her fingers were white around her pint glass.

The bar maid came over and pulled up a seat when the crowd thinned out slightly. "Now, my lovely. You didn't come here for our fine piss water nor the genteel crowd. Maybe I can help with something, lass?"

Alex turned towards her, and her smile looked surprisingly genuine. "The beer was just fine. Better than the swill on my ship, it was."

Temp frowned slightly. Alex's accent had changed. Come to think of it, she'd sounded like Temp had expected her to when she'd captured her. But on the ship that accent had softened, and it had become more sophisticated. It had been subtle enough that Temp had missed it, but now it was clear as day. *She's a chameleon.* So who was the real Alex Minty? That little niggling feeling tickled her brain again, like she was missing something. And missing something when it came to Alex could be deadly.

Chapter Twelve

If Alex had been convinced that Temp wouldn't give them away, she would have kicked her shin with the blade sticking out of the front of her boot. Could she possibly look any more uncomfortable or superior? She wasn't kidding when she said she couldn't fit into places where she didn't belong. She stuck out here like a peacock among hyenas. "Molly, is it?" she asked, pulling up a long ago memory of Nottingham's accent. "I've heard tell that you're the one who knows what's up and what's down 'round here. And I'm in need of...down." Alex smiled and gave Molly a quick wink.

"Aye, but no need for flattery. We had a lad who worked on your ship for a time. Kel McKay. Boy was damn near as useful as a broom in a fire when his pa sent him off to find his way. Took him to you, it did. Now, he runs the best tannery in the city. Married a nice girl. Settled down." She nodded sagely. "We heard the stories he brought back. We know—"

"And so you know my business isn't best talked about with those who aren't one of us, eh?" She tilted her head towards Temp, who grimaced and looked away. "I'm in need of a guide. Someone who knows the caves and how to get through them."

Molly looked at her for a moment then shrugged. "Well, you already know one. Kel is a tanner, and he and his missus use a few of them caves for their work. Keeps the nasty smell and chemicals down there." She looked around and then gave a shrill whistle. A girl of maybe ten came running out of the back room, a miniature version of Molly in a coarse linen dress and apron. "Go tell Kel his former employer is here to have a word."

Alex smiled as the little girl ran from the room. "I think the time for people not knowing I'm here has passed. But thanks."

Molly nodded. "Do I want to know what takes you into the caves? They're dangerous places these days, lass. What with the sky cities taking all the rich folks, we've got the poor and the really poor, and the ones living in the caves who take the brunt of it, who don't even have a label for how poor they are. Desperate folk do desperate things."

"That's the truth," Temp mumbled and took another sip of her beer.

Alex ignored her. "You don't want to know, and it's best you don't tell anyone why I came about." She kicked Temp's shin this time, earning her a disgruntled look. "We should be real grateful for Molly's help."

Temp reached into her inside jacket pocket and pulled out a money pouch. She took out five sovereigns and pushed them across the table. "Thank you for your assistance."

Molly's eyebrow quirked, and her gaze followed the pouch's path back into Temp's pocket even as she slid the sovereigns off the table. "You're keeping mighty strange company, Captain," she said, glancing at Alex.

"Strange company for strange times." Alex shrugged and threw back the last of her pint of beer. Alex was certain truer words hadn't been spoken. Here she was, on the trail of an arcane item that could lead to all kinds of wealth, with a woman who could set the bedsheets on fire with just the smoulder in her gaze. The same woman who would have seen Alex hanged without flinching if it weren't for her need of Alex's particular skills. And gods only knew where the Urchin was holed up.

The door opened, and the young man looked around, his hair sticking up in all directions, a thick leather apron with a million pockets flapping about in front of him. He saw Alex, and a broad smile creased his face. He ran over and pulled her up from the chair to swing her around like a doll.

"Well, I never!" He finally put her down as she batted at his head. "You really are here."

Alex smiled warmly at him, happy to find he truly had made his way. "Good to see you too, Kel. Sit with us." She slid back into the seat and noticed the way he looked her over.

"Must say, Cap, you're looking pretty smart these days. Ted finally convinced you to start looking a little more ladylike, eh?" He grinned, showing the tooth he'd chipped when they'd hit a particularly strange air pocket that had caught them off guard. It had sent him sprawling onto the deck, and that bit of his missing tooth was still caught in the wood.

"Just a little disguise thanks to a job I'm on." She leaned forwards. "Any word of the Urchin?"

He looked surprised. "No...should there be?" His expression turned sombre. "Why aren't you with her?"

It had been a longshot. She'd gone down over the water beyond Land's End. The likelihood of information making its way this far up the country was nearly nil. "No worries. Now, we have a favour to ask." She made a small motion at the room around them. "Can we talk here?"

He looked thoughtful, then shook his head. "Nah. Besides, my missus would have my hide in the tub with the leathers if I didn't bring you round to meet her." He stood and glanced at Strud, his bushy, caterpillar eyebrows raised.

"For the moment, she's with me." Alex stood too and bumped him with her shoulder. "Come on. Show me the woman daft enough to tie herself to an ex-pirate."

Fortunately, Strud followed without comment, and this time, her expression was impassive as they made their way out of the pub into the murky, squalid night air. Silently, she followed Kel down narrow alleys and over cobbled streets, noting the indentations in the rocks they passed that were clearly entrances to caves. A church loomed out of the mist, with neglected and forgotten gravestones rising ominously from the tall grass. Alex shivered. This was a place of ghosts.

They stopped at a mid-terraced house not far from the church and beyond it, she saw something else. "Bloody hellfire, Kel." She pulled her hood closer around her head. "You live next to the gaol?"

"Aye." He grimaced, glancing that way as he unlocked the door. "Haven't hung anyone in public for about fifteen years now, thankfully. Jumpy Jack Alcock was hanged behind them walls last year for killin' his wife. Said she didn't want to share a bed w' him, so she wouldn't share a bed w' no one." He looked at Alex over his shoulder as the door opened. "Treason and piracy are still hangable offences too, eh?"

She gave a short nod and followed him inside, ready to be away from the ghosts of the dead swirling around the cobbled streets that probably ran with the blood of innocents and guilty alike.

Inside, it was warm and cozy. A small fire blazed in the fireplace, and the furniture was near enough to new to still have some padding. Low, broad wood beams made Strud duck her head, and she looked almost comical in the space, like a giant in Lilliput. The thought of the old fairytale her nurse often read to her made her smile briefly before she shut it down. There was no place for memories in this world.

"Kel?" a woman's voice called before she stepped out of the kitchen. "Oh." She stopped, staring.

"Mary, this here is Captain Alex Minty. Fiercest pirate on land or in the air and best person I've ever known."

Alex flushed under the praise and elbowed him hard enough to make him grunt. "Stop yammering." She held out her hand. "Nice to meet you, Mary, even if you've got poor taste in men." She winked, and Mary laughed.

"Well, I can tell you he's the best down here." She tugged hard on Alex's hand, pulling her forwards into an embrace. "And if it weren't for you, we'd never have been able to afford our own place."

Alex nearly sighed out loud. She didn't want Strud to know her business or how she ran it, but it seemed there were plenty of folk about who were determined to open that window into her life. "Well, nothing is free. I've come to ask a favour."

Though Mary looked wary, Kel leaned forwards. "Anything at all, Cap. What is it?"

"We need you to take us through the caves to Wollaton."

Kel and Mary looked at one another and then at Alex. "Cap, I mean no disrespect, and I know full well you can handle yourself, but that's no place for anyone who wants to keep all their bits attached to their body."

Briefly, Alex wondered at Strud's continued silence. It wasn't like her to stay quiet and unopinionated for so long. Understanding dawned sharp and clear. If Strud never said anything, if no one could properly identify her, then she'd avoid the noose if it came to that. Not that someone like her would get the kind of punishment the rest of the thieves would. "Yeah, well, I've made a deal with this one, and that means I need to get my hands a little dirtier than usual. All I ask is that you take us to Wollaton Hall, and then we'll make our own way from there." She tilted her head towards Strud. "She'll pay well."

He bit his lip, frowning. "I guess we could—"

"Not her. Just you. Or you and another person." Strud's low voice seemed to fill the room.

Alex looked at her, incredulous. "Are you saying this is too dangerous for a woman? Does your hypocrisy know—"

Strud held up her hand and looked at Mary. "You're with child, yes?"

Mary's blush was apparent, even in the dimly lit room. "Aye. Doesn't mean I can't walk the caves. Ain't nothing wrong with my legs."

"She's right." Alex couldn't fathom how Strud had known. "It's dangerous enough, but now you need to think for two, I'm of a mind to tell you to stand down and find us someone else too, Kel. Don't need your lass raising a child on her own."

He shook his head, his hair moving with its own kind of emphaticness. "No, Cap. As you say, I can take you through the tunnels, and then I'll leave, and they'll be none the wiser. At the hall...well, no sense in having a lookout standing still to be spotted outside them walls. Once you're in, you'll want to get a move on. But don't go gettin' caught doin' whatever it is you're doin'."

Mary got up and went into a back room, then came out and handed something to Alex. "You'll need this."

Alex peered at it, trying to work it out. "What is it?"

"It's a flash lantern." Strud reached out and gently took it. "A fine one, at that."

The copper lantern seemed mostly clockwork in nature, with the gears exposed and visible inside a cage of hair-like copper strings. Strud turned a key at the back, cranking it, and as the gears began to move, small flashes of blue light sparked between the copper threads until a blue glow filled the room.

"Where did you come by this?" Strud asked, her tone curious, not accusatory.

"There's a tinker in the market. Lad's probably only about seventeen or so but has a mind like you've never known. I traded him some good, tanned leather for his family. This works well when we're tanning in the caves. No smoke, no flame. Just have to make sure to keep it cranked up. If it goes out down there, it's a nightmare to find it and get it going again. It's darker than a dead sky with no moon in those tunnels."

Strud continued to admire it, holding it at a distance and turning it this way and that. "We'll make sure you get it back."

She almost sounds genuinely impressed. Just when Alex was ready to write her off as a posh, arrogant sky person, Strud said or did something that made her think twice. She didn't like not understanding what made someone tick. It meant she didn't know if she could trust them. "We'd like to go now, if it's all the same to you," Alex said. "Time is pressing."

Kel stood and grabbed a regular lantern, which he lit from a stick out of the fireplace. "Let's be off then." He gave Mary a quick kiss. "Back in a tick."

Her smile didn't match the worry in her eyes. "Be quick. Mind the turtle."

He nodded, then opened the front door. "We'll stick to the walls and shadows and use the fog to hide us as well as possible. We've got about two miles before we drop into the tunnel head, and there's bound to be Willoughby's men watching for trouble."

Alex pulled up her hood and startled back when Strud raised her hand. Strud's eyebrow quirked, and she kept her hand still for a moment before tucking an errant strand of hair deeper into Alex's hood. The intimacy of the simple act made Alex's breath catch, and a shiver ran over her. She pulled the hood low. "Thank you."

Strud nodded and turned to Mary. "I've left something there on the table for you. It should be more than enough to help with the babe."

Alex looked at the table and schooled her expression. The amount of coin Strud had left on the table would be enough to move the family to another home and then some, if that's what they wanted.

"Crikey," Kel said, looking over Alex's shoulder. "Who are you?"

Strud clapped him on the back and strode past him into the fog. "Best you not know. Shall we?"

Alex winked at Kel, who continued to stare at the money. "Just don't forget that I'm your favourite fairy godmother."

He laughed and shook it off. "Right. At least Mary and the baby will be taken care of if Willoughby's thugs decide my arms look better in the river than they do on me." He moved into the fog, and they followed.

Any lightness that they'd found in the little house was quickly absorbed into the tension of the stealthy walk back through Nottingham's corridors and alleys. Alex caught sight of the main road running parallel and stopped to watch as a group of three men shoved a smaller, slighter one who held his cap in his hand

and looked like a rabbit facing down foxes. Alex took a step that direction.

"No." Strud grabbed her arm, and her breath was a whisper against Alex's ear. "That isn't our fight. And if you get caught, you'll not make it back to the Urchin."

She looked at Strud, and an irrational fury filled her. "Is anything other than ancient treasure or depraved rich folk ever your fight?" she hissed, and then spun when someone cried out.

The man hit his knees, and the three jackals closed in, weapons raised. Alex pulled her knife from her thigh holster and ran forwards, moving like the dancer she'd once been, light on her feet and soundless.

"Stop."

Alex's breath went out of her as Strud pushed her against the stone wall, thrust the copper lantern into her arms, and moved past her just as noiselessly. Alex watched, stunned, as Strud moved up behind one man, her hand moving forwards and back lightning fast. She spun just as one of the other jackals turned towards her, sword drawn. She lifted the absurd walking stick she hardly ever let go of, and steel glinted from the end as she pushed it forwards, straight through the man's throat before he could shout.

The third man, however, did manage to shout before she relieved him of his head, which bounced off the cobbles and into the mist.

She wiped the end of her sword on the dead man's coat, and then it disappeared back into the innocuous wood casing with a click. The man they'd been about to beat, likely to death, stared up at her from the foetal position he'd curled into. She gave him a brief nod, then jogged back, her expression hard.

"Now. If you don't mind, can we continue on? We can't save everyone in this godforsaken city."

Alex glared at her, hands on hips. "How did a genteel captain of a posh ship learn to fight that way?"

Temp looked away, her jaw clenching. "If you must know, I was trained to special operations in a secret branch of the American government. Now, for the sake of all that is holy, can we please move on?"

Alex grinned and followed Strud back to the street where Kel waited. He, too, looked somewhat awed.

"How much further?" Strud asked. "I don't want to be here when their friends come upon their bodies."

"Nearly there." Kel backed up, then looked at Alex. "You've finally met your match, Cap."

She narrowed her eyes and waved him on. Was that true? Strud wasn't at all what she seemed. Though, what she seemed, Alex still wasn't entirely sure.

Kel led them through a small, rusty gate nearly overgrown with brush. If you didn't know it was there, it would be easy to walk right past it. That made Alex feel a little better, until she saw what was beyond it.

An abandoned cemetery lurked in the mist, stones fallen and cracked. Like wraiths looking for companions, the mist swirled and danced around the stones. She stopped, wincing.

Strud looked back. "A superstitious pirate. How disappointing," she said, her tone surprisingly gentle as she repeated words from when they'd met.

Goaded, Alex tilted her head and walked after them, but she nearly groaned aloud when Kel ducked low and disappeared into an old crypt.

Strud stopped at the entrance and motioned impatiently. "Go. I'll watch your back, though I'm quite certain it's not the dead you need to worry about. It's the living who will come after us."

Alex took a deep breath and ducked into the crypt. It was empty, except for Kel, who was only a head on the ground. She yelped and leapt back.

"Cap, come on. There are stairs down. Just watch your feet. Some of 'em have crumbled. And you should turn that lantern on now." Kel's head went below ground, and she could see the hole he'd dropped into.

"Bollocks and bull's brains," she whispered. Why had she agreed to this? She *hated* enclosed spaces. Quickly, she turned the winding mechanism on the clock as tight as it would go, and the gears kicked in. The blue glow chased away a little of the darkness, and she breathed easier. One step forwards. Then another. Down, down, down.

She grew dizzy as the stone walls touched both shoulders, and the slant of the stairwell meant wet stone grazed her head too. It became harder to breathe, and her knees turned to water.

"Damn it all."

The sound of a thud and scrape brought Alex back to the present, and she shifted to look back.

Strud had to turn sideways to navigate the narrow stairwell and was far too tall for it. She was rubbing her head, where a welt had already begun to rise. She looked sheepish as she tried to crouch, like a crab too big for a stone bucket.

Alex laughed and found she could breathe again. She could do this. She wasn't alone. She wasn't trapped. She was on an adventure, one that had the potential to make her a rich woman who would never, *ever* have to crawl through caves or be locked in rooms *ever* again.

Chapter Thirteen

Temp hated killing people. Yes, it was occasionally necessary, and there were bad people who didn't make the world a better place, people who preyed on others for a whole host of unsavoury reasons. Still, killing them always made her feel a little too close to actually being one of them. The ends justifying the means had never been a saying she cared for. When she'd seen Alex running forwards to take them on with nothing but a small knife, she'd had no choice but to intervene. She needed Alex's stealth and connections and despite her earlier willingness to see Alex hanged by the law, she had no intention of watching her die on Nottingham's squalid streets.

As she hit her head against the low cave ceiling yet again and barely refrained from swearing out loud, she tried to push those thoughts away. She needed to stay focused. Kel's genuine feeling for his old captain was puzzling. She was fully aware that people who sailed together, no matter which form it took, developed a bond. But pirates weren't known as the forgiving sort, and she'd never heard of a group remaining close once a pirate had abandoned ship for any reason. And yet, she now knew of at least two people who'd left the Urchin and made their lives elsewhere.

That nagging feeling was getting louder. The one that said she was missing something right in front of her. She ducked a millisecond before she hit her head again and took in a deep breath to slide between the walls as they narrowed.

Kel had stopped ahead of them, holding his lantern high. "This here is what we call the turtle. Looks like the path goes off to the right, eh?" He swung the light in that direction, showing a widening corridor. "But look here." He swung the light the other way and illuminated a shadowed path, easily overlooked. "That's the one you want. If you take the other, you'll find your feet getting wet as it leads you right into the River Trent." He turned away from them and held the lantern high. "This is the turtle's head. See it?"

Temp did see it, and she couldn't help but grin. The rounded section of cave between the forks looked very much like a turtle's head, especially with the eyes and mouth someone had drawn on it.

"Don't know why, but it's the same on the other side. Same head, same fork in the path. Make sure you take the right one on your way back."

Temp made a mental note. They'd gone down forty-two steps and walked another hundred and eleven to this point. At least they'd know how far they had to go once they got to this point upon their return. The lantern's glow briefly illuminated Alex's face, and Temp nearly reached out to her. She looked haunted and pale, her eyes wide, the hand with the lantern trembling. But just as Temp wouldn't want anyone to see her weakness, she knew full well that Alex would feel the same. "We've got it. Lead on." Temp took a step forwards, and the other two moved ahead of her in response. She thought back to Alex's reaction to being locked in a cell on the ship. This was a woman who didn't like enclosed spaces. Why? There were many, many things she didn't know about Alex.

The caves were cold, dark, and dank. The smell of ancient mildew and limescale rose with every step they took, but it wasn't that holding Temp's attention. These caves had been lived in for centuries. Markings in the wall were clear indications, as were the simple benches carved here and there into the sandstone. Occasionally, she heard the scuffle and whispers of other people somewhere in the stone network, too distant to be worrying but clear enough to make Alex's back stiffen and her head move as though she was looking for the ghostly source.

Finally, Kel stopped at a set of stairs, though the tunnel continued past them. He raised his lantern and tapped a large red blotch of paint that looked vaguely like a little demon. "We're here. These stairs will take you to outside the old priest's cottage on the edge of the property. From there, stick to the woods. After that..." He shook his head. "Cap, there's a lot of open space before you get to the manor."

"I'll figure it out. Thank you, Kel." She drew him into a quick hug and then swatted at his head. "Get out of the way."

He tipped his head and moved, then looked at Temp as she started to climb after Alex. "I don't know who you are, but remember that you don't know who she is either," he said, grasping her forearm. "If I hear you've done 'owt to hurt her, I'll rejoin the Urchin, and we'll hunt you down."

The pirate in him was still firmly in place, apparently. His tone held no malice, just fact. "It's my intention to see to it we both come out of this with what we want. I assure you I'll watch her back." Temp flexed her arm under his hand, and he removed it.

"I'll keep my ear to the ground, and if I hear you've got into a tight spot, I'll see what can be done to help." He looked up at Alex's retreating form. "Take care of her. No one really does, you know?"

Once again taken aback by the gentle and genuine behaviour, she simply nodded and quickly ascended the steps. There was a moment when his lantern light and the light from the one Alex carried didn't cover her, and she shuddered at the darkness sliding over her like a damp blanket. She wasn't superstitious; she simply didn't like the feel of it.

And then her head crested the opening, and she was up and out of the system below. Alex stood nearby, her back against a tree, her head tilted back, and her eyes closed. Temp let her have the moment of quiet to centre herself while she looked around. As Kel said, they'd come out beside Beeston Lodge, which Wade had suggested was the best option. All the windows were dark, and cobwebs acting as curtains suggested it hadn't been used in a very long time. The woods ahead were shadowy, and mist danced through them. As the wind bent the branches, she caught occasional glances of flickering torches in the distance.

"That's the hall," Alex said, coming up beside her.

"Not too far." She glanced down, glad to see Alex's expression back to its usual wary, curious self. "Any plan yet?"

Alex set off, and Temp walked beside her. "I've only been to Wollaton Hall twice." She glanced over and rolled her eyes at Temp's incredulous look. "No, I didn't tell you I'd already been. And I probably won't tell you plenty of other things. But that's how I know Willoughby is ruthless."

They stopped and waited in the cover of the forest when voices floated through the air, moving away from them. Then they walked on again.

"A while back, he heard I'd stolen something from Duke Villiers: a jewel the duke got as a gift from some sultan or other on a hunting trip. Willoughby wanted it because of some feud he has going with Villiers. He thought it would serve him right for it to be on the neck of someone in Low Nottingham instead of High Buckingham."

"So you offered to sell it to him?" Temp wasn't sure what the rules of low societies were but that sounded unlikely.

"Not exactly." Alex stopped and peered around the tree, her face illuminated by the soft blue glow of the lantern, which was dimming. "He sent thugs to the Urchin who suggested that I *wanted* to sell it to him." She glanced at Temp. "The message was clear, and I wasn't about to go to war with someone over a jewel I didn't even want. I only took it from Villiers because I was irritated by him hunting a beautiful animal for sport."

"So you do have principles." Temp chuckled and took the lantern from Alex. She unwound the gears, and the light flickered out. "We're too close for this."

"Anyway, I came down and met Willoughby in the main reception. But I had to wait..." Alex stared at the massive hall ahead of them. "He was dealing with someone he thought had double-crossed him. He slit the man's throat while he was pleading, saying things about his wife and kids. Willoughby told him not to worry, that they'd be next so they could all be together in the afterlife."

"Lord have mercy," Temp murmured. "Did he do it?"

Alex shrugged. "Don't know. He called me forwards as they carried the man's body out, we conducted our business, and I left. I've done my best to stay out of his sight ever since—" She stopped abruptly and shook her head. "Until now."

Temp wondered what the rest of that sentence might have been, but her attention was diverted when she saw how close they were. "What now?"

"Follow me. Try not to make so much noise with those big feet of yours."

Temp frowned. "I warned you I wasn't stealthy."

"Not stealthy? You're like an elephant walking over glass." Alex ducked a low hanging branch, and it swung back, nearly hitting Temp in the face. She grunted.

They made their way in the shadows past the impressive frontage of Wollaton Hall, where candles lit most windows, and lantern flames danced along the outer walls. At the back, the woods were closer to the building. Temp pointed. "There?"

Alex shook her head. "You don't want any main door. We want...that one." She pointed towards a door at the bottom of some steps leading below ground. "Delivery entrance. There won't be any this late at night, so there won't be many servants about." She darted across the open space, light and swift, her cloak pulled tight around her.

Temp scanned the edge of the woods and the ledges above, and they were empty. That felt...wrong. But she wasn't about to start doubting their luck. She darted after Alex, unreasonably aware of how heavy-footed and large she was in comparison.

She pressed her back to the wall and looked at Alex, who knelt on one knee, her fingers already moving over the lock. It clicked open, and she stood. Temp leaned down, grasped the thick iron handle, and hefted it open to a ninety-degree angle. It would be obvious if anyone passed by, but there was no choice. She wasn't about to close it behind them and find it locked when they were in a hurry to leave.

Alex dropped in first, and Temp followed. The dim space was full of bottles and barrels. They crept to the door, and Alex opened it slowly, peering out. Temp blinked against the light from the hallway.

"He'll probably have it in his study," Alex whispered. "He's paranoid and likes control, so I'm going to guess that his study will face the front of the house, so he can see who's coming and going."

That made sense. "So we find the study."

Alex made a face. "Obviously. We just have to hope we can get through the house without being seen." She set off, moving lightly. "But I don't think that's going to happen."

Temp followed her down the hallway, where old wallpaper peeled away at the edges and damp patches coloured the corners. Light became brighter, and Temp heard voices. They stopped, and Temp looked back. There were no rooms on either side of them. They'd have to retrace their steps. She took a step back, then heard the voices coming up the hall behind them. "Christ," she murmured. "We're trapped, and we didn't even get through half the house."

Alex looked at her, her expression inscrutable. "You're not going to like this," she murmured back, then took a step towards the light.

Temp reached out to pull Alex back but was too late.

Alex walked straight into the reception room, her head high, a wide smile on her face. "Baron. Nice to see you again."

Temp froze, and then felt the pistol at the back of her head. She raised her hands slowly, keeping a firm grip on the cane, and followed Alex into the room.

"Minty! What's my favourite pirate doing skulking around my house? You know you're always welcome to use the front door. When my guards told me they'd seen you and your companion go around to the back of the house, it got me thinking you're up to no good."

Alex laughed, low and sexy. "I'm always up to no good. You know that well." She glanced over her shoulder. "I have someone with me who needed more than just my reassurance as we came in. I'm afraid I had to play the game. You know how it is."

There was something in Alex's glance, in the look in her eyes, that telegraphed a warning. It was hard to look past her betrayal to wonder what it meant.

"Bloody pirate," Temp said, her voice nearly a growl.

"I do indeed." He moved away from the dining table, throwing his napkin on the floor and shoving aside a feral-looking dog waiting at his feet. "And so does she, I think." He stopped in front of Temp, his eyes narrowed. "It's good to meet my opponent. As hard as I've searched for you so I can get my trinket back, I couldn't find any trace. And then you walk right into my home." He laughed, bits of food from his meal falling from the gaps in his teeth. "Captain Minty, you've gone above and beyond."

Alex gave him what almost looked like a sarcastic curtsy, if there were such a thing. "I heard the rumours on the wind and knew which way they were blowing. When Lady Dee Grey approached me, I mustered a plan."

Temp kept her expression neutral, but her mind whirled. It was his men in the cave. His men had killed Duncan. Now she knew, but what good did that information do her? And what was Alex doing, giving Temp a false name? D. Grey. Dorian Grey. The fictional man who wasn't who he seemed because there was something else at play. Someone who disobeyed the rules of time. If Alex was really betraying her, why not just tell him who she really was? What was she doing?

"And how did you get her to follow you, Minty?" He turned, his smile nowhere near his eyes. "What is it you promised her?"

Alex shrugged. "We had a...scuffle, she and I. Our deal was that I bring her to you, because you have something she wants. Then she doesn't get me hanged." Again, Alex glanced over at her, clearly trying to telegraph something in the brief look before she turned to the baron. "And I did exactly what I promised, didn't I? I didn't ask what it was she wanted from you. We both know too much knowledge is bad for one's health."

He nodded and touched the side of his nose. "Truth in that, lass, truth in that. Now, what can I give you in return for your generosity? We both know nothing comes free."

Alex grinned. "A finder's fee and a place to sleep the night wouldn't go amiss. I don't fancy going back through those damned mists. Give me the right creeps, they do."

"My home is at your disposal. And in the meantime, I'll get to know our guest." He flicked at Temp's suit jacket. "Too bad she's not properly attired, though I doubt you could ever make *Lady* Grey look like a woman you'd want to bed." He and the guards around him laughed.

Alex shrugged and yawned loudly behind her hand. "Well, while you play with your new friend, I'd like to put my head on a pillow, if you don't mind." She tilted her head, giving Temp a wry smile. "'Punctuality is the thief of time,'" she said, quoting the book with the character's name she'd given Temp. "'For there is such little time that your youth will last.'"

It was an amalgamation of passages from the book, but Temp thought she understood. She damn well *hoped* she understood that Alex was buying them time and telling her that she'd hurry. If she was wrong, then Alex was simply giving her a strange goodbye message.

The pistol against the back of her head pushed her forwards as Alex followed a maid through a door at the other end of the room.

The baron leaned against the large, pockmarked dining table. "I'm not familiar with your lineage, Lady Grey. But women of rank don't generally go gallivanting around caves looking for ancient artefacts or wander about dressed in men's clothing. So who are you, really?"

Temp grit her teeth and glared at him. "You killed my friend."

He shrugged. "And you killed mine. Such is life. Now I get to kill you, but not until you tell me where I'll find the Firebird." He nodded at the man behind her, and a blow to the head knocked her to her knees. "We can make this quick and painful, or we can make it slow and painful. One of these is guaranteed; the other is your choice." There was another blow to Temp's head, making her ears ring. *Buy Alex time. Pray she doesn't take off with the orb and leave me here.* She repeated it like a mantra.

"Take her into the back room. Let's get her *un*comfortable."

She couldn't help but struggle as two beefy men dragged her upright and yanked her arms behind her back. Her cane lay discarded beside the table. *Damn it.* She continued to fight her captors anyway, putting up an appearance but nothing real. *Buy Alex time.* They led her into a smaller, dimly lit room where shadows danced on the walls. The marble floor seemed to shift as she was dragged over it to a chair in the middle. They pushed her into it, and she got a moment of satisfaction, and an instant headache, as she slammed her head back into one of the thug's and made contact with his nose. The break was audible.

She held her hands at an angle even as they were tied behind her back, which they didn't seem to notice. When they stepped away, she relaxed them and felt the rope loosen. It would be enough. *Buy Alex time.*

"Why do you want the orb?" she said, trying to ignore the spots in her vision.

"Why do you?" the baron said, sitting in a chair opposite her, his legs crossed and a cigar between his fingers. He puffed out smoke. "Why does anyone want immortality?"

So he didn't know the full extent of the orb's power. It was a small victory, at least. "No one should have that power. It won't lead to anything good."

He puffed out a circle of smoke. "I disagree. I think it would be very good for me. I'd finally get out of this damned hellhole and make it up to the sky cities. I'd be one of them, and they'd eventually bow down to me. I'd watch them all age and die while I stay young and beautiful."

Temp coughed. "I don't think any orb could manage that for you."

A hard cuff to the back of her head made the headache throb that much harder.

"The use of electricity is on the rise, but steam will always be needed. I'll be there to make sure I'm part of it all. As our mutual friend said, knowing which way the wind blows will mean I become the richest man in history. And the future."

Alex hadn't said that, but it would probably mean another knock to make her headache worse if she said so. "There's always someone bigger and stronger to take what you've got."

His eyes hardened, and she saw at once the ruthless man Alex had said he was.

"No one takes what's mine. Which leads us back to you. Where have you stashed the Firebird?"

Temp stared at him, mute. He stepped forwards and his punch connected with her jaw, snapping her head to the side. A second punch to her abdomen made her double over as far as her bound hands would allow.

"You know, if you were dressed like a woman, I'd have a moment of doubt about this," he said, punching her in the stomach again. "But you've made it easier on my conscience."

She wheezed, her breath burning. "You don't have a conscience. Don't pretend on my account."

And so it went. He'd ask, and she'd either not answer or answer with sarcasm. Blood welled in her mouth, and she spit it on his shoes, earning her another blow. The longer it went on, the more she understood that Alex had played her. She was going to die because she'd trusted a pirate. Baron Bastard wouldn't get the Firebird though. Thanks to Alex not giving her real name, at least the crew of the Chimera were safe, and the baron wouldn't ever get the next piece of the puzzle.

"I could admire you, if you weren't so stubborn," the baron said, sipping from a glass of wine, his knuckles red, his hands splattered with her blood. "I could use someone like you on my crew, in fact. Tell me where the Firebird is, and we'll make a deal. I'll let you live, and you can work for me."

She spit again, this time with less energy. "I'd sooner work for a pig in a bacon factory."

He was quiet, staring at her thoughtfully. Or at least she thought that's what his expression looked like. With a swelling eye, it was hard to tell.

"Maybe I go wake up Minty. Give her the same treatment I've given you and let you watch. Maybe that'll loosen your tongue."

Temp's stomach turned. He'd found a button she didn't even know she had. "You think I care what you'd do to a pirate who betrayed me? I'll see her hanged anyway if I get the chance."

"Lady Grey, I grow tired of this game." The baron's tone was steel covered in blood-soaked velvet. "Tell me, or I'll hand you over to my men, and you'll wish you'd taken me up on my generous offer."

A glint of steel in the shadows caught Temp's good eye. A flash of red hair, a swirl of a cloak. Her heart began to race, and pumping blood helped dull the pain. She shifted as though trying to get comfortable and felt the rope around her wrists slacken and slide over her hands. Still, she didn't move off the chair. "If I tell you where to get the Firebird, you'll let me go? Let me go back to my sky city in the north and leave me be?" She softened her tone, hoping it sounded almost pleading. She wasn't good at pretending.

"You have my word." His shrewd gaze looked her over. "But you don't leave until I have the Firebird in hand. Insurance, you see."

She nodded slowly. "Fine. I was only going to destroy it anyway." What else could she say? "It's—"

Alex leapt from the shadows onto a chair and then onto the table. Her airgun discharged, hitting first one guard, and then the other. The charge was so close to Temp's head, she felt it singe her hair. She pushed out of the chair and her ribs groaned in response, but she tackled Willoughby to the ground, punching him solidly in the face and knocking him unconscious.

She got up and looked at Alex, who stood by the door, a bag slung across her back.

"Are you waiting for a royal escort?" she hissed, waving Temp forwards. "Let's go!"

Temp tried to move quickly, but it was hard to breathe, let alone see. Her vision wavered, and she stumbled.

Alex draped Temp's arm over her shoulder, but she was too short to really be of help. "Come on, Temp. Don't go all floppy on me now."

She used my first name. She was fairly certain it was the first time, though why it should matter in this moment wasn't clear. They hurried down a dark corridor, and Temp lost track of where they were. She could only trust to Alex's direction, and when she staggered up stone steps into the cold, damp darkness, it was at least one good indication that they'd made it out of the house. Wet leaves felt good on her hot face, and she listened hard for the sound of Alex in the forest ahead of her, moving as fast as they dared. And then there were more stairs, wet stone walls, and the cold dankness of the caves.

They walked carefully through the darkness. The lantern had been left behind, as had Temp's cane, which she could have used right about now. They felt their way in the pitched gloom, hands sliding along walls. She followed Alex's voice, murmuring to her, telling her silly jokes, stories of debauchery that would have made pirates blush, and even calling her names when she faltered and fell to one knee.

"Left or right?" Alex knelt beside her and whispered. "We're at the turtle, Temp. But I don't remember if we go left or right. I'm all turned around."

Temp's head swam, and she lurched sideways to retch. It was odd, doing it in such total darkness. She'd had this kind of head injury before and knew it was a bad one, but not one that couldn't be overcome with rest. Rest. If she could just rest...

"Damn it, Strud!" Alex pinched her underarm, hard.

"Ow." Temp yanked her arm back, awake again. "Left." She struggled to her feet and grasped the bit of cloak Alex tucked into her hand, like a child being led. And then, too soon, there was a splash, and her feet were cold.

"Shite sticks and god's balls," Alex said, bumping into Temp as she backed up. "We're at the river entrance. We'll have to retrace our steps to the turtle—"

A shout bounced off the walls around them, echoing like a gong in Temp's head.

"Bollocks. I hope you can swim." Alex grabbed Temp's arm and dragged her forwards.

"We can't go in that water. God only knows what's in it." Temp's words felt like slugs leaving her lips.

"I'd rather take my chance with the river than with Willoughby. I can't believe you didn't kill the bastard." She tugged at Temp's arm and their legs were quickly wet through as they entered deeper water. When it was at their shoulders, Alex's teeth were audibly chattering. "If there's a grate ahead, we're dead. Let's hope that isn't the case."

Temp didn't have the extra energy for words. She shrugged out of her suit jacket, put the pouch of money in her trouser pocket, and took Alex's hand. They both took a deep breath and dove under the icy black water.

At least if she was going to die, she'd be holding the hand of a beautiful woman who hadn't betrayed her after all.

Chapter Fourteen

They swam through total blackness, surfacing for air only to find little more than a handspan of space between the cave and the water. It was enough to get a breath and then keep going. Twice, Temp's grip loosed on Alex's cloak, which she'd have taken off if it weren't for the fact that Temp seemed to be holding it like a lifeline. Twice, Alex reached back and pinched whatever skin she could find, knowing the silly pain would bring Temp back, even if only momentarily.

The water grew even colder, which Alex hadn't thought possible, and then the current was on them, pulling them forwards at a furious pace into the massive river itself. Temp's grip on Alex's cloak made it a noose, yanking her back as the current dragged her onward. Flailing, she managed to release the tie at her throat, and she was propelled forwards. She kept the cloak wrapped around her hand and could only hope that Temp didn't let go. There'd be no saving her now.

They surfaced at the same time, Temp spluttering and coughing behind her. Alex spotted a metal ladder on the wall ahead and with the very last of her energy, swam towards it, almost towing Temp along behind her. She grasped the metal and clung to it, pulling hard on the cloak to draw Temp to the only thing that could save them right now. Temp reached out, and her hand slipped off, and Alex grabbed the neck of her shirt.

"Damn you to all the dogs of hell, you good-looking bastard," she said, her arm burning with the effort of not letting go. "Grab the ladder."

Temp reached out and wrapped her arms around the ladder,

and Alex let out a sob of relief. They hung there together for some minutes, getting their breath, before Temp tapped Alex's arm.

"Need to get out of the water," she said, and it sounded like it was painful for her to speak. "Freeze."

"You first. At least I can shove your arse from behind if you forget how to move." Thankfully, Temp didn't argue. She moved onto the ladder and slowly, so very slowly, climbed up and over the ledge onto dry land. Alex followed, grateful that Temp didn't slip or fall back and take them both to a watery grave.

They collapsed on the dewy grass, the smell of earth rising around them. Rain fell in fat, heavy drops that helped wash the river grit from Alex's eyes. She shivered hard, feeling the pain in every nerve from her toes to her skull. A noise penetrated her exhaustion, and she struggled to place it. Horse's hooves and cart's wheels.

She pushed herself to her knees and looked. A hansom cab was trundling their way. She pushed to her feet and stumbled onto the hardpacked dirt road. "Here!"

The cab pulled up and slowed to a stop. The driver tipped his hat back and looked at her. "Cripes, love. Did you go in the river? It's a miracle you're alive. Come on now, I'll take you home."

Alex nearly wept but held herself together. "My friend, there. She went in too, but I don't think she can walk."

He jumped down from his seat and hurried over to Temp, then looked at Alex quizzically. "She?"

"She." There was no time for explanation or quibble about standards of dress. "Can you help?"

He shrugged and pulled Temp up, draping her arm over his shoulder and half dragging her to the cab. The horses snorted and pawed at the ground, seeming to understand the distress around them. "Open the door, miss, if you wouldn't mind."

Alex swung it open and did her best to help tumble Temp into the cab. She climbed in after. "The Old Angel, please."

He tipped his hat. "There's a blanket under the seat. I use it to keep the horse warm, but I don't imagine the smell will bother you right now."

She pulled the blanket out, which did very much smell of horse, and sat close to Temp, who was drifting in and out of consciousness. Her eyes were swollen, and bruises were already spreading across her cheeks. Her jaw looked wrong somehow. And the wheezing sound when she breathed couldn't be a good thing. Alex had known there was only one way forwards at Willoughby's, but she hadn't counted on him getting so violent so quickly. She'd underestimated him, and she swallowed the bile that rose in her throat at being the reason Temp was in this condition. Not that it would have been Alex's choice to rob the bastard in the first place.

The cab bouncing over the cobbles made her head ache, but she kept chafing Temp's hands in an effort to warm them, though it did little good since Alex's were just as cold. The cab stopped, and the door opened.

"I'll just pop in and get someone to help with your friend," the driver said.

"Ask for Molly, please. She'll know what to do."

He left, and Alex cupped Temp's cheek. "Temp, I need you to wake enough to get into the pub. Can you do that?" For some reason, she kissed Temp's forehead. "Please?"

Temp tipped her head back. "That one was too high. I'll respond better if you do it lower." She pursed her lips.

Alex patted her leg. "You're going to be fine, I think." She stepped down from the hansom and moved out of the way as one large man got into the cab and helped hand Temp down to another, waiting below. Someone wrapped a thick blanket around Alex's shoulders.

"Let's get you both inside and into a hot bath," Molly said, her arm around Alex's waist. "Wait here, good sir, and we'll get you paid," she said, glancing back at the cab driver, who tipped his hat.

Alex, numb now that the need to survive had fled, followed as they nearly carried Temp inside and up the stairs to a room. They dropped her on the bed and left without a word. Alex dug in

Temp's trouser pocket and didn't miss the small grin on Temp's lips. She pulled out the money pouch and shoved it at Molly. "Will you pay the cab driver enough to keep quiet? And take what you need for the room and bath. And some food, if you can spare it."

Molly pocketed the pouch. "I'm having the bath brought up now, and we'll get it filled nice and hot soon as we can. In the meantime, take off all that wet stuff, or you'll never get warm." She moved to the fireplace and quickly got a roaring fire going. "I'll have some clothes sent up while we get those clean and dry." She eyed Temp. "It might take me a minute to find something to suit."

"Much appreciated, Molly." Alex sank into a chair, almost too tired to move. "Trouble might be out there looking for us."

"Darlin', trouble is always lookin' for someone. It's us in the know who keep the doors closed to it." Molly winked and left.

As she'd said, it was only a moment before the door opened again, and a large copper bath was brought in by the men who'd helped bring Temp up the stairs. Two young girls took repeated trips, their eyes downcast as they filled it with steaming water nearly to the rim.

Once they were gone and the door was locked behind them, Alex sighed and looked at Temp. "I'm not undressing you. I'm too tired, and you're too heavy to move."

"That's incredibly unromantic. The love poets would be deeply distressed." Temp pushed herself upright with a groan. "I feel like I've been in a fight."

"You haven't. To fight you need to actually throw a punch. You were just mashed like a potato." Alex hesitated, and then decided there was no more time for decorum. "Look away." She undid the stays on her corset with difficulty, her fingers trembling as she fiddled at the wet cord refusing to come free. Large hands covered hers, stopping her.

"Let me help," Temp said. "I can't see very well, but this is something I could do in my sleep."

"Braggart." Alex didn't mind the heat that swept through her at

Temp's deft touch. Temp didn't need to know that it set her aflame.

True to her word, Temp got the stays undone quickly and slipped the corset from Alex's body, letting it fall to the floor. When her hands came up again, Alex stepped back.

"I can handle the rest, thank you." It came out more primly than she meant it to, but Temp still smiled and sat back down on the bed. She turned towards the wall, even though her eyes were swollen enough to make seeing impossible.

Alex disrobed quickly, trying not to be disappointed that she couldn't put on a show, exhausted as they were. Leaving the clothes in a pile, she slipped into the bath and grimaced at the pins and needles that shot through her as the heat met her icy flesh. She sat back, gingerly, then sighed with pleasure.

"Thank you," Temp said, still not looking at her.

"For putting you in a situation that means you look like you got in a fight with the devil's demons? My pleasure," Alex said, unable to acknowledge fully the guilt she felt.

"For saving my life." Temp's tone was soft, vulnerable. "If you hadn't kept pushing me, I'd be dead in those caves right now."

That was, without question, true. "You'd have drowned too, if we're keeping track." Alex kept her voice light. There'd been enough seriousness for the day.

"That too." Temp turned towards her, her head tilted, her eyes closed. "Why *did* you save me? You could have escaped, left me to die, and been on your way back to the Urchin. Why not leave me?"

Alex didn't have an answer, so she slid beneath the water and let it wash over her face. She ran her hands through her hair, getting out whatever the river had sifted into it. After a quick wash with coarse soap, she rose from the water, though she'd have liked to have stayed in much longer and breathed in the fire-warmed air. "I don't know how to answer that," she said, stepping from the bath. "What I do know is you should get in the hot water and not look like something dredged from a river bottom."

Temp looked almost disappointed, but she stood and

unbuttoned her waistcoat. Alex watched, unabashed and feeling no need whatsoever to look away, as Temp removed her button-down linen shirt, leaving her in a tight white vest. Her small breasts were clearly visible beneath the wet fabric, and then her nipples were hard and tight in the warm air as she shed that too.

Alex nearly doubled over with desire as it flooded through her. Temp's body was trim and muscled, with hardly an ounce of fat on her. As she slid off the wet trousers to reveal the short underpants beneath, Alex was ready to fall to her knees. When the underpants came off too, Alex had to cross her legs against the throbbing at her centre. Had this been any other situation, at any other time, she'd have pushed Temp back onto the bed and straddled her. Instead, she pulled a blanket from the bed, wrapped it around herself, and curled up on the mattress, her back against the wall. Only then did she really see what she was looking at.

Bruises spread in a constellation over Temp's abdomen and chest. Her jaw and eyes were swollen, and a cut was oozing blood on her side. "Christ on the cross," Alex said and went to the door. She opened it and looked out. As she'd expected, a maid was posted outside. "Tell Molly we need a doctor."

The girl darted away down the hall, her shoes clattering on the stairs. Alex went back inside and stared at the vision of Temp in the bath, her legs hanging off the end, her head resting on the edge, her short dark hair slicked back. Even battered and bruised, she was a heady example of strength and sensuality. And Alex had very nearly gotten her killed. She leaned against the wall.

A knock came at the door, and she cracked it open, then stepped aside as Molly entered with two maids, all of them carrying food and pints of beer.

Molly looked at Temp in the bath, who hadn't stirred. Her eyes narrowed, and she tilted her head, as though taking in all the injuries. "I needed to see for myself which doc to call on." She nodded and motioned at the trays. "Get her to eat and drink if you can. I'll be back with someone soon."

Alex thanked her and locked the door behind them. Then she brought a pint of beer to the bath and knelt beside it. "Temp, can you drink this? Maybe it will kill off whatever we swallowed in the river."

"I doubt anything will kill that off. We'll be growing tentacles by morning." Temp pushed up a little and water sloshed around her breasts. Alex tried, unsuccessfully, not to look. "Thank you," Temp said, taking a drink, and then a longer one.

Alex went and got hers, then sat beside the bath, facing the fire. "I'm having a doctor brought in. I think you need stitches in your side. How'd that one happen?"

Temp shrugged and instantly winced. "I took a hit from one of the thugs in the side, and I think he had a ring on. But it could have happened any other time too." She seemed to open one eye. "Are you hurt at all?"

Alex shook her head. "Not a scratch. Just cold to my bones, and I likely have a small dose of the plague from our swim."

"What's a little plague among friends?" Temp settled back in the tub and continued to sip more slowly at her beer.

They sat quietly for a time, and Alex let the crackling of the flames lull her to a doze. The knock at the door startled her, and it took a moment to remember where she was. She rose and opened the door to Molly and a man who looked more than a little disgruntled at being woken in the middle of the night.

He came in and set his physician's bag on the table, then looked over Alex. "You don't need me." He turned and looked at Temp, then grunted. "She does. Get her out of the bath, please."

Together, Molly and Alex helped Temp out of the now cold bath and onto the bed. Molly winked at Alex as they wrapped a blanket around Temp and then helped her lay down. Alex grinned back, feeling the heat in her cheeks.

"You're the least virtuous woman I've ever met," Temp mumbled. "It's downright lecherous to ogle me in this state."

"Pirate," Alex said, pointing to herself. "No virtue, all ogle." She moved aside when the doctor cleared his throat and began his examination. He kept clucking in disapproval as he moved from Temp's head and face to her ribs and side.

"She's got at least two broken ribs. She'll need to be very careful about how she moves and keep all activity to an absolute minimum, or it may go all the way through and puncture a lung. If that happens, she'll die. Quite painfully, may I add." He went to his bag and pulled out a needle and thread. "She'll require three stitches in her side. I don't think any bones in her face are broken, though her jaw is dislocated, and I'm going to have to reset it. And you both need to drink this." He pulled out two small glass bottles. "It's called Coca-Cola. We're seeing good results in it killing bacteria from bad water."

Alex pulled the cork from hers and sniffed, then took a sip. It was odd but not bad. She drank the fizzy brown liquid, hoping it did as the doctor said.

"Do you have bread that's gone off, Molly?" the doctor said, ignoring Temp's hiss as he began to suture the wound in her side.

"Aye. Hungry?" Molly asked, her hands on her hips.

"Wet some and place it over this wound. It could easily get infected thanks to the river water. The mould on the bread will help prevent that."

Molly shrugged and looked at Alex. "Who knew?"

Alex just shook her head. The exhaustion overtaking her made it hard to stay upright.

The doctor tied off the stitch and put his things away. Then he turned back to Temp, placed his hands on her face and said, "This will hurt." He seemed to simultaneously push and pull, and Temp groaned, then grew still as consciousness left her. He stepped back, nodding. "That will do it. Now it will heal properly. Molly, can I get an old sheet torn into strips, please? I'd like to bind her ribs, so they don't move much. Once she's in a place where she needs to be ambulatory, she can remove the bandages and allow them to heal naturally."

Molly bundled up their wet clothes, handed them to a girl waiting in the hallway, and gave the order for the bandages. The maid outside returned quickly with torn sheets. Between the three of them, they held Temp in place and got them bound around her before letting her collapse back onto the bed.

"Right. We'll leave you to get some rest. Try to eat before you sleep, and I'll wait for you to ring the bell for breakfast." Molly gave Alex's arm a squeeze. "You're safe here, so sleep easy."

"Thank you. Oh, will you get word to Kel that we made it back? He'll be worried."

"Will do. And I've a notion that you won't need new clothes after all. Yours will be dry by morning." Molly left, closing the door softly behind her.

Alex crawled up the bed beside Temp. She was too tired to eat, and by the way Temp was breathing, she wasn't going to be awake for a while either. Alex curled up next to her, combining their body heat, and pulled a rough-spun blanket over them. Temp grunted slightly and shifted, putting her arm under Alex and pulling her close. Alex lay her head on Temp's shoulder, feeling safer than she could remember feeling in her life, and drifted to sleep.

At one point in the night the door opened, and she came awake, realising she was naked and had no weapons. But it was just one of the young maids, who crept to the fireplace and stoked it from the embers, warming the room once again. She crept out just as silently, taking with her the tray of uneaten food.

Alex's body complained bitterly as she left Temp's side and sidled off the bed. On the small table were her knife and airgun, still sheathed in their leather pouches. She took them both and crawled back into bed, and didn't mind when Temp once again pulled her close. She settled one weapon under each pillow, and then drifted to sleep once more.

Chapter Fifteen

For just a moment, Temp wondered if she had, in fact, died and been dropped onto shards of glass in hell. There wasn't an inch of her body that didn't hurt in some way, though her head seemed to be winning the contest for most painful. As hard as she tried, she couldn't open her left eye very well. Through the slit in her right eye, she saw a fire throwing shadows across the walls, food on a tray that she immediately wanted to crawl to, and a pile of neatly folded clothes on a chair.

Not hell then.

When she tried to move, she found herself pinned. Alex was keeping her in place. Her head was pillowed on Temp's shoulder, and Temp's arm was numb. She moved a piece of hair away from Alex's cheek and tucked it behind her ear. Although she hadn't been hurt, even in sleep, she looked weary and paler than usual. The feeling that Alex fit too perfectly against her forced her to clear her throat.

"Why in blazes are you awake?" Alex mumbled, her eyes still closed.

"Because you snore like a flyer with engine trouble."

Alex's eyes opened to slits. "Liar. I do no such thing."

It was a moment, a slip, but Temp heard it. Alex's accent had the formal training of education, the Queen's English. Once again, that nagging feeling rose.

And then Alex sat up, the sheet falling away to her waist, and Temp forgot everything, including how to breathe. Alex's full breasts were bare to the firelight, her thick red hair hung loose down her slim back, and... "A tattoo?"

Alex looked over her shoulder. "All miscreants have them."

Temp traced the thin, simple lines with her fingertip. A sun was punctured by a crescent moon directly below it, and below that, with a line connecting it to the moon, was a star. "What does it mean?" She'd never seen a woman with a tattoo before, and she found it incredibly alluring.

Alex shivered under Temp's touch. "The North Star will always lead me through darkness and into light. But all three shine their own light, so even the dark doesn't need to be feared."

It was surprisingly philosophical and meaningful, but Temp had learned there were layers to Alex she had yet to suss out. "That's lovely. Deep, for a pirate, but lovely just the same."

Alex scooted off the bed, taking the sheet with her. She tossed her hair over her shoulder as she wrapped it around her, providing a mind-numbing view of her rather perfect backside before she covered it. Then she looked over her shoulder at Temp, a wicked gleam in her eye that suggested she knew exactly what effect she was having.

"How are you feeling?" she asked.

"Like Hades himself used me for target practice with his pitchfork." Temp groaned as she sat up, her ribs protesting every inch.

"I think you've got your mythologies mixed up, handsome." Alex's gaze moved over Temp's torso, naked but for the bandages. "That doesn't bode well for our continued adventure."

Temp sighed and rubbed at her sore temples, then winced at the pain of touching her temples at all. "What further adventure? Without the orb, and with Willoughby knowing we're after it, we'll never get close again."

"Whoever said we don't have the orb?" Alex grinned and picked up a leather bag by its long handle, swinging it gently. "You don't possibly think I handed you over only to fail? You hired me because I'm the best at what I do. I'm insulted you'd think otherwise."

Temp stared at the bag, and then at Alex. "You actually got it?"

"All I needed was time to search the house with everyone else's attention elsewhere. You gave me that." Alex handed her the bag and then turned towards the food. "I never give up when I want something desperately enough. And the situation was certainly nothing if not desperate." She layered cheese and bread and took a massive bite as she watched Temp.

Temp opened the bag and removed the glass ball. It was covered in etchings, and a red swirl ran through the middle like a thick thread. On each side was a small groove, and she could picture the way the Firebird would settle into place perfectly atop it. "It's incredible." She held it up to the light, but her vision was too corrupted to see it properly. "Alex, this is...I thought..." She swallowed hard.

"You thought I betrayed you. You thought I sold you out, was going to take the money and then run off back to the Urchin." Alex shrugged. "I tried to tell you."

"I understood when you quoted Dorian Grey to me. Before that, I wasn't sure. And the longer it took..." She leaned back against the wall, all movement making it hard to breathe. "I'm glad I was wrong."

Alex sat on the edge of the bed, bread and cheese in one hand, and took the orb in the other. She ate as she turned it this way and that, studying it. "I recognise some of these symbols as ancient Celtic. The others I'm not sure about."

"Do you think Molly could get us some paper and a pen? I'd like to get started transcribing and see if we can make sense of it." She hesitated, thoroughly irritated at her helplessness. "If you wouldn't mind doing it, since I can barely see you, let alone those tiny characters on the orb."

Alex handed her the orb, went to the door, poked her head out, and spoke to someone in the hallway. She came back in and sat next to Temp, who took the food from her hand and ate slowly, her jaw protesting every bite. Alex set the orb on her stomach and got up to get more food. She also poured them both a cup of strong tea.

"Good thing we can trust Molly, or we'd both be dead. Neither of us moved when they brought this in." Alex sighed happily as she took a sip of tea.

"Very true." Temp finished the bread and cheese and sipped her tea, enjoying the warmth of it as it slid down her throat. "Honestly, I don't even remember getting here last night. It's all a blasted blur after the river." She shuddered and drew the blanket over her. "That's something I never want to experience again."

There was a knock at the door, and Alex retrieved paper and pen from someone, then moved the food to another table so she could use the one nearest the fire. She set the orb between two books and began to copy the symbols. She looked completely comfortable wrapped in nothing but a blanket, her long, thick hair cascading down her back, tucked behind her ear to keep it out of her way.

Temp watched her, thinking of the training and education Alex clearly hid from the world. Her accent, her casual delicacy, even the way she ate, all indicated that she'd once been part of upper-class society. What had made her give it up? What could possibly be so bad she'd turned to piracy and even murder?

"Staring is rude." Alex didn't look up from her work as she drew quick, simple lines.

"My apologies." Temp rested her head on the pillow and closed her eyes against the throbbing headache.

Another knock at the door came, and Molly entered without waiting for Alex to open it. "Well, good to see you're not dead. I do hate having to clear bodies from the rooms. Make an awful stench, they do." She glanced at the table Alex was at and then away again. "I'll have some hot food brought up too, seein' as how you're eatin' now." She moved to Temp's beside and handed her a mug of water and two small white pills. "They're called aspirin. New cure for headaches. I swear by 'em. Will help your pain."

Temp took them, willing to take opium if it would just dampen the throbbing. There was some on the ship if she grew that desperate. "Thank you, Molly, for everything you've done. We'd be in dire circumstances indeed without you."

Molly grinned. "You were in dire enough circumstances *with* me. Now, sit up. Doc says I need to check that wound in your side for infection."

Temp wanted to argue that it was fine, but she wasn't so stubborn that she'd risk dying of something preventable. If it was. She frowned when the wrapping fell away, and she saw a piece of mouldy green bread over the wound. "Well, that's disturbing."

Molly threw the bread into the fire, and it crackled. "Doc says the mould will help prevent infection. Looks all right so far. Bit red, but it isn't hot to the touch." She pulled a mostly clean-looking rag from her apron pocket, dipped it in the cup of water, and cleaned the wound with a surprisingly gentle touch. "Now," she said, moving away. "I'll leave you to it, but you should know the streets are abuzz with news of a reward for the capture of thieves who look an awful lot like you two. No one here will say a word, but the longer you're here, the shorter your time for safe exit. If two people can keep a secret only if one is dead, then you're looking at a whole lot of folk who need to be gone before you're really safe." She looked at them shrewdly. "You got here somehow, so I suggest you make good use of Kel to get home."

She squeezed Temp's leg, patted Alex's shoulder, and left them in silence. The whole time she'd been tending Temp, Alex had been drawing and turning the orb to look at the next section. The sheafs of paper were full of intricate designs. She was fast and clearly precise. Temp moved gingerly, swinging her legs off the bed, and reached for her clothes. "We should get back to the airship, assuming it's still docked where we left it."

Alex looked up, and her gaze slid over Temp like silk. "I'll get a message to Kel and ask him to bring a hansom. You clearly can't ride, and walking would take too much time in your condition."

Temp couldn't argue that, but a hansom cab wasn't exactly

inconspicuous. It would have to do. She pulled her clothes on slowly, the pain in her ribs making her breathing difficult. It was her shoes she couldn't manage and with a quiet swear, she decided she'd just have to walk barefoot. No one here would be upset about her lack of decorum.

Alex pulled her corset over her blouse and laced the stays, her eyes following Temp's moves. Temp was sorry she'd been too focused on getting ready to watch Alex get dressed. There was something just as sensual about watching a woman dress as there was about watching her undress. Well, almost as sensual, anyway.

Alex finished and then knelt at Temp's feet. She pulled on her socks and shoes, and Temp didn't say anything. The visual made her throat dry, and she couldn't look away if she'd wanted to.

She put her hands on Temp's thighs and stood, and Temp swayed at her nearness.

"Be right back." Alex's gaze lingered briefly on Temp's lips and then she turned away and left the room.

Temp dropped her head into her hands. What was happening? Being attracted to Alex was one thing. Sleeping naked beside her and wanting to pull her back into bed was another entirely. But they had the orb, and that meant their deal was concluded. Why did it bother her that Alex was now free to go?

Alex came back in. "Molly got the same driver who dropped us here last night to take us to the airship. He'll take a variety of routes, but that dock is going to be compromised and unusable from now on. Figured that doesn't really matter right now though. I don't want to involve Kel any more than we already have."

She wrapped the orb in a piece of cloth and placed it in the leather satchel that still looked damp. She also added two parchment packets but didn't explain what they were. She laid the etchings in parchment too and rolled them up before tying the bundle with a piece of string. Temp watched it all through vision still slightly blurry, unable to help and hating the feeling of being a lump of useless clay.

"Let's go." Alex looked her over. "Can you walk? Or should I get those big orcs to come carry you down like the princess you are?"

Temp grunted. "Like hell they will." She followed Alex down the steps, careful to keep one hand on the railing. Flailing her way downstairs would only serve to make Alex see her as weak and useless, which to this point, she had been.

Outside, rain fell in sheets, and they moved as quickly as possible into the cab. Alex whispered directions to the dock, and the driver frowned but shrugged and climbed into the driver's seat. They set off, and the jarring made Temp swear silently and repeatedly in her head.

"Alex," Temp said, finally forcing the words out. "You got us the orb. That was our deal. You don't have to stay with me any longer. You can make your way–"

"You're daft as a bat with silver wings if you think I'm staying down here for Willoughby to grab me." Alex crossed her arms and glared at her. "You think you can get rid of me that way?"

Temp held up her hands. "No! I wasn't saying that. Of course you're free to come back to the Chimera with me and leave from there. I was just giving you the option. If you wanted to leave now and go find the Urchin, I wouldn't try to stop you."

"Oh, well, thank you for giving me your *permission*." Alex's tone could have pierced armour. "I could have left you at any time, your majesty. And I'll leave when I'm good and ready."

Confounded, Temp couldn't think of a response. Alex didn't want to leave? Why not?

A shout sounded, and the hansom rocked. The horses whinnied, and the driver cried out. Alex pulled the knife from her boot, extended the silver tips in her boot tips, and grabbed the curtain. She peeked out the side. "I can see the airship. That's the good news. The less good news is that Willoughby is on a horse with four men in front of him, and I think they've killed the driver."

Temp sighed. "I wish I had my cane."

"Because you'd be right useful that way, swinging it about

when you can barely see. You'd probably cut my ear off instead of killing one of them." Alex tapped the wall with her fingertips. "You may have to fight anyway." She pulled the small airgun from her arm holster and pressed it into Temp's hand. "We'll use the clock system."

Without another word, they exited the cab.

"Baron. It has been *such* a long time since we crossed paths. I was hoping to call on you for tea later, but it seems you've rather inconvenienced us by causing our driver to stop breathing," Alex said. "Rather rude, if you don't mind my saying."

There it was. That way of speaking that meant Alex was more than just a pirate. Temp decided she'd get to the bottom of it at some point, if Alex stayed in her orbit.

"No games. I want the orb back. Hand it over, and I'll kill you quickly. Lady Grey looks like it won't take much to push her over the edge, though I admit to admiring her ability to take a beating and continue on to steal from me. Don't hand it over, and I'll kill you slowly and still take the orb."

Alex sighed. "Eleven o'clock," she murmured, then said more loudly, "I'm afraid we have no wish to die, nor do we wish to hand over the orb. It's a difficult choice, isn't it?"

Temp raised the airgun and hoped to hell the shadow at eleven o'clock was what she was aiming for. She squeezed the trigger, and blue light flashed. The shadow fell to the ground.

"Down!" Alex dropped beside her, and Temp followed, her body protesting every millimetre of movement.

"Three o'clock," she said, and Temp aimed that direction. She saw Alex throw her knife just as Temp squeezed the trigger again, and two more shadows hit the ground. "Six o'clock." Another went down, and only Willoughby was left, but she couldn't see him.

Alex yelped and scrabbled at the dirt as someone grabbed her from beneath the cab and pulled her backwards by her feet. Temp grabbed for her but only got a handful of gravel.

"Now," Willoughby said, his voice cold. "Come where I can see you, Lady Grey, and lay down the weapon. I'm out of patience and will happily break Minty's neck."

Temp moved carefully around the cab. Through slitted eyes and pounding rain, she could see Alex being held against the front of Willoughby's body, one hand on her neck, the other on the side of her head. It was a killing move, one Temp had been forced to use herself on occasion.

"Give me the orb. Now."

Temp reached down to the satchel laying in a puddle. She pulled the orb from it, holding it up. "Here. Let her go. I'll hand it over, and we'll be done."

"No," Alex whispered hoarsely as she struggled to speak over his crushing hold. "My life isn't worth it. He'll only kill us both. Get him first—" She choked as he tightened his hold.

Temp took a breath. Alex was right. He'd kill them both anyway. If he got the orb, he would ruin the world and kill how many more? But they could go after it again. Try to beat him to the Apple somehow. But it wouldn't be possible to raise Alex from the dead. She lifted her head. "I'm rolling it to you. I'm the one who wanted it stolen. Alex is just a pirate I hired to help me. She didn't even want to. She told me you were dangerous, and I shouldn't have any dealings with you. I didn't listen. Leave her alive. It's me you should kill."

She bent and rolled the orb, still clad in its wrapping towards him. He raised his airgun. "I'll kill you first, since you're so eager to meet your maker. Then Minty and I will have a lover's chat before I send her after you." He stepped on the orb, lightly resting his foot atop it.

Before he could pull the trigger, Temp pulled the knife from the pocket in her boot and threw it, aiming as best she could. It hit true, burying itself in his thigh. He dropped the gun and let go of Alex as he fell to the ground, clasping his leg. The orb was trapped beneath him.

A shout came from somewhere nearby, along with the sound

of running footsteps. More of Willoughby's men, most likely.

"Run!" Temp grabbed the satchel as she lurched forwards, then held Alex's hand as they ran through the deluge of rain, splashing their way up the ladder to the dock, where their little airship bobbed in the storm. Temp dropped awkwardly into the passenger seat, and Alex dove into the pilot's seat. She pulled the dome shut, cranked the gears, and flipped the switch that released the mooring rope. She pulled hard, and they rose into the storm, leaving Low Nottingham, and the orb, behind.

Temp closed her eyes. "Press the silver crow and then follow the compass. It will lead you back to the Chimera."

Alex did as she was told, without comment. Once again, they were both wet through and shivering. Temp couldn't wait to get into her warm bed and wake without someone trying to kill her. For a few days anyway.

Silence filled the cockpit, and Temp let herself drift into a place where the pain lessened, though it kept pulling her back to reality. The airship slid through the wet ink of the night sky, putting distance between them and the villain of their story.

Alex, held in the grip of a ruthless madman...her eyes wide, her voice trembling even as she told Temp to let her die, the gun pressed to her temple...

Temp jerked awake and groaned as fresh pain assailed her.

"I'd very much like to talk to Wade about how this mechanism works." Alex's voice drifted back to her. "I truly can't begin to fathom how the crow somehow speaks to a ship leagues away."

"I told you before. Wade is something special when it comes to makers."

"So why does he work for you?" Alex asked.

Temp debated but then didn't have the mental energy to question the ethical dilemmas regarding someone else's story. "He's too good. He comes from a land town in the far north, near Hadrian's wall. Knowledge there is a sort of taboo. When the railroad went through, Wade made suggestions about the gears, the steam, and how to make it more efficient. He didn't even work for them. He just knew, in that way special people do." Temp shifted, trying to get comfortable with the pain in her ribs. It was no use. "His town turned on him. Said he was unnatural, that he was in league with the devil. The sort of nonsense propagated by ignorance and fear of the unknown and misunderstood. They were going to hang him."

Alex glanced back over her shoulder. "That's monstrous."

Temp snorted. "Says the superstitious pirate." She closed her eyes again. "I happened to be working in the area and heard about it as I was passing through. I put him on a horse, then an airship, and he's been with me ever since."

"You gather the people who aren't welcome among their peers like a sheep gathers grass," Alex said softly, distant. "I understand that desire."

Temp wanted to ask questions, but her mind was fuzzy, and she drifted off yet again. A bump woke her, and she blinked against lamplight. The flyer was hooked to its lift ropes and was being pulled into the belly of the Chimera. Tension slid from her shoulders and made her dizzier. She went to step from the flyer and lost her balance, tilting sideways, unable to keep from falling.

Strong clay arms caught her and hoisted her into a cradle position like she wasn't tall and stoutly built. She looked into glowing eyes. "Thank you, Crispin." And then she fainted.

Chapter Sixteen

Alex propped her bare feet on the edge of a chair. "I think you're bluffing. I call."

"I do bluff ever so well," Ginny said, laying her cards on the table. "But I never do it if I think I'll get caught."

Vee laughed heartily, making Alex grin in return even though she'd just lost a third game of cards for which she had no money to add to the pot. She'd grown bored in her room, and the staff were busy looking after the passengers who seemed to appear and vanish like strange circus folk. Only Ginny and Vee had come out of their room and stayed for a bit after lunch. Alex had slept long and well, and when she'd woken, she'd gone to see how Temp was faring. But one of the golems stood outside her door, and Alex had backed away quickly. Someone would let her know when Temp was up. No need to get near that thing.

"Why are you here?" Alex asked, shuffling the deck quickly. "You could be card sharks in London-on-Ground and make a killing instead of up here doing...whatever it is that happens up here."

Vee's eyes narrowed, but her smile remained. "That was rather unsubtle, if you don't mind my saying so, Lady Pirate. Do you have a question you truly want to ask?"

Alex continued to shuffle, but she kept her gaze on Vee's. "Why are you on this ship?"

"Because we're writers in love," Ginny said, smiling with obvious affection at Vee. "As writers, we want to experience as many situations as humanly possible. As writers in *love* with each other, our opportunities are more limited when it comes to experiencing those situations *together*." She turned her attention to Alex. "This ship allows us to fall into our deepest desires, our most decadent fantasies, and explore our most secretly held inhibitions, without any fear of judgement or reprisal. It's amazing inspiration for the characters in our novels and lends veracity to the situations we put them in."

"And it gives us time together without worrying that anyone will turn us over to the authorities." Vee took Ginny's hand, then kissed her knuckles.

"But the queen herself—"

"Is a lovely, highly capable woman who also enjoys her privacy." Temp slowly lowered herself into the chair beside Alex and gave her a wry smile. "Good evening, ladies."

Vee sat up, all levity gone from her expression. "Good God, Captain. You look as though you got in a fight with one of your golems. Are you quite all right?"

Ginny placed her hand over her mouth, her eyes wide. "Surely this didn't happen to you on the ship? Were you not careful when you left it?"

Alex turned and studied Temp and saw what they were seeing. She laughed. "You really do look like the dog's back end after bad pork."

Temp winced. "And you really do have a way with words, Alex." She waved away their concerns. "It looks worse than it is, although your reactions suggest I should remain in my quarters for a few days until I look respectable again." She stood and looked down at Alex. "I was looking for you to discuss our business and was told you were here taking advantage of my guests."

Vee laughed, though it didn't quite mask the concern in her eyes. "You'll find it's very hard to take advantage of us. No need to worry on our behalf."

Ginny stood and moved around the table. She placed her hand on Temp's arm. "Truly, Captain. If we can do anything to help, please don't hesitate to ask. We're at your disposal."

Temp moved Ginny's hand from her arm and kissed it much the same way Vee had. "Sweet lady, if I were to call on you both outside the ship, you can be sure it wouldn't be for anything beyond the boudoir."

Vee's laugh was louder and more genuine this time, and Ginny blushed a pretty pink. Alex ignored the odd flare of irritation that ran through her.

"We'll hold you to that, Captain." Vee shifted so Ginny could sit on her lap.

Alex and Temp left them there, and they headed for Temp's office. Temp had replaced her cane, but whereas it had been an accessory before, now she leaned on it. Was there a blade hidden in this one too? Alex looked down the length of it and saw the small protuberance that likely made it come out. How amazing it would be to afford more than one of that kind of thing.

Inside, two mugs of tea were already letting off steam on Temp's desk. Alex slid into a chair and cradled the mug. "You may look worse than a dog's dinner, but you clean up well."

Temp ran her hand over the wool waistcoat. "Thank you. I find that if I look good, it helps me feel better." She looked down and shook her head. "And you're walking the ship barefoot like an urchin."

Alex wiggled her toes. "Your carpet is too fine to be crushed under my boots. Besides, they're still too wet to put back on."

Temp nodded. "I can have new ones brought to your room later."

Alex stared into her tea and then looked up. "You could have let him kill me. If you had, you might have been able to get the orb after you threw the knife. One you could have buried in his chest, if I hadn't been standing in front of it."

Temp didn't look away. "I could have done that, yes. And if things go wrong, I may regret that decision when all of humanity is at risk. What is one life weighed against many?" Temp gave a tired half smile. "In that moment, your life weighed more. I wasn't about to watch him kill you."

"The way his people killed your last partner." She wasn't trying to be insensitive, but she liked the truth.

Temp swallowed a gulp of tea. "Yes."

It became clear she wasn't going to say more on the subject, and Alex could respect that. "Well, thank you. I wasn't ready to meet my maker, whoever She might be and whatever climate She might be living in."

"Well, you may still get your chance. Without the orb, we're back to where we started."

Alex shook her head and reached down beside the chair. "Even half dead and with broken bones, you managed to grab this." She held up the satchel. "And in it are the drawings I made from the orb. We don't have the original, and we don't know what it would have shown with the Firebird attached, but maybe we can still come up with something."

Temp nearly leapt to her feet, and then winced and leaned on the desk. "Alex, I could kiss you. I forgot that I grabbed it. Most of the fight is a blur, to be honest." She reached out and took the satchel, then emptied the contents onto the desk. The wrapped parchment parcels fell out. "What are the small ones?"

"One is from the doctor. Aspirin to help with the pain." She motioned towards the other small packet. "That's something I nicked off Willoughby's desk. I don't know why, but it seemed important, what with the way it was placed near the orb."

Temp unwrapped the small rune stone. "Futhark rune. The Nauthiz, representing need."

"Or conflict." Alex rolled her eyes at Temp's look of surprise. "You were coming to me for my expertise. You shouldn't be surprised at my knowledge base."

"Point taken." Temp looked back at the rune. "We didn't even know this was part of it. What does it have to do with the orb?"

Alex shrugged. "I think we should gather your people and put our heads together to see if we can decipher the sketching I made.

Maybe that will explain it."

Temp nodded, then sat back in her seat and looked at Alex through her swollen, bruised eyes. "You're staying."

It wasn't a question, but Alex answered anyway. "I'm curious, and I still want to see what treasure is at the end of this. I have my reasons, beyond just that of being a pirate and it being what I do." She didn't need to add anything about wanting to stick around to make sure Temp was really okay. And she certainly didn't need to add anything about the concoction of emotions she felt when she thought Temp *wasn't* going to be okay, or how she'd nearly vomited when she saw how beaten Temp had been. Saying anything about the dreams of caressing Temp's face and taking care of her would certainly be out of the question.

Temp's gaze searched hers, and Alex wondered what it was she was looking for.

"Okay then." Temp looked away and picked up a copper tube type thing, then spoke into it. "Please ring Wade and Joe and have them come to my office."

Alex shook her head. "I really want that for the Urchin."

"Just what we need. An advanced pirate ship." Temp smiled, and she still looked tired.

Wade, Joe, and Peter arrived a few minutes later. Temp and Alex had vacated to the little secret room and spread the sketchings on the table with the Firebird holding the parchment down on one end and the little rune on the other. Alex smoothed fresh paper down on another table and placed an ink pot with a fresh pen beside it.

Joe's gaze was measuring as he looked at Temp. "You should be on bedrest."

"And you should be in the kitchen. But here we are." She flashed a grin at him and then motioned to the table. "These are the drawings that Alex managed to take from the orb. She may not have got them all, as time wasn't on our side, but I have a feeling she got most." She looked at Alex, who nodded.

"There weren't any English words, which isn't surprising given the time period and origin of the Golden Apple myth." Alex crossed her arms, scanning the drawings. "I copied them, but I haven't had time to study them."

"And it's possible that you won't make sense of them without the orb attached to the Firebird anyway." Wade circled the table slowly, his big owl eyes moving over the drawings like he was searching a field for prey.

"Cap," Peter said, looking at her with his big brown eyes shimmering with tears. "I don't know what we woulda done without you." He shook his head and looked down at his boots. "If you hadn't escaped—"

"I didn't, technically." Temp ruffled his hair. "Captain Minty saved me. She leapt onto the table like a pirate from a book, brandishing her gun, and shot two of them before I could blink."

Peter looked at Alex, who winked at him. Interesting, that Temp would give her that credit. She'd assumed her to be too full of pride to admit to being saved by someone else.

"We're indebted to you," Joe said, looking at Alex briefly before refocusing on the papers.

She wasn't sure how to respond. Would anyone on the Urchin other than Tom care a whiff that she was gone? It wasn't likely. But then, there were some who'd come to like her, based on people like Kel.

They posited various theories for the following two hours, with Joe and Peter leaving to attend to passengers and then returning. Joe brought in dinner when it was clear none of them would be leaving, and Wade left to see to the visions for the evening. When he returned, he looked at Temp. "Any new ideas?"

"None—"

"I see it!" Peter said.

They turned to see that he'd stacked a box on a chair and was standing on it, looking down.

"It's the stars above rivers." He drew lines in the air. "That there is the Plough, and below it is the Thames. See, that bendy bit there?

That's headed towards Arcturus, above it."

Temp looked like she was going to climb onto her chair, and Alex pulled it away from her. "I rather think not, Captain. All we need is for you to lose your balance and hit your head on the desk. You'd be dead, and all that nonsense last night would be for nothing." She looked around and smiled as Wade put a box on the chair, and then held Alex's hand as she climbed up. Then he handed her the fresh paper on a serving tray, along with a dipped pen.

"Say that again, Peter. Show me." She drew as he talked, and she saw what he meant. Constellations were drawn above the major waterways, and it wasn't hard to figure out which were which. But the remaining symbols didn't correlate to either air or water. "Air or water..." Alex bit the end of the pen, thinking. "I wonder if the ones we don't understand are to do with fire and earth."

Temp nodded, her brow furrowed. "The Norse were deeply attached to the elements. It would make sense."

"Something strange though." Peter tilted dangerously on his box as he leaned over. "The North Star is wrong."

Alex frowned, also tilting precariously. "You're right. It's too low. Even if it isn't an accurate map, that's a strange placement of it." She checked her drawing and placed the star, then handed the paper down to Temp. "Tell me what you see."

"Winchester." Temp traced the Thames below the constellation marker. "The home of Alfred the Great when the Vikings took London in the seventh century."

"And who better to entrust something of that importance to than a great warrior king set to rule the known world?" Alex's skin warmed with excitement. "Is that where the Apple will be?"

"It seems too simple." Wade finally spoke up. He'd been silently mulling over the inscriptions and designs, hardly saying a word. "And nothing worth having is ever that simple."

Temp sighed, and Alex took in the paleness of her skin and slump of her shoulders. "Right. That's it for tonight. We've got one small piece of the puzzle, and we're all tired. Let's start again tomorrow."

She caught Temp's eye and got a subtle nod of thanks in response. The men left after brief discussions with Temp about the passenger needs and status.

"Room six has requested more laudanum." Joe looked at Temp, his expression neutral.

"Use formula forty-two. Let me know if he gets out of hand."

Joe nodded and left, leaving Alex and Temp alone in the small room.

"I'm surprised you allow that foul concoction on your beloved ship," Alex said, her irritation with that subject coming back now that they weren't running for their lives.

"It's useful for the visions and lets them sink into them in a way not otherwise possible. It removes inhibitions and provides a semblance of peace." Temp rose and motioned Alex out of the room ahead of her. "I'm fully aware of how noxious that weed is, and we monitor the use of it closely. We're no opium den."

"Formula forty-two?"

"Always the answer to this particular problem. It has a significantly smaller dose of opium and a much higher dose of sugar. At the point it's needed, the person taking it will often be just fine thinking they've had the real thing. The mind is a wonderous and easily tricked thing."

She locked the small door behind them, and they moved through her office, stopping only so she could pick up her cane.

"And the man unconscious in the hallway? I recognised the symptoms. He clearly didn't get your precious formula." Alex wasn't in the least concerned that there was distinct judgement in her tone.

"No, he didn't." Temp gave a small shrug, and even that made her wince. "Every passenger is asked about their health before boarding. He wasn't honest about his, and his system didn't respond well to his desires." She glanced down at Alex. "He's fine now."

Temp made it sound so simple, but Alex had seen enough people fall under its spell to know it was anything but. If Temp hadn't looked weary enough to keel over, she might have pursued the matter. As it was, she wondered if she should call for a golem. Only then did she realise that Temp had walked her all the way to her room.

"Thank you. Your mind is as sharp as your reputation suggests. I'm very glad to have you on this project." Temp's eyes, still swollen, gave away nothing of her emotions, but her voice was husky.

"You know, you don't have to walk all the way back to your room. You could share mine." Alex swung the door open and backed into it, not taking her gaze from Temp's face. "I could check those bandages of yours, make sure you're healing."

Temp seemed to hesitate, but then she took a step back and tipped her head. "Good night, Alex. Sleep well."

Alex sighed and dropped back onto her bed as she listened to Temp's slow stride down the hall. *You can't blame a girl for trying.*

Would it be such a bad idea? They'd come to terms, and after what they'd been through, trust had been established. Temp didn't want to see her hanged anymore, and they were even working on the next part of the puzzle together. Alex missed her crew and her ship. She missed being at the helm and in control. But this adventure had turned into something interesting, and if the Urchin was back in the sky, she'd find it when this was over. For now, she was happy to enjoy the lush accommodation and food, as well as the knowledge that no one was looking for her.

Winchester. That put a hitch in her breath. London was one area she'd stayed away from for many years, and she had no desire to go back. If she was to be recognised from her old life, it would be by going there. But then, Temp hadn't recognised her as Alex Minty. Would anyone else? If she showed up looking the way she had when she'd boarded the Chimera, her chances of remaining unseen were good, if not perfect. Could she risk it?

Chapter Seventeen

"It won't be in London-on-Ground, in the original Winchester." Temp had slept poorly and eventually, unable to get comfortable, had risen and gone to her office. A cigar and whisky were soothing, and she'd managed to drift off at her desk. When she woke, ideas on how to move ahead were already in place. "It will be in London-on-High. The question is, who moved it, whatever it may be? Who is watching over it? And where did they move it to?"

Alex, dressed in the skirt she'd been wearing when she'd boarded the Chimera, sat sideways in the chair, her legs swinging over the arm. Her wild red curls were pulled into a messy chignon, and she looked ready to be tumbled straight into Temp's bed.

"First, what makes you think it was moved?" Alex asked, then sipped her cup of tea.

"Original Winchester Cathedral is barely a mark on the ground anymore. It's been dismantled, and much of the stone was moved to London-on-High for the new one." Temp tapped the huge, leatherbound book in front of her. "I was studying the orb map last night, particularly in relation to the symbols we didn't recognise." She grinned and tossed the small rune stone to Alex. "Several of them are runes."

Alex flipped the small stone between her fingers, making it travel her knuckles. "Your desire for the dramatic is making me want to go back to sleep."

Temp opened the book, ignoring Alex's surly attitude. It had become clear she wasn't a morning person. She pointed to a section of the map. "The Algiz. Symbol of Heimdallr, the god of protection who hid Valhalla from unworthy persons. We thought it was a river, and it very well might be. But we can't ignore that it mirrors the symbol perfectly. I believe what we're looking for has a protector of some sort. Maybe one passed down through the ages."

Alex scoffed and tossed the rune on the table. "That's absurd. You can't really think someone has been actively watching over an artefact for more than a thousand years."

Temp looked at her seriously. "An artefact created by the gods? I think it could be possible." She picked up her tea and sat in the seat opposite Alex. "Three years ago, I searched for the Cintamani in Siam. It promised great power, and I was aware that some very bad people were after it. I found it in a temple deep in the jungle. The monk watching over it was rumoured to be more ancient than the trees, some of which were more than a thousand years old. He looked it too."

"You stole from a monk?" Alex's eyes widened. "That's very impressive. Not even I would stoop that low."

"I didn't *steal* it. He gave it to me for safe keeping when the enemy showed up at the gates. He said he'd known the time had come, and that I was the one he'd been waiting for." Temp wiggled her eyebrows. "It's a phrase I hear often."

Alex laughed. "You said I was the superstitious one. But you believe someone can live for a thousand years to protect a bit of stone or glass?"

Temp sobered. "Alex, you search out these items the same way I do. You can't tell me you don't believe in them in some way."

Alex shook her head and drained her teacup. "I believe in greed. I believe in money and people's desire to have it. I believe that people will do whatever they can to have power over other people, and that they pursue myths and legends in order to find that power. I don't believe that anything *actually* grants it."

"But you believe in ghosts and that golems are evil." Temp shook her head, genuinely puzzled. "How do you reconcile the two?"

"Stone and glass don't hold power. The spirit does. Golems

shouldn't have spirits, and the spirits of the dead don't always want to rest." Alex stated it so simply, as though it were fact from the university, not opinion based on her own belief system.

"I've seen enough to disagree with you on that front, but I'll respect that you think otherwise." Temp motioned towards the map. "I think it will have had a guardian, and that guardian would keep it safe by placing it where it belonged. In this case, the cathedral, which was built by Alfred the Great. And that exists in London-on-High."

Alex sighed, and there was something in her expression Temp couldn't read. It most certainly wasn't excitement. "Are you reticent to go to London-on-High for some reason?" she asked.

Alex slowly turned her gaze to Temp, and the look in her eyes was hollow. "I'm not afraid of anything."

"I didn't say you were. I asked if you were reticent. But interesting way to twist my words to suit your feelings." Temp didn't look away, challenging Alex to tell her the truth.

"Winchester is on the outskirts of the sky city. Far from London proper. It's a labyrinth. They wanted it to echo the original, but cleaner. They've put the cathedral right in the centre, so we'd have to dock and then make our way to it. There are no mid-city docks there, because they've built everything so close together. The only park is an airship-free zone."

Temp took all that in. She knew it too, of course. She'd lived in London-on-High, once. But it seemed, so had Alex. No pirate would know the layout that way, because their skies were well patrolled, and the city was the best protected of all the sky cities. It made sense, given the queen's residence there. Alex had spent time in the sky city, and not as a pirate.

"Stop it," Alex said quietly as she studied Temp's face. "Stop trying to figure me out. Let me have my secrets. We all have a past, Temp."

Temp inclined her head. "Very well." The vulnerability in Alex's tone tugged at her and she relented. It was nice that she was letting her guard down, and Temp didn't want them to go backwards. "My suggestion is that I go into Winchester and look around. I won't stand out there, so I can go alone. If anyone does recognise me, there won't be an issue. I'll walk the cathedral and look for any matching symbols that may lead me to a hiding place."

She didn't miss the flicker of relief in Alex's eyes, nor the indication of internal struggle as she tugged at the material of her skirt, pulling at one of the many safety pins on it.

"You shouldn't go alone." Alex stood, smoothing her skirt and readjusting her spiked gloves. "Baron Willoughby may have figured out these symbols too. And just because we haven't seen the Kaiser's men yet doesn't mean they don't have information of their own. You'd be outnumbered, and I simply don't have the patience to save your arse yet again."

"Then I'll take Joe. Or Peter." Temp didn't want to take either of them. Not after losing Duncan. But she couldn't ask Alex to go somewhere she clearly wanted to stay away from.

Alex sighed and glared at Temp. "We both know they'd be as useful as a stalk of corn in a duel. I'll go with you." She hesitated, her palms pressed to her skirt. "We'll just have to go at night and stick to the shadows. Same as any other job." She looked Temp over. "But you can't go like that. You're still not breathing right. We need to give it a few days, until you can move easily."

Temp laughed, and it *did* hurt. "Busted ribs take a more than month to heal. We don't have that kind of time. Too many people want the Apple for us to delay. I'll just have to move carefully and do my utmost not to get involved in any more fights."

Alex shrugged. "It's your neck. When do you want to go?"

"I have some correspondence to deal with and a few crows to send out. Tomorrow evening should suffice." She stood and rubbed at the back of her neck. "In the meantime, we can continue to study the map. I'd like to see if we can gain some understanding of what purpose the Firebird serves. It can't simply be decorative."

"No." Alex picked it up and turned it in her hands. Her stomach rumbled, and she set it back down. "I want some of that porridge."

"I'll join you." They walked to the kitchen, and all the staff stopped and curtsied or bowed when she passed, then went about their duties.

"You don't really notice, do you?" Alex asked with that bit of steel in her tone that suggested the person she was speaking to should be wary.

"Notice what?" Temp opened the kitchen door for her, and the smell of food made her glad her jaw only ached and wasn't broken.

"The way your staff kowtow to you. The bows and curtsies. The obedience they know is expected from them." Alex practically hissed the words.

Temp held up her hands. "I've never asked them to do it. I've never required it. You're right, I don't notice. But that's because I don't expect it one way or another. These people have trained in some of the wealthiest houses in the world. That's why they work on the Chimera. I wanted the best service, and they provide it. If that's how they were trained and they want to continue it, then I won't stop them." She handed Alex a bowl, uncertain as to whether or not she was about to get it broken over her head. Or against her arm anyway, since Alex was too short to reach the top of her head.

Alex seemed to deflate, and she spooned a large portion of porridge into her bowl, then dropped in strawberries and chopped dates. "I assumed they did it on your command."

"Sorry to disappoint you." Temp smiled and sat across from Alex at the staff table. She said hello to some of the staff who came and went, and they smiled back but kept moving, not stopping to talk.

"Where are you from?" Alex asked suddenly, her gaze still on her porridge like it was the most interesting thing in the room.

"London." Temp ate, wondering how much personal information she wanted to hand over. At the end of the day, Alex was still a pirate. But what could she do with information about Temp's past? "London-on-High, actually. The Strud family have been there since the sky city went up. My father was an ambassador, and my mother was a translator."

Something crossed Alex's eyes. "Was?"

That same sense of loss from years ago rose in her chest. "The fever took them both when it spread though the city. I was already on a military airship away on a mission where I couldn't be reached when they passed." There it was again. That strange sense that she was missing something. A flash of green eyes, a cheeky smile...

"And your father encouraged you to be a pilot?" Alex continued to eat, her tone strangely flat. "Joe told me."

Well, that was surprising. Joe was usually extremely circumspect when it came to sharing personal information. "Yes. He flew for the Air Corp before he became an ambassador, and when it became clear I wasn't going to be a proper young lady, he taught me to fly and how to do my best to make the world one worthy of living in. I'm aware that I was quite lucky."

Alex nodded. "Most women could only wish for that kind of freedom."

"Freedom you managed to claim for yourself too." Temp wanted to touch her. She wanted to reach out and wipe away the frown line that showed Alex's deeper conflict.

The frown cleared, and Alex grinned. "That I did."

"Alex, have we met before?" Temp finally asked the question that had been bothering her. "I'm not asking for anything you don't want to share. But there's something about you, something that keeps pushing at the back of my mind."

For a moment, it looked like Alex might give in and divulge some answers. Instead, she gave a wink and smile. "If you'd met me before, you can be sure you wouldn't have forgotten me, Captain. No one forgets a night with Alex Minty."

Temp flushed. "Good Lord. I wasn't implying we knew each other *that* way."

Alex laughed and stood. She placed her porridge bowl in the sink and gave it a quick wash. "Would it be so terrible?" She glanced over her shoulder, a mischievous grin in place. "Somehow, I don't think you'd mind."

Temp shook her head and stretched out her legs. "I wouldn't. I just didn't mean to imply otherwise. Have you always been this feisty?" She wanted to take the question back instantly when Alex frowned again, her shoulders dropping. "Never mind. Let's go play with ancient symbols, shall we?"

The relief in Alex's eyes was obvious before she turned away and led them back to Temp's office and the little room beyond it. "Do you have any books on Norse mythology? I'd like to refresh my memory."

Temp motioned towards a section of bookshelf. "That's the mythology and fairytale section. There should be plenty to occupy you."

Alex pulled over a step stool and began tracing the spines as she read them. Tempting though it was to watch her move gracefully along the shelves, Temp turned back into her office. She sat down and moved the Firebird this way and that, placing it at various points on the diagram simply to see if it looked like it might fit. But it never did, simply looking like a bird out of place. Quickly, she penned several notes and put them in crows, which she had Peter dispatch. The sooner she got responses, the better, and she had little doubt she'd get the answers she needed. She pulled up the book of runes again and began to study. She glanced up when Alex came in and draped herself over the chair, a book in her lap. She looked so at ease in her loose blouse, threadbare waist belt, and skirt with a million pockets. The person in the clothes Temp had given her and the person across from her seemed years apart. She didn't ask why Alex had gone back to her old clothing instead of wearing the nice things Temp had provided on her first morning. That was Alex's preference, and Temp wasn't about to force her to conform. She went back to her studies when Alex pointed at the book on Temp's desk without looking at her.

Bleary-eyed, and sometime later, she saw that it was dark

outside the dragon's eye window when she looked up at a noise outside the small room. The door opened, and Wade and Joe came in, breathless as they wheeled a medium-sized circle into the room on its side.

"Hold it steady," Wade said, his goggles pushed back on his head so his hair stood up like he'd been shocked. He pulled a slim piece of wood out and placed it over the huge wooden map. Then he turned back to the one Joe was holding. "Lift and place on three. Three, two, one..." They hefted it and set it on top of the other wood map.

Alex stood and stretched, and Temp looked away when the blouse pulled taut against her breasts.

"What do we have here, gents?" Alex tapped the book she'd been reading against her thigh.

Wade pulled a small lever on the side, and the map sprang to life. It was a parameter piercer of Winchester, including the narrow streets and houses clustered around the cathedral, which sat above the rest.

"How on earth did you put this together so quickly?" Temp asked. "We only figured this out yesterday."

Wade lightly touched one of the buildings. "I have loads of them in my workspace. I add to them every time we visit a city. This one happened to be nearly finished anyway. Figured it was as good a time as any to put the finishing touches on it."

"Wade, you're truly a master craftsman." Temp clapped him on the back. "This means we don't go in blind."

"You haven't seen the best part." Wade tapped a spire on the cathedral, and it sprang open like a flower, revealing multiple tiny rooms inside. "My best yet," he murmured, a glint in his eye as he sighed.

"I agree." Temp peered into the cathedral. There were rooms everywhere. In the towers, in the main section, and even what seemed to be below ground. "I know there was a section underground in the one on land, but surely there isn't one in the sky city?"

He grinned. "Not technically. They built it with an extra level. Stairs lead up to it, and it makes you think you've entered on the ground floor. Good design, really. Means they keep the underground bit like it was in the original." He grimaced and stepped back. "I couldn't recreate all the symbols and such though. Plenty of them carved into the walls and floors throughout."

"What are these?" Alex dipped her finger into the main section and pointed towards the rectangular boxes.

"Those are the mortuary chests. Filled with bones when they opened them, but there's no writing to say to whom they belonged. I remember being fascinated by them when I was child." Temp recalled those happy trips with her mother, who had enjoyed all things mysterious and historical.

"Could the Apple be in one of those?" Alex asked, looking hopeful.

"No, I wouldn't think so. They've been opened, and the bones have even been shuttled from chest to chest. In light of what we've learned, I'd like to look at the symbols carved on them though." She had a vague impression of cherubs but nothing more.

Peter came in holding a metal crow messenger. "For you, Cap."

She pulled out the missive and saw the eagle with its outstretched claws. A quick read let her know she had the funds and contact she'd been hoping for. She looked up and saw Alex's sharp gaze watching her, and that she clearly took in the symbol. Temp raised an eyebrow, but Alex didn't look away.

"I've been offered a private tour by Gabriela Cunninghame Graham. She was a friend of my mother's, and I was hoping she was still in the city; she's an expert on the cathedral as well as many other things. This will mean we don't need to sneak in or stay in the shadows. We can investigate in the full light of day under the cover of being simple tourists."

Alex was already shaking her head, sending locks of red hair falling from the clasp. "I told you. Shadows only."

Temp crossed her arms as Joe and Wade took a few steps back, clearly feeling the oncoming storm. "We did things your way in your world. This is mine, and I'll do this my way. If you like, you can stay behind and accompany me later, if I need to go back and do some less than public searching." She narrowed her eyes. "Or you can dress like a proper London lady, and no one will recognise the great pirate Minty."

If a person could spit flame, Alex would clearly have done so, leaving Temp in a heap of ashes. "Have it your way." She turned and left without another word.

Temp slid back into her seat. "God save us from the devil's women."

Joe laughed, and Wade just shook his head.

"I'll come with you, Temp." Joe smoothed his hand over his hair. "I haven't seen my family in some time, and they live just outside Winchester. We can stop and see my wife and boys, and it will lend credence to us visiting instead of doing any treasure hunting." When Temp went to protest, he held up his hand. "Alex is right. Any real hunting will need to be done at night. But I can be an extra set of eyes and watch your back while you focus."

She sighed. "Very well. But if any thugs show up, we leave. I won't put you in danger, Joe."

His expression spoke volumes. He'd been close to Duncan too. "And I appreciate that, Cap." He grinned and elbowed Wade. "Besides, Alex will be a tiger by the time you return. We'll be glad to see the back of you two in the evening if you go back."

"Thank you for your everlasting support." Temp tossed a piece of wadded up paper at him. "She's like to kill me before anyone else does."

Wade shook his head and headed out, his multitude of pockets jingling with the gears and such he carried at all times. "Makes me glad I stick with my machines."

"What it makes you is odd," Joe said, giving Temp a quick salute as he backed out of the room. "When do we go?"

"We're meeting her at ten a.m., and we can't be late. She's funny about punctuality." She waved them off and then the quiet of the small room enveloped her. She scanned the wooden Winchester, letting the maze of streets sink in, using her internal compass to map them as best she could. Then her thoughts began to wander, and she closed her eyes, letting her head fall back.

Alex's secrets clearly had to do with her past in London. Her fear was palpable, and her eyes when she'd looked at the eagle symbol had grown hard. Fear and anger. A secret past. A need to stay hidden. Temp was reminded of the men from the Dawn who'd asked about her. Pieces of the puzzle were sliding together, and she wasn't sure she liked the picture they were forming.

Chapter Eighteen

"She's the most stubborn donkey's arse ever to have existed." Alex paced her room as she talked to herself, so the frustration didn't come out in her breaking something. "Why would she want to expose herself that way during the day? What if someone connects her to whatever we take? Then they'll know who she is. The only reason they haven't come after the Chimera is because she kept her identity secret. That won't happen if anyone figures out it was her at the cathedral during the day. Then we'll all be dropped in the pot, won't we?"

They were good arguments, and ones she should have made when Temp was in the room. But that damn symbol had jumped out at her, and the fact that the Golden Dawn had asked about her far too recently had made her freeze. Did Temp even know that the organisation she was helping was in league with the Dawn? She must, given that they'd come onto the ship to ask for her help. Two organisations that could tear Alex's world to pieces, and she was working with the woman connected to both.

She flopped onto her bed. "Hades' hairy bollocks," she muttered.

The thing was, Temp was right, though it galled her to admit it. This was Temp's world, and she could tour the cathedral with some fancy lady on her arm without drawing much attention. Except for the fact that she was stupidly handsome and wore men's clothes. That might get her noticed. Still, since Queen Victoria herself had deemed it appropriate for women to wear the clothing necessary for them to do their jobs, more and more women were wearing trousers of some sort. It wouldn't get her hanged anyway.

So all Alex needed to do was wait.

And wait.

And wait.

God in heaven, how she *loathed* waiting.

Finally, she got up and headed back to Temp's little research room. She and Joe had left an hour ago, and Alex had stayed away, afraid she'd do something absurd like change her mind and decide to go with. What would Temp learn? What would she find? Alex's fingers itched like she wanted to touch whatever it was Temp might be touching as well.

"Well now, this is new." She stopped and leaned against the doorframe of Temp's office.

Peter leapt up from the chair behind the desk, turning red right to the tips of his ears. "I didn't mean nothing by it. Please, don't tell Cap. I don't want her thinking I'm overstepping—"

"Whoa, young 'un." Alex held up her hands. "I think you're allowed to sit in a seat, Peter. Cap's arse is nice, but I don't think it means you can't sit where it's been. It isn't royal."

Peter's shoulders dropped, and he grinned. "Are you sorry you didn't go with them?"

Alex groaned and nudged an expensive-looking vase with her toe. It would serve Temp right if it broke while she was gone. "Going would be stupid. I'm supposed to be dead, after all, which is only to the good in the long run. But not knowing what's going on is making me crazy."

Peter nodded. "I hate being left behind, even if Cap is trusting me with the Chimera. I read all the adventure stories but never get to go on any."

Alex laughed and motioned to the room. "You don't think being on a ship of dreams, sailing through the skies with the highest members of British society is an adventure? What more do you want, lad?"

He shrugged a little. "Something with swords and dragons. Coming up against the Devil's Urchin was more exciting than anything else we've ever done." He bit his lip, his eyes shining. "And it brought us a real-life pirate. I bet you've had some amazing adventures."

His enthusiasm was catching, and she thought back. "I have. Big fights with airguns and airships larger than the Urchin. A crew I could laugh and fight with. Sailing through storms so vast I wasn't sure there'd ever be an end to them."

"And the other adventures. The ones Cap heard so she was going to search you out?" He looked like a child waiting for a bedtime story.

"Those have been pretty amazing too." She sat on the edge of the desk. "I've found things that would make Temp's heart stop if she knew whose hands they were in."

"I won't tell her if you don't." Peter gave that same cheeky grin. "Long as you don't steal nothin' from her."

Alex studied him. His clothes were tailored and fit well, but he wore them like they were slightly too tight, too awkward. He brushed his hair out of his eyes, and she saw the scars on his forearm. When he was with Temp, his accent mimicked hers, like he was being taught how to speak properly. But when he was with Alex, his accent was anything but the Queen's English. "How did you come to be on the ship, Peter? Tell me your story." She moved to the chair she liked best and plopped into it, sideways on like always, her legs dangling over the edge.

He pressed his lips together and hesitated, then shrugged and flopped into the chair opposite her. "Guess there's no reason not to tell it. After all, it isn't like you won't understand the way other people on the ship mightn't." He plucked at a loose thread on his pant leg. "I grew up in an orphanage. Left on the doorstep of a church, I was. No name, no nothing. Just an old blanket. When I got to an age, they were going to send me down t'mines with some other lads. But I couldn't imagine living my life underground, going down when the sun came up and coming out when it had gone down." He shuddered. "So I ran away. Lived on the streets for a bit, then one night I saw a dragon fly through the sky and land nearby. It was the wee hours of the morning, and no one was about but me. I saw the people get off, and the dragon didn't leave right away. It was silver and black, and it had these red eyes that seemed to tell me it was meant for me." He grimaced. "Sounds dumb, doesn't it?"

"Not at all. If anyone understands the call of a ship, it's me." She motioned. "Go on."

"So I snuck on board, into the cargo hold when they were loading up supplies. Had no idea where it was going or who was in charge, but I didn't care. I just knew I had to be on it when it left."

"But Temp found you?" And she hadn't thrown him off. Why not?

"Aye. Found me when I was trying to nab some food from the kitchen and take it back to the cargo hold. I told her my story, and she offered me a job. Said she'd train me up, if that's what I wanted." He wiped at his eyes, not looking at Alex. "No one had ever given me a chance before. Like, I was expected to live and die doing what other people wanted, not what I wanted." He stood and looked at Temp's desk. "I owe her everything."

Alex nodded, understanding his loyalty now. Being tossed a lifeline could create a far stronger bond than most people realised. Plenty of her own crew felt the same way about her and for the same reason. The question about why she hadn't thrown Peter off was one she could answer herself. People deserved a chance at a better life. Did she and Temp really have that sentiment in common?

"I need to get back to work." Peter picked up a piece of paper from the desk. "I was checking tonight's guide to give to Wade for the vitascopes."

She nodded. "Temp must have incredible faith in you to leave such important people in your hands on a ship like this."

He beamed, his eyes lighting up. "I'd better make sure she's right to trust me then, eh?" He waved and left her there alone.

Now what? She dropped her head back and sighed. She let her vision blur and her thoughts wander. That book yesterday...

She jumped up and looked around, and eventually found it under a stack. She opened it to the place she'd stopped and turned to the following page.

The Firebird rose from an ocean of silver, its feathers a garish cacophony of colour.

She brings blessings or doom to her captor, using the truth of their heart to lead them to the ending they've brought on themselves. The journey ahead will be hard, the reward great or terrible. If she should feed from aught but the Golden Apple, she will turn to a demon and devour all that is good. Be wary, traveller, of the pearls that fall from the sharp beak. Treasure they may be, or the seeds that grow destruction. To seek what your heart desires, follow the flight of fire.

Well, that was non-committal and vague. Alex read it again and then beyond it to the following pages. Nothing more was said. She picked up the Firebird, noting the strange trail of pink that followed her fingers as she stroked it, only to disappear when she stopped. Follow the flight of fire. If they could attach it to the orb, would it somehow show them an actual trail to the Apple? Would it just lead them to Winchester anyway?

Somehow, she doubted it. What was it they'd find at the cathedral if not the Apple? She settled down to read and found another strange passage.

The Norns, who knew all that was fated, grew irate at the beauty and charm of the gods who never died, and snuck one night into their orchard. Where the apples had contained only light, beauty, and youth, once the Norns breathed upon the apples, they were suffused with their envy and the rictus of age. Those gods who remained pure of heart and who wished only to make the lives of the humans who served them better continued to eat the fruit and receive its blessings. But those gods who had become hardened to the suffering of the mortal world, or worse, who created yet more suffering, were turned to väsen, to live out their days in the protection of the land and the detritus the gods have left behind.

For even that which has been discarded by the gods may be capable of terrible destruction in the hands of a mortal.

What were Norns? Väsen? Alex was familiar with the general Viking pantheon, but these were aspects she'd never come across. And did it help them in any way with their search?

She took the book to Temp's desk and pulled out a fresh piece of paper. Dipping the pen, she began to transcribe the relevant sections for them to study later without having to carry the book about with them. *Detritus.* What did the gods consider trash? And was the Apple one of those things? *Maybe we're just looking for an old apple core.* The thought made her smile.

It was early evening, and the crescent moon lit the dragon's eye window when Alex heard the chime of the bell that signalled the small flyer was back and needed to be let into the belly of the dragon. She blinked and yawned, then headed towards the flyer bay after tucking the pages of her notes into the large pocket on the side of her skirt. When Wade and Peter pulled the ropes to bring it in, Alex's heart stuttered.

Joe was alone. He leapt out, pulled off the hat and goggles, and held them out to Alex.

"I've done my bit and seen my people." He smoothed back his hair. "It's your turn. Some extremely interesting things for you to have a look at in there. Temp will be waiting for you at the back entrance." He hesitated and lowered his arm, pulling the goggles and hat away. "Actually, you might want to change. You have to dock at the main station and walk through the town to get there."

"Does light shine out of their arses and eyes in the sky city?" Alex asked, crossing her arms. Being recognised as her old self was more dangerous than being recognised as the pirate she was now. "The only reason for me to go dressed as a clown would be if there aren't any shadows I can blend in with."

He shook his head. "Up to you. Good luck."

She tucked her hair beneath the cap as best she could and pulled on the goggles. The last time she'd flown, it had been with

Temp badly injured in the back. Now they were handing her the keys to a flyer and letting her go. For a moment, she saw that same thought pass through Joe's eyes, and he touched her shoulder.

"She's waiting because she trusts you." He tilted his head and said more softly, "And I know the stories of what you really do out there."

She didn't say anything. There wasn't anything to say. She got in, and Peter and Wade lowered the flyer back out of the dragon, and she flipped the switches for the bags that hadn't even had time to deflate yet. Gears shifted, the propeller whirred, and she dropped away from the Chimera. The rush filled her, and she smiled as she deployed the sail. It caught and pushed the little craft through the air. The last bit of sunset threw a soft orange glow over the dark water below, and she wanted to linger, but it wasn't the time for a pleasure flight. She shifted sail and flew up through the cloud layer. That same soft orange glow painted the sky cities, their lanterns coming on like electric stars.

She flew true and as she came to London-on-High, she gripped the controls hard to still her trembling. *What am I doing? This is madness.* She'd long ago sworn to stay as far from here as humanly possible. Now she was heading directly into the lion's gaping maw. She circled from a distance, looking at the various docks and port stations and noting what ships were where. When she saw what she needed, she grew dizzy with relief.

She canted the sail and swooped down like a hawk headed for prey, drawing up at the last second near the docking station by the hospital that was still being built. The dock, which would usually have the airships of the contractors attached, was empty at this time of night. There wasn't another ship in sight, and she moored quickly without having to look over her shoulder. This would make for a better escape area too, if they needed one.

The hospital was also blessedly close to the cathedral, and after only a few streets, she was within view of it. She stood on a corner in the shadows, watching to make certain there were no unsavoury characters, other than herself, watching the building. She thought one man looked out of place, but then he wandered away from the cathedral and into a pub. A quick tug of the collar on her coat helped hide some of her hair, and she pulled her hat low. It would have to do. She set off quickly across the wide road to the cathedral and moved away from the front entrance, where the huge wood doors were closed for the night.

Staying close to the wall she moved easily, trying to look like any random pirate in tatty clothes out for an evening stroll. She was just passing the large stone columns leading into an open courtyard when someone grabbed her arm and yanked her through a doorway. She yelped and dropped into a fighting stance, her knife in one hand.

"I'd rather you not stab me before we begin. I'd hate to lose even more time, and though I hate to admit it, I'm already not feeling my best."

Temp's voice came out of the dark, and Alex narrowed her gaze to see Temp leaning against the wall, her ankles crossed, looking for all the world like she was sizing up a potential bed partner instead of being threatened with a puncture wound.

Alex sheathed the knife in her thigh holster and didn't miss the way Temp's gaze tracked the motion. "Pulling women into dark rooms isn't very gentlemanly."

"Good thing I'm not a gentleman then." Temp pushed away from the wall. "This way."

Alex saw that they weren't in the cathedral proper but rather in an offshoot building. "Where are we going?" she asked, the hairs on the back of her neck standing up as the statues of various dead saints watched them from niches in the stone above them.

"The Norman section includes the transepts and tower in the northern partition. This will take us there without having to go through the nave, where we'd surely be seen by the staff."

"Are they called staff in a cathedral?" Alex asked, drawing her coat tighter around her. "I'm sure there must be a more holy word for them."

Temp glanced back with a wry look but didn't respond. Alex looked up and grew cross-eyed at the height of the room, where the ceiling was made with clover leaf tiles in a light brown that contrasted with the dense, heavy grey stone that led to them. She blinked and focused on catching up to Temp, who had stopped at the entryway to a larger t-section of the nave.

"This is the Norman transept. Look at the floor."

Alex looked, and her pulse began to race. She knelt, not worried about dirt on her skirt, and looked more closely at the tiles with what appeared at first blush to be random designs. "They're runes."

Temp nodded, crouching beside her. "Some are, some aren't. I think they did it intentionally, so it wouldn't be obvious." She pointed to the ceiling. "What do you see?"

Alex tried to look up, but the position was too awkward, so she flopped onto her back to stare up at it. "The constellations we saw in the map," she whispered.

Temp grinned. "Almost exactly, as far as I can tell."

Alex scanned it, twisting to see the parts beyond her. "I don't see the North Star."

Temp grimaced and stood, offering her hand to help Alex to her feet. "I tried on my own earlier when I realised what I was seeing, but as I had company, I couldn't make it obvious."

Alex's stomach turned a little at the idea of Temp having female company, which was absurd. "I have something that may relate," she said, pulling the papers from her skirt pocket and unfolding them, hoping it hid the irritation that probably showed in her expression. "Read these." She pointed towards the passages about the Firebird and the Norns.

Temp read quickly and then looked around. "Do you see any fruit or monsters?"

Alex shuddered. "I always see monsters in these places. All the twists and turns they put into the stonework make me think of

Greek labyrinths that hold beasts meant to eat people."

"Exactly what people who go to church think of, I'm sure." Temp gave her a half grin and shook her head. "Let's split up and look for anything that looks like fruit, demons, or phoenixes."

Alex was sorely tempted to suggest they stick together. The cathedral was far too large though, and it made sense to look in different sections. "I think we need to be more logical about it. Consider the map and the time period we're looking in. We know we want to concentrate on the Norman section, right?" She dragged the toe of her boot over a rune tile and traced a similar line along the ceiling with her finger. "It's almost an arrow. Those two parallel lines that link with the short lines at the end..." She followed the constellation with her eyes even as she shifted her body the way that the rune pointed. "I say we concentrate on the far wall, below that window."

Temp looked impressed, and Alex tried not to let that make her happy. They moved slowly, watching the runes and ceiling, and it led them to an area directly below the huge archway.

"I thought you said there'd be some strange ancient person waiting for us," Alex whispered, and it seemed like even that echoed through the huge space. She looked above the archway to the balcony, where a large chest sat on the ledge, a round rose window looking over it like the stern eyes of a guardian.

"Are you disappointed?" Temp grinned, her gaze still on the area above them. "The centre of the window is the same as the tiles in the ceiling."

Alex saw it, as well as something else. "Look at the positioning of the chest under it."

"We need to get up there. Let's find a stairwell." They split up, each of them taking one side.

Alex slid her hands over the stone and into the statueless niches, but there was no doorway apparent.

"Here," Temp said, her soft voice floating through the dim space between them.

Alex hurried over. Temp was already moving up a circular stairwell barely large enough for her broad frame, with deep steps that meant Alex was practically climbing them, thanks to her short stature. By the time she reached the top, she was sweating and irritated. "At least the cave steps weren't made for giants." She wiped a strand of hair away from her damp cheek.

"I made it just fine." Temp gave her that mischievous grin and then moved onto the balcony. "It's really something from up here."

Alex agreed. The narrow balcony in front of the massive round window had looked small from down below. From here, the view of the nave and the branches feeding off of it was truly spectacular. She turned in a circle to look at the window and grabbed Temp's hand. "Look. The North Star."

It was right in the centre of the round window, the clover design framing it perfectly. They moved apart, and the light from the star shone directly onto the chest on the ledge. Alex dropped to her knees in front of it, her nose nearly touching it as she read the inscription. "An unknown woman. May she rest with the angels."

"You read Old English." Temp shook her head and bent to look at the end of the chest. "Of course you do." She ran her hand over the end. "What do you see on the other end?"

Alex was glad she let the topic of ability drop. She had no desire to discuss her education level, which would water the seeds of Temp's memory. She moved to the other end of the chest, which was only about four feet in length, but appeared to be made of an intricate combination of stone and metal. She nearly yelled with excitement. "I've got something that looks rather like a phoenix."

Temp grinned and nodded. "And I've got what look like apples."

"Neither of you have anything, if you don't mind."

Alex's head snapped around at the soft voice that seemed to come out of the darkness. A figure in a long, deep red robe stood in the shadows at the opposite end of the balcony they'd entered from.

"Please step away from the chest." A glint of silver slid through the air.

Alex stepped back, moving to Temp's side. "We mean no harm." It wasn't exactly true. She'd been contemplating the possibility that they'd have to push it off the ledge to the floor below to break it open. But the stranger didn't need to know that.

Temp tapped her cane gently on the stone floor. "We're trying to keep the Apple from some very bad people who will likely be here very soon. The kind of people who were meant to be kept far from the power it holds."

The figure stayed still, blanketed by shadows. "And I will keep those people from taking it as well."

Temp took a step forwards but stopped when silver flashed again, and this time, the razor-thin blade of a sword showed clearly in the star's light. "They're not coming with steel. They're coming with guns, and you won't be able to stop them. Please."

The figure moved with preternatural grace towards them, seeming to glide. They pushed back the hood to reveal thick blond hair around an angular face. It was a woman with eyes as dark as the night sky. Alex shivered and took a step behind Temp. She could take the brunt of ghost woman's ire if she wanted to.

"Do you understand what it is you seek? I'm not the only guardian you will have to convince." Her voice was time made physical, sandpaper sliding over silk.

"The väsen." Alex peered around Temp's shoulder. "They watch over the apples now."

The figure inclined her head, her black eyes staring into Alex's soul and finding it wanting. At least, that was how it felt.

A noise rang through the church, a clanging and the sound of stone breaking. The figure looked past them, down into the long dark nave. She moved her hand, and the lid of the chest clicked open. "Hurry," she said, not looking at them, her sword raised.

They moved as one and had to work to get the lid up. "Interesting and rather unexpected," Alex said, reaching in to take out the abnormally small skull and holding it up for Temp to remove the ornate, pure crystal crown that circled the dry, cracked bone.

Temp lifted it reverently and set it in a velvet bag she pulled from the leather pouch on her hip. She bowed to the figure like an old-style courtier. "I swear by the gods that I'll protect this with my life."

"It won't be your sacrifice to make," the figure said, her gaze moving slowly from the noise growing louder below to focus on Alex. "The gods were torn apart when they lost their way and forgot what they were meant to be. What will you choose when the star guides you to your destiny, lady?" She waved them towards the entryway behind her. "You must leave. Do not tarry. I will aid your escape as best I may."

Alex's stomach turned at what felt very much like the kind of thing an ancient oracle said to people just before they got eaten or chopped to bits. She gave the figure a wide berth as she passed but not wide enough. It grabbed at her, and Alex whimpered when she saw the bony claws wrapped around her forearm.

"Deny who you are, and you deny the gifts given you. You can only run so far before the road runs out, and you must either fall from the cliff or turn to face that which you run from. Väsen know the will of your heart. Choose wrong and join them for eternity."

"Can I choose to leave now?" Alex whispered, tugging her arm away.

The being—she couldn't allow that it was an actual person—let go and turned away, effectively dismissing her.

She followed Temp down the spiral staircase, refusing to look back for fear of turning to a pillar of salt or a pile of dust or something. Her arm, where the entity had clasped her, burned as though it had touched skin, even though her coat had been in the way. The words ran through her head, shifting and blowing like they were caught in the wind.

Once they were back on the ground level, she and Temp stood by the doorway, and she forced herself to consider the situation in front of them. Male voices rang out, bouncing against the vaulted ceiling and off ancient stone. Alex looked over her shoulder and then tapped Temp. "This way," she whispered.

Thankfully, Temp followed without question. Alex crept slowly, watching her step so as not to kick over anything or dislodge any loose stone. She frowned as she stepped on a grave marker, and then on another. Of course. The original had a crypt, and as Wade said, they'd managed to put one under the new cathedral as well. Once again, she was walking on graves.

Shouts rang out, and there was the sound of steel meeting steel. They made it to a small, low door that would easily go unnoticed in the great hall, and Alex twisted the metal ring handle, opening it surprisingly easily. It let them into a small, rectangular courtyard.

There were no other doors but the one they'd come through.

"Athena's tits," Alex hissed, searching, hoping she'd missed an exit.

"We'll have to go back." Temp took a deep breath and turned.

"Or we wait them out." Alex stopped her, grabbing her wrist. Her own arm continued to tingle. "They'll think we escaped, and they'll go looking for us. We just have to wait here until they're gone and then make our way back to the ship."

Temp shook her head slowly. "Look up. We're surrounded by windows on every side. All they need to do is look out, and they'll see us. We have to go back."

Alex didn't like it, but she saw what Temp meant. This bloody cathedral must have twenty sets of windows, one high, one low, facing them. "Lead on, Captain."

Temp opened the door, looked in, and then slipped inside with Alex close behind. They darted between pillars as they moved towards a larger door in the middle of the nave. Shadows jerked over the walls as some small battle continued where they'd left the being.

A crash and splintered stone made Alex jump and look back. The chest had been shoved off the ledge, much as she'd considered doing, and men were looking over the railing at it.

And at them.

"Run!" Temp reached back and grabbed Alex's hand, and they shot out of the cathedral, shouts following in their wake.

Wet mist clung to Alex's cloak and face and made the moss-covered stones underfoot slippery. A shot rang out, and blue light sizzled the air overhead. Alex lost her footing and went down hard, letting go of Temp's hand as she fell. She rolled to her side, wincing at the pain in her knees.

"Stop!" a man yelled.

Alex got to her feet and looked back. She froze, staring into eyes she'd hoped never to see again.

"I knew it," he said, his words echoing through the cavernous space. "I knew you were too stubborn to die, Lady Billinghurst. And I knew I'd find you again, one day."

"Blast," Temp said, her voice hoarse. "Run, Alex!"

Shaking, Alex began to move, and her feet were ahead of her brain as she ran, following Temp down the narrow streets. "No!" she said, grabbing at Temp's waistcoat. "This way." She turned and was grateful Temp followed. She'd heard the recognition, the realisation, in Temp's voice in that single swear. Was this to be the end of their partnership?

Light sizzled past them, striking the side of a house and blowing chunks of stone into the air. They ducked and made it past the construction materials for the hospital, the sound of pounding footfalls behind them. She climbed the ladder to the little docking station and felt the ladder shudder with Temp's weight behind her. She threw off the front mooring rope and jumped into the pilot's seat, while Temp ran to the back to release the other rope.

Blue light flashed, singeing the air, and Temp flattened herself to the dock. "Upship!" she yelled. "Go!"

Alex hesitated. She couldn't leave Temp behind. But there was no way in any of the seven hells she could get caught. Not now. Not after all this time... She pushed the lever, inflated the bags, set the gears whirring, and the ship lifted. Temp leapt to her feet and reached for the side, but another bolt sent her to the dock again.

Within seconds, the ship was too far from the dock for her to reach.

Tears filled Alex's eyes, and she gasped for breath as the ship lifted into the air. Then it jerked, and she had to hold hard to the throttle. She looked over and saw Temp holding the mooring rope, arms and legs wrapped around it.

Dangling, she looked up. "Fly!" she shouted, then closed her eyes against the wind.

Alex set her course for the Chimera, locking in the magnetic signal, and prayed that Temp could hang on. But then...if she didn't...if she fell, and Alex didn't have to go back to the Chimera...if she could leave it all behind and escape back to the Urchin to pick up the life she'd created for herself...

With a small sob, she headed for the coast.

Chapter Nineteen

Arms burning, legs cramping, lungs heaving, eyes watering... Temp hung on to the rope, determined not to fall to her death. At least, not before confronting Alex.

The air warmed slightly, and the wind whipping against her lessened. She opened her eyes to find that Alex was bringing the flyer in to land on the cliff edge before they headed out over open water. *Thank the gods.* When her feet touched down, she unwound the rope quickly and moved away so Alex could land. For a split second, she caught Alex's eye and saw the doubt in her expression. Would she fly off, content not to have Temp's death on her conscience? Now that her secret had been exposed, Temp had no doubt Alex would want to bolt.

The flyer landed with a soft thump, the bags wheezing as they deflated enough to keep her grounded. Alex slowly climbed out and slid to the ground, her gaze never moving from Temp's.

"I *knew* I recognised you. It was always there, in the back of my mind. I don't know how I didn't know it right from the start, what with that hair of yours." Temp shook her head, bewildered at her own ignorance. "Lady Miranda Billinghurst, heir to the Billinghurst fortune. Why didn't you just tell me? For goodness sake, we played together as children."

Alex sighed. Her eyes glistened with unshed tears. Rain clung her to red hair like dew drops on an exotic flower. "You didn't remember me, and that's the way I wanted it. I admit, I was surprised that you didn't, but then, you and your family left for America when we were both still very young. I never expected you to come back, and when you did..." She laughed without humour. "I didn't recognise you either. When you left, you were a little girl in a dress and pigtails who liked to play in mud puddles. You weren't..." she motioned, "this."

"And you weren't a ruthless pirate." Temp crossed her arms, weary and wanting to get back to the ship. "But here we are. Let's get back to the Chimera, and we can talk some more. Maybe we can even be honest with each other. I need you to tell me who those men were. The older one...that was your father, wasn't it? I seem to remember those eyes. I can't believe I didn't recognise either of you. In God's name, Alex, how could you not have told me?" She waited, wondering if Alex would get back on the flyer or if she'd allow fear to make her run. She'd heard what the strange being at the cathedral had said, and here they were, on a cliff's edge as Alex had to choose.

It seemed like an eternity, standing there in the rain as the wind blew Alex's long hair around her face, before she gave a small nod and turned to the flyer without saying another word. This time she got in the back, leaving the controls to Temp. Relieved but unsure exactly why, Temp got in and they headed out over the water towards the ship.

When they finally boarded the Chimera, Alex brushed past her. "I'm exhausted. We can talk in the morning."

Irritated at the brusque brush-off, Temp grabbed her arm. "I think you could stay awake long enough to explain."

"Um, Cap?" Peter said, his tone uncertain. "I could do with some of your time, what with the passenger requests and such."

Temp and Alex glared at each other, and she let go. "Very well. Until breakfast. Sleep well, lady."

Alex winced like she'd been struck, then stomped off, her head held high.

Temp sighed and rubbed at her temples. "Okay, Peter. Let's go to my office though. I need a drink."

Once they were in her office, Temp kicked off her shoes, not caring for once that she was less than perfectly suited. She threw her jacket on the back of a chair and winced as she sat down. Swinging from a rope high above the earth hadn't done her ribs any good, and breathing was uncomfortable at best. In fact, her whole body ached. "Pour me a whisky, will you, Peter?"

He moved with alacrity and slid it across the desk to her. "You okay, Cap?"

She shook her head. "I don't know, lad. Tell me what's going on with the ship. That will take my mind off things."

He ran through the passenger list. Most were happy, though a few were asking for more intricate dreamscapes. She listened, her mind only partly on what he was saying.

Miranda Billinghurst. A child who had talked about types of flyers and who read adventure books instead of doing needlework and learning how to serve tea. They'd had plenty of arguments about who would fly the fastest and who would be the more daring hero. There was a day in the garden when they'd been in their own world, when Temp was set to rescue the damsel in distress, and when she'd helped her climb down from the tree, Alex had given her hero a kiss that had left Temp's knees weak and made her stomach feel funny. It had taken years before she understood what that feeling betokened. *She was my first kiss.* The thought made Temp smile a little.

"Cap?"

She opened her eyes. "It's fine, Peter. Take the requests to Wade and see if they're viable. If they aren't, tell him to do his best approximation, and I'll talk to the guests at lunch tomorrow to make certain they're satisfied."

Peter made slow, careful notes on the sheet in front of him. "Also, we've had a crow from Camden-in-Middle. Mr. Wilde would like to be picked up when we're next in port."

She nodded again, sipping her whisky. "Send a return message that we'll dock there soon and will send a crow the day before so he can be ready."

"Did you find what you were hoping to in Winchester, Cap?"

Peter's tone was hopeful.

She rolled her head to the side and smiled. "Always want the tales of adventure, don't you?" She tilted her glass towards the satchel. "Have a look."

Eagerly, he removed the bundle of material and unwrapped it slowly to reveal the small crystal crown. "What is it?" He breathed softly, as though afraid he'd break it.

"No idea. It was set atop a skull as small as a child's, but there was something odd about it. I'd have liked to bring it too, but we were only steps ahead of Willoughby's men and had to take what we could to escape with our lives." She shook her head a little at the excitement in his eyes and the pink in his cheeks as he looked at her, wide-eyed. "Tell me what you see."

He held it up in both hands, cupping it and eyeing it critically. "It's shaped funny. Look here, it curves in a little at the top. Like it's meant to hold something else."

She hissed as she sat up too quickly and her ribs caught. "Show me."

He leaned forwards, tilting it to and fro to show her what he meant. The small tines encircling the crown curved inward, and it was easy to picture what was missing. "The orb would fit perfectly on top."

"So it's not a crown. It's a stand. But you said it was on top of a skull?" He frowned, tipping it as though he could picture the skull attached. "Does that mean someone wore the orb on their head, like a hat?"

Temp laughed. "Would be an odd one, that's for sure. But if you saw the person who was guarding it, you might believe lots of strange things."

His eyes lit up again as she told him about the person with the fathomless dark eyes and mysterious demeanour, and how she'd opened the chest with just a wave of her hand.

"Crikey, Cap." He sat back in his chair, shaking his head. "Why do you think she gave it to you and not them others?"

She traced the cold crystal, feeling the engraving under her fingertips. "It was like she knew we were coming. She said that Alex would have to sacrifice something." For some reason, she couldn't remember the being's exact words, which was strange, since Temp's memory was usually spot on.

"If you don't mind me sayin', Cap, things didn't seem right between you when you got back to the ship." Peter seemed to shrink a little as he waited for her to tell him to mind his business.

"They're not exactly right, no." She gave him a small smile. "But we wouldn't expect everyone to be exactly what they seem on this ship, would we?"

His shoulders dropped, and he grinned. "I suppose not. What's next?"

What indeed? "I'm not sure. I think all I want is sleep. The four of us will meet after breakfast tomorrow to put our heads together again."

He stood up to leave and hesitated at the door. "Cap, it's none of my nevermind, I know. But you've seemed happier with Captain Minty onboard. Less...lonely, like."

She raised her eyebrow and her glass. "You're right, lad. It's none of your nevermind."

He flushed and ducked his head as he pulled the door open to leave.

"And Peter?" She waited until he popped his head back into the room. "You've done a mighty good job running the Chimera, lad. I'm proud of you."

His eyes grew glassy, and he swallowed audibly. "Thanks, Cap."

Alone in her office, she gave free rein to her thoughts, letting them run any direction they chose. Hanging in the bitter chill wind by a rope, praying she was strong enough to hold on. Thinking of Alex's true identity and what it meant. And why. Why had she become what she had? Willoughby's men had been right behind them in the cathedral. How close were they to the next clue, without the crown in hand? And without the orb, could they figure out where to go next? Or were they at an impasse?

A soft knock roused her from a drifting sleep, and she rose to open it. If it were Joe, Peter, or Wade, they'd have simply come in after knocking.

"No talking." Alex put her arms around Temp's neck, then pressed her body to Temp's. "Just this." She kissed her.

Temp stood still, frozen. Sure, she'd dreamt of this since Alex had come onboard, but dreams were meant to stay in the imagination. Slowly, and seemingly of their own volition, her arms wrapped around Alex and pulled her close, returning the kiss as she walked backwards into the office, kicking the door shut behind her.

It wasn't gentle. It wasn't a slow, romantic seduction. She pulled Alex's thick hair and exposed her neck. She bit and sucked and drank in Alex's breathy moans. With her other hand, she unlaced the corset and tossed it aside, then followed it with the blouse, which lost a few buttons as she jerked it from Alex's body. She broke away just long enough to pull the linen chemise off to expose Alex's full, soft breasts. Temp groaned and lifted Alex onto the desk, swiping everything off it and onto the floor.

Alex caught the crown just as it was about to be swept off as well. She flashed a grin and held it out. "Maybe set this down more carefully."

Temp ground her teeth but set it on a shelf out of the way, then she turned back and pushed Alex's thick, tattered skirt up around her waist. Silk slid under Temp's hand, and she breathed out. "Silk and lace drawers. At least you continued to wear something I gave you," she murmured against Alex's neck as she unbuttoned them at the back and then undid the silk ribbon that held them around Alex's hips. They dropped to the floor, leaving Alex open to her gaze.

Lust and desire was going to drive her mad. She knelt on the desk and covered Alex's body with her own, kissing her hard as she found the wetness between Alex's legs and entered her quickly. She swallowed Alex's gasp and pressed her to the desk, the feel of Alex's breasts against her chest and her clenching around her fingers making her crazy with need. She drove deep, kissing her way down Alex's neck to her breast and sucking in her nipple. Alex arched, crying out, her hand hard around the back of Temp's neck.

"If you stop I'll throw you overboard, I swear it," Alex said, gasping out the words, her eyes closed tight.

Temp nipped at her nipple and got a slap against the head for it. She bit a little harder, and Alex cried out, her head thrown back, her hair spread across the desk. Temp nearly froze again, but this time at the excess of beauty she couldn't have imagined even in her wildest fantasies. Alex's pale, perfect skin shone against the dark wood of the desk, her wild red hair catching the lamplight, her beautiful lips parted as she moaned and begged Temp not to stop.

And she didn't. She wouldn't, not until Alex was limp with sated desire. Thankfully, Alex was as unrelenting in her ability to keep cresting as she was in her search for freedom and treasure. Over and over again, she filled Temp's hand, only to beg her to keep going.

Eventually, she dropped flat to the desk, breathing hard. She put her hand over Temp's, which rested between her legs. "No more," she whispered, a small grin touching her lips. "It would be a nice way to die, but I'm not ready yet."

Temp removed her hand slowly and slid from the desk. When Alex's eyes opened, her expression wary, Temp held out her hand. "I'm not done with you. But I'm content enough for the moment for us to move somewhere more comfortable."

Alex's expression cleared, and she scooted to the end of the desk, where Temp pulled her into her arms. Alex wrapped her legs around Temp's waist and kissed her way along Temp's jaw as she was carried from the room, using one of the secret passages to get to her cabin. She didn't set Alex down though. She carried her straight to the bed and lay her down, keeping only a hair's breadth between them. This time though, Alex fidgeted until Temp rolled off her.

Alex pushed gently on Temp's shoulder to get her to lay back, and then began unhurriedly unbuttoning Temp's white shirt to reveal the vest beneath. She pulled it off and traced her fingertips over the bruises on Temp's biceps, making her shiver. She did the same again when she pulled off Temp's vest to reveal her fully, including the bruises around her midsection, which she kissed softly, each in turn.

Temp closed her eyes and felt the silken curls of Alex's hair slide over her skin like a balm. Could she drown in the pleasure of a woman's touch? She'd never thought so before, but Alex's sure handling made her think maybe she'd been made for this woman alone. Alex tugged off her trousers, long johns, and socks, leaving her naked and wanting.

But not for long. Alex moved over her like a wave, her hands and hair making every inch of Temp's skin tingle, and it wasn't long before she was on the edge of begging. Before she got to that point, Alex moved between her legs and took Temp into her mouth.

She bucked, her hand tangled in Alex's hair, and her world crashed and spun around her as she let her guard down and allowed her desire to crest. She gasped out a plea for it not to end, and then slumped back, empty of anything but languid contentment.

Alex crawled up her body.

"Take the rest of your clothes off, please," Temp murmured.

Alex left the bed and dropped her skirt, then sat on the edge and unlaced her boots. Temp took in her naked back, the way her curls draped over her shoulders and brushed the very base of her back, and the black ink of the tattoo. "You're something out of a sailor's fairy tale. A sylph sent to wreck sailors on the rocks," she said softly, her thumb moving over the base of Alex's spine.

Alex turned in her full naked splendour and curled up against Temp on the bed. "No talking." She rested her head on Temp's shoulder and draped her arm over Temp's waist.

Temp could handle that. She reached down and pulled a blanket over them, then held Alex to her. Whatever this was, whatever it betokened of their future, tonight she'd take it just as it was.

Pre-dawn light filtered into the room, and she grimaced at the pain in her side. Alex's arm rested over the most bruised bit, and she gently nudged it downward.

"Moving. Stop." Alex nestled closer.

"I have duties to attend to, beautiful." Temp kissed the top of her head. "There are other women on this ship who need my attention." She jumped when Alex pinched her side.

"They can have you. I've had my fill." Alex grinned and shoved the blanket down to her thighs. She stretched, her arms above her head. "Really. Go right ahead."

Temp grumbled and took Alex again, this time more slowly. She lavished attention on her breasts, cupping them in her hands, figuring out exactly what pressure Alex liked on her nipples and between her legs. Alex was almost wanton in her desire and open, naked pleasure, and Temp had never been so enthralled by a woman's willingness to take what she wanted from her lover. By the time Alex had cried out through multiple orgasms and lay in a heap on the rumpled bed, Temp was convinced she'd never get enough of the way Alex's body moved or the sounds she made.

"Okay. Now you can go deal with your other women." Alex pulled up the blanket and curled against the pillow.

"Hussy." Temp kissed her cheek. "We have a discussion to endure after breakfast, remember. And there's the little issue of what to do with the information we have in hand."

Alex groaned and pulled the pillow over her head. "Talk without me. A boor kept me awake all night, and I've not the capacity for conversation of any consequence."

Temp laughed and moved to the washbowl. "There's the Lady Billinghurst." A pillow flew through the air and hit her in the back.

"Unless you want the next one to be a knife, you won't call me that again." Alex sat up and swept her hair back into a loose bun.

Temp held up her hands. "I have no desire for death at your hands." She finished washing her face and turned to Alex, liking the way Alex's gaze travelled over her like a physical thing. "But we do need to talk," she said softly. "Meet me in my office after you've eaten?"

Alex's expression went from languorous to guarded, and Temp felt the loss of their connection like a tug at her heart.

"Very well." She made a shooing motion. "But you need to leave so I can take care of my bodily functions. Nothing ruins romance like the need to pee."

Temp laughed and bowed. "As you say. I'll take mine elsewhere." She left, wondering if it was smart to leave Alex in her quarters. But then, she kept most everything of real value in her office, and Alex had full run of that. She winced at the moment of distrust. Would she always feel that way? No matter who Alex had been, she was a pirate of some renown now, and Temp couldn't just set that aside. And despite Alex's assertion that she was no longer the Lady Billinghurst, that person was still in there. If Temp could bring her back out, then perhaps it would be possible to pursue something of substance. Because while Temp couldn't have a relationship with the notorious pirate Alex Minty, relations with the Lady Billinghurst were most acceptable.

Temp whistled as she made her way to the kitchen. She'd certainly never expected Alex to show up at her office that way, but maybe things were going to change for the better...

Chapter Twenty

If ever there had been a time when Alex needed to steel herself, this was it.

Her clothes had mostly been left in Temp's office, but there was nothing for it. She'd have to walk back to her room without them. At least she still had her boots. She rifled quickly through Temp's wardrobe and found a shirt that would work as a dress, thanks to their height disparity, though it would be incredibly indecent given the amount of leg it would show. She put it on quickly and gave a cursory look around Temp's most private space. It was strong, with earth tones and hardwoods. A physical image of Temp, really. She lightly touched the black and white photo of Temp on the wall, where she stood beside a man who couldn't have looked any prouder. Her father, most likely. What a memory to have. Alex could only imagine.

Get out of here, you sentimental fool. She picked up her boots then crept out of Temp's room. She'd paid little attention to their hurried sojourn to Temp's room, but the door led to a normal hallway. Damn. Where was the hidden one they'd come through? She searched the walls but couldn't find any indication. Damn Wade. He was far too good at his craft.

Giving up in the interest of time, she made her way back to her room, trying to look unhurried and as though her heart wasn't pounding itself into splinters. Once in her room, she wondered if Wade would know she was there. Of course. The light would have gone on to show the room was inhabited. She moved as slowly as possible, stripping off Temp's shirt and shoving it into her satchel, which Temp had returned, sans arcane object. She wore a combination of her own clothes and the ones Temp had provided, and somehow that felt quite right. She hesitated as she was about to leave the room, wondering if she should take the small vase or the statue in the hallway. They could fetch a good price at market.

But she couldn't bring herself to do it. They'd come too far together and now the thought of pilfering from Temp felt...wrong, like stealing from a saint. Damn woman. Who was she to change a pirate's nature? Alex huffed and made her way to the corridor that led to the belly of the ship. Fortunately, all the staff were busy with breakfast supplicants, so her passage went unnoticed.

She reached the flyer and held to the side of it. What was she thinking? She had the chance to find something truly spectacular. Treasure that could set up the Urchin for years. It was, as Peter reckoned, the kind of adventure someone like her lived for.

And there was Temp.

The lever to open the hatch pushed easily to reveal the sea far, far below. She loosed the front rope and jumped into the flyer. That, right there, was the issue. Last night had been the kind of magic reserved for fairytales. And Alex was no princess, though Temp could easily be the hero on a white horse. Or steering a silver dragon, as was the case. The fact that Temp now knew who she'd been changed everything. It changed the game entirely. She'd have expectations now. She'd have ideas and want to change Alex. She could see it in her eyes when she'd left this morning. And it put her in even greater danger. She had no idea what she'd gotten into when they'd identified her in the cathedral.

She reached back and grabbed the rear rope, then let the front one go, forcing the flyer to drop forwards, nose first towards the ground. She settled into the pilot's seat, took a deep breath, and let go of the rear rope, freeing the flyer to drop from the belly of the dragon.

She steered away from the ship, dropping low and fast before she engaged the gears and sail, then swooped away. A quick glance over her shoulder was all she'd allow, even as the tears streamed down her cheeks and grief churned in her stomach. *Not a princess. Not a fairy tale. There is no happy ending here.*

Sunshine disappeared as she dropped through the ever-present cloud layer that hung above the land, and she saw the white cliffs of Dover shine like a beacon in the grey mist. She wasn't sure where the Urchin was, but if word had got out, then she'd be sure to find it in Low London, the grottiest section of London-on-Ground. The flight was uneventful, and she saw a few flyers here and there going about their own business. By the time she made it to the dock, her nerves were on edge and bile churned the back of her throat. Did Temp know she'd left? Had she gone looking for her when she hadn't gone for breakfast? Did she feel betrayed?

She threw the rope to a lad at the docking station. It was the same one she'd come to know. He tied the mooring lines expertly and gave her the gap-toothed grin.

"Heya, Cap!"

"Hello, lad." She flipped him a coin. "Any of the Urchin crew about?"

He frowned. "Aye, Cap. Tom has been coming by every few days to see if there's been word of you." He ducked his head, his eyes wide. "They say you fell from a dragon."

She laughed. "That I did, lad. But not even a dragon can kill me. Any idea where Tom is laying low?"

He shook his head. "Nah. Said he'd be back though."

"Righto. Well, when he sees fit to check again, tell him I'm at the Dirty Squirrel, and he owes me a pint, eh?"

With a wave, she set off. Good ol' Tom. Trust him to not give up on her. She made her way to the Dirty Squirrel and breathed in the raucous laughter along with the undertone of violence about to erupt at any moment. This was the world she understood. One she could control. She stood still, just inside the doorway, and scanned the room. But she didn't see a single member of the Urchin's crew. Damnation. Why couldn't it have been easy? With a shrug, she went to the bar. "I need a room."

The bartender looked up from where he was spilling beer outside a pint glass. "I don't want no trouble from the likes of you, Minty."

She rolled her eyes and held up her hands. "Do I look like I'm causing trouble? I just need a room."

He shook his head, wiped his hands on a dirty towel attached to an equally dirty apron, and reached below the bar. He tossed her a key. "You can have room six, in the attic. It's all I've got free." He held out his hand, palm up. "Payment now, if you please."

She couldn't blame him, though she'd never stiffed him before. But pirates around here weren't always trustworthy. "Here. And another for tonight's finest food."

He spat into a jug. "You can be sure of it."

She climbed the three flights of stairs to the attic room. After her time on the Chimera, she couldn't help but notice the worn patches on the single chair by the scratched, dented table and the threadbare excuse for a blanket on the bed that seemed to tilt slightly to the left. Well and good. She shouldn't be getting used to the kind of luxury available on the Chimera anyway. She'd given up that life, left it behind for the wolves of memory to devour.

She took a seat by the window and looked out at the grimy, grey cobbles below. Horse dung sat in piles in the road, and children played not far from it, trying to lure a rat out of hiding with a mouldy bit of bread.

Now what? She rested her head in her hands. She'd not thought much beyond the need to flee now that Temp knew who she really was. Anyone with that kind of information could hold power over her she'd sworn never to give away again. But the only way she could be truly safe was if she was back on the Urchin. Irritated by the quiet of her room, she left her satchel tucked under the thin mattress, put a few coins in her pocket, checked that the knife on her arm was secure and the gun on her thigh was loaded, then headed back downstairs.

"You seen Tom around?" she asked, accepting the beer the

bartender shoved at her.

"Not today. Been a few days actually." He wiped at the bar, looking at her from the corner of his eye. "He's staying down t'Goose. You want me to send a lad?"

She shook her head. "I'll head down there myself."

He tapped the counter in front of her. "He's not the only one 'as been lookin' for you, Minty." He shrugged. "You might want to stick about here until you've got a few of your lads with you."

Ice ran down her spine. "Who else?"

"Toffs. Posh gits who don't belong on t'ground. But there was no information to give, since you hadn't been seen." This time he looked directly at her. "Offered a mighty sum for information on you. And you know what that means."

She stood, pushing a coin across the table. In a tavern full of pirates, she knew exactly what it meant. "Thanks for the warning."

He slipped the coin off the counter and into a pocket on the front of his apron. "So you want me to send for Tom?"

Indecision was paralysing. Run, and run now? Or wait it out and find her crew so she wasn't running alone? In her attic space, she had the ability to see anyone coming, but she was also trapped up there with no way out. If she got caught on the street, she might be able to run and lose pursuers in the maze of streets. If she had Temp and her wicked way with that cane, she might not worry... *Stupid.* Why think of the woman she'd left behind at a time like this? "Send for Tom. Tell him to meet me here after dark."

He nodded and turned away. She took her pint of beer to her room, and though she sat to drink it, she found she couldn't settle and drank as she paced. Would Temp come after her? She'd stolen the Chimera's flyer, after all. But somehow, she didn't think that would bother Temp. Would she feel betrayed? They'd gone through so much together in a short amount of time.

Last night, Alex had needed to have at least one moment of passion with Temp before she left. She'd gotten that, and more. Emotions had flowed as freely as the wind in a storm, buffeting her, turning her around, making her fall and rise like a bird over the sea. Every touch, every kiss, every moment that Temp had made her cry out for more... She sighed and rested her head against the wall. The memories would have to be enough.

If Temp didn't find the Apple, if the Dawn or the Kaiser got it instead, she figured she'd know soon enough, when one or the other tried to take over the world. If that didn't happen, then she could assume Temp found her way to the Apple and saved them all. As much as Alex would love to have the chance to see the quest to its conclusion, it wasn't worth the risk.

She set down the warm beer and leaned against the windowpane, not seeing the world below as she considered her position. What did she know? First, she knew that the Dawn had come looking for Alex Minty on Temp's ship. That meant they'd made the connection between Alex and Miranda. As far as the Dawn was concerned, that person was also dead. At least there was one plus to the equation. Second, she'd been recognised at the cathedral, and the voice she'd heard still occasionally haunted her dreams, even years after she'd last heard it. That meant the Dawn now knew she *wasn't* dead, and was, in fact, still very much alive and in the company of another treasure hunter. And since it was the Dawn who'd gone to Temp in the first place, they knew Alex was with her.

Alex shuddered and sat on the edge of the bed. Was Temp in danger? Even if she was, she could handle herself. The Chimera, with the golems and automatons, with the big guns and capable crew, wasn't to be trifled with, and the Dawn probably knew it.

Would Temp, too, put all these pieces together and decide she was better off with Alex gone? The thought made Alex's chest ache, and she rubbed it as though to make it better.

A soft knock sounded on the door, and she startled. The light outside had dimmed. Had she been lost in thought so long? Blinking hard, she shook her head at the slight dizziness that assailed her. Unsteady, she pulled the knife from its pouch and moved to the door.

"Aye?" she said, keeping her voice low.

"It's Tom. Let me in, you lucky idiot."

She grinned and opened the door, but stepped back, confused when two hulking shapes pushed their way in. Neither was Tom. Both wore menacing expressions like they'd been born with them in place.

"Your presence is required. Come nice and quiet, and we won't need to hurt you," one of the hulking shapes said. He reminded her a little of Crispin the golem.

She lifted the knife and stepped into fighting stance, but the men seemed to tilt. *The beer. Damn the bartender to the deepest hells.* The men flanked her, and she swung wildly, the movement making her ill. When she stumbled and went to her knees, she could have wept with frustration. She lashed out when one got close, striking tender tissue, and she grinned when he hit the floor.

Before she could lash out at the other, something hard struck the back of her head, pain flashed behind her eyes, and the world went black.

$$***$$

"Bear's bollocks." Alex groaned and turned onto her side, letting the vomit spill onto the floor beside whatever it was she was laying on. Her skull pounded to the beat of her heart, and the bile in her mouth tasted of metallic beer.

Slowly she sat up, fighting the urge to drop back down and close her eyes. Candlelight sent shadows dancing over the wallpapered walls. Heavy brocade curtains covered large windows, and a silver pitcher sat beside crystal glasses on a table beside the bed.

She poured herself some water and drank gratefully. Reaching back, she prodded the lump on the back of her head and winced when she felt the hair matted with blood.

The lock clicked on the door, and it opened slowly. A young

woman wearing a white cap and equally white apron looked in. "Oh, good, you're awake. His Lordship said we should get you ready for tea, miss." She looked away from Alex and at the floor. Her expression turned to one of sympathy. "They said you weren't well when they brought you in. No worries, we'll get you cleaned up and feeling better shortly."

Alex stood, inwardly cursing the feeling of fragility. "Where am I?"

The girl looked surprised. "Why, you're home, my lady. At Billinghurst Manor."

Alex's knees gave out, and she slid to the floor, her boots slipping through the muck she'd thrown up. She didn't care. After all these years, they'd finally caught up to her.

"Oh no." The girl came into the room, but then quickly turned and locked the door behind her and shoved the key into one of the many pockets in her apron. Then she came and helped Alex to her feet and over to the table. "My lady, after all you've been through, being captured and held by pirates all this time, you should really go easy. The bath is being filled now, and that will help you feel right as rain."

Alex let out a semi-hysterical laugh. "And the reason you're keeping me locked in?"

"They said you're going to be a little..." The young woman paused. "Well, a little like a feral cat. For a while, until you get used to being back where you belong again. It's just for your safety, my lady."

Her safety. She was lucky they hadn't just outright killed her. But then, they wouldn't get what they wanted, would they?

There was a knock, and the young maid opened the door. Soft words were spoken, and then she turned to Alex. "Your bath is ready, my lady. Let me help you." She put her arm around Alex's waist, and the door was pushed open further.

Belatedly, Alex realised her knife and gun holsters were gone. She had no desire to punch her way out of this, but she would if necessary. If, of course, she could stand on her own. Whatever the bartender had put in her beer had yet to wear off and, combined with the head injury, she couldn't fight her way out of a wet sheet right now.

Waiting at the entryway was a large woman, built like a brick wall with a stoney expression to match. She'd likely never smiled a day in her life, Alex thought. Then she noticed the metal ear, along with a length of metal that looked like it had been burned into her collar bone. She glared at Alex with eyes that were hard and mean.

The young woman helped Alex down the hall to a large, too bright, too ornate washroom. A large copper tub sat in the middle, steam rising from it, and suddenly Alex desperately wanted to get in it.

"Allow me, my lady," the girl said, expertly undoing the stays of Alex's corset. "Goodness. You're lucky you didn't expose yourself to all of London. Your stays look like you did them without any attention at all."

"I was in a hurry," Alex mumbled, tears stinging her eyes as she thought of the way she'd left Temp's room. She'd left Temp only to fling herself right into the arms of the people she'd been running from for years. Would Temp appreciate the irony?

Naked, she sat on the edge of the bath and swung her legs over, then slid in. She heard the small gasp and looked over to see the girl staring at her tattoo.

"Did the pirates make you get that?" she asked, raising her hand almost like she was going to touch it, then remembered herself and dropped her hand to her side.

"Something like that." Alex slid deeper, letting her head sink below the hot water and muffle the sound around her. Hands disturbed the water and began washing her hair, and she let the girl do it. In truth, it felt wonderful, and after three washes, it began to squeak.

The water was cooling when she took the soap and scrubbed herself clean. Between her legs was deliciously sore, a heartbreaking reminder of the last beautiful moment she was likely to have in this life. Tears blurred her vision once again.

"Oh, my lady. I can't imagine what you've been through, but it's all right now. You're safe." The young girl sounded so sincere, so sure.

Alex stood and accepted the thick towel to dry herself as she stepped out of the bath. "There's nothing safe for me here."

The girl's eyes dropped, and she stayed silent as Alex sat and let her brush out her tangled hair. She put something in it, an oil of some sort, that smelled of roses.

"It's his lordship's favourite scent," she whispered. "It will keep him sweet."

Alex quaked inside. She'd rather have him dead than sweet. But if this young girl was to be her jailor, then she needed to make sure she wasn't wary, and saying something like that out loud would only get that key tucked further away.

The key. It was time to stop feeling sorry for herself and start planning an escape. She'd done it once. She could do it again. The silk robe slid over her shoulders, and she barely noticed, her thoughts whirling as she followed the girl back to her room, with Brick Hilda following close behind as though divining Alex's line of thought.

Back in her room, the door locked from outside this time, and she gritted her teeth. So she was to be guarded. She'd just have to find a way around that too.

"Where are my things?" she asked, looking around.

"Goodness, my lady. They've gone right in the bin. They weren't fit for someone of your station."

Alex groaned. "My knife? My gun?"

The girl once again looked bemused. "I believe his lordship has them, my lady. But you've no need of them here. You're safe now."

The repetition of the phrase made Alex grind her teeth, but she said nothing. "What's your name?"

"Lily, my lady." She pulled a pale pink skirt from the wardrobe and laid it over a chair, then added the chemise, drawers, pink bodice, and a beautifully worked magenta corset.

"I'm not wearing that." Alex crossed her arms. "I'm not here to be dressed like a doll that escaped from an asylum."

Lily swallowed, her hand stopping on the corset. "Please, my lady." She bit her lip and her eyes grew glassy. "His lordship made it very clear what he wants, and you know...he isn't one who likes his orders ignored."

Alex saw the fear then, in the way she held still, like a mouse trying to avoid a cat's gaze, and the way her eyes flicked around the room. For all she kept espousing the idea that Alex was safe, this young woman knew full well of the danger that lurked in the hallways.

"Very well." She sighed and stood. "Let's get this done with."

Everything was slightly too tight, and the skirt narrowed at the ankles, making it hard to take regular strides, let alone run or even send out a good kick.

"It's a hobble skirt, my lady. All the fashion right now." Lily looked up from where she was lacing Alex's short boots.

"Like hobbling a horse. I can see how it got its name." Alex grimaced and took a few short steps.

A knock came at the door, and the lock clicked. "Dinner," Brick Hilda barked.

Lily gave Alex a quick smile. "I imagine you'll enjoy having a meal at a real table again."

"Do you think pirates eat at fake ones?" Alex said, hobbling from the room. As soon as she could get a knife, she'd cut slits in it. And then use it on the man who would keep her a captive for as long as she breathed.

"Well, no. I mean, I don't think so. Do they?" Lily trailed along just behind her.

Alex didn't answer. She had no desire to talk about the life she'd left behind. Would Tom even know she'd been at the Dirty Squirrel? Would word go round? Would Temp try to find her? Of course not. Why would she? Alex had run. This was her fault. It was a good thing she'd left her heart on the ship of dreams. At least this way, she had nothing left to lose.

Chapter Twenty-One

Temp threw back the whisky in a gulp, then poured another. It only served to add fuel to the flames of betrayal and frustration that engulfed her. Not even a note. Alex had just up and gone after the magic of their night together. At least, Temp had thought of it that way. Apparently, Alex hadn't even felt enough to say goodbye. Why had she snuck off? They had a deal and if she'd simply said she wanted to go, Temp would have arranged it without losing the Chimera's small flyer. As it was, she'd had to send a crow to order a replacement that would be waiting when they next docked.

"Come in." She didn't care that her tone was less than welcoming when someone knocked.

"Captain, my Captain, how I wish you'd sail into my seas and drink the waters of my desire." Ginny and Vee appeared, with Peter looking on anxiously behind them.

Temp set down her glass and schooled her expression. "Ladies. I'm sorry I've been neglecting you. But this isn't a place for passengers. If you don't mind, I'll escort—"

"Nonsense." Vee plopped into a chair, her eyes clear and bright. "Peter told us you're trying to solve a riddle, and you should know that Ginny is one of the very best at those. You won't find one better. And as you've been terribly remiss in allowing us to lavish your body with our gazes or caress your intellect with our admiration, you owe us something interesting to delve into."

Temp glanced at Peter, her eyebrow raised.

"Sorry, Cap. They were asking after you, and I..." He shrugged, his face red, his hands stuffed in his pockets.

"Let me see," Ginny said, holding out her hand. "Please do. I love a good mystery."

Temp sighed and went into the small room. She gathered the pieces of paper with the drawings of the orb and lifted the firebird and crystal crown as well. She set them all on her desk in front of Ginny and Vee. "We figured out the map that took us to the place we found the crown. But there are runes and symbols we can't decipher and haven't been able to translate into anything useful."

Vee's eyes narrowed, and she tossed a stone into the air and caught it. "You're in a foul temper, my friend. Does it have to do with the lady pirate having made away with sapphic treasure?"

Ginny picked up the sheets and studied them, then asked for a magnifying glass, which Temp handed her. In the other hand, she held the crystal crown in her palm, turning it this way and that in the light.

"Bloody pirates." Temp poured two glasses of whisky and handed them over. "Peter, you can go back to your duties. I'll escort our guests back when we're done."

"Yes, Cap. Sorry." He looked truly chagrined.

"Don't be too hard on the boy. You understand how relentless we can be." Vee winked at her. "And as for your pirate, it does make for quite the romantic tale."

"Right now, it makes for a tale of thievery and idiocy. She stole my flyer, and I trusted her."

"If one brings a lion into the house, they can't get upset when it eats the children." Vee craned her neck to look at Ginny, who had her nose almost pressed to the paper. "You knew what she was when you captured her and when she captured your heart in turn."

"My heart is quite a bit further north than what she captured. And plenty of women can claim the same, so I won't give her the pleasure of thinking she was more than that." The words were tied with the coarse rope of a lie, but she refused to acknowledge the ache in her chest and soul when she'd found out Alex had left.

"Say what you will to make it bearable." Vee sighed and got up to look over Ginny's shoulder. "Anything, my darling?"

"It's fascinating." Ginny looked up, exhilaration making her eyes bright. "Look. Look at what happens when we hold the crown to the light, over the symbols Alex drew from the orb. See how it highlights certain ones?"

Temp moved behind Ginny and looked over her shoulder to see what she was talking about. It was true. Each prong of the crown pointed directly to a specific symbol, and the valleys left others in shadow. It was a kind of cryptic code. Her heart raced at the simplicity of the system.

"Even better, I know what it means when you put those highlighted symbols together. It's a Norse fairytale. I had a nanny from Norway for a time when I was young, and she taught me to read runic symbols not just as individual words, but as stories." Ginny sounded like an excited child on Christmas morning.

Temp moved aside, anticipation helping her set aside her anger. "What does it say?"

Ginny traced the lines like she was reading slowly. "On the Isle of Mists, where the Blue Men play beneath the merry dancers, turquoise pools call to the silken skins of the selkies. Where waters fall..." She frowned. "I'm not sure about this, as it makes little sense. Where waters fall, they arch beneath the pyramids. Beware the kelpie who would take you to the depths." She shook her head, tracing the symbols again. "That's what it says."

Temp went over the sentences in her head. "The Isle of Mists. That must be the Isle of Skye, right?"

Vee ran her hand over Ginny's back. "Selkies were mythical creatures who lived in rock pools in sacred areas."

"And the merry dancers were what they called the northern lights. The Blue Men?" Ginny looked between them. "Any ideas?"

Temp went into her office and picked up the book Alex had been reading from. "Maybe there's a reference in here."

Vee took it from her and sat back in the chair, legs outstretched, trousers much like Temp's pulled tight over her slim legs. She flipped pages, scanning.

Ginny went back to the translation and continued to sketch out words and then scratch them out again.

"Here." Vee looked up from the book. "The Blue Men were storm folk, mostly relegated to a narrow section of sea called the Minch."

Temp sipped her whisky, more slowly now. "Where the storm folk play under the northern lights, there are turquoise pools with selkies. Is there a picture to show the difference between kelpies and selkies? Not that I expect to see one and need to know the difference."

Vee turned more pages. "Here." She held the book up for them to see.

The image for the selkie showed what looked very much like a seal that shed its skin once on land and had become a lovely human woman, albeit with eyes too big and too dark. The kelpie, on the other hand, looked like a vaguely demonic horse, with seaweed in its mane and sharp teeth in a gaping mouth.

"It says the selkie is generally good-natured if it isn't upset, but it's responsible for the storms that come up without warning. The kelpie," Vee grimaced, "will drown its victims and then feed on their flesh, leaving only entrails to wash up on shore as evidence of a lost soul."

"Gruesome. But I hardly think I'll encounter mythical creatures." She closed her eyes and considered. "The northern lights are easy to see this time of year and will be visible from anywhere on the island. But the worst of the storms hit the west coast. Is there anything in the book about turquoise pools or the Minch?"

Vee flipped through the book again, stopping occasionally to read and then continuing on. "Fairy pools!" She held up the book that showed a series of waterfalls dropping into pools at various levels, and the water was coloured a vibrant hue.

"Beautiful." Temp took the book and read the passage about the mythical creatures that called the fairy pools their home. "And they're near to the west coast. It gives me a starting point anyway.

Perhaps I'll find something once I'm there to take me the rest of the way. Maybe towards the arch and pyramid, whatever those may be."

Vee picked up the Firebird and made a sound of appreciation when the pink lines followed her touch. She then held the crown and looked at it. "It's easy to see how the three pieces will fit together. But what will it show you that you can't find out from the verse alone?"

Temp sighed, deflating a little. "I don't know. The orb is being held by someone who is rather inclined not to release it." She didn't miss the way they looked her over. She'd been a mess after Willoughby's, and she was moving even more gingerly after the escape and her night with Alex.

"Best left alone then." Ginny lightly touched her arm. "Few things beyond love are worth dying for."

Temp stood, unable to bear the look of adoration between the women. For the briefest moment, she'd thought maybe that kind of thing was in her future. "I can't thank you enough for your assistance, which truly, I hadn't expected in the least."

Ginny gave her a sweet smile. "We're writers, Captain. We delve into worlds like this one as often as is feasible without someone wanting to put us in an asylum." She slid her arm around Vee's waist. "And now that we know you're sound of mind, if not of heart, we will leave you to your mysteries. We wanted to tell you in person that we've had a truly spectacular experience. We've already sent a crow requesting another booking in a year's time."

Temp was glad to hear it, though she couldn't imagine being on the ship a year from now. Surely her life would take a different direction. It was a thought that wouldn't have occurred to her before she'd met Alex. "I'll look forwards to your company on my lonely nights then."

They laughed, and she walked them back to the dining room, as she'd said she would. But her mind was racing. She picked up a copper talk-tube and asked the switchboard automaton to tell Joe and Wade she wanted to see them in her office. On her way back, she detoured to Alex's room. It was empty, of course. But Temp wanted to breathe in her scent one more time before it faded like she'd never been there. The simple wood walls were unadorned, and there was no illusion. It was just a room with a few pieces of furniture. Nothing special.

Like my world. A façade of something interesting. She shook off the thought. She wasn't prone to being morose and wouldn't give in to it now. She just hoped...well, she just hoped that Alex was safe, wherever she was. Maybe she'd already found her ship and was regaling her crew with stories of odd visions and odder passengers. It was strange, how quickly she'd grown accustomed to Alex's presence and input, and how at ease they'd become after a short time. She'd never felt that with anyone else. Had Alex really not felt the same?

"Cap?"

She turned to find Peter a distance away, looking worried. "Yes?"

"Wade and Joe are in your office." He blinked rapidly and looked at his feet. "Said you wanted to meet with them."

She strode away from the room, leaving the questions and memories behind for the moment. Clasping his shoulder, she led him back down the hallway. "I did. And the only reason I didn't ask for you as well is because you're doing a damn sight better job taking care of our guests than I am, and I need you to keep doing it for a while longer."

His frown cleared, and he nodded quickly. "Sure, Cap. I've got everything covered."

They branched off, Temp back to her office and Peter back to the lounge, where he said several passengers were taking afternoon tea. Wade and Joe sat in her office, reading over Ginny's transcription.

"What do you think?" she asked, leaning on the desk.

"I think we're going to have to fly the Chimera to the Isle of

Skye." Wade tapped the sheet, head tilted, owl eyes narrowed in thought. "A flyer won't handle that trip, not all the way from the mainland. The sea's currents are wild, and the winds are no better. We'll need steady hands and nerves to do that trip."

She nodded. She tried to stay away from the northern coast of Scotland for just that reason. Edinburgh-upon-Wind was the only sky city in the country. The rest remained land-based, and she had little need to visit except for the occasional myth to follow, of which Scotland had many. But she'd never needed to do the outer islands, which were often shrouded in mist and rain. "We'll still need a flyer to get all our gear down there. We can pick it up when we next dock. Damn pirate." She gritted her teeth against the unwelcome surge of hurt that rose once again.

"You found out who she was. Before she took the Urchin." Joe rested the papers in his lap and looked at her solemnly. "Right?"

She frowned. "You knew?"

With a sigh, he picked up his glass of whisky, his metal hand catching the light and making it gleam. "I've heard stories. She showed up in the sky like some dark angel. Kept away from the sky cities, vented her anger on anyone who took from poor folk. And when she got a good haul from a raid, she always set aside at least half and then divided the rest among her crew. The bit she set aside she took to the land cities and gave to the poor. Any of her crew who wanted to leave the ship and go their own way, she made sure had enough funds so they wouldn't struggle. There's a rumour she even helped fund an orphanage, but that could be part of the legend growing around her. But it's true enough about her helping her crew and the poor. My nephew sailed on the Urchin. Said Alex was one of the best people he'd ever known."

Various pieces of conversation clicked into place like puzzle pieces. Alex had clearly wanted to keep her moments of charity a secret. A pirate who had a soft spot for the poor and downtrodden wouldn't keep her ruthless reputation for long. But enough people had mentioned owing their lives to Alex that it rang true. "But you say I found out who she was? Did you know?" The thought that he might have and not told her made the situation even worse.

He shook his head. "No. But anyone who shows up like she did and looks over her shoulder the way she did? She's running from powerful people."

"Billinghurst." The name tasted like acid on her tongue. "She's Lady Miranda Billinghurst."

They stared at her, stunned into silence.

"Well. It explains her education." Wade lifted his goggles, setting them atop his head. "When she got found out, it must have put the fear of God into her, if she's been running all this time. Probably doesn't know how *not* to run. He's got a nasty reputation."

Temp hadn't considered the fear Alex must have felt. She'd been angry at being deceived but hadn't given a second of consideration to Alex's reasons for becoming what she had. "What do you know of Billinghurst? He and my father were acquaintances before we moved to the Americas, but I don't remember much of him."

"Big investor in mining." Joe leaned back, his brow furrowed as he thought. "No one knows what happened to Mrs Billinghurst, but there's plenty of speculation. Staff don't stay long. They say he's quick with physical violence when he doesn't get what he wants. I heard that he even cut off the ear of one servant because she wasn't listening to his instructions well enough. Said she wouldn't need the ear since she didn't use it."

Temp shook her head. "And that's the house that Alex grew up in, likely without anyone to protect her."

"Did you know Alex when you were children?" Wade asked, still studying the translation.

"I did. But I never matched the quiet child I played with to the deadly pirate. I wish my father was here. I'd get his opinion and advice."

Joe gave her an understanding smile. "Me too. But a crow to your contacts would provide information, wouldn't it?"

Temp sighed and pinched the bridge of her nose. "Probably.

But that feels like an invasion of Alex's privacy. And now that she's gone and likely already back on the Urchin, or at least with her crew, Billinghurst no longer matters. That said, he knows who I am now. He was one of the two men from the Dawn who came asking about the Apple and about Alex. I said she was dead, but there's no question he knows that isn't true now." She rubbed at her temples. "I need to stay focused on getting to the Apple before everyone else. If Alex wanted me to know her business, or if she wanted help, she'd have told me herself."

They didn't seem to have any response to that, and the room stayed silent for a moment. Finally, Joe said, "Well, what do you propose to do about your passengers? We have no reason to fly that far north."

"I don't think the passengers generally care where we are in the sky, since what they pay for is on the ship." She looked at Wade. "I don't suppose you have an amazing wooden map of the Isle of Skye?"

He shook his head, looking almost wistful. "Never had reason to go there. I'll be sure to get the lay of it for a base though, when we do."

She went to a shelf and pulled down a large leather volume. "Then we'll have to hope traditional maps will suffice." The page for the Isle of Skye was oddly sparse. "Is there really so little habitation on it? Or is the map incomplete?"

Joe shook his head. "I think that's right. You have to be hard as nails to live out there, and even the Scottish prefer the mainland. Like Wade said, the weather is prone to outbursts of temper. Neither land nor sea are reliable."

Temp rubbed at her eyes, tiredness washing over her. She needed rest to recuperate and process what had happened with Alex, but there simply wasn't time. "Can we sail towards Eynort, then?" She traced it with her finger, noticing the mountain markings. "The Black Cuillin mountain range looks imposing and like it would take far too long to traverse. If we flew into Loch Harport, near

Carbost, we'd have a straighter shot and not have to cross the foothills." She looked at them, and they seemed to agree.

"Then we leave tomorrow."

Wade stood. "We're not due to sail for another week, so I need to make some adjustments. And we'll have to make port in order to pick up the flyer. Are you letting the passengers know?"

Temp considered her options. "Yes. I'll make an announcement to anyone who shows up at dinner, and then I'll knock on the doors of those who don't. You'll need to power down the illusions, so I don't interrupt anything. They'll have the option to disembark if they want to, with the knowledge that they can come back on board at a later time if they wish. Otherwise, it won't affect their journey in any way."

"When we stop for the flyer, I'll bring in more supplies. We need to be prepared for storms and for whatever you might need on the ground." Joe stood and looked at her, frown lines creasing his eyes as he ran his metal hand through his hair. "You can't go alone."

"And you'll rust out there in the rain." She gave him a quick smile. "And Wade isn't made for outdoor pursuits. That means it'll be me and Peter." She didn't like it in the least. He was too young, too inexperienced, and God forbid she let something happen to him the way it had to Duncan. "Damn the pirate for abandoning us." Fortunately, neither of her crew members reminded her that Alex hadn't agreed to do anything other than help her in Low Nottingham.

"You could hire someone when we stop for the flyer," Wade said, though he sounded far from convinced.

"We all know that bringing in anyone else at this point would be foolhardy. We don't know who we can trust, and there are already too many players in the game. No, it will be me and Peter, and he'll have strict instructions to get back to the ship if anything goes wrong. And if it does, you need to get the Chimera into the air. Keep her safe, as well as the passengers." She held up her hand to forestall arguments. "I'll make it back somehow, if I can. If it's more than a week, leave and carry on with the schedule. I'll send a crow with my coordinates if it comes to that."

Neither of them looked happy about it, but they didn't protest any further. They left, and shortly after, one of the kitchen staff brought in a meal with a note from Joe that said she'd be useless if she starved to death. It made her smile, and a tiny corner of the sadness filling her brightened. Alex didn't want her, but she still had people around her who cared. Why didn't that feel like enough?

Chapter Twenty-Two

Alex shook from the inside out. The cocktail of emotions made her want to scream like an Amazonian warrior and upend the table. The gun on the table, however, made that inadvisable. The fact that it was turned towards her made it extra so.

"You look beautiful, Miranda."

She glared at the old man, unwilling to give him a response. Her father, Lord Billinghurst, looked older but no less imposing, and the sting of the back of his hand on her cheek flared up like it had been yesterday, not years ago. Beside him, slurping his soup and spilling more of it on his shirt than he got in his mouth, was Lord Cambrick Whisenhunt, whose dark eyes had followed her like prey from the moment she'd come into the dining room. It had been him with her father the day they'd boarded the Chimera to ask Temp for her help, and seeing his face brought back the ice in her blood.

"It's good that you're back where you belong, and before anyone made the connection between the despicable lady pirate and yourself. God knows you should swing for all you've done, if even half the rumours are true." He lightly tapped the butt of the airgun, almost playfully. "But we don't have to worry about that, do we? You'll behave yourself now."

Cambrick pushed the bowl aside, sloshing broth onto the table, and waved at the servant to take it away. Alex was fairly certain he groped her when she leaned over the table, based on the way she stiffened and gritted her teeth. If Alex could get hold the of the gun, he'd be the first to die.

"Did you really think you'd get away forever?" Cambrick asked.

"You're not nearly so clever as you think."

"And we need to discuss your relationship with Temperance Strud." Her father gave a curt nod to the servant who set his roast down in front of him. "I was fully aware of the Dawn requesting her help, as unnatural as she may be. She's extremely good at finding the things no one else can." He tilted his head slightly and stared at her as he speared a piece of rare meat that dripped blood onto his plate. "Though you've developed a certain reputation in that area as well."

"And the other," Cambrick muttered as he forked a large chunk of potato into his mouth.

"That we'll discuss another day. I'm sure you can put those urges to rest once you've reacquainted yourselves," he said, not looking at Cambrick, but keeping his steady gaze on her. "Where is Captain Strud headed next?" her father asked and took another bite of meat.

"You mean the Dawn hasn't included you in their updates? Why go after it yourself when you know she's going to get it anyway? Why not just sit back and wait?" Something wasn't adding up, but she couldn't figure out what it was. Direct questions weren't a good idea, as her father had never liked her way of plain speaking, but she needed to keep him talking, if only to delay the night ahead.

"The Golden Dawn is weak." Cambrick licked a drop of meat blood from his fingertip and winked at her. "They started out with the right ideas, but their desire to hold items of power for some moment in the future instead of using them right away is ludicrous. We could take control now. Partnerships with other men who understand power—"

"Shut up, Cambrick." Her father turned his steel gaze towards him. "She's a girl. She has no need for that information. It will only infect her brain even further." He looked away from him slowly, and Cambrick's faced flushed an unbecoming blotchy red. "Now, Miranda—"

"My name is Alex. Miranda died the moment she left this house."

She refused to blanch as her father raised the gun almost idly.

"I named you Miranda, and that's what you will be called and what you will answer to. I have no patience for your continued rebellion. I would rather kill you now, frankly, than not know where you are or in what ways you're debasing yourself. Not to mention tarnishing our family name and your mother's memory."

She picked up her glass and flung the crystal at the wall, where it shattered. "How dare you say a word about her. You have no right."

"No!" He slammed his free hand on the table, making everything rattle. "No. *You* have no right, and you will obey or by God, I swear I will take you out to the stable and put you down like a lame horse. And then I'll deal with Strud, who should join you in hell."

Alex settled her hands in her lap, clasping them hard to keep from lashing out again. "I'd rather you kill me than live life under your roof. Or his." She raised her chin, but the threat against Temp had made her pulse race. "And if you'd ever seen Temp fight, you'd know you have no chance against her."

"What a silly statement from a silly girl." Cambrick shook his head, looking at her pityingly. "You don't have to worry about how good a fighter a woman is, no matter what she uses. And she won't even see us coming."

Cold slid up Alex's spine. "What does that mean? That you'll be cowards and shoot her in the back?"

"Where. Is. She. Headed?" Her father stood and moved to her side of the table, where he pressed the muzzle of the gun to her cheek. "I won't ask again."

"Hey now." Cambrick sat back, his hands folded over his stomach. "I think you might be rushing, old fellow. No need to kill her too quickly. There are other ways to get answers out of her." His gaze slid over her, leaving an oil slick of longing behind. "More pleasant and less messy ways."

Her father grunted and pressed the gun hard to her face before pulling it away. "As distasteful as I find that option, if it's necessary, you have the right."

"He doesn't." Alex thought she might vomit, though she'd eaten nothing and didn't have anything to bring up. Still, bile burned the back of her throat. "Do you really hate me so much?"

He took his seat again and pulled a cigarette case from his coat pocket. "Yes." He tapped the cigarette on the table and lit it. "You have no loyalty. Just like your mother. Where is Strud going next?"

Alex laughed, hysteria and fear nearly making her faint. "I don't know. She had a clue, but I left before we could analyse it." This time, the laugh held less hysteria. "Do what you will to me; you won't get another answer because I genuinely don't know."

"We'll decide the usefulness of the information you do have. We may be able to piece more of it together than your weak women's brains have."

She shuddered again at the look in Cambrick's gaze. "The last information I had was at the cathedral. You were there so you know exactly as much as I do."

"What did you retrieve before we got to you? That...creature..." Cambrick grimaced and took a sip of wine, as though to wash away a foul taste in his mouth. "It fought like something possessed. If we'd had to use only blades, I daresay it would have won the day. Thankfully, it wasn't impervious to airguns, which made short work of it. Odd, though, the way it left no body behind. Just a bit of dust, like you'd find in an attic." He waved his hand. "Anyway, it's dead. What did you get from it?"

"Nothing." Alex wasn't about to tell them about the crown. The least amount of information they had, the better Temp's chances of getting there ahead of her competition.

"I don't believe you." Her father stood and took something from the credenza. He held up a slim bit of black metal with a forked end. With a soft click, light bounced and buzzed between the tines. "Miranda, do not force me to be the monster you've made me out to be. I understand this is an extremely unpleasant experience."

She swallowed hard and looked down at the table, hoping

she looked properly intimidated when she really just wanted him to bring it closer so she could shove the thing in his mouth and turn it on. "Gibberish. She said, 'Väsen know the will of your heart. Choose wrong and join them for eternity.'" Alex shrugged like it didn't mean anything. A large part of lying meant telling the truth. At least, enough of it to feel real. "I don't know what she meant by it or how it was going to help Temp find the answers to the orb."

His eyes flickered like he was taking in new information, and she continued to look at her lap, placid as a mouse.

"Come, Miranda. We all know that you wouldn't give up information so easily. I believe that's an element of it, but you're a liar and a thief. I'm aware this may be a more drawn-out process than I'd like it to be, but needs must." He looked over his shoulder at Cambrick. "Unless you'd like to try to get information out of her before I make markings which will certainly undermine her worth?"

Cambrick nodded slowly, his eyes half-lidded as he licked his lips. "I'd be happy to try that route first."

"Try it, and I will find ways to gut you that would make Jack the Ripper proud." She meant it with every fibre of her being, and it was clear he believed her when he paled slightly. "Indeed, I'll take great pleasure in it."

Her father sighed, and the zapping of the light between the metal tines sizzled in the air. "Then we'll need to take a different route." He rang a bell, and a behemoth of a servant came into the room, strangely light-footed for one so big. "Take my daughter to the information room and see that she's secured. Make sure there's a pen and paper set up so I can make notes as we progress through the evening."

Fear, an emotion she'd shut down the moment she'd escaped from this house before, sent a wave of nausea through her. She leaned over and vomited on the thick Persian rug. *I can't. I'm not strong enough. Please, don't...* But no. She'd be damned to the devil if she'd beg. She had to keep her head and watch for any way out, any moment unguarded enough for her to slip through.

The massive servant stepped to her side, and she saw that gears attached three of his fingers on each hand, slim metal rods running all the way to his elbow. Despite his size and the cold metal that gripped her arm, his expression was surprisingly sympathetic. "Come along, miss. Don't let's make this any harder, eh?"

She shrank from him, and he took her by both arms, pinioning them to her sides and forcing her to walk awkwardly ahead of him. She looked over her shoulder just before they left the room. "Be certain you kill me before letting me go free, because if you don't, you'll find out just how true the legend of Alex Minty is."

"Thank you for the warning, my dear. I'll take it to heart." Her father dipped his head in acknowledgment.

Well and so. Tears blurred her vision as they continued their stilted walk down the long, carpeted hallway that muffled their steps until they got to the wood floors that marked the entrance to the servant's area.

Brick Hilda frowned when they entered and shook her head as she picked up a large ring of keys and then opened the door. "You should have told him what he wanted to hear." Her tone was flat, but even in the hardness of her gaze there was something of the empathetic.

"I don't actually have the information he wants," Alex said, looking at her evenly. "Did he do that to you?" She tilted her head to look up and back at the man holding her. "And to you?"

They looked at each other, and Brick Hilda looked away first. "That's what I said. You should have told him what he wanted to know. Even if it wasn't true."

"Mayhap you'll remember something that will shorten the process for you, miss." The big man moved her forwards into the dimly lit entryway with stairs leading down into darkness. "Would be good if you did."

He let go of her arms when the door closed behind them, cutting off all sound from the servants in the kitchen. He stepped forwards, forcing her to take a step down. And so it went until she got to the bottom and then stepped backwards into him as the horror of what was in front of her made her knees weak.

A thick, long wooden table sat in the middle of the room. Metal shackles were attached by metal rings at each end, covered in what at first glance looked like rust, but at second glance was clearly old blood. Lantern flame sent eerie shadows through the room, highlighting the metal rack against the back wall, also covered with things she didn't want to imagine.

"Tell him what he wants to know, miss. Trust me when I say you don't want to go through this." Again, his tone suggested sympathy, but his bulk pressed her forwards.

She lurched towards the table and then around it, putting it between them. "You expect me to just hold still while you tie me down to be tortured?"

He shrugged. "It will happen anyway. You can put up a fight, but then you'll be too tired to hold out when the baron and the lord come down."

"They do this together, do they?" She gave a sickly laugh. "Of course they do. I imagine my father is teaching him everything he knows."

"Please, miss." He held up his half metal hands, the gears at his elbows creaking. "I'm just doing as I'm told." He glanced at his hands and sighed. "There's a...a medicine, of sorts. Some of the maids use it when the baron or the lord take a shine to them, before..." He grimaced. "It can take some of the pain away before it starts, make it feel like it's happening to someone else. I can get it for you, if you'll just..." He motioned to the table.

Slowly, she shook her head. This was what her father's domain had come to in the time she'd been gone. "No. I'm sorry..." She stopped. "What's your name?"

"Wally, miss." He tilted his head at a sound at the stairs.

"Wally, I left here many years ago and swore I'd never return. I became the most feared pirate in the skies by using my wits and never giving in to bastards who would take advantage of people who can't defend themselves. I don't plan to literally lay down and simply drug myself into a stupor so he can do what he wants to me."

He frowned, his big head tilting to the other side. "Most feared pirate..." His eyes brightened, a wide smile splitting his big face. "Alex Minty! The lady pirate said to be the most ruthless pirate in history."

"That's right. And if you help me, I swear to you on all that's holy, I will set this house to rights." She waited, holding her breath as he studied her in the flickering shadows.

"Okay, miss." He closed his eyes tightly and then reopened them. "I can't let you out of here. That would be too much, as I can't rightly risk the safety of the others. But maybe some of that fighting skill will come in handy. I won't tie you down the way I'm supposed to. I hope it's enough, and I hope you fight your way out and make it so this isn't the gateway to hell."

It wasn't much, but it was more than she'd hoped for. "Thank you, Wally. I'll do my best, and if I don't succeed, I'll make sure I tell them you did your job, and I just managed to get out of the bindings because I'm that good."

"I'd appreciate that, miss." He turned and headed up the stairs, his metal fingers sliding over the handrail. "Good luck."

At the top, light shined in from the kitchen and the clatter of dishes filtered down, and then the door clicked shut, the lock turned, and she was left in silence. She gave herself a moment to take deep breaths. Relief swished through her like a new river, and she leaned on the table for support. Thank the gods her father's staff didn't like him. He'd tried to cow them into obedience through torture, and while it may have worked, it had also served to create an enmity that might just be a way to destroy him.

In the meantime, she needed to find a weapon. After tugging at each of the shackles on the table and finding them solidly worked in, she moved to the metal rack. That was too well crafted for her to remove so much as a sliver of metal. A large wardrobe sat in the dark corner of the far wall, but it was locked. If she had access to her skirt, she'd have had lock picks in one of the pockets as well as a number of safety pins that would have worked to open it, but as it was, she had nothing at all thanks to the stupid outfit they'd put her in. The pink stood out like a beacon of purity in the dark room, an ironic touch if ever there was one. She jerked at the door, tugging and pushing, until sweat ran down her back. Finally, she gave up. There was nothing else in the barren room, which meant it was down to her fighting skills.

She considered that. Both men were well-built and strong but also used to soft living and people who didn't fight back. They expected her to be tied down when they arrived, and it would give her the element of surprise. It was something, at least. She could only conserve her strength and be ready. She found a sliver of wall that didn't seem to have dried gore on it and tried not to think of the horrors this room had witnessed as she sat down on the cold stone, her back to the wall.

Time slowed to a crawl. One after another, the lanterns flickered out until she was in total darkness. Memories assailed her, and she brought her knees to her chest and hugged them to her. So many nights when she was a child, she'd listened to her mother scream from somewhere in the house. Her father's low, evil laughter filtered under the door of her room. One night, she'd been driven out of her room by the sound of her mother's panic. It was in their room where she saw her father straddling her mother, his hands around her neck. She'd thrown herself at him, batting at him with her small hands, shrieking and crying. He'd flicked her aside as carelessly as though she were a fly, but it had given her mother the second she needed to gasp for breath, coughing, her eyes streaming tears.

He'd stood, looking down at her like she was an apparition sent to puzzle him, and then he'd dragged her back to her room by her hair. He'd thrown her in and locked the door behind him.

The maid who let her out in the morning didn't meet her eyes, and when she asked at breakfast where her mother was, his short reply as he read the paper was, "She's gone."

From that time forwards, she'd been locked in her room every night, and she'd never seen her mother again. None of the staff would say a word about her, no matter how she pressed, demanded, or begged.

Which was why she'd hated that moment on Temp's ship when she'd been locked in. When she got out of here, she'd never live in a place that had doors. She'd have them all removed.

Temp. What was she doing now? Was she following up on the origin of the crystal crown? Was she recovering physically? The thought made her smile a little, despite the darkness. Their night hadn't been the kind of relaxing a physician would have recommended, but it had been beyond pleasurable, that was without question. But Alex's fear of being found out, her fear of unfamiliar emotions building to something she couldn't name, and her fear of being expected to become something from the world she'd already fled, had made it so she'd run from the safety at Temp's side right into the fires of her past.

No one knew where she was. No one was coming to save her. She'd lost her crew, she'd betrayed Temp, and the only people who knew where she was were going to torture her for information she didn't have.

She rested her head on her knees and let the tears fall.

Chapter Twenty-Three

Temp tapped her fingers on the missive that had just arrived via crow in response to the one she'd sent the evening before. Outside, clouds drifted past as the Chimera headed along the coast of Wales. She'd made the decision to stay over water until they had to dock at Cardiff-over-Coal to get the new flyer. From there, they'd head up the coastline to the Inner Hebrides, where she'd take the flyer down and begin the land portion of her journey.

"Something wrong?" Wade asked as he tinkered with a vitascope tube attached to the Artful Artifice Contraption.

"I asked my contact at the Golden Dawn if they had knowledge about Billinghurst." When he looked up, his eyebrows raised above his owl-eyes, she shrugged. "I know, I said I wouldn't. But something about what happened at the cathedral has been bothering me. The man said Alex's real name and didn't sound surprised. It was like he was expecting her. I couldn't shake the feeling that I was missing something."

"And?" He glanced at the paper.

"And Billinghurst is no longer a member of the Dawn. They say they've ex-communicated him because he had outlandish ideas that weren't in keeping with their values. They had no idea he'd come to ask my assistance on anything. He and his crony figured I wouldn't check up on them, and I didn't."

"And they killed two birds with one stone. They wanted to find out if Alex was here, and they got your help and then followed you to make sure they got what they wanted and also watched to see if Alex was with you. And she was."

Temp nodded, her stomach starting to hurt. "I told them she

was dead, and then they saw that she wasn't. No wonder they keep trying to kill me."

He swore as he pinched his finger on something and shook out his hand. "But if they killed you, they wouldn't have gotten the Firebird or the crystal. That doesn't make sense."

"It does when we realise that they knew where to get it once it was in my hands. They know it's here on the Chimera. But they also know that the ship is heavily weaponed, and they wouldn't dare move against it. So they hoped to catch me out in the open and take what I had in hand, and then they could come aboard with me gone and take what they wanted in the name of the Dawn, and no one here would have stopped them."

"Is there any chance they'll know where we're headed now?" he said, stopping to look at her. "Are we putting the ship in danger?"

She considered that for a long moment. "No. I don't think so. We only just figured it out, and only the four of us know where we're headed. Alex left before she got that information. So there's no danger, not while I'm alive, at any rate. The crystal is what showed us how to interpret the story in the orb. Without that, the other searchers are wandering about blind right now."

He sat back on his haunches and pushed his goggles up onto his head, making his hair stand up at odd angles. "That's a little bit of good news, at least. But what about Alex?"

"What about her?" Temp had no answers at all regarding Alex, regardless of the meaning of his question.

"Well, it puts her in danger, doesn't it? Right in the baron's crosshairs because he knows she's the famed pirate, and he knows she's alive and searching for the Apple."

Temp shrugged. "I'm not sure she's in any more danger now than she was when we met. He clearly knew she was the pirate Minty before he came to ask for my help, because he knew to ask after her in the first place. As long as she stays clear of him, she'll be as safe as she was before she met us. Given that she left, she's clearly not going to keep searching for the Apple anyway."

He didn't look convinced, but he went back to fiddling with the machine without further comment.

A bell in the room tinkled, and she got up to answer the call coming through the telephone system.

"We're coming up on Cardiff-over-Coal, Captain," the pilot said.

"On my way." She patted Wade on the shoulder and left him tinkering. The walk through the belly of the dragon was even colder now, and she grimaced against the wind that caught at her jacket. Soon she'd have to use the main corridors of the ship, as it would be too cold to take the outlier passages. In the gondola, she took control and manoeuvred the ship towards the docking station. Cardiff-over-Coal was a mid-city, not as high as London but still rising above the mines in the land far below. Carefully, she brought it dockside and confirmed that the lines had been dropped. She held steady as the ship was tied off from below and the plank raised to the main door.

She handed control off to the pilot once again and then headed to her room, where she put on her finest coat and hat and grabbed her new walking stick that matched the sea green of her cravat. Wade was already waiting at the door, and they went down the plank to the docking station office together. He looked around, his large pad cradled in one arm as he sketched what he was seeing without even looking at the paper. It was a solid reminder of how truly talented he was and how lucky she was to have found him.

They signed the docking register and paid the fee. The clerk looked at them wide-eyed, his young face pale. "That's a ship like I've never seen," he whispered, as though sharing a secret with them. "It must be something right special."

"That she is, lad." Temp gave him a quick smile. "Can you point us to the Airship Guild? We've business to attend to, and they're expecting us."

He nodded so quickly his hat fell forwards over his eyes, and he shoved it back, so it nearly fell off the back of his head. "I'll get a boy to show you the way."

Before she could stop him and say they just needed directions, he blew on a whistle that made her and Wade wince. A child of about ten ran into the room, lank hair covering their eyes, holes in both trouser knees, and a bruise down the side of their cheek.

"Aye?" they panted, shoving hair out of their face.

"Take these fine people to the Airship Guild. No nonsense, you hear?"

The child glanced at them and away again. "Aye. You gonna pay me this time? Or you gonna keep it again to *save* it for me?"

The lad flushed red to the tips of his ears and leaned over the desk. "Listen, you little mutt. You take these nice people where they want to go, and then you and I will have a talk about money and manners." He looked almost apologetically at them. "These street urchins don't know nothing. I try to give 'em work, but..."

The child glared at him, hands on their hips. "You can sod off and find another guide. I'm not working for nothin' but a sharp poke."

Temp put her hand on the child's shoulder. "I'll pay you personally. Shall we go?"

The child's eyes narrowed, and they looked her over. "All right. But only as you look like you mightn't stiff me."

She smiled and released the kid's shoulder. She liked the fight in one so small who was clearly intent on standing up for themselves. They followed the kid out of the clerk's office and into the chill sunlight of the day.

"This way." The child waved them on and looked back. "I'm the best guide in the city, you know. I know all the ways in and out."

"What's your name?" Wade asked, continuing to draw as he looked around.

"Black Betty." She raised her chin. "I'm gonna be the fiercest pirate in the sky one day. Even worser than Captain Minty."

A smaller child, sucking her thumb, ran out from an alley and took Betty's hand.

"What are you doin', Sal? I told you to stay put until I was done workin'." Betty grimaced and shrugged. "Sorry about this. Me sister don't like stayin' alone."

Temp met Wade's eye before he looked away again, shaking his head. "You live on the streets here? How is it you've come to live in a sky city?"

The child shrugged, tugging her small sister along with her. "Ma died of a fever, and Pa decided we'd have a better chance here. He sold his coal mine to a posh git who lives up here in exchange for a house for us. But then the man said Pa stole from him and got him sent back down. Pa hid us, said we'd be better off on the streets here than down there, and that we might make somethin' of our sens here. Become a lady's maid or summat." She sniffed like she smelled something sickly. "Not me. I'm going to be a pirate."

They turned a corner, and the little girl tripped, skinning her knee beneath the threadbare skirt. She began to cry, and Betty squatted down in front of her, giving Temp and Wade a worried look. "She'll be fine. Just give us a second."

Wade thrust the book and pencil at Temp, then scooped the little girl into his arms and rubbed her back. She rested her head on his shoulder, thumb in her mouth, and closed her eyes. "It's no problem. Lead on."

Betty stared at them, wide-eyed, and then seemed to really look at Temp. Her eyes went round, and she pointed. "You're a girl! A girl like me!" She reached out like she was going to touch Temp's trousers then pulled back and looked down at her own, and her expression flashed from embarrassment to anger to awe to defiance. "Are you some posh git like the one as sold my pa out?"

"No, Betty. I'm a ship's captain too. On one of the finest ships in the sky." She heard Wade humming softly, rocking as he cradled the child. She didn't even know he liked children, let alone was good with them. "Lead the way?"

She nodded and walked beside Temp this time, looking up at

her as they walked down the cobbles. "How did you do it? How do I do it? Become a captain of a fine ship, I mean? I want to dress fine like you. Everyone says Minty wears skirts and corsets, which is fine for her, but I don't want that."

Temp had no idea what to say. She'd been so incredibly lucky to be born to the parents she had; it had given her advantages other children didn't get. That included her training to fly under her father's tutelage. This child had none of those things.

"When you're older, probably about fifteen or so, you can take an apprenticeship on an airship. We have a lad, Peter, who did just that. He started at the very bottom, cleaning and watching, then trained up until he became a second-in-command."

"Fifteen?" Betty's voice rose. "That's forever away. Another five years. Why do I have to wait so long? Can't I start training now?" Her eyes brightened. "In fact, I could do it on your ship. We wouldn't be no hassle, I swear it!" She stopped and pointed. "This is the Airship Guild."

Wade sat down on the stairs and looked at Temp, and she read the despair and sadness in his eyes. "I'll wait here."

She nodded and ruffled Betty's hair. "Back in a minute. Stay with Wade."

Betty sat next to him and started in with a barrage of questions. Temp went in and was met by a smart-looking young man who rose and saluted. "Captain Strud? We've been expecting you." He looked over her shoulder at the threesome on the steps. "I hope the little lasses haven't bothered you. They're harmless."

She shook her head. "Is there no one here willing to take them in?"

He looked at the paperwork under his hands. "Things don't work here the way they do in other sky cities." He tilted his head. "Or mayhap they do. I don't know; I've never been to the others. But here, there are three families who run everything, and they're not kindly disposed towards helping others. If they knew the lasses were here, they'd have them flown right down to the land, and anyone who helped them would be sent off too, most like. So we try to keep an eye and give them little jobs when we can. Tell them to keep out of sight."

"The sky cities were supposed to make things better, not become bastions of greed and cruelty." When it was clear he didn't have an answer to that, she shrugged. "Anyway. It's good you keep an eye out. Is my flyer ready?"

He grinned, clearly relieved. "Yes, Captain. Here's the paperwork. She's a real beauty. Made from the lightest wood but a nice strong frame. Even has a crow system built in so you can send and receive messages. Real handy, I imagine, for someone who sails the way you do."

Temp looked over the paperwork, which was all in order, and noticed the little additions Wade had suggested. It would work perfectly for the upcoming flight. "Do you have any waterproof covers available? And maybe a small pot of pitch in case of emergency?"

"Covers and pitch? Are you already planning on having problems on her?" He grinned. "I've got both. Come on out back, and you can choose your own."

She followed him out, hearing Wade's low voice answer one of Betty's many questions. They reached a stack of coverings and a shelf of pitch and brushes, and she chose based on what she thought she might need as she headed for the fairy pools. He wrote everything down and said he'd personally place it in the flyer.

"Thank you." She shook his hand and returned to the threesome on the steps. Betty had gone quiet, her head resting against Wade's arm.

"Got everything?" he asked, looking up at her.

"I did." She crouched next to Betty. "Now, can you lead me to a tailor who could provide me with winter clothes?"

Betty bit her lip. "I could. Thing is, the best one is in the really posh bit, and Pa warned us to stay away from there. Christopher too," she tilted her head back towards the lad inside, "says it's best to stay away from the mean-looking ones. You know, the ones in fancy clothes who look like there are golems behind the eyes."

It was an apt description of some of the society people Temp had known. "Well, if they ask, we'll say you're with us, and they won't give you any problems. Is that okay? If it isn't, I can pay you now, and you can just direct us. I don't want you in trouble."

Betty stood, yawning widely. She probably hadn't been able to relax her guard in a long time, and this moment with Wade had given her that. "Long as you say we're with you, I'm good with it. Come on," she said, slipping her small hand into Temp's and tugging.

She wondered what they looked like, walking along the street as a foursome. Wade, with his hair unbrushed and the ever-present goggles atop his head, his many pockets bulging with gears, tools, and other sundry things, holding a sleeping child in threadbare clothing. And then Temp, dressed in her finest clothing tailored just for her by Ede and Ravenscroft in London-on-High, being led by a child who wore more dirt than clothing. All they needed now was Alex in her pirate garb to complete the odd picture.

What would Alex think? What would she do? Temp knew, really. There was no way on earth Alex would leave these children on the street to fend for themselves. "But a pirate ship is a better place for them than the Chimera," she murmured.

Wade glanced over. "Strange, isn't it? I was just thinking the same. Chimera is no place for children. And yet?" He shook his head, falling silent.

While the city was nice enough by the docks, it grew steadily nicer until the stairs were made of marble, and the roads were swept so clean, meals could be served on them. Ladies in hobble skirts and absurdly wide-brimmed hats full of feathers strolled the streets looking in shop windows. Two-person steam carriages made their way up the streets, gears working quietly as though they knew better than to make extra noise.

Betty stopped and nodded towards a shop. "That there is

where the people go to get fine clothes."

Temp thought of Alex and nodded. "In we go then."

Betty yanked her hand out of Temp's and looked like she might grab her sister right out of Wade's arms. "You said we'd be safe with you. We won't be if you take us in there."

Temp knelt on one knee in front of her, placing her hand gently on Betty's shoulder. "I'd like to get you and your sister some new clothes, as a way to say thank you for the excellent service you've provided me today. It's going to get cold, and you'll both need better than what you have on."

Betty's look turned mutinous. "We can't eat clothes. Better you just pay me so we can go on our way, and I can get us some food."

"I'll pay you as well, don't worry. This is extra. Please allow me to do it, as I believe any future captain should wear the appropriate clothing."

Betty stared at her for a moment, still biting her lip, then glanced at her sister. "If you want to, it's your dosh." For a moment, her vulnerability slipped out from behind her mask. "You swear you won't let them throw us off?"

"I swear it, by my captain's oath." She held out her hand and smiled when Betty shook it solemnly. "Now, let's get inside before it gets much colder."

Wade winked at her, and he and the children followed her inside. A severe-looking man in a fine suit came out from behind the desk. His smile faltered a little when she saw the group, but he recovered quickly after giving Temp a once over.

"How may I be of assistance? I can see you've fine taste. That's an Ede and Ravenscroft creation, if I'm not mistaken? We have several items from their new fall collection." His tone was smooth and if he had misgivings, he didn't voice them.

"I'm in need of a full outfit that can handle the Scottish coastal weather. And my three friends here need to be fully outfitted as well." She motioned behind her. "You can outfit the children, I assume? Or do I need to go elsewhere for that?"

He looked past her at the girls, and she could see the way his mind was working to figure out their connection. He likely assumed Wade was their father, given his somewhat messy presentation. So he'd think Wade was staff and the girls his children. That would work well for them, since Temp wasn't known to travel with anyone. It would help keep them low profile. She grinned at the thought. Alex would say there was nothing low profile about Temp in her suit and tie.

"I can bring someone in to help the children, and if you don't mind me saying, I think I know someone who might be able to outfit your man in a style that seems more fitting to him."

Temp arched her eyebrow. "And in what manner would that be?"

"In the manner of a maker, I believe?" He wasn't put off by her tone. "He seems a man who needs ways to transport the many things of his trade."

She smiled and was glad to see some light in his eyes in the returning smile. "You're right. He does at that."

He nodded and motioned towards a small room. "Please sit, and I'll make the necessary arrangements. I assume you want this done today? Very well," he said when she nodded. "I'll have refreshments brought in."

Temp, Wade, and the girls went into the small reception area, and Temp took a seat on a plush leather settee. Wade settled into a chair and moved the sleeping child into a better position. She barely stirred. Betty stood in the middle of the room, mouth agape as she took it all in.

"Crikey," she whispered. "And this is just a shop. What do people's houses look like?"

"Some look like this. Some look even lovelier. Some aren't as nice."

"Like people." Betty nodded sagely and sat on the carpet at Temp's feet.

"You can sit up here next to me, Betty." Temp felt strange having the little girl sit on the floor.

"Nah. I'd get it dirty, and he'd get cross." Betty spread her fingers in the carpet. "And this feels nice anyway." She yawned and lay on her side. "I'll just take a kip while we wait." Her eyes closed, and her breathing slowed.

Wade looked at Temp. "Ideas?"

She shook her head. "We can't leave them. The boy at the Airship Guild said no one here will take them in. Something to do with the politics. We could take them aboard and then find them an orphanage in London."

He winced. "Those aren't nice places."

"But the Chimera isn't a place for kids. A ship where dreams and vices are made reality isn't safe for them." It was the first time she'd had cause to doubt the services she rendered. "Peter had a good head on him. I didn't need to worry, and he was older."

Wade nodded, softly caressing the hair of the child on his lap. "These are young. Imagine their father leaving them?"

"I can't. But if his reasoning was true, then he gave them the best shot. At least there's no crime here for them to contend with."

Wade shook his head. "They'd be better off with their father, even if it meant working in the mines. They could starve or freeze to death up here. It's amazing they've made it this far."

"Did you ever want a family, Wade?" she asked, hoping it wasn't crossing a line.

He looked thoughtful. "Sometimes. But I've always liked my machines better than people. No one ever wants to be with a maker who probably won't make enough to feed them, let alone little ones."

"But like Alex said, your work is truly incredible craftmanship. You could make more than you think, and probably end up being in demand. If you wanted that life, you could have it." Temp had no doubt of that, and though she'd hate to lose him, she wanted him to be happy.

"Thank you." He smiled, looking directly at her for a moment.

"But I'm happy where I'm at. If the day comes when that changes, I'll let you know."

The tailor came in, his hands behind his back. "The other clothiers are on their way. We could start with you, if you'd like, Miss...?"

"Captain." Temp stood. "American Naval Airship Captain." It had been true at one time, and it would stand for the moment.

He nodded and looked suitably impressed. "Very well, Captain. If you'll come this way, we'll get started."

The rest of the afternoon was spent choosing materials and discussing what was needed. Three other tailors came in, all followed by assistants carrying a multitude of cases and cloth. Wade stood aside with a man who was attired similarly, and they talked about clothing as much as they talked about gears and materials for building.

The women went to the girls and began to make a fuss, and Temp had to intervene when she heard Betty's voice raised.

"I don't want no skirt!" She stamped her little foot.

Temp put her hand on the girl's shoulder and looked at the woman. "Please outfit Betty as you would a young lad about to be apprenticed on a prestigious ship. And provide extra trousers and shirts."

The adoration in Betty's eyes could have rivalled the stars in the sky. "Thank you," she whispered.

The woman looked horrified, however. "But...but..."

"Women are wearing trousers more often now, are they not? For riding bicycles and horses? She can just get used to it now." Temp kept her tone firm. "Thank you."

The woman swallowed and shook her head. "Very well."

Temp settled the bill, which was low in comparison to the shops in London, and gave extra to the assistants who'd helped with Wade and the girls' clothing. It wasn't a great idea to make an impression as someone with plenty of money, but she was fully aware of what it meant to deal with customers who wanted specific things and wanted them quickly. She arranged to have most of the new clothing sent on to the ship, but Betty and her sister wore a set of their new items, and her little sister twirled and twirled in the new dress until she grew dizzy and sat down with a thump.

"Dinner, I think." Temp led the way out, and her heart swelled at the sight of Betty striding proudly beside her, chin held high, her face aglow with pride. *That's how every child should feel.* The thought brought her back to Alex and what she'd likely endured at the hands of her father. They walked into a dining establishment and the maître d' guided them to a table without hesitation, though he did look a little askance at Wade, who still looked like he'd been sleeping under a hedge.

The meal was good, and Temp didn't mind that the girls ordered more than they could eat. Betty said they hadn't had anything but a burned loaf of bread the baker had tossed out the back door to them the day before.

When they were done, Betty grew quiet. "Are you leaving now?"

Temp looked at Wade, who raised his eyebrows. "We are."

She nodded. "Well, it was good while it lasted. Greatest day we've ever had, I reckon. And we'll take right good care of these clothes, I swear it."

Temp nodded and could only pray she was making the right choice. "Betty, how would you and your sister like to come with us?"

Betty stared at her, and then slowly moved to kneel on the chair so she was looking Temp in the eye. "And live on the ship, with you and Wade?"

"Not permanently. Our ship...it isn't a good place for kids. But we'll take you away from here, and we'll find somewhere appropriate for you and your sister to grow up. Somewhere you won't have to beg or sleep on the streets. Where you'll be safe."

Betty bit her lip, her expression dimming a little with the news it wouldn't be forever. She looked at her sister, who had fallen asleep, her head pillowed on her arms on the table. "What about my pa?

What if he comes back looking for us?"

The hopefulness of a child. What a thing to have. Temp hadn't given him another thought, and she doubted he'd ever come back. "We can leave our information with the dock clerk. If your father comes asking after you, the clerk will know where to find you. But you'll have to earn your keep, you know. Learn your letters, help in the kitchen. That kind of thing."

Betty's face lit up. "Then we have a deal." She stuck out her hand, and Temp shook it.

"Very well. Off we go." They made their way back to the ship, and Temp continued to wonder if she'd done the right thing. Wade carried Betty's little sister, and Betty walked alongside Temp, her arms swinging freely as she asked questions about airships. At the dock, Temp was assured the new flyer had been loaded into the Chimera's belly and all the packages had been taken by her staff. She went in and gave Wade's information to the clerk, using the address they had in London-on-High instead of giving the Chimera's name. A basic description of the ship would give them away, but it was better than nothing.

Outside, Betty stood leaning against Wade's side, her mouth open as she stared at the ship. "You have a dragon," she breathed out softly. "A real dragon."

"Not quite. But she's beautiful, isn't she?" She walked forwards. "Time to go."

Betty was, likely for the first time, lost for words as they made their way onboard.

Joe and Peter were waiting, and their puzzled expressions meant she'd have to explain, though she wasn't certain she had an explanation that made any sense. "This is Betty and Sally. They're going to be staying with us for a time, until we find suitable arrangements. Joe, can you please take them and get them set up in a room in the servants' quarters?"

"Do they..." Joe looked around. "Is there a nanny?" He didn't seem to know quite what to say.

Temp sighed. "I should have thought of that. No. Can you spare any member of staff who might have that capability?"

He smiled at Betty and took Sally from Wade. She barely murmured before settling back to sleep in Joe's arms. "We'll figure it out, won't we, girls?" He tilted his head. "Betty, this here is Peter. He runs the ship when Captain Strud isn't about. If you need anything, until we get someone to look out for you, you can come to us. Is that acceptable?"

She looked up at Temp, who nodded. "All right then. But you're not going to separate us, are you?"

He shook his head and held out his hand. "No, not at all. Come, I'll show you to a room."

Betty looked back over her shoulder as they walked away, fear in her eyes.

"Hold on, Joe." Temp went over and crouched down. "Are you okay? Are you sure you want to come with us?"

Betty swallowed hard. "It's just...*I'm* not scared." She said it as though to convince herself. "I'm not scared for me, mind you. Just for Sally. What if she gets scared in the night because we're somewhere new?"

Peter knelt next to Temp. "I'll be sleeping in the room right next to yours. If you...if Sally gets scared in the night, then I'll be right there. You just have to knock on the wall."

She took a deep breath. "All right then."

Temp watched as the four of them walked away.

"Now that they're settled, we'd better get on with our own planning." Wade patted her shoulder. "You did the right thing."

"I hope so." They walked to her office together, talking through the items she'd ordered. "I like the new touches you made to the flyer. They'll be useful."

In her office, they went over the map again, and then were joined by Joe and Peter, who looked at her expectantly. She explained the situation, and Joe smiled.

"Your parents would be proud, Temp." He clapped her on the

shoulder. "Don't worry. We'll keep an eye on them and make sure they stay away from the passenger areas."

"Good. Thank you. I'm going to take the ship up, and we'll head north. Did you get all the supplies you needed?"

"Everything, plus some extra. We're as ready as we can be." He frowned. "I'm still not happy about you taking Peter with you, Temp."

Peter frowned. "But I want to go. I'm ready."

"I know you are. Which is why you're going with me. But Peter, these people are dangerous. More than any we've encountered before, and they won't refrain from firing just because you're young. You have to promise me you won't take any extra risks."

He nearly glowed with excitement. "I promise, Cap."

She looked at the small team of people she considered family. "Then let's go find some treasure."

Chapter Twenty-Four

ALEX WOKE, CONFUSED AS to where she was, when a creaking sound bounced off the walls of the gruesome room. Light made her blink, and realisation brought her quickly to her feet. Her father stood backlit, a menacing shadow.

"Get up. You've been given a reprieve."

She stayed where she was. "What do you mean?"

"Captain Strud's ship is on the move, and we're going to follow it. I'm taking you along for insurance. She has a reputation for chivalry, and if I put a gun to your head, she might see enough value in you to give me what I want. Don't make me drag you onto the ship, Miranda. I'll gladly do so and save myself the idiocy of the things you say."

Anything was better than this locked room, and being on a ship meant a thousand options of escape. She moved forwards, her body aching from having slept on the cold stone floor. She stopped ten feet from him, waiting for him to move. Behind him were two large men.

"Hold out your wrists." After she did so, he turned aside. "Make sure she's properly bound. If she escapes, I will kill you both." He walked away without a backwards glance.

The men moved in, and their faces may as well have been carved of stone, so little expression did they have. She was too tired to care. Cold metal slid around her wrists and locked into place, and then one of them shoved her forwards into the house. They marched her out the front to a growler carriage. She climbed in awkwardly without the use of her hands and stumbled, only to be shoved aside into the seat.

Her father and Cambrick sat facing her, and a man with an air rifle attached to his back sat beside her. One of the men who'd escorted her through the house reached in and attached manacles to her ankles, a chain linked between them. Then he handed her father the key and shut the door.

"I stole her flyer and left without a word. She won't care if you kill me." It wasn't true. No matter what Temp felt about her right now, her father was right. Temp was too good a person to watch someone be killed outright. But then...what was one life weighed against the threat to millions? Temp was also practical, and she'd faced the same choice once before. How often would she choose Alex over the fate of the world?

"Say anything more, and I'll have you gagged as well." Her father looked out the window and tapped the roof. The carriage jerked, and they moved forwards through the dark.

The ship they boarded wasn't anything special. A small airship with air cannons attached to the sides, it was functional rather than luxurious, which surprised her a little. Her father wasn't one to give up his finery. It was only when she saw more men in uniform and heard the accents that she understood another piece of the puzzle.

"You're in league with the Kaiser."

Cambrick shrugged, stretching his legs out in front of him. "It's important to ally yourself with the people who have the most power. Once the Dawn showed us they weren't worthy of our loyalty, we found someone who was."

"Why not just take it for yourselves? Rule the world as despots." The more information she had, the more she might be able to use when the time came for her to escape, and hopefully help Temp do so as well.

"Who says we won't?" Cambrick scanned the men around them, busy getting ready to upship. "The man who lays his hand on the Apple first will be the one to win the day."

"My father will kill you before he lets you anywhere near it. You're a fool if you think he isn't planning getting to it first."

His eyes darkened as he stared at her. "And maybe I have a plan in place for that too." He leaned forwards. "And when I'm the one in charge, you'll fall into line. You'll be so grateful, so in *love*," he sneered at this, the word a mockery, "that you'll never want to leave my side."

"There isn't enough magic in the world to make that happen." She leaned closer too, able to smell his cigar-laden breath. "There will never be a moment I won't want to stick a knife between your ribs."

He sat back and folded his hands over his stomach. "Then I guess I'll have to kill you the moment I've got it in my hands."

Her father sat in the seat beside Cambrick. "Trying to woo her, are you?"

"Doing my best."

Alex looked away, sickened by the sight of them. Despite her decision to be stoic, fear flooded her at the thought that Temp had no idea she was being followed, nor that there was a small army coming at her. Somehow, she had to find a way to help her.

$$***$$

The journey was long and dull. She refused to fall asleep, lest Cambrick decide to molest her in some way, but he fell asleep and snored for most of the trip. Her father read a paper, then stared out the window. There was quiet conversation between the other men, but she'd never felt the need to learn German, and her father's men remained as silent as he was.

"Why?" she asked, after hours left alone with her own thoughts.

He looked at her. "Why what, Miranda?"

"Why did you care when I left?"

"Unfortunately, you're my only child." He tilted his head, looking at her like one might a cow at auction. "Marrying you to Cambrick and combining our families' wealth was a way to leave a legacy. That was before I knew about the Apple, which will make the need for a legacy via my offspring unnecessary. But that's why, to answer your question."

Alex couldn't quite follow. "Why not just go into business with him? Why involve me at all?"

"Because you carry the family name, Miranda, much as I wish it were otherwise. When I die, I want what I've built to stay in the family, not be portioned out to business partners. I have it in writing that any child created within the confines of your marriage to Cambrick would be my true heir."

Alex laughed dryly. "Then you'll be waiting until you're reborn as the cockroach you are. I'm *never* having children. I'd never bring them into a world where men like you exist."

He yawned. "Once I have the Apple, I won't care. I'll continue to build my empire, and Cambrick will be nothing more than a servant like all the others. You will no longer be able to besmirch my good name."

She thought she saw Cambrick shift, just a little, his eyes flutter. But his breathing evened out, and she couldn't be sure. "No loyalty among thieves," she said.

"Loyalty is irrelevant when you're immortal."

"It's good you think so, since no one in their right mind would give it to you."

Before he could respond, one of the crew came up from the gondola hatch. "The dragon ship has dropped anchor. If we do so as well, we risk being seen."

Alex looked out the window. The horizon dipped as the ship was buffeted by the winds, and the sea churned below, white caps frothing like wild animals. Dawn seemed a long way off, and any stars were blocked by a layer of dark clouds.

"Where are we?" her father asked, standing and kicking at Cambrick's feet to wake him.

"The Inner Hebrides, sir. The dragon has docked at a village called Eynort."

Her father looked at her, and she shrugged. "Like I said, I left before I had the next clue. I have no idea."

He turned back to the crewman. "Watch for movement from the ship. As soon as anyone leaves it, drop ropes, and we'll follow."

Alex desperately wanted to go to the other port window to see the Chimera, but she knew full well her father wouldn't allow it.

Cambrick yawned and went over himself. "That's some ship," he said, looking over his shoulder at her. "You've been on it?"

She simply stared at him.

"I thought so. You were on it when we came looking for you, weren't you? We should have just burned it out of the sky right then." He looked back outside. "Look. There."

Her father looked outside as well. "A lone flyer. How stupid is she to head out there alone?" He turned to the crewman. "Dock and get us a few flyers to follow far enough behind she won't see us."

"Sir, the winds—"

"Do it."

The man hesitated, then went below to the gondola to confer with the pilot.

Her father held up the key to Alex's shackles. "I'm going to undo the ankle chain, as I need you to be able to move quickly." He tapped the key against the airgun at his side. "Have no doubt whatsoever that I will shoot you if you so much as blink the wrong way. I want you as insurance, but I don't need you. Do you understand me?"

Alex gave a short nod. She wanted to be near Temp, and if this was the way it happened, so be it. She could escape when they were closer.

He undid the metal cuffs around her ankles, and they clanged against the floor as he dropped them. "Let's go."

She followed the line of men to the plank leading to the dock and was struck by the intense cold as well as the depth of the darkness. It was pitch black beyond the lanterns lighting the dock office. No lights burned in windows or on roads. It was nearly impossible to see anything other than the shadows of a large mountain range in the distance.

"Flying in this light is madness," Cambrick muttered, also looking into the darkness.

"You're right. We shouldn't do it. Let's wait until full light so she can see you coming and know exactly where to aim her weapon." Alex smiled sweetly, and her head slammed to the side when the back of his hand made contact with her cheek.

"There are three flyers available, sir." One of the German crew came over, his gaze sliding over her like oil before returning to her father. "There are two three-seaters and one two-seater."

"Eight against one. Seems like reasonable odds." Her father's white teeth shone in the dark as he gave a wolfish smile. "You saw the direction she went?"

The man frowned. "We did. But it will be easy to miss her in this light. If she turned, or even if she landed in a valley, we may not see her."

Her father pulled his airgun and aimed it at the man's head. "I suggest you make sure that doesn't happen."

The man swallowed hard, gave a short nod, and headed to the flyers.

"Cambrick, you and I and Miranda will take one flyer and leave the other two to the crew. We'll stay in the middle so we're protected should she fire from the ground." He raised his voice slightly. "Remember, do *not* kill her. We need the information she has to get what we've come for. Maim or injure, but do not kill."

Alex swallowed the panic building in her throat that made her want to scream a warning into the night. It wouldn't do her or Temp any good for her to lose her head now. Getting into the flyer was awkward, and she twisted her ankle when she went down, her bound hands slipping on the condensation and making it so she fell into the seat. Within seconds, they were upship, all three flyers nearly silent as they set off into the darkness.

Please see us, Temp. Please don't get caught out. She watched the hilly scenery below as the wind whipped at the small crafts, sometimes forcing them nearly sideways. No sails were up, as the gusts would have caused them to spin out of control. Only the steam and gears propelled them forwards, but the crafts were nearly too light to handle the frigid Scottish weather.

A light blinked in the flyer next to them, and the pilot pointed. Ahead, a lone flyer sat on the ground, tilted awkwardly on the rocky hill. A shape moved in the dark, away from it.

Her father motioned, and all three flyers moved lightning fast to the ground, one ahead of the moving figure, the other two behind. They landed with thumps, and the military crew were up and out of the flyers in an instant, weapons raised.

Light flashed, and two of the men went down without discharging their guns.

Her father swore and stood on the wing of the flyer, yanking Alex out behind him. "Captain Strud," he yelled, holding Alex in front of him like a shield. "I believe we have a friend of yours who would look far less winsome with a hole in her head." He jabbed his gun hard into her kidney. "Say something," he hissed.

"Temp, run!" she yelled, and then gasped when he threw her from the wing of the flyer. She landed hard on her shoulder and heard a bone snap somewhere in her arm. "Bastards of Bell's tits, that hurts." She groaned and rolled to her other side, cradling her arm.

He jerked her up by her hair after jumping down next to her. "In fact, I think she might already be injured. Shall I put her out of her misery? Or will you be practical about this?"

"Let her go." Temp's voice came out of the darkness.

"No, I don't think so." Her father scanned the night, trying to spot her. Cambrick moved to the right, and the other crew to the left. "But we can make a deal. You help me get what I want, and I won't make her unrecognizable."

Alex shivered, and it wasn't from the cold. There was something else here, something not right. The shadows moved strangely against the base of the mountains. River water running towards the sea was the only other sound. Goosebumps ran over her arms. They weren't alone.

"Fine." Temp rose from a crouch, her gun held high. She tossed it aside. "Let her go. I'll need her knowledge to keep going anyway."

He grinned and shoved Alex forwards. "I knew you'd see reason."

Alex stumbled towards Temp, awkwardly holding her arm, her wrists still bound. Her sore ankle protested the uneven ground under the thin shoes. Temp opened her arms, and Alex fell into them. "I'm so sorry," she mumbled against Temp's chest. "I couldn't stop him."

Temp held onto her. "Are you hurt?"

Alex nodded. "But not so much I couldn't put a knife into his neck if I could use my hands."

Temp held her gently at arm's length. "Hopefully you'll get your chance. How many are there?"

"Six, including me."

Her father, Cambrick, and the German crew surrounded them, weapons still raised. "Now. Where are we going next, Captain?" her father asked.

Temp took a deep breath, clearly debating her next move. Alex was certain she had other weapons on her, but they were outnumbered, and Alex wasn't exactly in perfect shape.

"Before you waste any more time wondering, I will gladly shoot you both and continue to search the area myself if necessary. But it could be you both make it out of this alive, should you help me get what I want."

Temp glanced into Alex's eyes, and Alex shook her head a little. No, he wouldn't let them go.

"Very well. Use this to keep you steady." She handed Alex her cane and moved away. "I only have vague clues to work with. Do you have the orb?"

Alex had forgotten about the orb entirely. She thought

Willoughby had it, but her father motioned and one of the crew pulled it out of a canvas bag. She held the cane tightly. It was their only weapon, so she'd have to use it wisely. "You're working with him too?"

"No need to have all your eggs in one basket, my dear. Willoughby is a thug, like you, and like you, he had no loyalty. He gave me the orb in return for money which he'll never get the chance to spend."

Well, at least it was one less villain to deal with. It also explained how her father had tracked her to the Chimera and made the connection to Temp. "We should have killed him when we had the chance." Alex grimaced at the pain in her arm. "Now what?"

Temp's jaw clenched as she scanned the men surrounding them. "The last artefact suggests the Apple will be somewhere in the vicinity of these pools. Normal fairy pools are fairly shallow, where waterfalls drop into pools before they move on down the river and drop into lower pools. The story in the runes said there'd be an arch under water. That's what we're looking for. After that?" She shrugged.

"Get moving." Her father waved his gun.

Temp led the way, with Alex limping beside her. They walked along heather-clad boulders on one side and the rushing river on the other. Temp kept her hand out, helping steady Alex as they went. The sound of falling water made her look up, and she caught her breath. The waterfall was stunning. The pool at the bottom of it was wide and clear enough to reflect the stars, even as small fish swam among them.

"Fan out. Look for an arch." The group did as they were told, but there wasn't a moment when one of them didn't have a gun aimed at them.

"What's in the bag?" Alex asked, leaning against a boulder as Temp bent low to look at the water.

"Diving gear, towels, that kind of thing." Temp looked back at her with a small smile. "I don't know about you, but I have no desire to get into the water again."

Alex smiled back, her heart breaking a little at the gentle emotion she saw in Temp's eyes. Something caught her attention though. Movement, like fog in the shape of a person, just beyond the crest of the hill. It disappeared, and she shivered.

"What is it?" Temp asked softly, not looking at her.

"What did the guardian at the cathedral say about väsen?"

Temp frowned and scanned the area. "The gods who weren't pure enough were turned to väsen to protect the land and the detritus the other gods left behind." She glanced back. "And the guardian said you'd have to be the one to convince them you were done running."

"Guess I've already failed that one." Alex tipped her head towards the hill. "I'm sure there's something out there."

"There's no such thing as ghosts and goblins, Miranda."

She looked up to see her father on the small ridge above her.

"You believe in an apple that can give you immortality but not in a creature that might be in place to protect it?" Temp asked, continuing to walk the edge of the pool. "That's illogical. If you believe in the one, you should believe in the other."

He grunted but didn't respond, making Alex smile.

"I don't see anything like an arch. We should keep going." Temp looked at Alex for a moment, then up at her father. "Although I'm tempted to say you should kill us both now. I'm the only one with the clues, and if I'm dead, you won't find what you're looking for."

His ugly laugh echoed against the waterfall. "You might be willing to die, but will you watch me kill Miranda slowly? Are you willing to watch her suffer, Captain?" He kicked at the dirt, making it fall below onto Alex's head. "Because I assure you, I can make it last."

Temp closed her eyes. "We keep going."

Alex followed, holding Temp's arm not just to steady herself. "He's going to kill us anyway. You're just delaying it."

"I'm playing for time," Temp said, her voice low. "They don't know about the väsen. Just like we got away by swimming in the Trent, there might be a way out ahead. We just have to find it."

Alex hoped like hell that was true, and she stayed quiet to concentrate on the slippery, uneven footing. The sound of water crashing made her look up again. "Hades' boots," she said softly.

The waterfall was bigger, falling into a pool that looked green even in the dark. "Turquoise pools," Temp murmured. "Part of the story we deciphered."

"Look up," Alex whispered.

Light had started to shift in the sky. First, just a little emerald against the black, and then it became sheets of vibrant green that turned into red ribbons the higher it reached into the dark. The occasional purple ribbon shot through like a spirit dancer.

"There." Temp crouched at the edge of the pool, where the lights danced across the surface, mirroring the motion in the sky. And in the middle, beneath the water, a stone arch lay submerged. It was impossible to see through it into whatever lay beyond.

"What are you waiting for? Get in there," her father said. "Did you bring anyone with you, Captain?"

She frowned and looked at him. "I came alone. I wouldn't subject any of my crew to this. Why?"

He looked about them, his eyes wide. "I could have sworn I saw something…" He shook it off. "Get in there."

Temp stood and opened the sack. She pulled out a variety of odd-looking things.

"What are those? No tricks." Cambrick snapped at her, his gun gears clicking as he tightened his finger on the trigger.

Temp rolled her eyes. "It's a diving suit. I don't know how deep this pool is, but if I'm swimming under an arch, I'll need to hold my breath. Unless you brought a submersible? No?" She waved at the gear. "I'm going to need the orb. I'll take it down with me and see how it fits with the other pieces."

He shook his head. "Give you everything and have you lay hands on the Apple first? There is no way on God's green earth I will let that happen. You see what's down there first, and then we'll decide how to proceed."

"That's ludicrous. You know I won't leave Alex in your hands for any longer than necessary. Give me the orb so I can do what we came here to do."

Her father aimed the gun at Alex's head. "We do this my way."

Temp gritted her teeth and shook her head. "Idiots." She pulled two small packages from her sack, and Alex knew they were the Firebird and the crown. She tucked them into a leather pouch with a long strap.

"Hurry up."

Alex sat on a rock, her ankle and arm throbbing bad enough to make her eyes water. "What can I do?"

"I'll show you in a second." Temp proceeded to disrobe, laying her clothes neatly on a rock beside Alex. She stripped down to a one-piece bathing costume that covered her arms and went down to her knees. One of the men whistled, making the others laugh. Then the clinking and clanking began as she hung a thick bladder-like pouch on her chest and attached it to a copper cylinder that she hung on her back. Tubes attached to it that she then screwed into ports on a mask she pulled over her face. Last, she added the leather pouch, which she slung across her body, tightening it so it lay snug to her back.

It was eerie, and she could easily have been one of the väsen protecting the waterfalls. "Be careful," Alex said.

Temp nodded, and then added one more item to her gear. She tied a thick rope around her waist before handing Alex the rest of it. Alex set the cane beside her on the rock, then gripped the rope hard with her good hand and prayed like hell she wouldn't need to pull Temp out. She wouldn't have the strength with just one good arm.

Temp patted her shoulder and then waded into the pool. They could hear her swear at the cold even with the mask on. When she was halfway in, Alex stood, unable to sit still.

And then she saw it.

A strange blue face covered in whorls, framed with long dark hair, rose slowly out of the water, looked at her, and then dropped below again with barely a ripple. Alex screamed and tugged the rope to pull Temp back.

It floated to the surface, and Temp was gone.

Chapter Twenty-Five

Temp breathed slowly, just the way she'd been trained to when she'd met the maker of this device. It would only give her seven minutes, but she hadn't told them that. She hadn't wanted to worry Alex and risk being pulled back too soon.

Just as she went under, she thought she heard something, but the weight of the gear pulled her down and then she was swimming. The mask meant she could see the water churning below the fall, and the colours of the sky seemed to dance through the water like mystical creatures. It was surreal and serene, and the sound of her breathing seemed too loud for this place.

Forcing herself to focus, she turned towards the arch. It was attached to the sides of rock like an underwater bridge, and then she saw the carved stones far beneath. This had been a building of some kind. But how? She didn't have time to think about it. She dove deeper, swimming under it, and a flash of something ahead made her startle and back paddle. It was too big to be a fish, and she could swear she'd seen a foot. She shuddered and went to pat the rope around her waist for reassurance. Her groan in the mask was loud in her ears.

It was gone. So be it.

She swam on and then jerked back when golden eyes looked at her from up ahead. If it was something protecting the Apple, that was the direction she had to go, and she just had to hope it wasn't malicious. It receded as she got closer, so all she could see was the glowing eyes until it moved up and she followed, breaking the surface of another pool.

This one was unnaturally still, despite the small waterfall creating it. The cave it called home was high and wide, and every wall was covered in runic symbols, from the top to the bottom. She climbed up the mossy slope, glad she'd worn the thin swimming boots as they scraped on the jagged stones. She stopped when she saw the creature waiting for her, sitting on a rock, eating a fish that was still flopping slightly in its hand.

The Blue Men. More than a little concerned, Temp went over the rest of the clue in her head and promptly looked around, but there were no seal-people or demon horses in sight. There was just a human-looking creature with dark blue whorls covering their light blue skin from head to toe. Hair like seaweed hung lank to its waist, covering the chest and making it difficult to determine gender, though the clue might be in the name. Were there *female* Blue Men? It continued to rip at the fish with small, sharp teeth, all the while staring at her.

She took off the mask and let it hang around her neck. Then she shifted the bag and reached in. The creature stopped eating, teeth bared but not moving. Slowly, she pulled the crown and firebird out, unwrapped them and held them out in her palms. It looked from the items and back to her, and then went back to eating the fish.

"Okay," she murmured. "At least it didn't attack." She turned, keeping it in her periphery, and scanned the cave, repeating the clue in her head. It had said something about a pyramid. She moved cautiously, hands still outstretched with the items, so the creature didn't feel threatened. If only Ginny was here to read the runes, maybe Temp wouldn't be looking around blindly.

A sound caught her attention, and she looked back. The creature had dropped the fish to the ground, half-eaten. Its head was tilted, as though listening, and the little teeth were bared once again. Not at her, this time, but towards the pool. Instinctively, she knew she needed to hurry. These creatures weren't going to be patient with a bunch of men with guns surrounding their pools.

She moved a little quicker, looking at the runes and searching for anything that looked like any of the artefacts or some kind of pyramid. It was only when she got to the waterfall that she saw the shadow. Carefully, she slid along the narrow wedge of stone that led behind the fall and found herself in a smaller cave filled with dancing lights coming from the sky far above, let in via a hole in the ceiling that allowed a view of the purples and greens crossing the sky. Here, too, the walls were covered in red ochre runic symbols.

And then she saw what she was looking for.

The pyramid was made of large pebbles of varying colours and possibly even some gemstones, based on the way they glittered. Atop it was a model Viking ship, only about three feet long. The small boat floated in a pool of water coming from the top of the pyramid, the tiny oars moving as though it was being rowed. The empty middle was exactly the right size...

She placed the crown in the middle, where it began to spin idly, the crystal tines clicking against the oars. Without the orb, there was nothing more she could do. She'd have to go back for it.

Turning, she jumped away from the Blue Man standing directly behind her. It looked from the ship to her and shook its head.

"I'm sorry. I have to. Very bad men are coming to take it, and to keep it safe, I have to move it. I swear to Valhalla, I won't misuse it in any way."

Suddenly it looked back and leapt through the fall and out of sight. That same sense of urgency assailed her again, and she carefully placed the Firebird in the centre of the crown, where it dropped to the bottom, unmoving as the crown circled around it. Putting her mask back on as she hurried back to the pool, she figured she had about three minutes of air left in it. That would have to be enough.

She kicked out and down, swimming under the arch and into chaos.

Blood filled the water. A Blue Man floated past, a wound in his chest leaving an inky trail behind him. One of the Germans floated face down, a look of terror remaining in his dead eyes.

Alex. In a fight, she was probably the best equipped to handle herself. But she was injured and unarmed. Temp rose and looked towards where Alex had last been. She wasn't there. Temp stumbled ashore and shoved a German getting ready to shoot at two Blue Men baring their teeth from the water.

"Stop!" She waved frantically, ripping off the mask. "Damn it, stop!"

Amazingly, they did, though they didn't lower their weapons. There were only two on shore, and Cambrick and Lord Billinghurst stood to the side, Alex held in front of them. Blood dripped from her chin onto the pink blouse then blended into the maroon corset. Rage filled her eyes.

"Did you get it?" Billinghurst called. "Hand it over!"

"Of course I didn't get it, you idiot." Temp clambered onto the pool's edge, yanking at the diving gear and throwing it onto the rocks as she did so. "I need the orb. Just like I said I would. What the hell happened here?"

"Those...things." Cambrick looked over Alex's shoulder towards the pool. "They came out, five or six of them, and rushed us."

"They approached us and turned hostile when these fools started shooting at them." Alex's tone could have split the rock around them. "And then one of them dragged a soldier into the water, then another. They deserved it. And then these incredibly brave men hid behind me, hoping the creatures wouldn't hurt a woman."

Billinghurst shook Alex hard. "Shut up. Strud, where do we go? I'm not just handing over the orb. Take me to it."

"Can you hold your breath for more time than it takes to puff on a cigar? Can you swim in ice cold water?" She shrugged. "You have to swim under an arch into another pool. I'm happy to lead the way."

Billinghurst shoved Alex to her knees, his finger pressed against the wound in her head, making her wince. "I will kill her right now, Strud." His tone and expression were deadly calm. "You'd better find a way. You have to the count of three." He held up his hand. "One...two..."

"Kill her, and I'll never take you to it. We can all freeze and die out here. At least you won't get what you came for. These creatures won't let you anywhere near it." Temp glanced around quickly. None of the Blue Men were anywhere to be seen. Did they stay in the water? Were they even able to come out of it if they wanted to?

"But they let her near it." Cambrick's eyes narrowed. "They let her go in and come back."

Billinghurst looked at her thoughtfully. "Very well." With a sudden move, he shoved Alex hard, sending her sprawling, and then he aimed and fired.

Alex screamed, holding her side as blood pushed between her fingers. Temp leapt for her and pulled her onto her lap. "What the hell are you doing, you bastard?"

"Providing encouragement. She now needs medical treatment. The faster we get this done, the faster you can get her help. I imagine you'll find a way to get us in there now."

"Don't do it." Alex was breathing hard, her face pressed to Temp's shoulder. "Better we all die here and now."

"He'll kill these creatures and eventually find his way in anyway. I think we can stop him, but I'm going to need your help when we're in there. And I've become rather fond of you. I'd hate to see you die and become fish food for the Blue Men."

Alex shuddered. "That's the most romantic thing anyone has ever said to me."

Temp looked up, her mind flying at a thousand knots per second. "There's an opening, high above the cave. With enough rope, we could lower into the cave from there. Someone will have to stay up top to pull us back out."

"See? I knew you'd find a solution with the right motivation." Billinghurst turned towards the remaining soldiers. "Get all the rope you can find from all the flyers and follow us."

"I need to bind Alex's wound before she bleeds to death." Temp felt the edges of the wound and was relieved that the burn pattern from the airgun seemed to be along the outer edges of Alex's corset. The wound had likely missed anything important, hurt though it must. "Can you walk?"

"If she can't, she stays here." Cambrick's smile was hard. "Or I'll gladly drag her along behind us."

Alex pushed up, letting Temp support her. "I'm going to kill him, one way or another," she muttered. "I can walk."

They moved to Temp's pile of clothes, and she tore the fine linen shirt into strips that she then bound tightly around Alex's middle. "The cut on your head?"

"Cambrick wet his knickers when the creatures came out of the pool, and he shoved me aside to rush past. I hit my head on a rock. Nothing serious."

Temp nodded, relieved. "It's going to be steep. Use my cane and take it down into the cave with you." She looked into Alex's eyes and saw understanding.

"Always the chivalrous one." Alex nodded and waved. "Let's get this over with."

Temp led the way, heading back towards the flyer and more even ground, and then following the river from a higher vantage point. The arch disappeared from view, then they were beyond the main waterfall. Another hundred steps took them to a waterfall almost impossible to see from land. It fell out of the earth and into the hole that led to the cavern far below.

"This is it."

Cambrick moved past them to the other side, then knelt and looked in. "I don't see anything."

"Did you think it would be sitting just inside the opening, waiting for you to pick it up?" Alex's tone dripped acid.

He glared at her, the shifting purples in the sky making him look more monstrous than the creatures protecting the waterfall. "When we're done, I'll make sure you never speak to me that way again."

"When we're done, hopefully you'll be nothing more than a red stain on the stones." She glared back at him.

"Enough." Billinghurst turned towards the soldiers. "Knot the ropes together. Lower Miranda down first, in case it's a trap."

Alex held up her arm, the one holding the cane, the other pressed to her chest. "I'm not exactly in the shape necessary for rope climbing."

He stepped forwards and yanked her injured arm up, making her cry out.

Temp took one step forwards and punched him, knocking him onto his arse, and held Alex to her.

He stared up at her from the ground and cocked his airgun.

"Go ahead." Temp's jaw worked as she felt Alex tremble in pain. "You're so good at hurting other people, but you can't take a punch yourself."

He pushed himself to his feet, hatred filling his eyes. "When this is over, you'll beg me to kill you."

Temp looked at the soldier. "Tie us together. You'll just have to lower us down that way. She can't do it on her own."

The soldier didn't say anything; he and the other one simply did as she said.

Temp stepped to the edge of the hole. "Are you okay?" she asked, moving a piece of hair off Alex's cheek.

"I've been better." Alex gave her a weak smile. "I'm not a fan of walking off cliffs and falling into the earth when I can't use a rather large portion of my body."

The words rang a bell in Temp's mind. "The guardian at the cathedral. 'You can only run so far before the road runs out, and you must either fall from the cliff or turn to face that which you run from.' Remember?"

Alex nodded. "Do you really think this is that moment?" She looked over her shoulder and then back at Temp. "Maybe it is."

"Get moving." Cambrick's voice wasn't nearly as confident sounding as he probably wanted it to be. "I want to get out of here."

Temp nodded to the soldiers, held Alex tightly to her, and they stepped off the edge. Slowly they entered the cave, and she said, "Look at the walls."

Alex glanced around as best she could when they were strapped so tightly together. "Amazing. What I'd give to read them all."

Temp agreed. "Alex, there's no way this is going to be easy. The guardian at the cathedral suggested as much, and I think you're going to have to be the one to do it. There's bound to be a test of some kind, and we need to be slow and steady."

Alex nodded. "The cane? Is it the same as the one you used in Low Nottingham?"

"It is. But we're outnumbered, and it can't beat an airgun, not without the element of surprise. Use it to stay upright, and if the moment comes when you can make it work for us, go for it. Otherwise, we're just lucky to have it so you don't fall over."

Their feet touched down, and Temp undid the knots in the rope, then tugged on it to let them know it was free. "If only we could just stay down here until they got tired and left." She smiled at Alex and helped her to a boulder, where she sat down. For a moment, she considered mentioning that Peter had been with her, and she'd told him to stay in the shadows, just in case there was trouble. There'd been trouble, and he had orders to stay far from it and make his way back to the Chimera if he could. She didn't know where he was now, but he was out of the line of fire, and that's what mattered.

"This is incredible, Temp." Alex scanned the walls, the fingers of her good hand moving like she wanted to trace them. "If only Wade were here to copy them all. Or if I had paper."

"Who knows? Maybe we can make it back one day." In truth, Temp hoped they'd never see this place again. She'd see those floating bodies in her dreams for years.

There was the sound of a loud argument up above, and then Cambrick was being lowered into the cave. When he landed, he looked fit to punch someone. Temp moved in front of Alex.

"Bastard was going to come down first and leave me up there." He snorted. "Like I'd let that happen. If he wants the Apple, he's going to have to go through me."

"We can hope." Alex smiled, but there was pain in her eyes.

Cambrick walked around, staring at the walls. "What is this? What do they mean? And what is that?" He peered at the pyramid and the little ship in the water burbling beneath it.

"They're runic symbols, and we don't know. Neither of us can read them very well." Temp leaned against the rock, her arms folded. She was so cold, she ached, and the wet material wasn't helping. But damned if she'd show any weakness at all in front of him.

He looked up at the rope still ascending back to the surface, then turned to them. "Listen to me. Help me get the Apple, and I'll let you walk out of here. You'll never see me again, and I won't give a tinker's damn where on earth you go. He," he pointed up, "will make sure you never leave this cave." He raised his hands, almost beseeching as he looked at Alex. "Please. You owe me this for running out on our wedding day."

Temp choked on the breath she'd been taking and thumped her chest. "Excuse me? You're married?" Every ounce of blood in her body plummeted to her feet, and the world tilted in front of her.

"No!" Alex recoiled like she'd stepped on something that oozed between her toes. "I was seventeen and still under my father's control. He promised me to Cambrick. But on the day, I couldn't stand the idea of being chained to him for life, and I ran. I made my way to the docks, got work on an airship, and left that day."

"And you've been running ever since." Temp's world turned right again, and she took a deep breath. "But why? He can't force you to marry now that you're of age."

"Oh, but he can. They had a contract, you see, and in the sky cities, those are enforceable even when it comes to selling women of the household for financial gain." Alex shifted, obviously in pain. "We may be able to have contracts of our own now, thanks to your queenie friend, but they don't cancel out other contracts made in our names."

Never in her life had Temp needed to consider her gender in relation to her freedom, and the thought of Alex being sold off that way made her stomach turn.

"None of that matters now," Cambrick hissed, as Billinghurst's feet came into view above. "Help me, and you're free."

They didn't speak of it further, once Billinghurst was in the cave and looking around with interest as he descended. Temp mentally worried at the situation like a dog with an old piece of meat. She had no idea what would happen once they put the three pieces together, nor what they would lead to. The messages they'd received that had got them there had included warnings, but those weren't specific enough to tell them what to watch for.

One thing was certain though; no matter the cost, she was going to free Alex from her past.

Chapter Twenty-Six

Everything hurt. No, it didn't just hurt. Alex went through the various descriptions in her head of how bad it hurt. Like landing on rocks in hell maybe. Or like an elegant ball in the grandest ballroom in London-on-High, surrounded by witless people talking about witless things.

She watched Temp move along the walls, studying the symbols. She'd lied, of course. They were both at least a little proficient in them, if not conversant. Alex was too light-headed to get up and study them as well, which was a shame. Together, they might have deciphered some of it. The pyramid in the middle was clearly what they were there for, though she couldn't quite work out how it would operate. The small ship was beautifully crafted, and the crystal crown and Firebird were visible in the middle, where Temp had probably placed them for safe keeping.

There were no Blue Men in the cave, for which she was grateful. Not just because they'd been injured by the men around them, but because their sharp little teeth and unearthly appearance made her shiver with unease. Still, at least they weren't as bad as golems. The Blue Men were nature's creatures, and there was something soothing about that. Pain shot through her side, and she jerked, making her arm scream in response. Some pirate captain she'd turned out to be. She was going to die, land-bound, in a ridiculous pink outfit, surrounded by mythical creatures and ignorant men.

And Temp. That one hurt the most. There was no way they were getting out of here, and Temp deserved better than that. Seeing her again had lifted Alex's heart, and she had no doubts whatsoever that she had gone and fallen for the handsome enigma. But it was too late, and that emotion would crumble as surely as their bones down here.

Her father's heavy tread echoed off the walls as he released the rope and stepped forwards. "Incredible." He moved straight to the pyramid. "The crown and Firebird." He reached out to touch it.

"Wait!" Temp jumped forwards and pushed his arm away. "These things are often set up as tests and doing it wrong can set off a trap. We need to do this methodically."

He jerked away from her. "What do you suggest?"

She reached in and gingerly took out the Firebird. "Give me the orb."

He took it from his bag but hesitated before handing it over. "I *will* kill her—"

"For fuck's sake, we heard you the first ten times." Temp snatched it from him and turned to the little boat. She moved slowly, gently placing it into the cradle of the crown.

From somewhere deep in the walls, something grated, like a door that had been closed for a very long time. Dust and small rock rained down around them. Silence was thick as they all waited, but nothing more happened. Temp glanced back at Alex, who nodded encouragingly, though her heart was pounding.

The crown had continued to turn, tapping the little oars. The orb slowly began to turn in the opposite direction to the crown. Thin lines of colour appeared in the orb, moving between the symbols. Constellations, Alex thought, craning her head to see from where she sat. It was a culture dependent on the stars as they roamed the seas, so it made sense that was their primary way of communicating something celestial.

Temp held the Firebird over the orb. "There are notches in the orb that I think this fits into. If it goes on the wrong way, it could set off a trap."

"Or you're just stalling." Cambrick grabbed the Firebird from Temp's hand and dropped it almost carelessly onto the orb.

The stone he was standing on fell away.

He screamed as he plummeted into the darkness, grabbing onto the edge at the last second, his fingers scrabbling for purchase. "Help me! Damn it, Billinghurst! Grab my hand!"

Temp looked at Alex, who just stared at the scene. He'd been warned, and he'd rushed. It was a test, and he'd failed. There wasn't an iota of her being interested in trying to help him, nor did she feel anything in particular other than glad it hadn't been Temp standing on that stone instead.

Her father crouched down, shaking his head. "Such an impetuous fool. As much as I loathe my daughter, she's lucky to have avoided you after all." He pulled a knife from his boot and stabbed at the top of Cambrick's hand, forcing him to let go.

His scream echoed for a long time, too long, in the cavern. There was no thump or splash. Just a sudden end to his voice.

"That takes care of that problem. My condolences on the loss of your fiancé, Miranda. We'll find you another, more suitable one." Her father stood and turned towards Temp. "You were saying?"

Temp shook her head and studied the construction. The Firebird sat awkwardly on the orb, which continued to turn in the opposite direction to the crown. Alex could see her counting, her foot tapping out a rhythm.

With a deep breath, she plucked the Firebird off the orb. Nothing happened.

Alex breathed out a sigh of relief.

Temp continued to count, and it looked like she was combining the ticks of the crown against the oars with the turns of the orb. Yes, Alex was sure of it. The timing was perfect, like a complicated metronome.

"Now," Alex whispered, and Temp placed the Firebird onto the orb. The claws clicked against the glass, and it settled atop it perfectly, a mythic bird carrying the moon above the Viking ship. The pink lines in the Firebird seemed to twirl in time with the lines of colour in the orb, like it was flying across a sky at sunset.

For a long moment, nothing happened. And then the orb

slowed, the crown slowed, the ticking stopped, and it was silent.

"Well?" her father finally said.

Temp shrugged. "I told you I could go this far, and then we'd have to see what happened. It's not as though I've done this before."

His cheeks were red, and his eye was swollen from where Temp had punched him. He raised the ever-present airgun and aimed it at her. Just as he was clearly about to begin a tirade, a shard of light from high above came in like a spear, hitting the strange little setup in the middle. Prisms shot out of both ends of the Firebird, which had stopped with its head at one end of the ship and its beautiful tail at the other. A thick pink line flared through it and made it look like it was about to take flight. At each end of the pink line was an arrow, one at the tip of the tail, one at the very end of the beak.

The prisms of light pointed to each side wall, circling a section of writing.

Even Alex's father seemed taken aback by the beauty of it. For a moment anyway. "What does it mean?"

Temp looked at Alex, her eyebrows raised. Alex recited the passage from the book she'd read in Temp's office, which had stuck with her from the moment she'd read it out loud. "'She brings blessings or doom to her captor, using the truth of their heart to lead them to the ending they've brought on themselves. The journey ahead will be hard, the reward great or terrible. If she should feed from aught but the Golden Apple, she will turn to a demon and devour all that is good. To seek what your heart desires, follow the flight of fire.'" Her voice echoed strangely, like she was some kind of ancient oracle handing out vague prophecies.

Temp nodded, her expression thoughtful as she stared at it. "Follow the flight of fire." She moved her finger along the pink line in the Firebird. "I think that's this."

"But it points both directions." Her father looked at both walls. "What does it mean about turning someone to a demon?" He tugged at his hair. "What nonsense!"

"Again, Billinghurst, you can't believe in a mythical apple that gives you power and not pay attention to the stories that come with it."

Temp's tone was sharp, and it was clear she was only just refraining from punching him again. She glanced at the weapon in his hand and then away again. If she had the opportunity, she'd definitely take it from him.

Alex stood, drawn to the mystery, and hobbled over. She looked both ways. "Looking ahead or looking behind," she murmured.

"Over the cliff, or turning back to what you were running from," Temp said. "I think maybe you need to make the next decision."

Alex swallowed, but Temp was right. She moved towards the left wall, following the tail. "Face what you were running from," she said and touched the wall in the middle of the prism. A stone scraped at her palm, raised from the rest. She didn't press it. Instead, she turned back and hobbled towards the other wall. There, too, she put her palm to the centre and found a stone raised over the others. "Or go forwards, over the cliff." She looked over her shoulder. Her father, her past. Temp, her future. She turned back to the wall and pushed the stone.

Grinding echoed again, sending more dirt raining down on them. The waterfall behind them jumped and churned, and slowly, a huge section of the wall opened in front of her. A strange golden glow lit the space ahead.

Temp moved up beside her. "I knew it would be you." She jerked when Alex's father shoved the gun against the back of her neck.

"Ladies first. Don't touch anything."

Temp put her hand against Alex's back, and they walked forwards together. One of the Blue Men, this one with long, thick grey hair sat cross-legged in the middle of the room. The room, not much bigger than Alex's cabin on the Urchin, held shelves on each wall. On every shelf were three clay bowls, and in each bowl was a piece of fruit. Some looked like typical apples. Some looked exotic, some looked rotten.

The creature held up his hands. In his palms was the Firebird.

They hadn't even seen him in the cave with them.

"Move!" Alex's father shoved them aside. "That's going to lead me to the Apple." He took it from the creature, who looked at him, expressionless. Her father stopped, seeming to reconsider. He turned and grabbed Alex's arm, yanking her forwards. When Temp went to stop him, he raised the gun. "*You* find it. You opened the wall. Find the Apple. Now!"

Trembling, Alex took the Firebird and looked at the creature, who remained impassive. Except for one toe. The big toe facing her moved, seeming to point. It was a silly thing to take as a sign, but she had nothing else. She turned, holding the Firebird in her palm and moved to the first wall of fruit. Pink lines swirled gently inside it, no longer a straight line pointing to anything. *The truth of their heart.* She thought of her desire for freedom, of the way she felt when she was flying through the air, at no one's mercy, playing in the wind. She thought of the misery her father had blanketed her in from the day she was born. The Firebird suddenly grew so hot to the touch, she nearly dropped it.

She stopped in front of an apple the colour of summer cherries, without a blemish on it.

"Is that it?" her father demanded. "Is it that one?"

She looked at him as though from a million miles away, memories clouding her vision. "I don't know. Maybe."

He grunted and took the Firebird from her. "It's hot. That must be it." He pushed the carving back at her and then looked at the Blue Man. "Now what?"

The creature put its hand to its mouth, miming eating.

Her father turned and reached towards it, almost reverent. Holding it with both hands, he put it to his lips. "And now for immortality," he said and took a bite.

Alex stumbled back as he dropped the apple, a look of dawning horror on his face. His back arched hard, his neck twisted, and his face contorted in a rictus of pain. His scream was guttural, like he couldn't quite open his mouth.

Temp rushed over and pulled Alex to her as they watched the dreadful situation unfold. Alex couldn't look away, though it was the stuff of nightmares. The Blue Man watched as though it had seen it all before.

Bones snapped as his body hit the ground, twisting and writhing. His skin began to change, turning...blue. People with impure hearts were turned to monsters. But Alex had been the one to choose the apple. Did that mean it should have been her fate? She glanced at the guardian, who gave no indication one way or another...except that its toe flexed. She looked back at her father. This was his test. He'd failed because the Apple knew the truth of his heart.

Horns appeared on his forehead, and the noises he made were animalistic and grotesque. His clothes bagged around him as he seemed to shrink, and when he finally stopped moving and looked at them, it was with yellow eyes. He backed away, out of the room, looking from side to side as though trying to find a way out, and then darted on all fours from the room. There was a splash, and he was gone.

Alex buried her face in Temp's chest and gave in to a few tears. Not for her father's fate, which he deserved, but at the awfulness of it.

The Blue Man tapped the floor with a claw to get their attention. It pointed to Alex and motioned at the Firebird, then at the apples.

"No!" Alex shook her head and stepped away from the Firebird her father had dropped. "I don't want it. We just wanted to keep it from the bad people who would use it."

The creature motioned towards the ceiling, towards the soldiers who remained above.

"It's right," Temp said, kissing the top of Alex's head. "They know it's here. We could try to kill them before they leave, but if we didn't succeed, they'd bring people back. And they don't work for Willoughby or your father. They work for the Kaiser. If that power falls into his hands..."

"Then *you* do it. You're pure of heart. I used my heart and that happened." She nodded towards the room's opening. "I don't want that to happen to me."

"Tell me what you were thinking about." Temp smoothed her hair back. "What led you to that one?"

Alex sniffled. "I was thinking about how amazing it feels to fly. To be in the air and completely free. I was thinking about my childhood in my father's house."

"And your father is what kept you from being free. The one who took your freedom way back then. I don't think you would have chosen that apple for yourself. Because your feeling was true. His was greed, and you were leading him to it, not trying to find it for yourself. We were given that warning in the myth." She looked at Alex, and there was love in her eyes. "I'll do it if you want me to. But the guardian at the cathedral, and this one here, seems to think it should be you, pirate. This is your treasure to grab."

Alex laughed a little at that and pulled away. "Will you still want me in your bed if I turn into some blue demon thing?" She lifted the Firebird.

"Absolutely. I'll just have horns and a tail to play with as well, that's all."

Alex flinched. Her hand shook as she held up the carving again.

"Look forwards, Alex. What does your heart tell you about the future?" Temp asked softly.

What did the future look like? It had Temp in it, that was certain. But what about the Urchin? What about her freedom? She had it now. Her father and Cambrick were gone. She could live without looking over her shoulder. Well, maybe. The pirate Alex Minty was still a wanted fugitive, if anyone other than her father had put the clues together. But Temp didn't care. She wanted Alex as she was, not as she was expected to be. For perhaps the first time in Alex's life, she knew what the word unconditional meant.

Alex walked along, her eyes closed, as she let the feelings she'd long held at bay flow through her. Through all the turmoil, at the end of the emotional chain, was love. That was the last link, and it was warm and soft and kind and strong.

The Firebird grew so hot, she dropped it, and the silver figure shattered on the stone ground, leaving metal splinters spread out like a broken constellation. She stared at it with wide eyes and then looked at the Blue Man.

He tilted his head towards the bowl on the shelf.

It wasn't an apple exactly. It was a small, golden tree. At the end of each perfect branch was a tiny golden apple. She picked up the surprisingly heavy little sculpture and held it in her palm. It clicked three times, the apples turning on their branches, and then the trunk opened to reveal a small red stone, etched with a rune.

Temp looked over her shoulder. "The ending you brought on yourself is a cute little tree with a gem inside. I like that option."

Alex agreed. "Can you close it back up? I want to get out of here."

Temp took it from her and closed it, her touch gentle. "I think it might be actual gold. Wade is going to love looking at the way it's constructed." She gently slipped it into her pack and grunted a little as it pulled the bag down, making her readjust it.

The Blue Man guardian waited outside the room and shook his head when Temp pointed to the rope still dangling from the opening high above. He pointed to the waterfall.

"She's hurt. She can't swim all that way." Temp put her hand out, towards Alex's side. Blood had seeped through the wrapping.

He motioned again towards the waterfall, more insistently this time.

"I think..." Alex thought of the words of the other guardian. "I think I have to follow him off the cliff, Temp. No going back. It's okay to leave the past behind."

He nodded and held out his hand. Alex took it and smiled at Temp. "After all this, I don't think they'll let us drown. Do you?" She handed Temp the cane, and Temp took it and fixed it into the bag strapped across her back.

Temp grimaced. "Maybe? We found it. If we don't leave with it, then they know it's still safe."

The guardian shook his head and tugged Alex towards the water. The rope had begun to move like someone might be coming down.

Temp touched the creature's arm, making it jump. "She's everything to me. Please be careful with her."

It studied her, then nodded.

They went with it to the waterfall, and Alex held her breath as she slid into the icy pool.

Chapter Twenty-Seven

TEMP WATCHED ALEX'S SLIPPERS moving in the water ahead of her. The water churned around them, almost violent in its motion. Where it had been placid and clear before, it now seemed to feel the loss of the treasure it had been guarding. The water itself was grieving.

She took shorter gulps of air and saw when the creature led Alex to the surface to breathe, and then they dove again. When spots began to float in front of her eyes, she ripped off the mask and went to the surface herself, which wasn't more than two inches of air between the water and the cave ceiling, but it was enough. She dove again and swam forwards.

Alex and the creature were gone. The churning waters became confusing, and she kicked in a circle, trying to see the way forwards. Panic rose like a tide, and her breathing became too erratic. Deciding any way was better than none, she kicked forwards and mentally crossed her fingers.

Too long. It was taking too long. Her body jerked as she began to run out of air. She pushed towards the surface, but her time was up. Grief washed over her as she realised she'd never get to tell Alex she loved her. Bubbles rose from her mouth, lost in the chaos around her, and she began to sink.

Splashing made her blink hard, and she reached for the hands that appeared ahead of her in the water. She grabbed on and was pulled swiftly forwards and then above the surface. She flipped to her back, coughing, and let whoever it was tow her to the edge. Strong hands dragged her onto mossy stones, and she felt metal on her skin. She tilted her head back. "Joe. Good man." She flopped onto her back, breathing hard. "Alex?"

"Already on her way to the airship with Peter. We'll take her back to the village and find a doctor." He sat on the boulder next to her. "Looks like we're in for quite a story."

She forced herself up and nodded. They were alone, no Blue Men or soldiers in sight. "Let's get out of here. Take this, will you?" She took off all the gear, dropping it into a pile, and handed Joe the bag and cane.

"Your clothes were piled up over there. Dirty and a little wet, but better than your swim costume, I daresay." He nodded towards the clothes on the boulder behind them. "I'll load all this onto the flyer."

He gathered the diving gear and traipsed off into the morning light, leaving Temp to dress. She did so, watching the waterfall, and just as she was putting on her shoes, a Blue Man rose from the water and moved towards her, holding out its hands.

In them was a simple apple, yellow and medium-sized. It didn't look like anything special. She looked at it, and then at the creature. "I thought Alex found the Golden Apple."

It shook its head and pushed the Apple towards her.

"That's the one from the fable? The one that gives immortality?"

It nodded, and there was no mistaking the sadness in its yellow eyes.

"But why? You could let it sink to the bottom here, buried forever. No one would be able to make use of it." She still didn't take it, unwilling now to take on the burden of something so powerful.

Once again, it just proffered the Apple. Shaking her head, she took it. "Thank you, I guess. But what was Alex given, if it wasn't this?"

It backed towards the water, then turned away from her and raised its arms. Suddenly a long keening noise filled the air, and more chilling wailing joined it from all the pools. It filled the air, rending it with the end of a myth, with the freedom gained by the guardians who had been cursed to guard the Apple for as long as they could.

But the world was changing. One day, people would roam the

earth and even places like this one wouldn't be spared from prying eyes and greed. That's what the creature knew somehow. That's why Temp had the Apple cradled in her hands. The Blue Man didn't want to risk it being found by someone who wasn't worthy.

"That's incredibly disturbing." Joe moved to her side, his eyes wide. "What are they?"

"Free."

The keening stopped suddenly, a chord cut, and the creature dove into the water without a backwards glance. The ground began to rumble strangely in the sudden silence.

"Time to go." They ran towards the flyer, and Temp jumped into the pilot's seat with Joe behind her. She flipped the switches to inflate the airbags and watched the waterfall fling itself left and right, the hills around it seeming to crumble.

Gears worked and the sail went out, and the balloons lifted them off the ground just as the top of the waterfall crumbled. Water crested the falling hillside as it caved in on itself, and as the flyer rose, she saw the hole where they'd found the treasure. Now it was a crater with water flowing in on all sides, dropping into a wider pool. There was no trace of the soldiers, and Temp had no doubt they'd been taken into the water to feed the creatures there.

She headed back towards Carbost, where they'd taken Alex.

"I should ask if you're hurt at all," Joe said from the back. "Just figured you were fine, since nothing seems able to kill you. Not even blue creatures out of some weird fairy tale."

"I'm fine, thanks to you keeping me from drowning. It was a near one." She looked out over the empty landscape, glowing with the sunrise. "I'll be glad to get some sleep once I know Alex is okay."

"Did you get what you went for?"

Temp nodded slowly. "More than, I'd say. We still have some mysteries to solve, I think."

The trip back was quick, for which Temp was grateful. Worry about Alex was gnawing at her, and she couldn't relax until she knew she was safe. They docked the flyer beside the Old Inn at

Carbost, next to the one Peter had taken back.

Inside, there was a fire roaring, and the smell of food made her salivate. It was clean and welcoming, and her shoulders fell a few notches. A couple of hardy early risers sat at tables, looking curious but not saying anything.

"Right. You'll be the ones with the lad and lady. Come on this way." A woman came out from behind the bar and motioned with a bar towel.

They followed her up some stairs to a hallway and into a room where the door was already open. Temp stumbled when she saw the pile of bloody rags next to the bed where Alex lay motionless. The physician looked over his little spectacles at her as he wiped his hands clean of Alex's blood.

"You'll be Temp, I imagine? She was calling for you." He continued to wipe his hands as he spoke. "The airgun burn wasn't deep, but it did take a goodly amount of skin off her side. There was dirt in it, and I had to clean it out or risk infection." He looked at Alex. "That upper arm bone was snapped clean through. I've seen grown men weep like children from that kind of break, and they weren't traipsing out by the fairy pools, that's for certain." He shook his head. "The strength of women never stops surprising me."

"Will she recover?" Temp asked, finally getting her feet to move. "You should look at her ankle too."

He sighed and dropped the bloody cloth into the pile. "She didn't mention that."

"Why isn't she awake? Did you give her something?" Temp pulled a chair to Alex's side and gently took her hand. She looked so pale, so small and fragile in the white sheets spotted with her blood and wet from their swim. Her beautiful red hair was clumped and tangled. Maybe the inn had a maid who could help her brush it out. Temp would need to hire one for the ship...

"She passed out when I was cleaning the airgun wound, which was for the best. It let me get most of it done before she came to again. She kept asking where you were and whether the Blue Men had taken you after all." He glanced up from Alex's ankle, where he probed gently. "You're lucky they didn't."

"They saved us both." Temp didn't go into detail, but his raised eyebrows suggested they knew of the creatures who inhabited the empty moors and that wasn't the norm.

"Ankle is sprained, not broken. It will take a while to heal, and she'll need to stay off it as much as she can." He stood. "She'll need bed rest for all she's been through, and you'll need to watch for infection. The fairy pools are clean water, good for healing, but from the sounds reaching us from out that way, that may not be so right now."

"Thank you, Doctor." She looked at Joe, who pulled out a pouch of money and handed it over. A thought struck her. "I don't imagine it's easy to get to the people you need to out here, is it?" she asked, and he looked at her quizzically. "There are three flyers out by the pools; their owners no longer need them. It'd be a shame to let them rot there when they could be put to good use here."

His eyes lit, making him look younger. "Well, that's quite the boon. Three, you say? We can make good use of them up here, that's for certain." He held out the pouch of money. "I'd say we're square."

Temp shook her head and rested it on Alex's hand. "Take it and use it to help the people who need it."

"Very well. Will you be here for me to look in on the patient tomorrow?"

Temp raised her head and looked at Joe. Her energy was flagging, and decisions were becoming more difficult to make.

"Thank you, but no," Joe said. "We'll make our way back to the ship as soon as we can move Alex safely."

The doctor flicked a switch on his bag, and gears shifted as it shut and locked. "Give her some food and water, and make the trip back as smooth as possible. She should be moveable by teatime."

Temp nodded and heard Joe thank him. The door clicked shut. "Where's Peter?" she asked.

"Downstairs. Young lass working here has taken a shine to the young, heroic ship's captain. He couldn't handle the sight of blood and had to sit down with a pint."

Temp smiled a little. "I told him to get back to the ship if there was trouble."

"We'll tell you our side of it later. For now, rest. I'll have breakfast brought up in a bit."

Temp didn't respond, and she heard the door open and close again. Alex was safe. Badly injured, but safe. They'd completed their mission and had what they came for. The people who could hurt Alex were dead, and Temp had a feeling she'd be upset she hadn't been the one to kill them. But it was over.

She let herself drift to sleep, her head still pressed to the back of Alex's hand.

***

"Temp, if I don't get to the loo, we're going to introduce an element to our relationship neither of us is ready for."

Temp blinked and raised her head, her neck protesting the position she'd been sleeping in. Alex smiled at her from where she still lay against the pillow. "Remind me to tell you how we accomplish fulfilling that particular fetish on the Chimera," she said, standing and stretching out the kink in her back.

"Please don't. Ever." Alex looked at her side and arm. The broken one was strapped securely to her chest. Bandages wrapped around her waist. She winced. "I feel like something Hades' dog vomited."

"Descriptive." Temp pulled the blanket off her and whimpered. Alex was naked as the day she was born.

"Well, they couldn't very well leave me in wet clothes, could they?"

Temp closed her eyes and took a deep, steadying breath. "If you weren't hurt and the doctor hadn't instructed strict bed rest, I would ravish you this instant."

"And as I said, I need the loo. Or I'd beg you to." She pushed herself up using her good arm. "Wrap a sheet around me?"

"Give me two seconds." Temp went into the hallway and found Peter asleep in a chair, mouth open, head tilted at an awkward angle. "Hey, soldier on duty." Temp tapped the top of his head with her knuckles.

He startled awake and wiped his hand across his mouth. "Everything okay, Cap? Is Alex all right?"

"She is. Can you get her a dressing gown from the innkeeper? And where is the loo?"

He pointed at a door and then raced down the stairs. He was back moments later with a thick wool dressing gown in his hands. "Mary Margaret said she'll bring up a tray of food, unless we want to come down?"

She grinned at the hopeful expression on his face. "I think it would be good form if you and Joe ate downstairs. Alex isn't going to want to move yet, and she's going to need clothes. Is there someone who can get them in this village?"

His eyes lit up. "Aye, Cap. I'll figure it out and get Mary Margaret to help." He turned and trotted off.

Temp smiled and shook her head as she headed back into Alex's room. "Our Peter has a mash on the barmaid." She helped Alex put on the dressing gown and didn't begrudge herself the feel of Alex's skin under her fingertips as she did so.

Slowly, they made their way out of the room to the door Peter had indicated. "Do you need help in there?"

"Do you like having the use of working limbs?" Alex said, pushing Temp away with her good arm. "And don't just stand here listening either. Find something useful to do until I come out."

Temp laughed and held up her hands, backing away. "Far be it from me to cross swords with the pirate Minty."

Alex shook her head and closed the door. Temp went back to the room and straightened the bed. At some point, someone had cleaned up all the bloody rags and such. A small fire blazed in the hearth and beyond the window, it was raining, making it hard to see anything of interest.

At Alex's call, Temp hurried back out and put her arm around Alex's waist.

"I'm bloody starving," she said, looking up at Temp. "Please tell me they have food."

"They're bringing up a tray for you. Doctor said bed rest—"

"Bed rest can take a flying leap into the Thames." She tugged at the belt on the dressing robe. "Let's go down and join the others. I'll have plenty of time on my back once we're in the air."

"I can't express how much I like the sound of that." Temp grinned and took Alex's weight as they made their way slowly down the stairs.

"Oh!" The young barmaid stopped with her foot on the first stair, a large tray of food in her hands. "I'm sorry, did I take too long?"

"No, no." Alex waved her aside. "I just don't like the idea of being on my backside while everyone else does...whatever else they're doing." She gave Temp a quick smile as she helped her sit on the bench opposite Joe. "But that food smells like something the gods would enjoy."

The girl laid out the food as well as the pots of tea on the table, her face pink as Peter watched her adoringly. Joe just shook his head and tucked in, remarking on the quality of the eggs.

"Now," Alex said after taking a bit of toast and a sip of tea. "How did you come to be waiting outside the fairy pools like our guardian angels?"

Peter finally looked away from the barmaid. "I came down with Cap to search for the Apple. But when we left the flyer, I stayed apart to watch for any danger. When the other flyers landed, I kept to the shadows. I listened to what was going on, and when you all went up high to go underground, I took a flyer back to the Chimera to get Joe."

Alex looked at Temp. "You didn't tell me he was with you."

"I didn't want you to worry. Or to think we had extra help. I told him to leave the moment it looked like things might go awry." She tilted her head. "He did as he was told, in a way."

"When Peter told me what was happening, we weren't about to leave you to it." Joe took up the tale as he ate. "Everyone on board is taken care of, and the kitchen staff know what they're doing. Wade has it under control as long as he doesn't have to talk to anyone other than the children."

"Children?" Alex's brow furrowed. "There are children onboard?"

Joe laughed when Temp put her head in her hands. "Did you forget you became a parent yesterday, Captain?" He looked at Alex. "Our soft-hearted captain went and found some orphans in need of help and thought she'd bring them on board a ship meant for the delivery of vice and pleasure."

"I told them it was temporary, Joe. That it isn't a place for kids." Temp looked at Alex, wondering how she felt about family. It wasn't the time to ask. "It was one of those moments where you have to make a choice."

Alex's expression suggested she understood exactly what Temp meant. "I'm sure you made the right one."

"Your turn." Peter leaned forwards, his eyes bright. "Tell us what happened!"

Alex began with her betrayal and capture at the Dirty Squirrel, and then went on to tell them about waking in her father's house and the threats made against her. Temp felt ill at the idea that Alex had been locked away and nearly tortured, and she hadn't had any inkling she was in trouble.

They then took turns talking about the adventure at the falls, though both of them, without saying so, agreed not to talk about the items they'd brought out with them. That wasn't for a place where anyone could overhear them.

"Now what?" Peter asked, sitting back as though full from a feast. He always seemed contented that way after a good story.

"We get back to the Chimera. We have a schedule to keep for the passengers, and we need to get back to that. As for the things from the waterfall?" Temp looked at Alex, who smiled a little. "We have plenty to discuss."

The innkeeper came over and stood beside Alex. "Lady, I've got the local lass to come over with some clothes. They're not fancy, but they'll cover yer backside until you get where you're going."

Alex stood carefully, and Temp rose with her. Alex put her hand on Temp's shoulder and pushed her back down. "Relax, Cerberus. I'm safe and perfectly capable of letting these fine people help me cover my backside."

Temp did as she was told, watching as Alex moved slowly to a back room with the innkeeper and a young woman laden with material behind her.

Joe looked at her over his mug of tea. "Will the Chimera have two captains going forwards? Or will you become a pirate and fly on a black ship with spikes for sails?"

Peter snorted, then suddenly looked worried.

"I nearly drowned a few hours ago. My ribs hurt. My face aches. I have things in my possession no human should have. I have a beautiful, injured pirate who has her own decisions to make. And I have two orphans on my ship." Temp poured herself more tea. "I have plenty of questions and no answers. For now, we get back to the ship and get our routine back. We'll discuss everything else when we're safe and rested."

They discussed the schedule and where they needed to sail to next, and Temp felt a little better after resuming her normal role. Joe and Peter left, taking a flyer back to the ship. The least amount of time they left only Wade in charge, the better.

Temp looked up, and her heart skipped a beat when Alex re-entered the room. She wore a loose white shirt, forgoing a corset because of her side. The ankle-length skirt was an expensive-looking wool that flowed so she could move easily. She wore one leather boot with no heel, and one slipper with a thick wrapping around her ankle. Her hair was pulled back, with wisps down around her face. She looked drawn and tired, but she was the most beautiful thing Temp had ever seen.

"You shouldn't look at a woman that way in public. It's downright indecent." Alex bent to kiss Temp's cheek.

"I can't help it. I especially like your choice in footwear."

Alex laughed. "It will be all the rage in London-on-High. Just you see."

"Wait here. I'll get our things from your room, and we'll head to the flyer." She paused. "If that's okay?"

"Perfect." Alex lowered herself onto a bench. "You can be my cart horse any time."

Temp hurried up the stairs despite the ache inside, eager to get back to her ship and have some time alone with Alex in a more luxurious space, where they didn't have to worry about being overheard and where she could look after Alex properly. Her bag was heavy with the little golden tree and the Apple. Neither of which she had the foggiest idea what to do with.

She went back down and stopped when she saw Peter. "What's wrong? Why aren't you on the ship?"

He twisted his cap in his hand, his breathing erratic. "Cap, I've no right to ask, but I wouldn't forgive myself if I didn't. You see, Mary Margaret, she's right good with kids. She's been a governess for some kids on the mainland, but they're of an age now, and they don't need her anymore. She's been working here, but it isn't enough to pay her lodging—"

Temp relaxed, understanding dawning. "And the orphans need someone to look after them. It's an excellent idea, Peter, and well done. Follow us in the flyer when she's ready to go." She looked at him hard. "Does she understand the kind of ship she'll be living on?"

He nodded quickly. "The basics of it, Cap. I didn't tell any secrets, honest, but she knows the ship is special."

"Very well." She put her arm around Alex, and they started their slow walk out. "Did Joe give you any money for the innkeeper?"

Peter looked so relieved he might swoon. "Aye, Cap. He paid for everything afore he went to the ship."

"Good lad." She clapped him on the shoulder as she passed him. "See you aboard shortly. Don't tarry. We have a schedule to keep."

Getting Alex into the flyer wasn't easy, and when she was seated, she looked weary, the lines around her eyes tight. "I'm sorry, love. It'll be easier when we get to the ship."

Alex didn't respond, she just closed her eyes and let her head fall back. Temp inflated the airbags, lifting the ship off the ground, and then opened the sail, which caught instantly in the wet Scottish wind. She pulled into it, and they were headed towards the Chimera, still docked at Eynort, in a heartbeat.

"Love."

Temp turned her head. "Pardon?"

"You called me love. Do you? Love me?"

Temp smiled. "This isn't the place I was going to tell you. But yes, I love you. When you left the Chimera, you took a piece of me with you, and I realised it was my heart."

There was silence, and Temp wondered if she'd either fallen asleep or didn't know how to respond.

"When I was locked in that room," she finally said, "all I could think about was the fact that I'd fallen in love with you and wouldn't have a chance to tell you."

Temp's heart soared, and she would have danced the flyer across the sky, if it wouldn't have jarred Alex. "She loves me!" she yelled at the sky.

Alex laughed, and it was the most beautiful sound Temp had ever heard.

They came up under the Chimera. Joe and Wade stood at the opening and lowered the docking ropes. Temp hooked them to the sides, and they cranked it up from the inside. "Stop there for a second." Temp got out when the flyer opening was level with the floor. "Help me get Alex out here so she doesn't have to jump down."

The three of them took Alex's weight and helped her onto the ship. The fact that she didn't swear or call any of them names made Temp worry that she was in more pain than she was letting on. "We'll go on ahead," Temp said. "When Peter gets back, we'll have a second flyer, so you'll need to pull this one as high as you can to fit the other one in. The extra weight isn't ideal, and we'll need to drop that second flyer at the next port."

They started winching it up, and Joe called over his shoulder, "I fixed up your room, Cap. Figured you'd rather have the pirate in there under your watchful eye than in the passenger quarters."

Alex finally cracked a smile. "It won't keep me from stealing anything I want, Joe."

As soon as the door to the ship closed behind them, the silence was bliss.

Alex seemed to think so too, and she sighed softly. "It's good to be back here."

There was a bit of wistfulness in her tone. "But you miss the Urchin."

Alex nodded. "She was mine. I kept her pristine, and she was my Pegasus, my ride through the skies." She wiped at a tear tracing down her cheek. "And I really did like most of my crew. You know how they become family."

Temp knew that well. It was her own chosen family who'd saved them at the end. "I'm sorry, Alex."

They made it to Temp's cabin, and she helped Alex disrobe and slip into a simple cotton nightgown Joe had set on the bed. This time, worry kept her from making any comments of a sensual nature.

"Stop fretting." Alex had already closed her eyes. "The excitement has just caught up with me, that's all. I'll be fine after some rest and good food."

"I'm the captain here. I'll fret if I so wish." Temp sat on the edge of the bed. "I'm going to let you sleep while I see to the ship. I'll be back soon." She kissed Alex's temple, which felt warm. "I love you."

Alex's eyes fluttered, and she smiled. "I'm going to get used to hearing that."

Alex's breathing settled like she was already asleep before Temp had even closed the door. She made her way through the ship, checking on passengers, saying hello to those few in the dining area, and then went to the kitchen.

Betty and Sal were sitting at a table, happily looking at a picture book. When Temp walked in, Betty leapt from her seat and threw herself against Temp, wrapping her arms around Temp's legs. "You came back!"

"Of course I did." She ruffled Betty's hair. "Have you been well behaved?"

Betty grimaced. "Mostly. Everyone knows you shouldn't take a bath more than once a year. It lets the bad spirits in, otherwise. But they made us scrub like we'd been rolling around with the pigs!"

Temp laughed. "Being clean is an important part of being on this ship, and you'll most certainly bathe more than once a year, I assure you."

"We like Peter, and Joe, and Wade. They're really nice. Everyone here is really nice, and no one shouts at us." Betty climbed back onto her seat. "I don't ever want to leave."

Temp didn't miss the sadness in her tone, but there was nothing she could say yet about the children's future. "I'm glad everyone is being good to you. Peter is bringing a governess onto the ship for you right now. She'll see to your education and make sure you little devils don't turn the place upside down." She winked, and Betty smiled. Sal held up the picture book, her thumb in her mouth.

"I'm afraid I have to work, little one. But someone will be along to read to you soon."

Sal put the book down and leaned against her sister, and they went back to looking at the pictures.

Her heart full, Temp finished her rounds and blinked hard

against the tiredness spreading over her. Like Alex had said, perhaps it was catching up with her. She let Joe know she would be in her cabin and headed back.

Alex lay in much the same position she'd left her, with her beautiful hair spread over the pillow. But there was a sheen of sweat on her brow when Temp went to kiss her cheek, and her skin was hotter than it had been. She pulled down the blanket and put her hand above the bandage on her side. It was hot and red.

Infection.

She left her cabin and went to Peter, who was in the gondola giving orders. "We're heading to Mid Manchester. Because of the Tri-port, they have the biggest hospital in the north. Alex has an infection." She entered the coordinates and took control of the flight.

Peter stood behind her, seeming at a loss. "What can I do?"

"Tell Joe and Wade about the change, and let passengers know there'll be a detour. You never know; some may want to disembark. Let them know we may be in port for a few days. Send a crow to let the port know we're coming, and we need a discreet dock."

He left without another word, and she knew he'd do exactly as asked. Fear kept her hands locked on the tiller. She couldn't lose Alex. She simply couldn't.

Chapter Twenty-Eight

"Captain, please." The secondary pilot stood beside her. "I know where we're going, and I can call you when we're about to dock. Please let me take the tiller. You're nearly asleep on your feet, and the sky is getting busy with other ships."

Temp closed her eyes and let her hands slip from the tiller. "Very well. Tell me the moment we're about to dock. You have the coordinates for the docking station?"

"I promise, and I do." He nudged her aside, and she finally stepped back.

Rubbing her eyes, she turned and walked back to her cabin. Her first and only thought had been to get the Chimera to a sky city as fast as possible, so she could get Alex help. Fear had never driven her before, not when she was in the military and flying fighter ships, not when she'd been boarded by pirates. But the thought of losing Alex was nearly paralysing.

She opened her cabin door and stopped, staring.

Betty and Sal lay beside Alex on the bed, and Betty had a book open. She couldn't read, but she was telling Alex a story anyway.

Alex smiled and lifted her hand, then let it fall back to the bed. "I've got the best company a pirate could have."

Betty looked up from the book and half knelt on the bed. "You didn't tell me you had Captain Minty on the ship!" It was an accusation mixed with elation.

"And wasn't it a good surprise?" Temp smiled and sat on the edge of the bed. She stroked the hair from Alex's face. "How did you come to have such wonderful company?"

Alex laughed a little. "Little heads have big ears. They overheard

Joe and Peter talking, and they thought they'd come find me and help me feel better. They even brought me a ginger biscuit."

Temp looked at the barely eaten biscuit on the side table, along with the empty glass of water. "I'm going to refill this, and then we're both going to get some sleep." She stood and held out her hand. "Come on, girls. Come with me to the kitchen."

They followed, and Betty stopped at the door. "You promise you'll tell me more pirate stories later?"

Alex's smile was tinged with sadness. "I will, little pirate."

Temp's heart ached as she gathered water and a little food to take back to her cabin.

"There you are!" Mary Margaret threw up her hands when she saw them. "Where on earth have you been hiding?"

"They were keeping Alex company in my cabin," Temp said, glancing at her with a raised eyebrow.

She went pale and put her hands to her mouth. "I'm so sorry, Captain Strud. This ship is so big, and it has so many hiding places—"

Temp held up her hand. "It's okay, Mary Margaret. They just wanted to help Alex." She looked at the girls. "But you know to stay in the staff sections of the ship, right? Not to go anywhere near the passenger sections?"

Betty nodded solemnly. "We know. We won't do anything to get us chucked off the ship, we swear."

"Okay. Listen to your governess and be good." Temp took the tray back to her cabin, where Alex was still awake and staring at the wall.

"Infection, eh?" She laughed weakly. "After all I've done, after all I've been through, I'm going to die of a stinking wound."

"You're not going to die." Temp set down the tray. "You're the fiercest pirate in the sky. The strongest woman to fly on the deadliest ship beneath the stars." She caressed Alex's hot cheek. "And I love you, and I refuse to give you up just yet."

Alex turned her face to kiss her hand. "If only agreeing with you meant it was true."

"We're heading to Mid Manchester. I'm taking you to a hospital."

Alex nodded and let her head fall to the side. "I'm so tired," she murmured.

Temp kicked off her shoes and climbed into bed beside her. "Sleep. I'm here." She got as close as she could without touching any of Alex's injuries and drifted off.

When she woke, Alex's breathing was laboured and wheezy. She didn't stir when Temp shook her gently, and Temp tapped her cheek. "Alex? Love, please. Please wake up."

She didn't.

Temp eyes filled, and it hurt to breathe. The bell in her cabin rang, and she shuffled to it, keeping her eyes on Alex.

"Coming into dock, Captain."

"Good. I'll be right there." She hung up and called the switchboard. "Please tell Joe to come and sit with Alex." She kissed Alex's brow and left, her heart developing slow cracks that would allow it to shatter if the worst came to pass.

She took the tiller and brought the Chimera in to dock. The Triport was busy, but they'd been allowed to dock at a lower station towards the rear of the city, away from the main ports. Once the docking ropes were secure, she went back to her cabin.

Joe looked up, worry in his eyes. "It's bad."

She nodded sharply. "We need to get her to the hospital."

"Peter has already gone down to get transport. They're using passenger flyers on the streets here. That'll be best to keep from jarring her."

Together, they lifted her from the bed, and Temp ignored the shooting pain in her side as she carried Alex through the ship and down the plank to the dock. Peter waited beside a small flyer with a bench seat in the back, a propeller attached to the rear, and a small balloon holding it aloft. A man sat at the single-stick tiller, looking down at her.

Temp climbed in, and Peter hit the side. It set off, flying slowly down the middle of the street, passing others going in every direction. Temp kept her eyes on Alex, willing her to wake. She'd love to see these new little personal transporters, and Temp wanted to show them to her.

They pulled up outside the hospital, and Temp climbed down carefully. She carried her inside and was met right away by several nurses, who brought over a rolling bed. Laying her down, she kissed Alex's brow, and then explained the various injuries and likelihood of infection. They wheeled her away, and she sat in a chair with no idea what to do with herself next.

Hours went by. Joe, Peter, and even Wade visited to see how she was doing and if there was any news. There wasn't, and she ate only half the sandwich Joe brought her.

By the time the doctor came in, she was about to go in search of answers.

He sat down beside her, his expression grim. "She's very ill. We're going to do what we can, but the wound in her side has become infected, and the infection has spread to her blood. We've put a proper cast on her arm and wrapped her ankle. Those will give her some pain relief. In the meantime, we have to wait." He stood. "You didn't give her name when she came in. We need her information."

Temp didn't know what to say. Alex Minty was a wanted pirate, so that name was out. But giving her real name felt like a betrayal. "Lady Alex Billinghurst." It was the best she could do.

His eyebrows rose. "I see. Please leave your contact details, and we'll send a crow if anything changes. There's really nothing you can do right now, and she simply needs rest. You can come back and visit in the evening, if you wish."

Temp loathed the idea of leaving Alex alone, but a thought had started to swirl in her head, and she simply couldn't get rid of it. She left, breathing in the damp air, and headed back to the ship.

They had a potential cure on board. She ran up the plank and into the ship, heading straight for her cabin. She put the bag on the bed and pulled out the Apple and the little tree.

"Temp..." Joe stood in the doorway, Wade behind him. "When you told us about what happened out there, you said you'd told the Blue Men you wouldn't use it."

"I told them I wouldn't *mis*use it." She held it in her palm. "It could save her."

"It could also kill her. Turn her into one of those creatures that will then go galloping through the hospital like a monster from their nightmares." Wade came in and picked up the tree, examining it closely. "Didn't you say this one was given to her, specifically?"

Temp frowned, lowering the Apple. "She chose it after her father loped off."

"Then doesn't it seem like this might be a better bet than that?" He tilted his head towards the Apple but didn't take his eyes off the tree. He touched the middle branch, the little apples turned, and the trunk opened to reveal the runestone inside. It fell into his palm, and he held it up, lowering his goggles to look at it more closely. "Do you know what the rune means?"

She shook her head. "We haven't had time to look."

The three of them headed to her office without another word. Still, she clasped the oddly firm Apple in her hand. If that's what it took, then so be it. Alex was dying anyway...but would she want to live forever? Or live forever as a creature on the moors? Temp shuddered at the thought.

In her office they each grabbed a book and started flipping pages.

"Healing." Joe held up his book, showing them the photo that matched the little red stone. "Temp, I think that creature gave her that because it knew she was hurt."

Temp flipped it over in her palm. "What do I do with it? Melt it down and get her to drink it?"

Wade snapped his book shut. "Whatever you do, you'd better do it quick. Take it down there and see if anything comes to you." He held out his hand. "But maybe leave the Apple here?"

Slowly, she handed it over, and then turned away, the rune in her hand. The streets were crowded, and she made her way on foot, able to move faster than the varied line of transport options clogging the road. Back in Alex's room, she sat beside her and caught her breath. The stone in her hand was bright against the white sheet covering Alex's barely moving chest.

Temp closed her eyes and bowed her head, her hand covering Alex's. For the first time in her life, she prayed. *I don't know if anyone out there can hear me. Norse gods, if you're there, this is your healing option. If there's a way to save her, show me. Please.*

She waited, hoping, but nothing happened. Tears slid down her face, and she let them fall. And then she felt the cold radiating from the stone, like she'd stuck her hand beneath arctic ice. It burned and hurt to hold it. An image flashed in her mind of Alex's wound, and she knew what she had to do.

She pulled the sheet back to reveal the bandage around her waist. The knife she kept sheathed in her boot cut through the material easily, and it fell away with a whisper to reveal the blackened and swollen red hole in Alex's side. Trembling, she placed the rune against her side.

Alex screamed.

Her back arched, and her eyes opened wide, and Temp gasped and tried to pull the rune away. But it was stuck to the skin, and then...it was gone. It disappeared into the wound, and Alex writhed on the bed, holding Temp's hand and gasping.

"I'm sorry," Temp said, over and over again. "I'm so sorry. I was hoping it would help. Fuck, I should have used the Apple. I'm so sorry, love."

Alex went limp, unconscious. Several nurses rushed in and asked what had happened, but Temp couldn't very well tell them she'd used an ancient artefact to heal Alex, and it had been sucked into the wound. "She woke in pain and then fainted again," she said. She couldn't figure out how to explain the state of the bandages, but they didn't ask. They simply muttered about people not knowing what they were doing and went about reapplying them.

Her shoulders fell, and the first shards of her heart fell away into nothingness. She lay her head on the edge of the bed and welcomed the exhausted sleep that came over her. At least she'd be beside Alex to the end.

Chapter Twenty-Nine

A SHARD OF ICE pierced Alex's soul, ripping it to shreds, the pain excruciating as cold, white light shot through every cell of her being. Images flew past her, and she tried to catch them, ask for help, demand the pain to stop. But when the images slowed, they stared accusingly. People she'd killed in raids, in fights, when they'd boarded ships. Their pleas, their hatred, their desire to hurt her in turn. She felt them all, heard them all, and was forced to remember the moments she'd used a knife or gun to end someone else's life.

A prism of life flung her backwards, back in time, and she was cowering against a wall as her father berated her mother, who stood in front of a tiny Alex, protecting her. And then she was gone, and Alex was locked in one room after another, never allowed any freedom, always fearful of the moment her father would strike out. Cambrick's ugly face leered at her, telling her what a good wife she'd be.

And then he fell through a black hole, screaming. She hadn't wanted to save him.

The images slowed, and she jolted forwards. Temp stood at the tiller of the Chimera, strong and courageous, determined to always do the right thing even as she flew a ship dedicated to the dubious.

Temp's body covering hers, her storm cloud eyes looking into Alex's with such longing, such...love.

The pain stopped like it hit a wall. Love. She was free, and she was loved. Life going forwards wouldn't be about reaction and running. She could do and be anything she wanted. But who was that? What would that life look like? The images faded into nothingness, and she drifted into a dreamless sleep.

Voices, muted and calm, filtered into her awareness. She thought she recognised a few of them, but everything was soft around the edges, like her senses were covered in wool. She moved her hand, and it was instantly caught and held.

"Alex? Love, can you hear me?"

Her eyes felt glued shut, but she forced them open. "You look like you've been dragged through a hedge backwards by an angry cow."

Temp laughed, the deep circles under her eyes lifting a little. "Good to see you too."

Alex rolled her head a little. "You look terrible too. Both of you."

Joe and Wade grinned back at her from the end of her bed. They were both rumpled, like they'd been sleeping in a chair. Wade's hair stuck up even more than usual, and things looked perilously close to falling out of his many pockets.

A man in a white coat stepped to her side. "You're a miracle case, Lady Billinghurst. I was certain you wouldn't live through the night, and yet, your fever is gone and the infection around your wound seems to have nearly healed overnight. Honestly, I can't fathom it."

Alex thought of the images and knowledge that had flowed through her with the ice. "Just lucky, I guess."

"Well, I think it's safe to get you back on the ship and back to your estate. I'm sure you have a physician who can take care of you at home, where you'll be more comfortable. I imagine your servants and your...companion, can assist you from this point forwards." He tipped his head at Temp and left the room.

"What happened?" Alex asked, looking at Temp.

"I was going to use the Apple." Her expression was haunted as she looked at a spot beyond Alex. "I couldn't bear the thought of losing you. Fortunately, Wade figured out another option."

"The rune stone." Alex suddenly understood. "What was the symbol?"

"Healing." Temp's grin turned into a smile. "And it seems to have worked. I put it against your side, and your wound just kind of sucked it in." Her smile faltered. "Though it seemed like it was extremely painful."

"Being shot is extremely painful. That was like being eaten alive by the demons of the underworld." She shivered. "And it wasn't just a healing of the body. I saw so many things...so many people I've hurt and the way I was hurt as a child. Things I can let go now."

Temp kissed her hand. "Then let's get you out of here."

Alex raised her hand. "He called me Lady Billinghurst. Why?"

"I couldn't very well say the famed pirate was here, could I? I'd save you only to have you hanged." Temp kept her voice low, and Wade and Joe nodded. "I couldn't bring myself to use the name your father called you, so I said you were Alex Billinghurst."

Alex rolled that around on her tongue. "I like it. Perhaps I'll keep it." At the relief in Temp's expression, she cupped her cheek. "Thank you for saving me."

"Thank you for not giving up."

A small group of nurses came in and said the visitors needed to leave, so they could get Alex ready to go. Temp, Wade, and Joe left the room. It was strange, being able to move about less gingerly than she had only days before, and after being so close to death. There were plenty of comments about how lucky she was, how it was a miracle, and how her "friend" had hardly ever left her side.

All of it was true, and yet it lacked truth as well. She was lucky, that was true in itself. But it hadn't been luck that had driven her to run from Temp and end up in her father's grasp. Her healing was a miracle, but one given to her by a kind of ancient mysticism that couldn't be explained. And Temp was far, far more than just a friend.

The clothes she had to put on were the ones she'd arrived in. Sadly, no one had thought to bring clean ones, and these stank of sweat and illness. She couldn't wait to get them off again. And maybe this time, she'd be more interested in how they came off.

Temp was waiting outside the door when the nurse brought her out of the room in a simple wheeled chair.

"I don't need this. I can walk." Alex wanted to get up and fling the chair away, but she was just a little too tired to do it effectively.

"Why not save your strength for later?" Temp asked, her expression not giving anything away.

Alex grinned. "Well, if that's on offer, wheel away."

The nurse flushed and averted her eyes and was silent on their trip to the front of the hospital, where a floating personal transport waited.

"Isn't this fabulous?" Alex said, getting out of the chair and walking around the little flyer. "People will hardly have to walk anywhere ever again."

Temp held out her hand and helped Alex onto the bench seat. "I'm not sure that's good for the body, but it's certainly a better alternative than walking the city streets and getting one's shoes filthy."

Alex rolled her eyes. "We need to get you used to being a little dirtier, Captain."

Temp laughed and put her arm around Alex's shoulders. "I'm sure you're up for that particular job."

They made their way back onto the ship easily enough, and Alex was glad Temp led the way to the dining room. Ginny and Vee were already ensconced at a table, and they both rose when she and Temp entered.

"It's so good to see you well," Vee said, giving her a hug and a kiss on the cheek. "Your captain has been the kind of company only another angry bear could withstand."

Ginny slapped her arm playfully. "That isn't true. Captain Strud was perfectly professional, if a little bruised around the emotional edges. But it is good to see you back. Will you tell us about your adventures?"

They sat, and over a sumptuous lunch, they told Ginny and Vee much of the tale, omitting a few pieces, like the fact that they had ancient artefacts on the ship, and that Alex had been healed by one of them. Those things felt like mysteries better kept to themselves.

"Goodness." Ginny sat back, pulling the pen and paper from the leather pouch bound around her arm. "My imagination is simply overwhelmed with possibilities for stories." She began scribbling furiously as the others laughed.

"We're disembarking in London-on-High. We've had a truly delicious time, and we so hope you'll come stay with us at our home in Fitzroy Square." Vee stroked Ginny's arm, though she didn't seem to notice. "Our kind should stick together, where we can."

Alex yawned. "I'm sorry. I think I still need to get my strength back. Let's have a drink before you leave the ship though."

Temp escorted her back to her cabin. "I need to upship and get us on course. I'll be back soon. You're sure you're okay?"

Alex kissed her, slow and soft, nipping at her bottom lip. "I'm sure. Just hurry back."

Temp growled low in her throat and shook her head as she left the room. "Damn pirate."

Alex undressed, leaving the rumpled clothes in a heap, and crawled into the soft bed. How was it that the days of flying on the Urchin felt so long ago? Where was it? Were they okay?

She lay on her good side and let her thoughts wander. She drifted to sleep, comforted and safe.

When she woke, it was dark outside the porthole, and Temp wasn't with her. She stretched and got out of bed fairly easily and saw the folded pile of clean clothes on the chair beside the bed. On top was a note in Temp's crisp handwriting.

You were sleeping too well for me to wake you. If you'll go to the kitchen when you wake, they'll know where on the ship to find me. Love, T.

She made use of the wash bowl. It would be nice to get an actual bath at their next port, if that was possible.

Possible. Anything and everything was possible, and that left her in limbo. What did she want? What did Temp want? What did her life look like now that she no longer had to run? She dressed, draping the blouse over her still bound arm, and made her way to the kitchen.

Joe looked up from where he sat with the children. "Well, Sleeping Beauty finally rose from her berth." He stood and motioned for her to take his seat. "I'll get you supper."

"Thank you. Is Temp around here somewhere?" She accepted the pencil Sal offered her and added a little heart to Sal's drawing of the ship and its people.

"She's with Wade in the Illusionary Lab. He wanted some input on the next desire requests for the incoming passengers." He set a plate of bread and cheese in front of her, along with slices of cold meat. "She told me on pain of death to call the moment you were up." He smiled and went to the copper tube on the wall. He pressed a button and spoke into it, then pulled up a seat at the table. "She'll be here in a moment, I imagine."

Alex ate and asked questions about the girls' drawing. Sal climbed off her chair and stood beside Alex's, looking at her expectantly, thumb, as ever, in her mouth.

"She wants to sit on your lap, Alex." Betty looked up from the drawing, a line of smeared charcoal on her cheek.

"Ah." Alex looked at Joe. "Would you mind? I can't lift her with one arm."

He obliged, picking up Sal and placing her gently on Alex's lap. She leaned her head against Alex's shoulder and watched her sister.

"Does she not speak, Betty?" Alex asked, caressing the little girl's hair.

"Nah. Not yet anyhow. We always had to be really quiet, you know, so we didn't get chucked off the sky city. Now she's quiet as a titmouse being hunted by a cat." Betty frowned at her sister. "You can talk now, you know. These people aren't like them others."

Sal pressed a little tighter to Alex and looked away.

"She'll do it in her own time." Alex looked towards the door when it opened, and Temp came in.

She took in the scene and met Alex's eyes. "That's quite the picture. I bet your old crew wouldn't recognise you."

Alex knew that was utterly true, on many levels. "Can we all have a drink together tonight? I think we have things to talk about."

Temp frowned a little. "Of course. Anything you want."

Mary Margaret came in, wiping her hands on her apron. "Right, you two. It's time for bed. Off we go."

Betty slid off her seat and handed Temp the drawing. "You should hang it somewhere special. It's the whole crew of the dragon ship, and me and Sal. That way you'll always remember us."

Mary Margaret lifted Sal off Alex's lap, though she tried to hold on, her eyes tearing up.

"I'll be right here when you wake up in the morning, little one." She kissed Sal's forehead, and she let go, going with her governess quietly.

"Let's take our drinks to my office," Temp said, putting her arm around Alex when she stood. "It will give us some privacy."

Joe picked up the copper phone and told Wade and Peter to join them, and he carried a tray of drinks into Temp's office. Alex sat on the couch, and Temp sat beside her, pulling her close. Joe poured the drinks and handed them out, with Wade and Peter taking seats opposite them. Joe took the last remaining seat, behind Temp's desk.

"Thank you," Alex said, looking at all of them. "For helping Temp save my life, and for giving a damn what happened to me at all." She raised her drink. "To living well."

They echoed the sentiment and drank.

"Have you thought at all about what's next?" Wade asked.

"I have. A little. But I have some questions first." Temp gently stroked Alex's arm. "Alex, do you want to go back to the Urchin? To being a pirate?"

Alex shook her head slowly. "No. The things I experienced after the runestone...I don't want to talk about it, but I know that isn't my path anymore."

Temp nodded, as though she'd expected as much. "Joe, are you tied to the Chimera? I know it's good work and you send money to the family, but if you could make that same money on any other ship, would you?"

He swirled his drink in its glass. "The Chimera is interesting, and I like the elegance of it. But it's you I like working for. If you went elsewhere?" He shrugged. "The ship itself has no particular hold on me, no."

Again, Temp nodded, still looking thoughtful. "Wade? Same question."

"And a slightly different answer." He stared at his big boots, and even those had small pockets on them. "I get to create amazing things on this ship, things not seen anywhere else in the world. Creating is a part of who I am, and I wouldn't get to do it, not like this, on any other ship." He looked up, worry in his eyes. "But without you, who would give me the room to invent the things I do? And...well, our past."

Temp seemed to understand, and Alex, having heard enough of their story, got what he wasn't saying in full. "Peter?"

"I'm with you, Cap. Anywhere and everywhere." He swallowed, and his face flushed. "But, now there's Mary Margaret too, and I sure would want her to come with, wherever I go."

Temp smiled at him. "I understand that feeling well, lad."

Alex shifted to look at her. "Where are you going with all this?"

"One moment. I'm not quite done." Temp kissed her forehead. "Alex, I know it's a tender subject, but I need to broach it. You're now the sole heir to the Billinghurst estate. The whole thing, which, if I'm not mistaken, is considerable. You're a wealthy woman, if you claim it."

Alex stared at her. "But so much of that legacy is tainted."

Temp twisted a strand of Alex's hair around her finger. "That's true. But you can untaint it, so to speak. Do good with it. Help people the way you have for so many years."

Alex grimaced. "A pirate who gives away treasure doesn't get much respect. But you found out, did you?"

"It wasn't a well-kept secret, love. Too many people sing your praises for it to have stayed quiet." She paused. "But that begs another question. With that money, you could buy your own home in any sky city, if that's what you wanted. You could have a house full of staff and do whatever you wanted to do."

The thought made Alex twitchy. "No. That's not what I want. A house somewhere might be nice, but not to live in permanently. I love being in the air too much for that."

Temp nodded again, and it was easy to see the gears moving her thoughts around. "That brings us to me. I've made the decision to leave the Followers. They won't be getting the Apple, though I will give them the story. I'm no longer willing to find artefacts for organisations that can be infiltrated or twisted to someone's agenda."

They tipped their glasses to her and drank.

"When I was sitting beside you in that hospital, Alex, I had a lot of time to think about what I'd do differently if you made it through. And I think it's time for me to leave the Chimera. Like you, I'm well-off and I've invested wisely. That gives me the option to do something different. That said, I have no intention of leaving behind the people I care about most in the world."

Alex shifted so she could sit side-on and look at Temp as she spoke. "What do you propose?"

"A new ship." Temp's grin held no small amount of mischief. "One we have built to our own specifications. One where each of us takes the opportunity to do something we love." She motioned at Wade. "We'd have a Creator Lab built just for you. You could make whatever you wanted to. But," she held up her finger, "no more hiding your talent. It's far too special for only a few of us to see it. I'd ask you to consider showing your work at the next World's Fair in America. And I'd like you to consider taking on an apprentice. There's a lad in Low Nottingham with talent, and I think it would do you good to talk to more than just your machines."

He sat back, looking stunned. "You'd do that for me?"

Temp turned to Joe. "You're also being wasted behind the scenes. I know you miss your family. I suggest we see if your wife and kids would like to take a place on the new ship. They'd have their own section, of course. What would you like to do, Joe? If you could do anything?"

He too looked as flummoxed as Wade. "I've never given it any thought, Temp. Can I get back to you?"

"Of course." Last, she turned to Peter. "Lad, I'd take you anywhere, you know that. And if you want to follow us and take the ship in a new direction, you know you're welcome." She paused. "But the Chimera needs a captain, and I can't think of anyone better to take my place."

He stared at her, open-mouthed. "But...but then I wouldn't be with you, Cap."

"No, lad, you wouldn't. But you'd be making your own way in the world, flying the most beautiful ship in the sky. And it would give a nice start to your life with Mary Margaret, should your relationship reach that level."

He blinked and wiped tears away with the back of his hand. "I don't know, Cap. It's...it's a lot to think about. I'll need to talk to Mary Margaret."

"Of course."

"The girls, Temp?" Joe asked.

Alex held Temp's hand as she turned to face her. She could see the internal doubts and squeezed. "Spit it out, Strud. This is no time to hold back."

Temp smiled, and her shoulders dropped a bit. "Pirate, I never wanted kids. My life never called for me to settle down that way. But those little girls feel like they were dropped into my lap, and I admit, I've become fond of them. Now, rumour has it you've been funding an orphanage for some time. If you don't feel like they belong with us, then I'll respect that, and maybe we can use the place you fund. If not..." Temp looked into her eyes, seeming to search for an answer. "Maybe we can have our own very unusual family."

Alex swallowed and looked down at their clasped hands. "I do fund the orphanage, and it looks like I'll be able to help it a lot more now that I've got access to money. I no longer need to steal from the rich, since I'll *be* one of the rich." She felt more than saw Temp's disappointment. "However, I think they'll be just fine without two more children to look after."

"Really? You mean it?" Temp squeezed her hand. "What about the rest of it? The custom ship and flying around the world?"

"Yes. Yes to all of it." Alex's heart soared with the knowledge that it was exactly what she wanted for the rest of her life. "We both need to fly like we need to breathe, and being able to share that with people we care about gives us the best of all worlds." She hesitated, those words pushing on a sore spot. "I have people I care about on the Urchin too. I don't know if or how they fit into our plans, but I need to track them down and see them."

Temp nodded, her eyes filled with understanding. "We'll send out crows and see if we can get information. No more wandering dangerous backstreets for either of us for a while."

"For a while." Alex wiggled her eyebrows. "My adventuring days aren't over, Captain Strud. I'll have you know I fully intend to continue looking for amazing mythological artefacts guarded by amazing mythological creatures."

"Agreed, Captain Minty." Temp leaned over and kissed her.

"And that's our cue to go about our business, gentlemen." Joe stood, finished his drink, and waved the other two out ahead of him. "We'll have answers for you by the time we make port."

He closed the door softly behind him, leaving them alone.

Alex rested her forehead against Temp's. "Life is going to be so different now."

"Life is going to be whatever we make of it." Temp wrapped her hand around the back of Alex's neck and pulled her forwards. "And I want to show you right now how much I love you."

Alex fell into the kiss that held so much promise, so much passion. She wrapped her arm around Temp and held tight. Silently, she gave thanks that when she'd finally stopped running, she'd run straight into the arms of the woman she'd love for eternity.

CHAPTER THIRTY

ALEX BIT HER LIP as the flyer bumped against the dock. Ropes were thrown down, and the plunking sound of the plank hitting the dock reverberated through her feet. She jumped down and took Temp's hand when she landed beside her.

"You're ready?" Temp gently moved a piece of hair from Alex's cheek.

Alex nodded and tugged at her hand. "More than. If I have to spend any more time in bed recuperating from wounds the runestone already healed, I'll turn to mayhem just for something to do."

"I don't think *all* the time in bed was wasted." Temp grinned and followed her down the stairs to land.

"You know what I mean." Alex took her hand again as they made their way through Camden-in-Middle towards the rendezvous point.

The light tap of Temp's cane hitting the pavement blended into the sound of merchants hawking wares and the drilling noise from the makers showing off their talent to passing trade. Hardly anyone glanced their way, which was a novel feeling. Alex hadn't been able to walk down streets in daylight in a very long time. Now, holding Temp's arm, it felt like a return to the sun after being below ground. The world was alive with promise.

"There it is."

Alex didn't hesitate. She opened the door to the Camden Head and swept inside. Her eyes adjusted quickly but not before she was swept into a tight hug.

"It is damnably good to see you not dead." Tom held her at

arm's length. "You're not, are you? Some spirit sent to haunt me after I took over the Urchin? You don't look much like the captain who left us."

She laughed and punched him in the stomach, knocking the wind out of him. "Do I feel like a spirit?"

He wheezed and motioned towards a table behind him.

There sat the crew of the Urchin, all waiting to welcome back their captain. There were hugs, bawdy jests, and plenty of questions. She moved among her old crew, her heart swelling at the genuine affection they still had for her.

"Trust a pirate." Polly stood up, hands on hips, glowering at her. "You bring me aboard and then leave me to this lot. Do you have any idea how much they eat?"

"Not that she couldn't feed Rome's army with nothing but a pot and a potato." Tom sidled up next to her and put his arm around her waist.

"Idiot." She kissed his cheek and then pulled Alex into a hug. "Your crew wept like children when they thought they'd lost you."

"They're all a bunch of pampered ninnies, aren't they? Softest pirates in the sky." Alex smiled as she looked around and accepted a pint of beer. "And the Urchin?"

She sat at the table among her crew, aware that Temp had settled herself at the bar near enough to hear the conversation but not so near as to intrude on the reunion. It was kind and thoughtful, but Alex missed her physical presence.

"Urchin was hit bad by that dragon's fire." Tom shook his head dolefully. "We managed to get her to land but had a hell of a time fixing her up to get her to a place where we could fix her proper. Once we got her to London-on-Ground, and then hid her away in Low London, we took shelter and worked on getting her airworthy again." He stopped, his gaze searching. "I sent for word of you. Offered up a reward, asked around. Went to the dock each day, just in case you made it back. Then I heard you'd been taken..."

Alex held up her hand. "No need to go there, Tom. I'll share some of my story but believe me when I say it's no one's fault but them who took me."

He looked at her for a moment longer, then nodded. "Well then. You know our story. Let's hear yours."

Alex told it the way they wanted to hear it. It was a pirate's tale of adventure, foes, and treasure, and they hardly made a sound as she shared it. She left out the parts about her real name, her family, and the artefacts. "Nearly died for real that time," she said, when she got to the part about being shot. "If it weren't for the captain of the Chimera, I'd be long dead and haunting you already." Alex grinned at Temp over the rim of her pint glass, and Temp tipped hers in response.

Tom looked over his shoulder at Temp. "And is she the one that has you all dressed up like a lady from a sky city?"

Alex kicked his shin, making him grunt. "You can't possibly think anyone could make me do anything I wouldn't want to." She took a deep drink and set the glass down. "No, lads. Truth is, my time on the Urchin is done. I needed to come see you, make sure you haven't all turned into dirtier beasts than you already are." She laughed at the groans and protests. "But I have a new path, and you have a new captain." She clapped Tom on the back. "And you're doing a damn fine job, sounds like."

The next two hours were ribald fun like she'd enjoyed for so many years, and Temp eventually joined them, though she didn't drink because she was flying them to another stop after this one. When it came time to leave, she gave Tom and Polly hugs outside the pub. "Take good care of yourselves. Be careful. Watch your backs. You can always get a crow to me if you need anything. Send word to the Billinghurst Manor, and they'll get the message to me no matter where I am."

Tom's eyebrows raised. "Never thought that name would pass your lips again."

She kissed his grizzled cheek. "Me either."

They made their way back to the flyer and after Alex had

climbed in, Temp stooped to kiss her. "You okay?"

Alex looked out over the city. "I am. A little sad, I suppose, but I know it's the right decision."

"Thank God for that. I'd hate to have to set the Urchin alight again just to keep you at my side." Temp laughed and dropped into the pilot's seat. "You sure about the next stop?"

Alex clenched and unclenched her fists. "That will be harder, but yes."

They dropped away from the dock and flew up above the clouds. In no time at all, they were back over London-on-High. Temp brought the flyer into the private Billinghurst dock behind the manor.

They climbed out, and Alex stood staring at it for a long moment. "I never thought I'd come back here," she said softly, taking Temp's hand absently. "And then when I did, I thought I was going to die here."

"And now?" Temp asked, kissing Alex's knuckles.

"Now..." Alex headed down the dock steps. "Now it's mine, and the horror of it can be washed away with the years."

They made their way to the front door, which was opened by the young, wide-eyed maid who had helped Alex on her first night.

"Lady Billinghurst." She curtsied low. "Welcome home. We weren't sure what was happening—"

"Cease speaking." A man's voice cut her off as he strode up next to her. "Lady, please forgive her. She speaks out of turn. May I take your coat?"

"There's nothing to forgive, and don't talk to her like that." Alex handed him her coat, and he took Temp's as well. "Please gather the staff in the receiving room."

He bowed his head and strode away, his back stiff. She'd probably hurt his pride by telling him not to talk to women like they were worthless. Well, he was going to be far more irritated in a moment. She walked through the hall, touching pieces of furniture her mother had loved and noting things of her father's that would need to be removed immediately.

"It's a beautiful house." Temp had her hands in her pockets as she looked around. "You're sure you don't want to make it your permanent home?"

"Don't make me want to kick you." Alex shook her head. "We have a plan. I just need to fix this before we go. We'll sell it and use the funds to buy something that doesn't make me want to light a match."

They waited together in the receiving room, and Alex allowed the memories of her mother's love and laughter to filter through the other emotions. The staff arrived one by one and waited.

"Thank you for stopping to speak with me. For those of you who don't know me, I'm Lady Billinghurst. My father is now deceased, and I'm his heir. As such, I have to decide what to do with the estate." She saw Brick Hilda at the back, her metal ear glinting in the buzzing lamplight. "I'm sorry for all my father put you through. He was an evil man, and he'll be missed about as much as you'd miss having a wasp in your nether regions." There were better, more descriptive ways to say that, but she wanted this over with. "I'm going to sell the manor. We'll be setting up a new home elsewhere, though we aren't certain where it will be yet. If you'd like to continue to work for me and my family, please leave word with my solicitor, and I'll be in touch when the new house is ready. If you would like to seek employ elsewhere, I will provide a letter of recommendation." She stopped, uncertain what more there was to say.

"When will the movers come, Lady Billinghurst?" the sweet young maid asked, and it was easy to see her hands trembling.

"By the end of the week. I'll place a marker on the items I wish to keep, which will be few. If there's a piece you'd particularly like for yourself, please let the solicitor know when he arrives with the movers." She blinked away sudden tears. "I don't know why you continued to work for him. I can't fathom what he may have put many of you through. I can't make it right. But I can help you find better futures. Thank you. That's all."

The servants moved from the room slowly, talking in low tones. Temp wrapped her arm around Alex and kissed her forehead. "I'm sorry. I know that was hard."

Alex leaned into her. "It was. It is. Let me just look around and mark things, and then we'll go." She took the roll of tape and moved from room to room. It was only when she got to her father's room that cold spread through her. Shaking, she placed bits of tape on a few items. In the back of the wardrobe, at the top and covered in dust, she saw a box.

"Can you reach that for me?" she asked Temp, who had quietly and unobtrusively followed her throughout.

Temp pulled it down and handed it to her. "What is it?"

"My mother's jewellery box." She lifted the lid, and tears slid down her cheeks when her mother's perfume wafted up from it. "I thought he'd thrown it all out." She snapped it closed and stood. "I'm done. Let's go home."

Temp took her hand, and they walked out of the manor. She took a last look behind her. The past fell away, crumbling like the old parchment from a story that no longer needed to be read. She stood on her toes and kissed Temp hard. Her future was yet to be written, and it didn't need four walls. All it needed was the woman in front of her and the open skies ahead.

EPILOGUE

One year later

TEMP SHADED HER EYES against the late day sun. The ocean crashed against the cliffs behind her, and Alex was silhouetted against the sky as she called Betty and Sal to come in for lunch.

"You need to watch out for that one," Joe said, pointing at Betty, his metal finger glinting in the sun. "She'll steal that ship right off the dock one day, just to see if she can."

Temp laughed. "True. She's already taking after Alex. Sal is a little more like me. Subdued. Quiet."

He scoffed and turned her towards the house. "Wade wants to show you his newest gadget, and Peter is due to show up with Mary Margaret any moment now."

They walked towards the new house in silence. Cornwall-on-Sea had turned out to be the perfect place for their home away from the ship. The sprawling old Rockhaven Manor held their extended family without issue when they weren't in the sky. Temp loved that it reminded her of her own family home, although this home was most definitely land-based instead of being in the sky city she'd enjoyed as a child.

They'd made the decision after discussing, and arguing, over which sky city might suit them best. So many were bogged down in shady politics and inequality, and none of them had felt right. In the end, they'd moved to Cornwall-on-Sea, a somewhat remote area that meant they could come and go without checking in with anyone.

A shadow passed overhead, and the children ran up the grass

slope, screaming. "It's the Urchin! The Urchin is here! The pirates are coming!"

Temp shook her head and turned to watch as the ship docked near their own. Tom and Polly came down the plank, and Tom swung Alex into a huge hug as she batted at his head. The children flung themselves at the couple, who greeted them with open arms. The ship's horn sounded, and several of the crew waved as it set off into the sky once again. Now that he was joining them on the new ship, he'd passed the mantle on to another lad with a good head on his shoulders. The Urchin continued to take on the desperate and those trying to make a better life for their families down on the land, and it was a legacy Alex was proud of, despite the violence that sometimes accompanied it.

The group walked towards the house, Sal on Tom's shoulders. He held out his hand to Temp when they arrived at the house. "Captain Strud."

"Tom. Good to see you." Temp turned and gave Polly, now his wife, a kiss on the cheek. "Good to see you too, Polly."

They went in, and Alex lingered with her on the doorstep. "The firepit is ready to go when the sun goes down. The girls threw all manner of debris on it."

Temp pulled her close. "Sounds about right. Any regrets before we set sail tomorrow, pirate?"

Alex sighed and looked out at the ship tilting in the light breeze. "I can't wait. It feels like it's taken forever to get the Green Man in the air. Wade is already sleeping on it. He couldn't stand it being ready for him and not getting everything just the way he wants it."

"He'll come down for the party this evening." Temp had no doubt he'd be itching to get underway too. "Thankfully, the lad working with him still needs to eat and likes talking to people outside their lab. He'll keep Wade from becoming a true recluse."

"Joe's boys are winding the girls up with tales of adventure. I don't think they'll sleep a wink tonight."

"I don't think we will either." Temp pulled her in tight and kissed her hard. "It's our last night of real privacy, and I plan to make the best of every second."

"Enough already, you lot." Tom stuck his head out the window. "Joe says you're needed in the kitchen."

Laughing, they entered the melee in the house, where children chased each other from room to room, and pirates and aristocracy drank and filled each other in on the happenings of the last year. Peter and Mary Margaret came in and were received with hugs and plenty of banter when it was clear Mary Margaret had a child on the way.

The food was carried out on platters to outdoor tables, the fire was lit, and they settled on the grass to watch the sunset as they picnicked outside.

"I have something for you," Temp said, pulling a large package off the table and handing it to Alex.

Alex tore into it and gasped. "They're beautiful. They look..." She broke off and pulled on a glove, then hit a button that flung out the clawed grips from the fingers. Then she yanked off her slippers and pulled on the boots. With a tap of the toe on the grass, a blade slid out of each one. "But how?"

Temp nodded towards Wade, who'd finally come off the ship for food. "We had a good talk about the day we met, and I mentioned that it was a shame you didn't have any of your old gear. It was fetching, and it also served a purpose. And with the adventure coming up, it seemed a shame you didn't have the gear that suits you so well."

Alex threw herself into Temp's arms after sheathing the glove blades. "Thank you so much!"

Tom whistled, and there was laughter as the kiss deepened.

"I have something for you too." Alex spun and took a smaller parcel from Joe, who was grinning.

Temp opened it a little more formally, and her heart leapt when she saw what was inside. "My father's gloves."

"We had the leather restored and the compass has been

recalibrated so it's utterly perfect." Alex put her hands on her hips. "We can't put our lives in the hands of a captain with no compass."

Temp pulled them on, emotion making it hard to breathe. "Thank you. He'll be right there in the sky with us." The soft leather fit perfectly, as it always had, and the compass on the back of her hand moved as she did, until it pointed true north. Right at Alex.

She looked at the people around her. "We set off on the next stage of our lives together tomorrow, and I'm so grateful you decided to join us. Joe, the young people you'll be training for air service will be lucky to learn from you. Wade, your inventions are going to set the world on fire, hopefully metaphorically. Peter, I'm so proud of you and all you achieved on the Chimera. Tom and Polly, you may regret coming aboard to help with all the kids. But once you're on the ship, you're stuck with us. Ginny and Vee will be boarding when we get to Mid-Bristol, and they've already offered to tutor the children as needed. We'll have a full ship, with enough room to take on the occasional stray if we come across one who's mad enough to want to join us."

"Thing is, Cap," Peter said, looking around. "Well, that is, we were wondering if you might have room for two more?" He grinned and touched Mary Margaret's protruding belly. "See, I once had someone tell me that the Chimera isn't a great place for kids. And since that person is someone I respect—"

Temp pulled him into a hard hug. "I'd be glad to have you as my first mate again, Peter."

A cheer went up, and there was toasting and jests all around.

The sun dipped below the horizon, and the fire crackled, sending sparks into the evening sky. Alex sat on the ground between Temp's legs, her head pillowed on Temp's shoulder.

"You ready for this?" Temp murmured in her ear.

"As long as I'm flying with you, I'm ready for anything." She traced a line along Temp's leg. "Trying to steal from your ship of dreams was the best decision I ever made."

Temp laughed, knowing the best dreams were yet to come.

Other Great Butterworth Books

Dark Haven by Brey Willows
Even vampires get tired of playing with their food...
Available on Amazon (ASIN B0C5P1HJXC)

Unwritten by Helena Harte
No strings is fun 'til it unravels.
Available from Amazon (ASIN B0DGQFFHYB)

Chucking Putty at the Queen by Simon Smalley
A heartbreaking, humorous, and courageous exploration of what it takes
to be ones authentic self.
Available from Amazon (ASIN B0DGGBV22W)

The Promise by Addison M Conley
When the world keeps pulling you under, who do you reach for?
Available on Amazon (ASIN B0DDY9FH6Z)

Back to Back by Jo Fletcher
."When Fred and Ruby's worlds collide, can love rise from the rubble?"
Available on Amazon (ASIN B0D6M499K2)

Heart of the Storm by Ally McGuire
Sometimes a storm is just what you need to clear the skies ahead.
Available on Amazon (ASIN B0CYTSQXWW)

Sanctuary by Helena Harte
*Passions ignite and possibilities unfold. Welcome to the Windy City Romance
series.*
Available from Amazon (ASIN B0D4B42RRW)

Brave Enough to Love by Valden Bush
In a dance between truth and sacrifice, can they rewrite the rules of love?
Available on Amazon (ASIN B0CQP8PMVB)

Dead Ringer by Robyn Nyx
Three bodies. One killer. No motive?
Available on Amazon (ASIN B0CPQ8HFK7)

Medea by JJ Taylor
Who will Medea become in her battle for freedom?
Available from Amazon (ASIN B0CK2FB7GW)

Virgin Flight by E.V. Bancroft
In the battle between duty and desire, can love win?
Available from Amazon (ASIN B0CKJWQZ45)

Fragments of the Heart by Ally McGuire
Love can be the greatest expedition of all.
Available on Amazon (ASIN B0CHBPHR6M)

Stunted Heart by Helena Harte
A stunt rider who lives in the fast lane. An ER doctor who can't take chances. A passion that could turn their worlds upside down.
Available on Amazon (ASIN B0C78GSWBV)

Here You Are by Jo Fletcher
.Can they unlock their hearts to find the true happiness they both deserve?
Available on Amazon (ASIN B0CBN935ZB)

Green for Love by E.V. Bancroft
All's fair in love and eco-war.
Available from Amazon (ASIN B0C28F7PX5)

Call of Love by Lee Haven
Separated by fear. Reunited by fate. Will they get a second chance at life and love?
Available from Amazon (ASIN B0BYC83HZD)

Where the Heart Leads by Ally McGuire
A writer. A celebrity. And a secret that could break their hearts.
Available on Amazon (ASIN B0BWFX5W9L)

Stolen Ambition by Robyn Nyx
Daughters of two worlds collide in a dangerous game of ambition and love.
Available on Amazon (ASIN B0BS1PRSCN)

Cabin Fever by Addison M Conley
She goes for the money, but will she stay for something deeper?
Available on Amazon (ASIN B0BQWY45GH)

Breakout for Love by Valden Bush
They're both running from their pasts. Together, they might make a new future.
Available from Amazon (ASIN B0CWHZ4SXL)

The Helion Band by AJ Mason
Rose's only crime was to show kindness to her royal mistress...
Available from Amazon (ASIN B09YM6TYFQ)

That Boy of Yours Wants Looking At by Simon Smalley
A riotously colourful and heart-rending journey of what it takes to live authentically.
Available from Amazon (ASIN B09V3CSQQW)

Sapphic Eclectic Volume Five edited by Nyx & Willows
A little something for everyone...
Available free from the Butterworth Books website

Of Light and Love by E.V. Bancroft
The deepest shadows paint the brightest love.
Available from Amazon (ASIN B0B64KJ3NP)

An Art to Love by Helena Harte
Second chances are an art form.
Available on Amazon (ASIN B0B1CD8Y42)

Music City Dreamers by Robyn Nyx
Music brings lovers together. In Music City, it can tear them apart. Available on Amazon (ASIN B0994XVDGR)

Let Love Be Enough by Robyn Nyx
When a killer sets her sights on her target, is there any stopping her?
Available on Amazon (ASIN B09YMMZ8XC)

Dead Pretty by Robyn Nyx
An FBI agent, a TV star, and a serial killer. Love hurts.
Available on Amazon (ASIN B09QRSKBVP)

Nero by Valden Bush
Banished and abandoned. Will destiny reunite her with the love of her life?
Available from Amazon (ASIN B0BHJKHK6S)

Warm Pearls and Paper Cranes by E.V. Bancroft
A family torn apart by secrets. The only way forward is love.
Available from Amazon (ASIN B09DTBCQ92)

Judge Me, Judge Me Not by James Merrick
One man's battle against the world and himself to find it's never too late to find, and use, your voice.
Available from Amazon (ASIN B09CLK91N5)

Scripted Love by Helena Harte
What good is a romance writer who doesn't believe in happy ever after?
Available on Amazon (ASIN B0993QFLNN)

Call to Me by Helena Harte
Sometimes the call you least expect is the one you need the most.
Available on Amazon (ASIN B08D9SR15H)

What's Your Story?

Global Wordsmiths, CIC, provides an all-encompassing service for all writers, ranging from basic proofreading and cover design to development editing, typesetting, and eBook services. A major part of our work is charity and community focused, delivering writing projects to under-served and under-represented groups across Nottinghamshire, giving voice to the voiceless and visibility to the unseen.

To learn more about what we offer, visit: www.globalwords.co.uk

A selection of books by Global Words Press:
Desire, Love, Identity: with the National Justice Museum
Aventuras en México: Farmilo Primary School
Times Past: with The Workhouse, National Trust
Young at Heart with AGE UK
In Different Shoes: Stories of Trans Lives

Self-published authors working with Global Wordsmiths:
Steve Bailey
Ravenna Castle
Jackie D
CJ DeBarra
Dee Griffiths
Iona Kane
Maggie McIntyre
Emma Nichols
Dani Lovelady Ryan
Erin Zak